RUINS

Book One

Corpses in Armor

A Novel in Two Parts

Part One

G. D. Giles

An imprint of Nouveau Classic Imprints, LLC
Brookneal Virginia USA
nouveauclassicimprints.com

To Billy:

Wanted to be as good as you are, wanted to be as unique, and I wish you were here so I could ask you what you think. Wish you were here so I could ask 'cause yes, you were right when you said, *"All the world's a stage"*. But, Billy, whatever do you do when you find out you've got stage fright?

RUINS

Memories of an Old Man

A Foreword

Excerpt from the Life and Times of
Major Evelyn Archibald Lee, R.F.
(1865-1953)

Compiled and organized by
Colonel, Sir Justin Henry Charles, Bt, R.A.F., R.A., O.B.E.,
and Jonathan Michael Palmer

March 8, 1932
A motorway north of London

Liz's quizzical and unconcerned comment, "How odd" had occurred about ten minutes into a lull in the general and unremarkable conversations of the car's occupants. Justin Charles would need more than his Black Box to confirm the object of Lady Charles's attention had been a black sedan she could have sworn had passed them only a few minutes before. In short then, the scenario Justin embraced of what happened was largely speculative even though no one was saying there wasn't another car out there on the road that cold silent day. There very well could have been.

The same as everyone was certain if something in particular had struck Liz's fancy, so would it have struck Henry's as he sat in the rear with Liz and Katy, his hand comfortably around his pipe.

As anything out of the ordinary would have caught Bob's attention as he sat in the driver's seat, the dowager Martha beside him.

The matter of fact neither Henry nor Bob were the sort to go off half-cocked supported Justin's conviction the continuing minutes of silence following Liz's remark were provocative. Even Justin's critics agreed with that. Confident the men's initial response would have taken the form of exchanging silent looks rather than unduly alarm the ladies. The only trouble with any of it was it was just theory. No rhyme, reason, or evidence to explain the apparent excessive rate of speed Bob was traveling when he went into a skid he could not pull out from, inspiring the next surviving recorded comment to be one of Martha's. A simple and chastising "Robert" moments before Bob spoke his quiet and chilling words of finality "We're lost".

Henry's intentions of shooting someone, possibly Liz out of mercy, dying with him as the town car plunged a hundred yards down a ravine, exploding before, after, or upon impact. By the time the local Constable's office arrived on the scene, there were about seven people standing around, most noticeably a rather shaken young woman of about twenty.

"Miss Maple Clarke." One of the footmen on the scene identified the visibly shaken young lady whose passport indicated she was just twenty.

"Mabel Clarke, perhaps?" the Chief Constable accepted the passport without so much a glance.

"Could be." The bobby was interested, young, though well trained, and not about to argue with his superiors. "They're both locals, sir. On their way to book passage for their honeymoon ... Heard the commotion, saw the car ..."

"And, of course, ran to see what they could do to help, which was nothing," the Chief swallowed a tablet of aspirin, dry. "Allergies."

"Wicked this time of year, sir," the bobby nodded. "You're right about that ... That's her fiancé with her ..." He called up a rather stunned looking young man identified as one John MacEnroe of the Chief's jurisdiction. His face and voice clearly Irish, the Chief never heard of or seen him before.

"McCoy," MacEnroe informed the Chief, correcting his name, and accepting his second-class citizenship without too much lip. "And it is Maple like the tree. Maple Clarke."

"Charmed." The Chief couldn't have been less interested though certain the girl's parents probably were about the sort of company she kept. "What's all this about a commotion?"

"Explosion, sir," his studious deputy assured. "Petrol ignited, is my guess. You can see the trail where they went over the edge ..."

John McCoy was frowning, of a different opinion apparently, or not quite sure either way?

"No?" the Chief waited impatiently. "Yes?"

"Yes ... Well, no, actually," McCoy acknowledged, changing his mind again immediately. "Perhaps."

The Chief would hate to be hanging waiting for this one to decide.

"What I mean is ..." McCoy attempted to clarify. "We saw the car explode, yes. But it was the first ... well, *sound*," he debated what to call it and couldn't think of anything else. "It certainly was loud enough ..."

"Hit a tree, sir," the public's attentive servant lent a helpful hand. "Took half the front ... Sheared it right off ..."

"As it went over the edge," the Chief nodded. "Couldn't have happened on the way down."

It was a statement, not a question, catching the bobby off guard and confusing him. "Beg your pardon?"

"What's Clarke have to say?" the Chief asked, dropping another tablet of aspirin, dry.

"Oh, just something about the fellow's hand. Thinks she saw it move."

As it protruded from under the crushed hood, blackened and fairly charred to the bone? The Chief glanced over their witness perspiring in his tweeds. "MacEnroe?"

"McCoy," the gent sighed, wanting his name at least right should he end up having to take credit for something he either did, or did not do. "John McCoy. You have to understand, she has had quite a fright—"

"Could it have moved?" the Chief interrupted, looking around for the verdict from someone with a badge.

"Wouldn't think so." He was answered. "It's a sight down there. Need a stomach. Why?"

"Let's have a look." The Chief headed down the ravine, the

ground crisp and frosty as the wind, the sky gray and trees barren.

"Service issue, sir." The Copper in charge produced a pistol dangling off the end of a pencil.

"So?"

"Found it on the ground," he explained with assurance in his tone. "Bullet's in the chamber. Looks to me like it might have jammed."

The Chief glanced back up the ravine, his assistant nodding and feeling sorry for the misguided lass, pretty little piece that she was, tear-streaked and chewing on her nails. "I'm sure she is just shaken, sir ... Interesting though, gun like that on the ground."

"Call in the number plate."

"This one?" the Copper's excitement heightened, apparently believing it was the guilty who always lost, in this case, died, rather than hang about posing and passing themselves off as witnesses to the unfortunate end.

The Chief was actually a fair man under all that stuffing. He tried to be. "Both."

"Right, sir." He got on it immediately with a jump for the hillside, careful of the evidence. Like there wasn't enough of it strewn around. Bits and pieces everywhere, black as the dirt and the shell of a car with much of its human remains still trapped inside. "There's a farm not too far. That's where they rang from. I'll send one of us on..."

"Do that." The Chief moved on to join the fellows working over the scene, the smell of cooked flesh souring the air.

"Yes?" A fair-haired man of above average height and apparent breeding opened the door to a crew of Macs from CID. Their boss, an Inspector, and therefore of presumed intelligence and experience, put the fellow's age at about thirty.

Or so. The fellow looked somewhat understated excepting his height, and the Inspector couldn't help wondering briefly how much the gent might be worth, while naturally wondering who he was. Country bloke, the Inspector settled on, rather than some visiting schoolmaster or priest, and worth plenty by the quality of his herringbone tweeds.

Actually, Joseph Lee was a schoolmaster, worth quite a bit more than what he looked, understated though he might be as his tweeds. Currently on sabbatical to reconsider his calling, that was neither here nor there. On his way out and running late for the day's planned affairs, it just by chance Joe happened to be there at all. That would never happen again. A few hours from now Justin would be making a note to make sure it never happened again. Joe, like the rest of them, would find himself locked behind those doors, a veritable army of technology and men surrounding and protecting the lot of them. Civil liberties lost to peace of mind gained.

To the point Justin could ensure it, anyway. No guarantees, of course, but Justin was a gambler at heart. Knew the odds. Born and raised to know and beat them, and worked hard to do just that. Today was no different from any other, just a little closer to home than most.

That it was. "Sorry to trouble you, sir," one of the plain-coats tipped a hat and flashed an identification tag, while the others looked the obvious gent over in surprise, "but would the Major Evelyn Lee happen to be at home?"

"An accident?" Joe repeated when told, his unblemished complexion twisting slightly in his effort to understand what it was they were saying. He was a peaceful man, pleasant, exactly as he seemed, comfortable and quiet as his surroundings, misleadingly at ease.

"Quite, sir," the Inspector nodded. "Car accident. Rather a bad one, I'm afraid. Vehicle has the Major's number plate. One of those newish Bentleys. Would you be familiar? Lend it out possibly to someone?"

"Yes, actually," Joe agreed tentatively, though certainly knowing how he ought not to say anything, least of all to strangers. It was just one of those odd situations where you are not quite sure what to do. "That would be Robert Lee, the Major's son."

"Concerned it might be something like that," the Inspector apologized. "You would be again?"

"Joseph Lee," Joe answered. "Major—Major Robert Lee that is," he clarified, "is my father. Evelyn would be his. My grandfather."

"Haven't had the privilege, sir," the Inspector smiled however slightly. "Sorry it had to be today. Never easy, but that car accident of your father's would be fatal, I'm afraid."

"I'll ring the Major," Joe stepped clear of the door. "Come in, please."

"Thank you, sir." The Inspector accepted the invitation, one, or two of his cronies following him inside to stand in a foyer larger than the collection of huts the lot of them owned. Sparse though, it was, serene and empty. A heavy flight of stairs, walls and closed doors of dark oak and mahogany, a simple table with a telephone resting on it, that was all. No furniture, draperies, or hangings of any sort, let alone a manservant or mistress in sight.

"Just moving in, sir," the Inspector agreed being he did not believe he knew these folks any more than he knew the couple they had down at the station. "Let her for the coming season?"

"No," Joe said.

"Out then," the Inspector nodded in understanding of the times and troubles some of the upper class were facing, though in thinking of it, he couldn't say he even knew this house was out here, never mind any tenants, established though it was on its foundation. A rambling, and respectable country estate parked rather firmly in a hilly glade of pastures and gardens, undoubtedly green and flowering in the springtime with a small stream in the background completing the scene. Picture perfect. A little, too.

"Fairytale she is at that, sir," he supported the notion. "You'll find your buyer."

"Yes, well, neither," Joe said.

"Right," the Inspector cleared his throat, returning to the facts and reason for his call. "Before you do that though, actually?" he stepped quickly, his hand down on the telephone.

"Yes?" Joe looked at him with a fair mixture of expectation and surprise.

"Any idea, sir," the Inspector verified, "who may have been with your father? There have been no survivors, I am sorry to say."

"And this was on the coach road?" Joe considered, thinking perhaps of somewhere else? Expecting them to be in London, or town? The car was heading north, the Mick MacEnroe and his fiancée Clarke claimed. The city well behind them, Cambridge still miles off.

"North of London," the Inspector assured. "On their way here possibly?"

"My mother Kathryn." Joe stared at the telephone. "The Major's wife Martha."

"Right." The Inspector had an idea this might be more than just the usual unpleasant call.

"And Sir Henry," Joe picked up the phone.

"Beg your pardon?" the three Macs startled.

"Sir Henry Charles," Joe replied. "I would think his wife. Elizabeth is her name. Excuse me."

"Not at all," the Inspector quickly stepped out of the way. "You said Sir Henry? MP?"

"Yes." Joe rang his grandfather's mill, a family hobby for a couple or so hundred years keeping them wealthy, legitimate, and sane. "The Major, please. Fairly urgent."

"I'll be there for tea," Evelyn promised Martha faithfully as he took her ring.

"No, it's Joseph," Joe confused him. "There's been an accident. Robert. Out on the coach road."

"Robert?" Joe could hear his grandfather frown. *"On the coach road?"*

"Fairly bad one, I'm afraid."

"Yes, yes, all right," Evelyn was nodding brusquely on his end. *"Who's there? Where's the car?"*

"CID, I think," Joe glanced at the Inspector. "Where's the car?"

"Still at the scene." The point of the question eluded the Inspector. "Would that be the Major you're speaking with?"

"Still at the scene," Joe repeated to the old man. "He wants to speak with you."

"CID?" Evelyn sputtered. *"The devil why?"*

"Bob's dead," Joe apologized. "Mum. Martha. All of them. Henry and Elizabeth I gather as well."

"Yes, well, there would be six of them to be all of them." Evelyn was reaching for a chair. *"Joseph, are you listening to me? Tell that Inspector—or whomever it is you have there—there were six people in that car. Henry. Elizabeth. And that daughter of Liz's, Joanna."*

"Joanna?" Joe stared at the Inspector who hadn't mentioned anything about a child.

"*Do it,*" Evelyn instructed. "*And do not go anywhere near that house. Understand me? Joanna's fine, yes, of course she is. But we want her to stay that way, don't we? Bastards find out they missed one they'll go after the one they missed. Doesn't matter it's a child, doesn't matter who it is. You're to stay away from that house of Henry's. You hear me?*"

"I understand," Joe felt cold under his shirt and jacket, prickly little shocks tickling his skin.

"*Good,*" Evelyn approved, certain Joe did understand even better than he wanted to. "*Soon as you get off this telephone with me, you're going to get Mike up there with you. I don't care what you tell him ... tell him Claudia's had a change of heart. I want Mike there, and I want you to keep him there if you have to lock him in a cupboard. Claudia should just about be on her way ...*"

"Yes, well, actually, I ..." Joe started to explain how he had been on his way to fetch Claudia in some mood or another about something.

"*I'll take care of Claudia,*" Evelyn assured, "*and I'll take care of Justin—And, well, all right,*" he reconsidered against his will, "*put that Inspector fellow you have there on the phone.*"

"Knox, sir." The fellow sounded somewhat flustered to Evelyn on his end. "Inspector Knox."

"*Yes, well, Knox,*" Evelyn assured the bastard, flustered or not, "*I know a Knox. Though I would rather think if the two of you were related, you wouldn't be standing there in my hall. In the meantime, however, since you are apparently, you should know you're going to have a few of my boys there in a short while—not in the damn hallway, there at the car. Wherever it is.*"

"On the coach road, sir," the Inspector peered at the telephone.

"*Understand that,*" Evelyn was called the Old Man because he was old, not stupid. "*Of course the damn road's a hundred miles long, but regardless, they'll be there—you say you traced Bob through the number plate on my car? They're there now. And I would appreciate any assistance you can give them, any information ...*"

"And then I would appreciate it," he fumed, *"if you would get and stay the hell out of the way. Understand? Hear any of this on the wire before I want to hear it, I'll know it came from you, and it'll be the damn mistake of your career—Care about your career?"*

"Course, sir," the Inspector stared at the telephone.

"Yes, well, we'll see, won't we?" Evelyn agreed. *"Off you myself if I have to, don't you think I won't. In the meantime, my son Robert had a heart. Got that? Robert had a heart. I believe you'll find he suffered an attack, lost control, and end of story. Unfortunate, but it happens."*

"A heart attack," the Inspector repeated.

"A heart attack," Evelyn assured and hung up to ring Justin, Henry's son, off in Ireland of all God forsaken places. More trouble Evelyn believed than the damn place was even worth.

"Palmer?"

"Aye, right here." Evelyn's man John appeared, Irish himself by blood and personality, though he kept the politics to himself and that was all that mattered.

"About time," Evelyn nodded. "Martha's dead. Bob. Katy. All of them. Get a crew out to Joe, and another to Teddy's for Claudia before I lose any more of them—and get someone over to that damn town house of Henry's," he insisted. "The child's not supposed to be with them, don't know if she was or not. One way to find out."

"Right," John took an unconscious step forward.

"No, I'm all right," Evelyn believed. After all, seen his first wife die, watched her. The look of pain spike across her face as that uterus of hers burst, drowning the sheets and his newborn son in blood. Now couldn't be any worse than that, just felt that way. "Not so sure about Joe, not exactly his cup of tea. But if he's a Lee ... and, well, he is a Lee and so that settles that. It's Mike I'm worried about. He takes that Italian blood of his to heart. Bit hotheaded, he is ...

"So he is ..." His fingers drummed on the table waiting for someone to pick up the damn telephone. They did. Ten minutes too long and he was finally talking to whom he wanted to talk to, someone who mattered. "Graham? This is Lee. Justin about? Need him. Yes, I need him. Not here, need him at home. Now. While you're at it, there's an Inspector Knox. Whitehall. Scotland Yard. Something like that. CID. Someone's giving out my damn home address. Take care of it. Have enough trouble for one day—yes, there's trouble. No there's nothing you can do. Nothing anyone can do, unfortunately."

"Nothing that will bring any of them back," Evelyn ruminated as he sat in a car near the spot where he lost better than half his family and two of his dearest friends, reading Joe's hastily scrawled press release of an ill-fated automobile trip on a country motorway outside London, north to Cambridge. Paid to have a teacher in the family, it did. Joe's statement was short and to the grisly point. Sir Henry Charles, honorable Member of Parliament, was dead at fifty-one. Cause of death, an automobile accident attributed to black ice, his body burned beyond recognition.

That brought a cluck of disapproval. "What the devil does that mean? We know it's Henry."

"Forensic." Justin answered, speaking the first word he had spoken in over an hour, and it was cold, sullen. Justin was angry, looked it, pipe clenched in five years growth of a woolly black beard. Scare the devil right about now with his fixed owl stare. Pupils as black as the beard and hair crowning his long thin frame. Dangerous in his air force fatigues, poised and wanting to kill, probably planning it as he stood there. Yes, he likely was. Do the deed himself that he would, too.

.   "Reads like a coroner's report," Evelyn grunted, continuing to screen what would be London's account of the death of Henry Charles and his thirty-one year old wife of six months, Lady Elizabeth Edwards Charles, and Liz's nine year old daughter Joanna by her previous marriage to Sir John Edwards.

"Another bright and upcoming politician," Evelyn evaluated Edwards who had met his own, rather untimely death two years earlier in the wilds of the Australian outback. "But it happens. It happens. Doesn't mean a thing."

He forewent qualifying what he meant. Fair to presume most would assume money, position, and power precluded bad luck.

"And, of course, most, as usual, would be wrong," Evelyn eyed Justin, Henry's son by his first marriage to a young and beautiful woman by the name of Phoebe Jones dead herself fifteen or so years.

"Flu epidemic, 1918," Evelyn recalled what took Phoebe's life, Justin glancing up from trying to read the damn tea leaves, or whatever it was he was doing, standing there like a statue, cup more or less frozen in his hand. "Not that that's either here or there. Other than it happened. Yes, like Henry happened. Liz—if I'd thought fast enough I would have told them you were in that automobile, not only Joanna. Didn't think though, and I apologize. Change it, if I could, but I can't. No more than I can change Henry. Liz. Martha."

Evelyn thought about Martha Douglas Lee for a little while, also dead, burned beyond recognition in the ill-fated automobile. Age sixty-one, beloved wife of veteran RF Major Evelyn Lee alive at sixty-seven, a former Cavalry officer and founding member of the Royal Air Corps, now with close ties to the Foreign Office.

"Foreign Office," Evelyn snorted, casting Joe's account aside. "Well, I suppose they have to call it something—for that matter, me something. I'm a damn spy, is what I am. Same as my father before me, and his father before him … Same as you," he reminded Justin, lest Justin forget his own cloak and dagger lineage. "Your father and his father before him—four centuries. The Charleses, Lees, and Drakes—doesn't mean a thing."

It hadn't at the beginning of his rumination, and twenty minutes later, it still didn't.

"Bob would agree with that," Evelyn assured Justin, knowing full well Justin believed otherwise and would proceed to the ends of the earth to prove it. "That is if Bob were alive to agree."

Which, no, Bob wasn't alive. RA Major Robert Lee, forty-eight, son of Evelyn Lee and the late Eleanor Lee likewise perished in the same automobile crash along with his lovely and beautiful wife Kathryn Allyn Lee, also forty-eight.

"Almost got us all," Evelyn reached to retrieve Joe's hard work and give it a second, fairer look.

"Didn't, but almost did. A little too close for comfort, is that what you're thinking? Could have been a bomb. That's true. Could have been the Irish, Shiites—Henry was heavily involved in the India situation. Always was and probably always would have been—"

"Irish," Justin interjected. Second word he'd spoken in over an hour, cold and lifeless as the first.

"Same as you with those damn Micks," Evelyn agreed. "What's that *box* of yours tell you? Or whatever the devil it is you call it."

"Flight recorder," Justin replied, though admittedly, the gadget had made its home in the dashboard of Evelyn's car rather than a cockpit of an airplane. But the principle and purpose were still the same: information. Speed, function, and those all-important voices. However, rather like the trouble encountered when a plane went down not too much of the recorder had survived the car crash. Justin gave up deciphering his tea, aiming for the Scotch Palmer had been thoughtful enough to pack.

"Well, it should have something to say, oughtn't it?" Evelyn ignored him other than to tell him that. "What's the sense of having one if it can't? Henry knew the damn thing was there, didn't he? Knew its purpose. Pretty damn stupid time to keep his mouth shut, wasn't it?"

"Quite."

"Quite is right," Evelyn was back to reading about the two young witnesses, neither of whom seemed to fit or figure in a world of espionage. "Same as Bob did. And neither of them said a damn word because there was nothing to say. So there you have it. Robert lost it plain and simple, for whatever reason—speed, more than likely. Car shot off that cliff like it was shot out of a cannon. From there the petrol exploded, is my guess. I don't care what those two young ones think they heard and saw. Sight and sound has a way of playing tricks, you should know that. Liz had to be thrown fifty feet."

"Fits nicely with your cannon theory," Justin agreed.

Evelyn eyed him, tempered, since the lad had just lost his father. "It's still a damn sight better than yours. Now that I've said that, there's a bit of a difference between shooting your wife so she doesn't suffer—know what it's like to have your skin burnt off your body?

"Yes, well, neither do I," he assured Justin looking at him. "Though I came close once and I can tell you it wasn't pleasant, not even the thought. That's the point. Bit of a difference between shooting your wife out of mercy and helping her out the damn door while you're rolling ass over teakettle down a damn cliff. It was an accident, my boy, an accident. Never convince you, or believe it myself, but it is what it was. Robert had that back of his, don't forget."

"And a heart," Justin reminded.

Evelyn chuckled, surprised he had one in him, for that matter any left. "Quite. And a heart. Good a reason as any. Thought fast enough I would have told them you were in the car, not only Joanna, and that would have taken care of ... well, most anyway ..." He eyed some young upstart bucking for a promotion. "What?"

"Ready to take you on to the morgue, sir."

"Bully for you," Evelyn retorted, but then this fellow hadn't lost anyone whereupon he had. He had lost his wife. His son. His daughter-in-law of almost thirty years who he loved as if she was his own blood and he was here to see where his family died.

"If that's all right with you," Evelyn slowly shifted his ponderous frame up from the seat of the car to its still towering height and reasonably secure stand despite the wooden pin he wore in place of his lower right leg. He was a large man, tall and large, fat and muscle resting on his waistband. Powerful in his younger days, strong. Still was that, too. Mean. Kill you quick as look at you, as they say. Slit your throat and cut his own damn leg off, if he had to, and so he had, because he had to, rather than die of certain gangrene. Hacked off what was left of it—snapped off, actually, since there wasn't much left of it. Wrapped up the stump and made it back to talk about it, the details softened, of course, if there were ladies around.

"If it breaks, it breaks," he assured the bloke glancing down on the handicap that had grounded one of England's first airborne sons. For fun before the Great War, for fun and business during and now after it. "About time I had a new one anyway, one with a foot. I'm single don't forget. Might want to go dancing—where's that damn shillelagh of mine?" He looked around, Justin handing it to him without comment.

"Smart boy," Evelyn approved, heaving himself forward, Justin's long limbs falling into their meandering lurch beside him. "Never lock horns with a bull. I should know, I'm a bull, the same as you are. So, what are you going to do—mind you, going to do, not want to do about those two 'witnesses'? They're either involved, or they aren't. You're right if you're thinking no one will ever find their bodies out here, because they won't. I'll back you one hundred percent whatever it is you decide to do, just make sure you know what you want to do.

Blood's a little harder to wash off when it's innocent, but it's not impossible. Take it from me ..."

He looked around for Palmer, right there, flask in one hand, cup of tea in the other. "True or false? Talking about those two young ones who claim they happened by. Want their necks if they're guilty, not sure I care if they're not."

"I can understand that," John gave the tea a healthy dose or two, holding it out with a wink at the old man. "Do your soul some good."

"Might at that," Evelyn accepted the offer. "It's the Irish who drink to get the edge on, English drink to take the edge off."

"Oh? Now, who says that?" John's wink eased into a salty grin.

"I do," Evelyn downed his tea and resumed drilling his peg into the dirt. "One sniff of a cork—I've never met a Mick who wasn't philosophical or suicidal and reaching for his gun either way. Justin, in the meantime, thinks a couple of your Catholic friends may want to take credit for this."

"Well, now if that's true," John reassured, sincere about it, too, "they better make themselves scarce, and that's the God's honest truth. The lads are one thing, the ladies quite another."

"My sentiment," Evelyn profoundly agreed. "Comes with the territory. Henry and Bob both knew that."

"Did," Justin paused to light his pipe and see what he could do about burning the rest of the forest down with a careless toss of the match that lay there flickering before it died.

"So does the ego," Evelyn roused himself from watching the match to remind Justin, "and I hate to be the one to deflate yours, but you're wrong. Henry was the target, not you. That's why it was Henry. The same as if the target were me, it would have been me. Robert's too far in the background to be given the time of day—or he was." His peg bore deep as he stopped at the edge of where Martha and Bob left this life for a better one, Justin and Palmer exchanging one of those silent glances.

"How old's my damn grandson, anyway?" Evelyn changed the subject, peering down on Joe trying his hand at playing detective— or Merlin. Not quite sure which, or what Joseph thought the trees could tell him, other than they, too, had surrendered without much of a fight.

"Oh ... twenty-six? Twenty-seven?" John was handy with the family affairs, not necessarily its bible.

"Never know it." Bitter cold March wind, two university degrees, one from Cambridge, the other from the Academy, and Joe was out there cavorting around in a pair of trousers and a shirt.

Of course, the fact Justin was standing there showing off half of everything he owned from the waist up with his shirt unbuttoned and chest bare, was beside the point. Evelyn never met a Charles with the slightest sense of public decency, except for possibly Henry, and that was only because his mother insisted on the social benefits of good manners and hygiene. Lord knows Henry didn't come by it naturally, not by way of his father Scotty, Evelyn's mentor when he was once a young cadet. Oliver Barnard Scot Charles was a devil of a man. A giant in Evelyn's memory, seven feet tall, and almost as tall in life, hair and eyes black as midnight. Scotty looked like a savage, dressed like a savage, and could be savage if someone got on his wrong side, and Justin was not only his grandfather incarnate, he was beginning to look like his grandfather more and more every day.

"Where's your jacket?" Evelyn lambasted Joe hiking his way back up to them. "Catch your death out here, and I think we've had enough of that for one day, don't you?"

To Joe's credit, he had enough of his own upbringing to accept the dressing down. "Quite. Sorry. Didn't think."

Evelyn softened, of course he did. Lad had just lost both his parents, and that was a lot to take, even at twenty-seven. "Yes, well, there's not thinking and then there's not thinking ... and, well," he admitted with a glance down the ravine, "probably should apply that rule to myself. Anything down there I need to see?"

"Well ..." Joe eyed the wreckage and gave it his best. "I guess if they used just enough powder to blow a tire ... or the door ... that could explain Bob losing control ...?

"I don't know. It's just an educated guess." His supporting smile was humble and apologetic. "I don't see anything out of the ordinary, but it's not exactly my cup of tea."

"You're allowed," Evelyn assured.

"Aye and it's a good guess. Done it myself," John added his support, offering the lad the flask. "Go on, takes the edge off."

"Right. Thanks," Joe borrowed Justin's teacup. "What do you think?" he asked him. "Can you prove it wasn't an accident?"

Yes, well, if Joe was going to be a stickler for proof, "Doubt it," Justin replied and Joe nodded, "Just an educated guess."

"That's about the size of it," Justin relit his pipe, turning his back on the ravine to ogle the roadway cleared now except for theirs and them. "Rifle, maybe. Take out one of the tires. Less chance of leaving any evidence. Toss the casing over the side. Never find it."

"Have to be a damn good shot," Joe frowned.

"Mike could do it."

"So could you."

"Probably," Justin imagined, turning his sights on Evelyn.

"Anything about this mortuary business I should know?" Evelyn beat him to it. "Realize Martha's burned, they're all burned, asking if there's anything else."

"Went through the windscreen?" Justin shrugged.

Evelyn had the picture. "Use your imagination from there. And, well, all right. I'm sure I've seen worse—in fact, I know I have." With that, he turned away but stopped, because quite frankly he could not do it. No, he could not. "Sorry, but I can't." He did not apologize, no reason to. He was the one who was going to have to forgive himself, no one else. "I've seen too much. Never gave me a turn. Never would, unless it was one of my own. I've seen Eleanor die, Teddy, Scotty, and Robert through those back surgeries of his and that was bad enough. I'd like to remember Martha the way I remember her. Not some charred hunk of ... well, mutton."

"I'll take care of it." Joe had his youth on his side to protect him and Evelyn was grateful for that.

"Thank you. Sure it's a violation of some protocol ... but, well, I've never been much for protocol and I'm not about to start now ... you?"

Justin just looked at him and Evelyn nodded again. "Understand Henry's funeral will have to be some sort of State affair, but I'd like to keep the rest of them private."

"Will," Justin agreed.

"Henry's, too, if you had your druthers. In the meantime, there's that child of Elizabeth's who has to be taken care of—"

"Joanna," Joe seemed particularly concerned, probably the schoolteacher in him.

"Quite. Joanna. Must have been found by now ..."

"Oh, yes, she's up at the house with Mike," Joe assured, "and Claudia. I've been thinking Claudia ..."

"Smart thinking." Joe did not have to explain any further. Claudia had nothing but time on her hands, anyway, even with that little Andrea of her own, and if she could be talked out of this divorce business with Michael, Liz's daughter would be all set. New mother, new father, and even a baby sister to play with. It all sounded good to Evelyn and he doubted if anyone had any better ideas, if they had any idea at all.

He knew one who didn't. "She's not about to end up in a work house," Evelyn directed that point to Justin, in this up to his neck whether he wanted to be or not. "Never live with myself if I let that happen. Realize she's no blood to anyone, and that none of us really even know her from Adam, but that's hardly the child's fault. We'll help you all we can you have my word on that. But your father married that little girl's mother. She's your sister. Stepsister, I'll grant you, she's still your moral responsibility, and be prepared or not, my boy, considering that child's age, I believe you've just had yourself a daughter."

With that, he did turn away, aiming himself for the car before Justin fell over the precipice to his own death, never mind anyone else. Ridiculous though, when you come to think of it, after all, spies, though they might be, instead of business men, bankers, or thieves, that had nothing do with sex or marriage or propagating the ranks by virtue of marriage or otherwise, the same as everyone else in the damn world. Evelyn should know. He had walked that path himself a few times; twice once, he would wink when asked, to the same damn woman. The same as every Lee, Drake, and Charles had for the last four centuries. Married, that is. Respectably and legitimately contributing to their family trees. Granted there weren't many of them, but that had more to do with the nature of their business and its limited life expectancy rather than it did with some physical or psychological failing.

"That is except for Justin," Evelyn confided to Palmer.

"Aye, you've got yourself a hard sell," John had his own ideas about that one.

"Yes, well, something short of Nancy boy, one would hope," Evelyn snorted. "Justin's no more one of them, than I am, any more than he's some sort of monk. He's self-centered, is what he is, a little too. He's got Scotty's arrogance, if you want to be kind. A snob, if you don't. And don't think they don't know it when he looks down on them because they do."

John supposed they did. It did not matter. John wasn't thinking anything about Justin other than him suddenly having a tot on his hands. It would never happen. Michael did not have a monopoly on shying away from that sort of responsibility.

"Think it may have been better if you stopped with reminding our boy Justin he had a sister," John proposed wisely. "Never met a fellow who ran at the idea of his mother having a child. Met plenty who'd run at the idea of someone giving them one."

"As well as plenty who'd drop him in his damn tracks unless he assumed his responsibility," was Evelyn's answer to that social problem.

"Oh, no, now you can't do that," John dissuaded him from any hasty action. "Not but, what? Twenty-five years old himself? He'll come around. Just not time yet. What's he going to do with a wife and family at his age? Nothing but drive himself and her crazy."

"So he's a man's man," Evelyn stopped to sputter about what had to be one of the most ridiculous things. "What the devil does that mean? Fear of women? Never heard of such a thing. Can someone explain it to me?"

If someone could it wasn't John.

"Didn't think so," Evelyn snorted again. "No one can. Just one of those things. Like fear of needles, or something. Yes, that's what it is, like fear of needles. Lord help me—and that child, while he's at it," he clucked sadly. "Yes, Lord help that little girl. Doubt if she woke up this morning expecting to lose her family, never mind me."

"Well, now, that other idea of yours," John could help all he could with that. "The one about Michael and my darling lady Claudia taking her in as one of their own?" he reminded. "Can't do much better than that. Like you said, they're already married, a child of their own. And Michael's not been in any hurry to leave since Henry's wedding, not that I can see ..."

"No, that's true," Evelyn considered, "that's true."

"Is," John promised, however tactfully, since Michael's sudden interest in staying around no doubt could be traced to the unexpected sight and scent of the lovely Elizabeth Charles rather than any renewed interest in his own wife. John wondered briefly if anyone had bothered to check Claudia's whereabouts at the time of the deed before settling on blaming the local Mick. Be a rather spicy twist to the tragic state of affairs if it were true. It wasn't, he was sure, and he dismissed the thought of a woman's revenge to focus on the here and now. "Little of the right sort of encouragement and I'm inclined to agree with you. Don't believe anyone's going to have to be concerned about a divorce between those two any time soon."

"That, and Claudia's Roman," Evelyn agreed. "Yes, she is. Converted to marry Mike. First Roman in the family to my knowledge—certainly the first Yank. Surprised Teddy didn't turn over in his grave, yes I am surprised that did not happen. If that didn't beat all."

"Talk to me about it when one of you brings home a Mick," John got the door, helping the old fellow load himself back inside as comfortably as possible. "That's what I want to be there to see."

"Oh, well, now, that will never happen," Evelyn was close to laughing to the point he had tears in his eyes. "Never happen. Every damn ancestor there ever was would be in an uproar. The closest any of us ever got to crossing that line was that smidgen of Scot Scotty had in him. Not enough so that it counted—it was on his mother's side in the first place. Just enough to make him a contrary son-of-a-bitch. I should know. I'm a contrary bastard myself. Word to the wise, word to the wise, don't let my jovial nature fool you. I am an evil old man ...

"Yes, I am an evil old man," Evelyn patted his shillelagh with a shake of his head. "Same as my father before me, and my son aft, and one of these days I'm going to have to figure out how the devil I ended up with a schoolteacher for a grandson. Love him dearly, don't get me wrong, I just have no idea where he came from ... must be from his mother's side. Yes, it must. Devil knows it's not from mine."

"Was Henry the target?" Joe watched the old man hulk away.

"Doubt it," Justin highly doubted it, also doubting if Joe really wanted to know the reason why he thought that.

"You're right," Joe cast a short, sunny smile around the gloomy hillside, "I don't. Sometimes I almost wish I did, but then I'm glad I don't—no disrespect intended, old chap," he cast his smile briefly over Justin. "You might be a bit barmy, but who isn't? And we'd be lost without you, just the same."

"Yes, well ..." In Justin's opinion, Mike was the one who was barmy, but he supposed Joe had his point. "At least my sister will have a good education."

Joe had to laugh a little at that. "The best. Take's care of my needing to find a new position as well, fancy that."

"Yes, well ..." Justin didn't have much to say about that.

"No," Joe didn't expect he would and let it drop there. "Well, you have my word, the old man's, too. As far as Claudia ..."

"Claudia can do what she's damn well told to do," Justin fell into his gangly lurch for the car. "That goes double for Mike. Stuff and nonsense, the two of them; Evelyn's right. Not to say a workhouse probably wouldn't be the fairer choice, because it probably would be. Were she a few years younger, it definitely would be. She's not though and so, quite, Claudia and Mike are it, like it or lump it, or there'll be two more bodies out here no one will ever find."

"Cold, Charles, cold," Joe paused in his own easygoing gait, a touch surprised by the venom. He looked up to Justin, fair to say. Not meaning in the sense of a pun considering Justin's rather extraordinary height, but looked up to the man himself. Though Joe was the elder of the two, Justin was the sage, old as Evelyn in his own way, at not but twenty-five. "She's a Drake, is all I was going to say, Teddy's daughter. Evelyn's cohort in crime ..."

The light dimmed briefly in Joe's eyes as he thought of the freakish way Teddy had died. A hunting accident, weekend outing. There was more to that story Joe was sure, the same as there was more to this one, though he doubted if one would find the answer to this one in the family stables.

"Your point, Lee?" Justin requested.

"Right," Joe roused himself. "Just Claudia, that's all. Fairly confident she'll go along without the need for your thumbscrews, or whatever it is you use. She knows enough to accept what she doesn't understand. The same as me." He looked around again, lost in thought for another moment or two. "Sorry. It's just me. I shouldn't even be here. But I couldn't just sit there. Not the sort of thing to just sit there."

"Yes, well, does that include a dead child quite alive and having free run of the parlor?"

"Sorry?" Joe looked at him.

"Claudia," Justin lit his pipe. "Somewhat less confident in Claudia than you are ... somewhat less confident in her than I am in Mike," he admitted. "Bit of a hag when she wants to be."

Joe smiled, "If you mean as far as the idea of a child having free run of Claudia's parlor. You're right. It will never happen."

"Yes, well, good," Justin said, because she certainly wouldn't have the run of his, and he didn't have the time or patience to train her.

"Oh, quite," Joe's gasp was contrived as Justin dug into the back seat for a jacket that out of spite turned out to be his. "That's what's really getting to you. With Henry gone, you have responsibilities. A house. A home. Furniture—"

Joe had the RAF eagle whammed into his chest.

"Chicken?" Justin drawled, as Joe looked the jacket over.

"About frostbitten," Joe admitted, and therefore would survive. He slipped the jacket on, the leather cold and well worn. "Wouldn't happen to have a cigarette hidden away in the glove box—or a pocket somewhere—that and a flask—"

"Yes, well ..." A flask and a match Justin had. The cigarettes he had to pinch from a subordinate strolling past.

"Thanks," Joe exhaled, unmindful of the fact they could have been to Killarney and back by now. "It's this mortuary business. You said Martha went through the windscreen?"

"Decapitated," Justin yanked the throttle and sat there revving the engine.

"Right," Joe's voice was tight. "No, the Old Man wouldn't have been able to take that. Still, Liz had to bear the brunt of it, didn't she, dashed on the rocks like that?"

"Did," Justin lied.

"Good," Joe exhaled that time in relief. "Sorry, but its Katy. Bob's one thing, but Katy? I realize she's my mother, not my wife ..."

"Yes, well ..." Justin realized Henry was his father, not his wife. Liz was one thing to him, Henry quite another. Not saying he did not like Liz, because he hardly knew her well enough to like or dislike her. Their relationship, had one evolved, would likely have been more of a respectful relative rather than some stepmother had Henry's and her marriage endured, which it had not. Unfortunately not because Henry had decided to come to his fifty-one year old senses.

"Do you remember Phoebe very much at all?" Joe was just curious, though knowing Justin had to remember his mother. Justin was young when she died, desperately sick himself, but certainly at eleven old enough to remember her quite vividly. And so did Justin remember, Joe supposed he was wondering, not her, but what it was like to have her, and then lose her so suddenly? Justin so difficult to know sometimes, what touched him and what did not.

"I remember my cot." Justin threw the car into gear and tore out of there like a bat out of hell, wrenched the steering, spun her around and hit the curve at forty, taking it clean.

"Brilliant!" Joe gasped when they came to a halt. "What's her top speed?"

"About eighty," Justin lit his pipe.

"The devil it is."

"The devil it's not," Justin took off again without any further shenanigans. "Mercedes invented the damn SS supercharge in '26."

"That's true," Joe admitted. "Rival Royce, if you can believe that."

Justin could. He nodded ruefully. "De Valera isn't the only rotten fish in the sea, there's Mosley and his gang and that bolshie Hitler."

"Of course," Joe sighed. "Mosley. Forgot about him. So what's next? If it's not the IRA responsible for this, you and the Old Man set your sights on the Blackshirts? Honestly, Charles, what a wretched life we lead, really. Thought the need for any of this would be over by now ... for that matter," he fingered the jacket, "thought you fellows were about disbanded."

Yes, well, if Joe meant grounded, he was right. Disbanded, was another thing. Not quite. But then flying wasn't all there was to it. Justin should know. Flying not exactly his cup of tea. Not because he did not have the skill, because he did. But more because he was more valuable on the ground—that and at six-foot five and a half, he could just about fit inside a damn cockpit, at least the modern ones, at least not comfortably. "It's De Valera," Justin assured.

Joe nodded. "And it's not over. Well, one step ahead of them is the best any of us could hope for, I guess. Two more bodies, you said, I mean when we were talking about Claudia and Mike. Two more bodies out here, you said as if there were already two. I take it, it's less important if those two witnesses are saints or sinners than simply not worth the risk."

"Quite," Justin said.

"War is hell," Joe sighed.

For some, Justin supposed. Personally, right about now it had the potential of being quite satisfying. "They're not going to get away with it, Lee." In the meantime, he did top it out at eighty along the road to London, just to prove it could be done, despite the damn black ice.

"That's an odd couple." Evelyn noted as Justin tore out of there like his tail was on fire after proving his point to himself. "Yes, that's an odd couple—trio, not to exclude Mike. But then, well, so were Teddy, Scotty, and I. That we were. That we were."

"Been a while," John agreed.

"Thirty years," Evelyn nodded. Thirty years since any of them died in the line of duty. That would be Scotty in the Boer War. Teddy's demise, quite, was a family affair. "Overdue, is that what you're saying?"

"No," John said. "Just that it's been a while."

So it had been. It was eight years later, almost nine, before the black wreath hung on the door again. That time for RAF pilot Joseph Lee who died in service to his country on or about the 20th of December 1940, age thirty-five. But then it came with the territory, yes, it did, whether it was the Irish, the Shiite, Dutch, and so forth and so on.

"So forth and so on." Evelyn Lee puffed on his pipe, putting aside the faded photographs of Teddy, Scotty, Robert, all of them. Joe now added to the chronicles. His young widow left behind. Joanna.

.Book One

Prologue

The Fezzan,
Territorio Militare, Libya
Sunday, March 8, 1942

Thirty-two year old Hauptmann Dieter Reineke raised his field glasses and scanned the surrounding sand dunes. It was so hot. Emaciated stalks of a benign species of plant life made no attempt to hide their shame beneath the scrutinizing eyes of his powerful lens. They would not want to. Gifts from nature, their mockery was intentional, and they grew as thorns along the sands that tried to strangle them. He believed them to be spurge flax, one of this desert's annuals. If he was in error, it was irrelevant because he wanted from those withered yellow shrubs an answer, that was all, an answer—

Answer me!

But the plants were sleeping, and the sand just stared, stubbornly refusing to disclose its secrets; and it was so very hot.

His glasses lowered. Tiny droplets of moisture momentarily blurring his piercing glare were blinked away and slid along the mask of stone that held the palest of blue eyes—and those eyes could not, would never accept the emptiness as a confirmation the silence was all there was to see ....

Answer me!

Narrower still, his eyes repeated their demand; lips parched and split tightening against his face frozen and silent. No throes of emotion evident, he lay in peace with only a vague reference to inner turmoil—

And it was a coverlet typical of births native to the month of September! Except he had been born in August. Such a hot day in August. So hot. So yellow. Rather like today ...

Answer me!

Yellow shrubs in barren pockets of dead yellow seas, it was not August. On fire, the sun flamed yellow in the sky, though it was not August. But it could have been. It could have been. Such a hot day in August, such a hot day today, it could have been the 23rd of August 1909—

And it WAS August. He could feel it in his chest. He could see it in the heat rising from the blistered sands around him, and he could hear the fossils moan, August. August …

ANSWER ME!

That silent scream was a howl, damning the quiet for he knew it lied. The unruffled sands claiming there was nothing to see for miles, lied, and the fire burning in the blue depths of his eyes brightened, becoming white. For as of late, as of the past few months, it had become increasingly difficult to contain the volatile thoughts beginning to metastasize to the muscles straining against flesh, cords that tightened and twisted in his throat, and sweating palms clenching into fists—

"ANSWER ME!" Reineke broke the unnerving silence. His scream so loud, demonic in its fierceness, it echoed—

(And two hundred meters in the distance, Oberleutnant Heinrich Thiele stood up in the rear seat of the wagen.)

But the desert took notice of the cry simply for pity's sake. The drowsy vegetation repeated its answer the silence was all to see today, *Madman.* That was all.

"Liar!" Reineke challenged the sand, and turned around to walk away, but it must have been the fossils, for the shiver started at the back of his neck, and slid along his spine. Its terrifying fingers spreading out across his back, and he heard them moan, *August.*

August.

And though it was March, it could have been August, and he had been born in August.

Born in the Rhineland, the Feast of Vulcanous, heir to its river, castles, and trees. *Living link!* to the fables and lore, Frederick the First greatest of all, surviving soul of his Prince dead some two centuries and immortal in its fetus Dieter Reineke. A reticent child, reclusive man, preferring the company of servants to friends ...

At fourteen, Reineke deposed his father. The fierceness of his hatred erupting during a fencing lesson and his father's foolish attempt to cut his son's cheek marking Reineke as the man he claimed Reineke would never be. Reineke was a man, his father's throat held at the mercy of his sword until the father bowed his head to the son who would not bend, retreating defeated and disgraced.

And later, after having humiliating his father, Reineke watched his reflection in a mirror, repeating his arrogant challenge a second time, "I am a man."

A flawless face of near-perfect symmetry, the flesh hugging his marvelous cheekbones needed no scars to entice the moist, approving glances of anyone feminine. For some time now, women twice his age had warmed themselves on the smoothness of his skin. And in the mirror, his smile changed to a rare grin, pleased in the knowledge of how sex also did not necessarily make anyone a man. "Mirror, mirror," his head cocked teasing, watching himself in the glass, waiting for his grandfather's call, the beloved giant passing nine years later, shrunken and old. His title and sacred Prince's Cross passed to Dieter Reineke, his grandson, not the beast sired by his loins.

At twenty-three Baron Dieter Reineke walked from the cemetery, master of his fate and empire. The allies long gone from his homeland, the French, the Rhineland Palatinate free and secure, it was winter, late fall, 1932, and more and more people were talking. He ate dinner at home alone that night. Sometime later, the younger of his two sisters, Alexia, decided to join him, explaining her interruption by confessing to a bad dream.

"Why a bad one?" Reineke inquired with a smile. She was a glorious child, Alexia, pure and gentle, so unlike the hated Helena who stole his face and longed to steal his throne.

"I don't know," she shrugged her shoulders, and if she did not know, he did.

"It is your birthday a few hours from now," he mentioned, and she looked up at him slyly from under her lashes.

"Is it too terribly callous of me?" she asked, what with her grandfather only just buried, she should be mourning, not thinking of jewels and pearls and cosmetic creams.

"No more than it is of me," Reineke agreed. "Only if either of us were to forget—which is inconceivable!" he set her down on the sofa next to him with a laugh.

"So what did you get me?" she asked as they studied the Baron's cognac together, admitting they would both rather drink poison, even the smell was just so vile.

"A house," Reineke shrugged.

"A house?" Alexia blinked. "I'm only nine."

"Ten, in a few hours," he reminded, though still not quite ready to marry her off just yet. "A house in Switzerland. A chalet. You like to ski, right?"

"I can ski here," she assured, "with you."

That was true. Though not as dangerously as either of them liked, not as extreme.

"What about the river?" she asked, viewing him suspiciously. "You made me promise we would never leave the river."

"It is right there," he assured. "Right outside the windows. Just like this."

"The same one?" she remained skeptical.

"The only one," he laughed again. "Indeed, the Rhine. So, what do you think? Is it acceptable or do I have to drive myself crazy trying to think of something else?"

"I'm considering it," Alexia waved away the smoke from his cigarette so she could rest her head comfortably and toy with his cross. "Why isn't there a princess's cross? I think there should be a princess's cross."

"No." It was the only thing he ever refused her. Death from an attempted suicide in 1939 did not count, Alexia mercifully surviving her ordeal, and he went on with his army to France.

"But I am the Baroness," she said.

"This is very true," he agreed, "and I am the Baron."

"I do not see where there's a difference," she shook her golden head, its color so much darker than his, the strands long and curly. "Is it big, my new house?"

"Very big," he promised.

"High on a hill?"

"Very high," he assured, "extremely; on a cliff. So, is it acceptable, or am I going to have to find some other Baroness to give it to for her birthday?"

"It's acceptable," she agreed, only teasing it might not be. She settled down, happy enough to fall asleep. "What did the Baron mean when he talked of unification?"

Reunification and it meant different things to different people, many of them afraid. "A newspaper story," Reineke sipped his wine. "A silly one. The Rhine is German and Germany. No one can ever change that. Not any man or any map."

"Do you think they will come back?"

"The outlanders? No." The Siegfried line of defense built four years from now would take care of any chance of that.

"And that there are no Nordics on the Rhine?" she smiled up at him.

Reineke had no idea. He was Nordic, the chancellor and champion of Aryan superiority without having to be taught or told. His family on the Rhine a thousand years, his manor built as a summer home for the prince in 1604 and never fallen. Alexia retired to Switzerland in 1936, the chalet her fortress against the mandatory conscription of beautiful young girls. He continued not to care about Helena, whom she married, or where she went. Death from a glass of cyanide waiting should she ever decide to return and avenge their father. She never did, afraid beneath her cold arrogance, possibly more afraid of Alexia than she was of him since he was not there.

He had no idea why he joined their party. It was a business decision, of course, little else. One he made to secure his family legacy, fortune, and home. He was an aristocrat, Lutheran, by 1936 few, if any of them left, their lives and lands gone, confiscated and consumed as the Nazi peaked in popularity and strength. A dethroned and treacherous father hovering in the background alongside his comrades with their rantings of the rights and ideals of the common life he knew nothing about. The son's existence, a flagrant example of everything so right and so wrong ...

And Reineke would be lying to say he did not believe in a truth beneath the rhetoric, the state of Germany critical, punished for a war they did not start and failed to win.

Lying, if he said he did not believe in a divine right, ultimate power, and new Reich, stronger than the Second, enduring as the First.

Lying to suggest if after three years of service in Germany's new uniformed army he understood or cared anything about politics, struggles, or strife, which he did not, familiar only with the name. Hitler. Some Austrian implant who seemed to think he knew what was best for his German cousins even if they did not, and who knew if they did. Exalted as a redeemer, the people's hero was a puppet for the party's headliners of bourgeois wealth with their own aristocratic dreams, and Reineke had no need or desire to mingle with the crowds drowning in the halls of their temple Berlin ...

Such arrogance or ignorance clearly chosen and contrived, he was an intelligent man, trained and skilled in the interests and excesses of his position and wealth. Sophisticated, successful, and perpetually bored. Few serious ventures extending beyond the cloistered existence of his estate. But four years spent at the universities of England and Germany, the degrees earned in architecture and engineering remained virginal. They were only whims anyway, interesting ways to stay the boredom. As was this army an adventure, a quest, opportunity to display his prowess at games and sport ...

But games can become tedious, and nerves ragged, watching the insanity multiply and there is no culmination, no relief, or satisfaction obtained ...

On September 1, 1939, they invaded Poland. In two days, war was declared between England and Germany, and on September 30, 1939, a new Polish government was formed in Paris while *Deutschland über Alles!* was sung to a country laid to ruin ...

Ruins.

Thirty-two year old Hauptmann Dieter Reineke stared at the sand listening to the fossils cry. In months, they rocked the foundations of Europe with Holland, with Norway, with France. To fight in the fields of France had been a game, indeed. Revenge for the near annihilation of his people lost in history and a hundred years of war. But revenge left a bitter taste, and he had been glad to leave France behind and come here.

Beneath the scornful eye of Nature, the shoulders of a still-young man bowed, hunching deeper into a shirt encrusted with layers of dirt and oil. The thin cotton, the bland color of this world, blended well with his skin turned yellow from sweat and creams protecting his body from the sun and heat. Gently, Reineke raked a fingernail over his arm, lifting a layer of the congealed creams clogging his pores.

"Paint me a picture," he murmured to the scum with its consistency of cheese. Posters and voices foretelling palm trees and salted breezes sweeping cliffs along such a beautiful, beautiful Mediterranean.

Liars.

He had not believed them, but they were liars still.

"Liars!" he snarled and wiped his hand clean. He could indeed taste the salt even buried this deep in the bowels of Libya, for you ate it with the sand. It burned your throat and seared your lungs as you ate it with the sand. Not in breezes, but in the sudden winds called *ghibli*.

Reineke shut his eyes, perspiration creeping out from under the band of his cap. The winds. The silence could be a foretelling of the winds, warn the rodents to run and hide.

"*Khamsin*," he whispered into the air, praying the desert might answer. It was the Englishman's word for the winds.

"*Khamsin*," he chanted to conjure an image the desert could not refuse to answer, the god himself, the Holy Man, master of the sand.

"Pierre?" Reineke opened his eyes because he thought he heard a sound. "Pierre?" he whispered. "Answer me."

But it was not ready yet, not yet—

"ANSWER ME!" Reineke screamed. "Pierre, answer me!"

But the desert refused to answer, and it was not fair! He knew the words, learned the words, used the words Pierre had taught him, and Pierre would know. It could be the winds. The silence a prophecy of the wind. It was SO quiet.

"PIERRE!" Reineke shouted and started to run. "ANSWER ME, PIERRE! ANSWER ME!"

(And two hundred meters in the distance, Oberleutnant Heinrich Thiele vaulted over the side of the wagen.)

But against the yellow Reineke had little chance, the shrubs springing to the defense of their desert, catching him, tripping him, and he watched himself crumble, such a helpless fledgling sobbing in fright.

He went down on one knee. One sharp branch had gouged his boot.

But not his boots! In dismay, Reineke touched the wound. Such a proud peacock, determined to flaunt his regal tail he wore the black leather accessories, not the brown, never the brown, and the black would never blend into this desert, never!

"Never!" he damned the sands. "Never!" Strong fingers digging deep, he tore at the roots. "Damn the devil, never!"

Madman! The fossils laughed. *Madman!*

"Devil!" Reineke cursed. "Devil—ANSWER ME!"

That scream pierced the yellow, and he stopped. Still shaking, he stopped. It was so hot. So quiet.

TOO quiet.

"Madman?" Reineke whispered, questioning the sand's condemnation, and started to smile.

Madman. The sand affirmed, though not with certainty.

"Indeed," Reineke whispered. "Answer me. In all your silence, answer me!"

But it could not. The desert could not. It was *too* quiet.

"Thank you!" Reineke said, and perfect white teeth flashed lethal in his smile. Madman or not, his mind was keen. Remember, he had wanted to come here. They needed peacocks. Proud, independent peacocks, adept at strategy, elusive foes, and he was one. SO adept that of the five installations he was the closest to the embattled coast road.

SO adept that of the five Hauptmanns he was first. As always first! Arriving with the first at Tripoli, and since coming here, his plots, his tricks, his games eluded the Allies—

From the background yet!

And he wanted to be in the background, to come this far south to perfect those tricks and games, never caring if his importance, or their importance, ever reached beyond the few of his sect.

And he wanted to stay in the background, safe from the blurry circle of ignoble defeat and victory, if only to bury with him the secret their existence was bound to be lost in the sand, the eternity of the sand ...

So hot ...

So yellow ... *August.*

The trance was threatening to return, but Reineke did not care. He had his answer. The desert answered. It was TOO quiet.

And through the yellow heat of August, the eyes of a handsome young man narrowed, fashioning into slits burning from a face made hideous from so much hatred.

And he knew he was right, because he felt the ground shudder, the long dead skeletons writhe in their tombs, and he heard the fossils resume their chant, *August.*

August.

And though it was March, it would soon be August, and before the heat of August, this desert would remember Dieter Reineke and admit he had won.

It would go down on its knees and bow its head, and remember Dieter Reineke.

"Indeed!" Reineke answered their quail, and started to laugh, loud. His head snapped back, eyes bright and burning as he continued to laugh, and in his insanity, he was up on his feet.

And the desert cowered, for in his triumph he started to mock, legs bounding forward, black boots swinging in glee as they ruptured the sand, and he started to sing, "You will remember me! You will remember me! You will remember the madman!"

"*Hauptmann!*" It was a voice. An actual voice that nearly shattered his daydream. Reineke turned around. Oberleutnant Heinrich Thiele stood less than two meters away. And Reineke was tempted to explain about the heat, about the fossils, but Thiele's face was saying, *Madman,* and he decided to explain nothing. Nothing.

For You

Corpses in Armor

In December 1941, five German officers, each equipped with a squad of men, ventured deep into the Sahara to establish a lifeline of munitions complexes in defiance of the idiosyncratic management of Berlin that threatened Rommel's North Afrikan Campaign.

In February, the British forces in chaos, near ruin, German victory seemingly on the brink, Rommel unexpectedly ended his major offensive at Gazala, west of the British stronghold in Tobruk, Libya, his army, and supplies equally spent.

But while General Rommel sat through those weeks in February and months to come, the idea of the complexes began to take shape and grow under the noses of the Allies, Italians, and Berlin alike ...

For a while, anyway, for a little while.

This is the story of one of those five officers, Baron Hauptmann Dieter Reineke. It is the story of what he found, and what he did, and the Englishman Charles who waited one step ahead.

Ruins, Book One

Corpses in Armor

Part One

The Axis

Chapter One

The Fezzan
March 8

Reineke wondered if Thiele knew what he looked like, never mind him, out here in the dust of man and mankind glittering like gold in the noon sun. He eyed him. The young lieutenant's flushed face frightened and confused. Reineke wasn't quite sure why. The twenty-seven year old son of a shopkeeper claimed to know his Captain well, understand him without difficulty, wealth, or university degrees. The Hauptmann, privileged and talented, infused with ego and eccentricities, was spoiled. By self and circumstances, deranged.

"Indeed," Reineke smiled, a superman long before the theories of Aryan purity proven in the unclean hybrids of carnations and pigs. Birthed, and bred from the loins of Nordic Kings.

"Indeed," Reineke smiled, an exotic being, beautiful, beguiling, powerful, and strong. A divine, god-like creature, fluid and flawless, near painful to behold ...

"Indeed," Reineke said, exhausted and worn, little more than a Frankenstein, manufactured son of his father, cousin to himself. The untainted pool of genetic matter tired, stagnant, and drained, crippling its offspring with emotions and ills far too unstable to survive in a world outside the pleasures of his estate. Grandeur and grace crumbling under the pressures of mortality and men, tortured and tormented, radiant on the outside, but hollow within; or so Reineke suggested, today, pretended to be, today. Embraced. Tomorrow, of course, would be different. An hour from now it would be different. Thiele was not any of those things, and never different, but always the same.

"Indeed," Reineke continued to eye Thiele, comfortable with himself, and with this Thiele, who was an asset beyond his flustered appearance and tempered impatience for the naughty Nordic royal who should know better but refused to.

"It is too quiet, Thiele," he suggested wryly as a reason for his overheated fit, but Thiele was not amused. In this heat, as tired as Thiele was, his massive chest still heaving from his maddened dash across the sand, his darker, rounder blue eyes studious and intelligent behind their sturdy wire frames were not appreciative of the coquettish flutter of the Hauptmann's lashes. The tolerance in Reineke's voice with its amusement directed at him, Thiele. Suitably shorter than the striking Captain an impressive 1.92 meters in height, the abundant muscles of Thiele's typically broad physique did not have him particularly skilled in acrobatics. Two hundred plus pounds, no matter how firmly packed, Thiele was not graceful or attractive in flight. But powerful biceps and equally powerful forearms carried hands quite capable of snapping any neck, never mind one as delicate as ...

"Waterholes," Reineke interjected, and Thiele frowned, "*Was?*"

The Hauptmann smiled, and Thiele eyed him, the androgynous figure before him who looked less like a man than an engaging woman except for that imposing height.

Thiele eyed him. The boned, porcelain features and brushed straight bang, the hair so blond it was white. The Hauptmann was almost albino, nearly invisible in the bright desert light, but he was still a man, not a god, or angel, or whatever he pretended to be. The superior Nordic race matured later than Thiele's common Western stock, and this one had yet to mature at all. "Herr Hauptmann," he replied with the look and tone of a parent scolding its child, "we are thirty kilometers from the ridge your men are waiting for you."

Down went Reineke's head, debating as he conducted his silent appraisal of ...? Of what? Thiele stared at him, not completely at ease for all he claimed to understand.

"It is too quiet, Thiele," Reineke decided finally and he was back to smiling coyly at the wary Oberleutnant with the grim face. "Find me a caravan, hm? Between here and the ridge? One full of natives? Their bodies as hot, tired, and dusty as ..." his gaze flickered over

Thiele, a swollen pumpkin in his uniform with his knotted tie strangling his throat, even in this heat formal and dignified. Reineke's tie was home somewhere at his compound, his stiff shirt collar limp and open. "We are Thiele. Their bodies as hot, and tired, and dusty as we are."

"A caravan?" Thiele gaped at the suggestion that could only mean danger, trouble for the small convoy of soldiers, certainly not something they should intentionally seek out. "We are only thirty kilometers from home."

"So you have said," Reineke agreed, "so you have said." And back down went his head as he walked a few meters away to stand with his back to Thiele who could not feign being amused.

"Herr Hauptmann ..." Thiele began again, restrained.

"Waterholes." Reineke turned around.

Thiele paused. "Waterholes?" he repeated. "The waterholes? What about them?"

"Yes," Reineke said simply. "You found them, did you not?"

Found them? Thiele had not found anything. They knew where the waterholes were already. It was what they were doing out there, inventorying the waterholes. The quality and quantity of the nature-made wells for comparison to the original reconnaissance a short three months ago. Thiele looked around though as if expecting to find a new one rising, bubbling up out of the sand. He didn't, and there wasn't.

"Hauptmann ..." he said with his frown and a tip of his sandy-blond head.

"Yes," Reineke was well aware of what they were doing out there. They were his squad, after all, following his orders, for that matter, and by claim, his waterholes.

"And they were full, Thiele, still full. Well done, Thiele, well done," he congratulated the efficiency of the man.

Thiele was going to say, "What?" His mouth opened, he knew he was gaping again, and damn you, he would not say—"*Was?*" his face twisted comically in frustration.

"Waterholes," Reineke smiled. "The waterholes. Is it me, or is it you? I think it is you."

Damn you! Thiele flushed. "Herr Hauptmann ..."

"No," Reineke shook his head. "No, it is very hot, Thiele. And it is quiet, *too* quiet," he whispered not to disturb the silence. "Find me a caravan between here and the ridge? One more? I want one."

And he was gone, off in the opposite direction of the wagens, Thiele shouting after him, "Hauptmann!"

"No, Thiele," Reineke refused, gaily bouncing away, "I want another caravan. We have seen only three caravans in four times as many days, and it is early ..."

He whirled back around, amusement gone from his face, "And it is quiet—*too* quiet. I want another caravan between here and the ridge. Order it!" he insisted. "Order it now!"

Order it. As if Thiele could. "Where are you going?" he questioned sullenly, Reineke walking away from him again.

"For a walk, Thiele. Pick me up on your way."

Single file, the kübelwagens bounced over the sand. Their idling engines springing to life, the column rolling as Thiele assumed his seat with a wave of his hand. He did not verbally direct the driver to secure Reineke. A snap of his fingers and the soldier understood, the motorcade purring along to reclaim its commander.

He did not repeat Reineke's orders. He said nothing and it would not have mattered if he had. Ten pairs of vacant, staring eyes, half-hidden beneath canvas helmets, would not have found anything peculiar with the Hauptmann's request.

Request! Thiele snorted, violently shuffling the maps. Reineke was, after all, the Hauptmann, their Hauptmann, and Reineke would not tolerate anything less than vacant, staring eyes.

Marionettes! Thiele labeled the soldiers lounging in various positions on the seats of the four kübelwagens. With painted smiles, and starry eyes they danced to the whims of the Hauptmann.

But Thiele was not a puppet, his meaty hand strangling the map as he clutched it, recalling a day not too long in the past.

Tunis, Tunisia
December 1941
"Herein lies the strength of the German Army, Oberleutnant Heinrich Thiele." had been Reineke's introduction of his squad to his newly

appointed First Officer Heinrich Thiele. "Mindless creatures, each and every one. Zombies."

The startled lieutenant disagreed, finding the comparison insulting, his posture stiffening in defense.

"Indeed. You think otherwise?" Reineke noted the defiance.

Thiele did. But the Hauptmann was right to question. It was not Thiele's place to think, and certainly not to say. He stood down immediately with apologies. "Order is necessary, Hauptmann," he agreed. "I believe I understand what you mean."

"Indeed," Reineke walked away from him to stand, looking at the picture of the Führer on the cool, stone wall. "You are different than what I anticipated," he said finally.

"In what way, Hauptmann?" Thiele asked.

"Order is strength," Reineke suggested.

"It is," Thiele said.

"It wears glasses," Reineke assured. He turned around. "You wear glasses, Oberleutnant," he pointed out with a dismissive wave of his hand, aborting any need for Thiele to explain or defend his imperfection. "It is all right. However distracting and unattractive, they are apparently necessary. I understand ... Indeed," he assured, "I understand completely. I know who you are, Heinrich Thiele. I know why you are here. You are my watchdog ... Yes, watchdog ..." he briefly considered the reasons why he needed a chaperon. "Tell me, watchdog, Thiele, what did Herr Oberst, our Colonel, tell you? What!" he gestured dramatically, "concerning I, did he have to say? That I am mad? Egotistical? Insane?"

He took a step closer like a movement in some dance. "Did he say, 'Watch my Hauptmann Reineke, for he is all that and more? Though he is good at what he does, you can never be too careful or too sure'? And what is it that I do, eh, Heinrich Thiele?" he requested. "What could he be talking about? What could he mean?"

Murder. Herr Colonel Schönfeld was talking about murder, the timely and coincidental deaths of those who had offended or defied Reineke. There had been three. Thiele knew of one. "I am aware of Oberleutnant Goetz," he acknowledged the unanticipated demise of his predecessor found shot to death at the tip of Reineke's prized and polished boots. A crime, whose evidence Thiele did not believe, any more than their Colonel who did not believe in anything except his Hauptmann Reineke who enjoyed his moments of notoriety.

"I killed him," Reineke assured, lest there be any lingering doubt to his guilty plea. "They say I did. They may say I killed you."

"They may," Thiele agreed with a shrug.

"Indeed," Reineke straightened up, intrigued. "We are not a suicidal race. That would be the Japanese."

A culture of barbarians Thiele knew little about, leaving its concerns to his superiors the way it should be. Still, he was not quite sure if Reineke was making a joke or what it was he was doing. Thiele studied him. What he thought he could see behind the bright pastel eyes a transparent blue-grey like a fading sea, large and curved like a sphinx or stone cat. There was a distinct hint of an animal in the Hauptmann's features with the stark, bold cheekbones and cut, firm jaw. A suggestion of seduction in his stance, seriousness in his tone and ordinance *we take no prisoners*, be they the enemy or his own.

"What we are is capable," Thiele replied, it seeming a fair compromise, a safe one. They were Rear Services after all, Transport and Supply, their ranks hardworking, occasionally undisciplined, and generally bored, hardly the knights of legend or lore.

"Capable." That was a bold claim. Reineke looked over his shoulder at the picture of Hitler on the wall. "Indeed. You are capable, Heinrich Thiele. I have your file. You are quite capable. Intelligent. Versatile. Why is this? How can it be? You are common, your people slaves to their factories, farms, and mills. What right do you have to rise in the ranks alongside someone such as myself ...

"Indeed, I question your capability!" his head snapped back with a hiss. "It simply cannot be. You are stupid, you have to be. How is it you are not? Why is it? Is it possible we are all truly equal after all? Answer the question!"

"What is the question?" Thiele verified.

"Do you ever dare to imagine," Reineke stretched forward across his desk, "that a man's background is not necessarily an accurate measure of his capability? Eh, my watchdog Heinrich Thiele? Do you ever dare to question what you have been taught, what you have been told? Is the East as great as the West as great as the Phalic, as great as I, the Nordic man?"

"No," Thiele replied without having to consider his answer. The truth indisputable in what he had been taught and told.

"Indeed," Reineke inclined his head. "You have a great deal to learn from me, Heinrich Thiele. I demand your loyalty."

"You have it," Thiele promised.

"Good." Reineke smiled. "Because I will kill you if I find out I do not. A *distinct* capability of mine."

The Fezzan
March 8
Reineke was also capable as a commander, despite his whims and moods. Extraordinarily overqualified to stock his complex of munitions and supplies and therefore, yes, bored. Thiele dismissed the memories of Tunis for here and now. The maps lay at his feet and were useless, anyway. Orders or wishes could not produce a caravan. He did not understand the sudden importance of finding some caravan when they had seen caravans that were not important at all. Because he could not understand it, he did not like it. He glanced forward at Reineke standing upright in the front seat of the wagen, arms draped leisurely over the windshield as they bounced along, and it was Thiele's turn to shiver despite the heat.

"My reputation precedes me, Oberleutnant. I am well aware of that. It is, after all, my reputation."

Madman. His sanity in question, Reineke was not insane. Calculating, manipulative, devious, and deliberate, he was above all, "Lucky!" Thiele whispered. "You are lucky!" But only because Reineke always somehow managed to get away with it whatever 'it' was, other than no act.

Deep in thought, Reineke shifted his weight as they rode. His high black boots, dramatic in appearance were not comfortable. The hard leather hot and heavy in this heat, he was contemplating sitting down for a while. This recent trip into the desert surrounding his compound had been uneventful, and as Thiele correctly surmised, like his squad, Reineke had spent the majority of his time bored. The dormant bulk of the German army lay far to the north, silent as the enemy on their side of the Gazala line. Here, two thousand kilometers south, contact and conflict with the Allies or French was distinctly nonexistent, and though they had wandered over quite an area, not to contradict the sand, the waterholes were also devoid of life.

And he had assumed there would be life. Locating a cigarette in the pocket of his shirt Reineke surrendered to his feet, folding his legs and easing himself down onto the seat of the wagen, the wheels busily devouring the last few kilometers to the oasis and home.

Home here in Libya was his compound. A magnificent ten thousand acre oasis, remnant of an ancient world uncharted on current maps, and artfully concealed in the sea of dunes. Wakes and waves of the sand rising and falling off the end of the earth, pouring down into a great hole of marble and limestone, alive and flourishing with vegetation and water, natives, and of course, sand. *Eden.* Eden in the middle of the great Sahara of nothing and nowhere.

A thousand feet below the desert, ringed by the scarred steep cliffs of an ancient dried riverbed, the oasis lay impenetrable to even an army of men. A working quarry at the time of Egyptian reign, wind, and sand seeded the rock, trees erupting from an old womb creating parcels of land ranging in size from mats to the ruins of a Roman city built upon the Pharaohs' past glory, and subject to the same decay wrought by time.

Three thousand years of conquest and civilization, now two thousand years forgotten and lost, and only briefly reborn to the Ottoman Empire in the late 16th century, until Turkish hold on the North Afrikan region weakened to pirates and the lore of the Barbary Coast. The oasis failed again, surrendering itself back to the sand, Egyptian and Roman triumph, and the Moor restoration overrun with desert nomads, most recently fleeing the Italian-Libyan war. At the time of Reineke's arrival, a league of pagan tribes populated the oasis, particularly along the northern court with its surviving Emperor's villa and labyrinth of lifeless stone gardens. Laying his claim to the oasis, Reineke did not expel them. Instead, the nomads' retreat to the ancient Roman ruins decorating the western sector of the oasis was an agreement. Their few hundred bodies providing an ideal facade for any curious French or Allied reconnaissance and were allowed, to a degree, the freedom to wander—

Reineke snapped to attention. It was *TOO* quiet. Warn the rodents to run and hide.

Even now, the emptiness reverberated, and he whirled around to Thiele. "How far are we?"

Was? Thiele bolted free of his daydream of the taming of Hell, Egypt, and his impetuous commander Reineke.

"How far are we?" Reineke demanded.

"Twenty kilometers?" Thiele guessed. "Wait!"

Except Reineke was not going to wait. He snatched the papers away from Thiele, glaring at the maps.

Twenty kilometers, and the civilization beyond remained anonymous, hidden.

Twenty kilometers, and his native facade allowed the freedom to wander was nowhere around. Not so ideal.

Of the five munitions installations, his was closest in proximity to the front, the first in line.

Reineke stared at Thiele. Only Thiele was not aware of any natives wandering, their movements disciplined and monitored or not. And only twenty kilometers ...

Yes! *Yes*! The swollen radiators agreed. Only twenty kilometers to the compound et al!

Nineteen! The squealing wheels corrected, gobbling the glassy sand.

"Verdammt!" Reineke hissed, and was off his seat, and out of the wagen, running to break his fall as his feet hit the ground.

Chapter Two

"Halt!" Thiele shouted. Hand up to stop the procession he grabbed the door for balance and support as the wagen's suspension groaned under the circle spun tightly in the sand.

Reineke had found them. Meters away, he glared through his binoculars and summoned, "Thiele!"

Field glasses in hand, Thiele could make out what appeared to be tracks drawn in the sand, but he waited for the wagen to stop rolling before heaving himself over the side and he was there, stooping to touch the ground, running his finger through the impression to calculate its depth. "A truck," he interpreted the first of the two sets. "Wide base—possibly a supply truck."

"Indeed," Reineke crouched beside him, poking at the second.

"Staff car," Thiele was convinced. "The tread is narrow."

"Indeed," Reineke said, and Thiele winced, "Their treads are narrow."

"How long ago?" Reineke was already standing, watching his collected clump of sand trickle down.

Thiele blinked. "That is impossible to know."

"Is it," Reineke said.

"It is not possible to know," Thiele insisted. "Their freshness could be deceiving—"

Reineke scoffed, discarding his handful of sand and walking away, hands on his hips, staring out over the silent, arid canvas.

"Hauptmann," Thiele persisted behind him, "there is no breeze to disturb them. Without a breeze ..."

But Reineke was not listening, and rising to his feet Thiele tried again. "It is longer than an hour ..."

"No dust." Reineke understood the rules of science as well as he understood his gift of the sixth sense. "I knew something was wrong,

Thiele, I knew it. Out there in the sand, I knew it." Even though he could not see it, touch it. He turned around. "Knowledge, Thiele. Not hallucination or guess. Knowledge."

"Yes," Thiele agreed after a moment. "But it still could be hours ago. Two. Three. Even four—"

"German," Reineke considered, a somber and annoying thought.

"The vehicles?" Thiele blinked. "Of course."

"Their occupants hopefully German as well," Reineke nodded. "Either way I will not have my caravan after all, will I? A convoy in the area and any natives would quickly make themselves quite unavailable ... to the Germans," he looked Thiele in his worried and wondering eyes. "You think so, Thiele?"

"Yes," Thiele thought so with confidence, but then he was German and the desert Arab was little more than a rat scurrying in and out of its hole.

"Indeed," Reineke said. "We are two thousand kilometers from the front lines."

"Yes," Thiele said.

"Still, this far to the south, is there something else I would like?" Reineke coldly agreed.

"Like?" Thiele repeated.

"Prefer, Thiele," Reineke clarified. "Would I prefer our visitors to be someone other than us? Indeed. If it were to be something I preferred, you are quite correct, it would not be a German convoy— of two, Thiele. Of two."

The emphasis on the number of suspected vehicles was unnecessary. Thiele thoughtfully studied the tracks. "The tire pressure is uneven," he observed, "the truck may be empty."

Empty or full was irrelevant. "A single truck is not a convoy, Thiele," Reineke assured. "Not of supplies or of men."

"No," Thiele agreed. "You are right. Something is wrong. I do not understand."

"Reconnaissance, perhaps?" Reineke suggested.

"Reconnaissance?" Thiele's warrior flared.

"German reconnaissance," Reineke assured. "We are an equally safe distance from the French as we are from the Coast Road. Indeed, I have no idea why anyone would be out here, Thiele—including us."

He returned to staring around the windless sea. "Neither am I pleased to have to be thinking of one now."

"No." Neither was Thiele. "Under the circumstances ..."

Yes. It was probably a good idea for them to get out of there. Reineke followed Thiele's glance back to the kübelwagens and the men, and the light weapons their squad carried. The small arms and number put them at an obvious disadvantage to anything larger than rats. Ironically that had been a complaint of Thiele's when they started out, now proven valid. "One of the kübelwagens," Reineke decided.

"What?" Thiele's scowl turned on him, apparently under the impression a good idea was the only idea.

"Two of the men," Reineke was nodding, "and you."

"To follow the tracks?" Thiele hissed. "*One* kübelwagen?"

"And I," Reineke volunteered. "The rest stay here."

"You?" Thiele choked.

"Order it."

"It might be a truck," Thiele reminded. "It might not be empty!"

"Order it," Reineke repeated. "I wish to find out what it is and who."

"They might not be German," Thiele screeched. "We are guessing!"

"Order it!" Reineke barked, and Thiele sputtered, "Damn you!" and bolted, shouting the orders as he ran.

"Du sau," Reineke pivoted, glaring down on the tracks running roughly parallel to those of his column, and would, the same as his column, in less than nineteen kilometers, come to an abrupt halt at the ridge unless the visitors had changed course, which he doubted they had. "Du sau!" he swore, and it was an oath.

"Du sau," Thiele also swore, though quietly when Reineke's long strides deposited him on the running board of the kübelwagen where he chose to remain. Standing there like a target in Thiele's opinion, not a king. Such grandstanding was not worth the risk.

Thiele was wrong. Reineke rode along on the running board not to impress but to ensure recognition by the unseen nomad he knew was out there. It was already almost certain he was a target, or they were, or could be, until the visitors were identified and perhaps even then. It remained to be seen. In the meantime, the reasons for the show were Reineke's, not something Thiele understood. More of what Thiele did not know, and distinctly present and pressing on both of their minds.

The demarcation point Reineke referred to as *the ridge* was the summit of a deep gorge, a savage rip in the earth's crust, where the desert fell into a valley of stone. Eden? Oberleutnant Heinrich Thiele moaned. Eden was little more than the skeletal remains of some ancient lake, or riverbed buried by Nature and unearthed from its tomb by man. A thousand years, two, or five, Thiele had no idea how long the quarry had actually been there, only that too much stone had been removed threatening the stability of the crumbling walls. Twice, in the three months they had occupied the oasis, portions of the ridge in the west had collapsed revealing an ambitious honeycomb of caves and tunnels supported by petrified wooden shoring. A mountain balancing on stilts, Thiele awaited the day when the dried, riddled props would surrender, bringing the desert crashing down around them.

Reineke would laugh. Never sound, the ridge had withstood ten thousand years of torment and would survive a few more. The tropical island below camouflaged by a canopy of date palms only appeared inaccessible. There had to be a way in. The task was to find it, which they did. At first, only an artery of what appeared to be steps fractured by wind, sand, and avalanches of rock, and then the Egyptian goat path impassable as the steps, and finally the smooth wonder of Roman engineers: a road. Built for their two horse carts, the narrow, harrowing twisting passage through the mountainside was wide enough for modern day trucks, and most importantly, intact.

And in the beginning, Reineke had initiated an effort to re-shore the mineshafts, for the deterioration in the west was acute, until suddenly he halted the work. It was not necessary. They did not use the land in the west. There was no reliable road to the west, and he confined their camp to the renovated north where man and Nature had been kinder to the mountain towering above the courtyard, its majesty glittering diamond white in the sunlight and ghostly sallow at night.

Thiele was not satisfied, steadfast in his refusal to believe man, ancient or modern, had also not sabotaged the northern wall that carried the weight of the road, and if the land were to shrug? If it were to shrug?

Hauptmann Dieter Reineke, riding atop his wagen's running board like a king, enjoyed Thiele's fear. If he ever were to admit to the possibility he might be wrong, and that the land beneath the road had been tunneled through so that every truck was in danger of causing the land to shrug, then let it shrug. When the time came there would be no way of stopping it, and until that eventuality, Reineke would forever be in awe of the frenzied and fantastic imagination of Nature and man who fought to control and use the great stone pit. A feat of engineering likewise embraced in the construction of the villa, for the ridge was not the only monstrosity balancing on stilts.

Oh, yes, Hauptmann Dieter Reineke would always enjoy the return trip home ...

Always?

It was Thiele's turn. Barricaded in the rear seat of the lone kübelwagen, Thiele knew the oasis really was an excellent location for their complex. It had water—an abundant supply of water, particularly in the west. It had more than ample space for storage, and you could search the area for hours and never find the road.

Thiele groaned. They had found the road only by accident, after a storm, though it would not have mattered. So in love was Reineke with the possibilities the oasis offered, he would have built a road, as narrow, winding, deceptive, a terrifying, confusing passage down the mountainside, barely wide enough to allow a single line of trucks. Only one road, and only in the north, no other road was ever found, just countless crumbling steps vanishing and reappearing in a mindless, pointless arrangement.

It was not mindless or pointless. It was a labyrinth constructed on the backs of Egyptian slaves as Rome flourished, and Egypt failed. Markings of an ancient prayer walk of some divine oracle where recessed stations provided the perfect camouflage for Reineke's sentries. Men, who could, from their posts, see for kilometers in every direction. In turn, inform the villa of any trespassers. Whereupon the villa with its conspicuous lack of uniformed patrols could, from the villa's twin towers, observe the road, the one road.

The only road up, and the same road down.

And anyone approaching along that dusty route was well within sight and range of the deadly 88 mm guns housed within those towers. Oberleutnant Heinrich Thiele, riding in the rear seat of the lone wagen, squelched the panic he felt.

Reineke stepped off the running board at the rim of his canyon to greet the tracks that had not turned off in another direction, but continued to run parallel to his column, stopping where he stopped, at the ridge, approximately thirty meters west of their position.

"Three o'clock and all is well, eh, Thiele?" he remarked softly to Thiele stealing up behind him. "We shall see."

Mute, disapproving, Thiele followed him back to the wagen, Reineke snapping his fingers in a brisk signal for the soldiers to disembark. "Take the men, Thiele. I will meet you at the gate."

Thiele's crawl changed quickly to a trot. "Hauptmann, it is foolish—"

"Now, Thiele." Reineke's knuckles rapped sharply against the armor plate of the wagen putting his reluctant driver on notice to hurry up and get out of the way, "You, too. Out."

"But, Hauptmann, your pistol is inadequate," Thiele insisted. "The rifles are inadequate at such a range—distance! It is useless," he swallowed, confidence waning under Reineke's lofty gaze. "It would be foolish?" he concluded, "To endanger yourself? I will go instead."

Particularly since it was far more likely simply foolish rather than potentially dangerous at all? Thiele had no knack for hiding his thoughts, saving Reineke the trouble of having to read his mind. "I said now, Thiele," he replied.

Thiele's eyes dropped, the driver sliding out from behind the steering wheel, wary as Thiele, but obediently relinquishing his seat to the Hauptmann. "I will meet you, Thiele?" Reineke verified. "At the gate?"

"Yes, Herr Hauptmann," Thiele acknowledged Reineke's foot burying the accelerator, the gears screaming from reverse to first as he sped away.

"But," Thiele whispered through the stinging cloud of sand kicked up by the wheels, "we would see." Regardless of who could or could not see them, did or did not see them, one lonely, even carelessly tossed grenade and they would know if their visitors were German, or the enemy instead as a thousand tons of ammunition erupted in flames. The volcanic explosions deafening and visible for miles instead of quiet like it was. So quiet. The broiling air silent, eerily still.

Thiele looked around. An uncomfortable sense of something out there mocking them, a feeling of being watched and not alone was difficult to ignore, but he ignored it. Tried to. "Move!" he turned angrily on the men waiting, but then he knew there had been no call over the radio to warn or advise them of anything whether the operator was desperate, concerned, or simply confused. That was wrong. If everything else was all right, that was wrong. Something was wrong.

Reineke drove as he had run, crazed and maddened, the air gasping with sand. Thiele quickly lost sight of him except for the billowing cloud of yellow dust. The cloud was intentional. Not wearing his goggles for protection was not. Reineke forgot about them and remembered them quickly when the stinging rain of sand stung his eyes. He needed the jolt perhaps. He had to focus, remain focused. Stopping, he strapped them on. This close, the nomads, if they were out there, could see him clearly. There would be no mistake, or mistaken identity insofar as who he was. He stopped again fifteen minutes later, in a private place, invisible against the peaceful scenery where no one watching from the towers could see. Adjusting his binoculars, he found Thiele. A smile briefly coated his tight lips as he watched Thiele and the men attempting to navigate the savage rock two hundred meters above the canyon floor. It would take Thiele an hour, perhaps more.

"They are German, Thiele," Reineke nodded, confident. "Indeed, our visitors are German, Thiele," he assured. But there was still a little time. Waiting for the intentional blinding cloud of sand to settle, Reineke still had a little time before he had to leave. The arc of his field glasses moved west, away from the northern face and the compound for the ruins of Rome and the nomad settlement, the broken white columns of marble marking the end of his territory, and the entranceway to theirs, coming into view.

"Talk to me," he encouraged his hidden audience he knew had to be watching him. But there was nothing to see, no sound, no one. The natives remained barricaded in their settlement, their spies, silent as the air, and the binoculars thudded against his breastbone when he dropped them in disgust. His little time was running out quickly. Thiele would think he stopped to check the perimeter. Thiele would watch the cloud of sand kicked up by the wagen, and too much time passing and Thiele would think that something was wrong. Reineke rolled his eyes. Thiele's concern for his safety however founded on the rules of engagement and war was nevertheless unwarranted. He was safe. Of them all, he was safe.

"Our visitors are most definitely German, Thiele," Reineke scowled. "Warn the rodents to run and hide, and so they have."

But he should perhaps still check. He should perhaps drive a bit further just to be sure. His annoyed return to his wagen, slowed. His hand stretching to retrieve his discarded pistol closed over the steel with reluctance. It was perhaps a wise idea to make sure.

It is always a wise idea to make sure. The haunting presence of the natives surrounding him agreed.

"Indeed." Reineke disarmed, emptying the ammunition from his gun into the sand and tossed the unloaded pistol into the back seat with his hat and holster. There would be no stinging clouds of sand this time. Carefully, Reineke eased the wagen down along the second treacherous road hidden in the mountain's side.

Hiking their way down the road was out of the question; it would take too long. Thiele aimed for the nearest cutback of steps, from there, straight for the bottom, skidding and sliding, his boots desperately seeking any foothold along the slippery rock. If this was some actual operation, instead of simply temperament, Thiele would have studied and planned the descent. It wasn't, and Thiele just wanted to get down to the bottom without killing himself. That would be a victory unto itself. Field maneuvers were not something at which Thiele excelled or enjoyed. A decorated marksman, deadly accurate, his skills were useless and laughable when his rifle was currently much more valuable to him as a crutch or brake to stop his body from falling. He had to slow down, plan what he did not want to spend time planning and that was where to put his feet. It was infuriating. He did not believe the intruders were the enemy. He knew they were not. Reineke was simply angry at the surprise appearance of guests and so they were denounced as the enemy, regardless of who they were, unmindful the probability of some French or Allied invasion was as thin as the air surrounding them.

"As thin, mein Hauptmann," Thiele muttered, successfully managing to twist his neck around and fix an irritated glare on the cloud of dust from Reineke's speeding wagen. Except it was gone. The air was clear. Thiele blinked, briefly uncertain in his conviction that the visitors were German. But then he rejected the idea of enemy infiltration as fiercely as he rejected this exercise in suicide. It was just more of the same nonsense. The cloud was a diversion, diverting the attention of the enemy's fists tightening around the handles of the cannons below away from Thiele and the men on the wall to Reineke. It would be the Hauptmann who died first. A martyr to the cause, sacrifice to his compound, hero to his men subsequently buried themselves in the ensuing avalanche of rock as a bombardment of anti-aircraft shells pounded into the mountain, the ridge disintegrating into rubble beneath them.

"Du sau!" Thiele seized his field glasses, his neck craning forward, searching for the road through the canopy of trees, imagining what the perplexed soldiers must be thinking watching their insane Hauptmann speed toward them, and the Oberleutnant who staggered down the canyon steps before plunging to his death.

"Du sau!" Thiele cursed the guards in the towers he knew had fallen laughing to the floor. Guards who could not hear Thiele's words, but could see a gesture, and gesture Thiele did, as obscenely as his precarious position would allow him.

And he was thinking. He was seriously thinking about demonstrating his opinion to the Hauptmann when the hot, sour breath of one of the men mumbled in his ear: "There are two vehicles parked just inside the gate, Oberleutnant."

Thiele's head twisted back around. "What?" he said, but did not really mean it.

"There are two," the soldier nodded with a point in the direction of the courtyard.

"TCH!" Thiele yanked his field glasses into place. There were two. One staff car, and one supply truck, both unmistakably German, their swastikas proudly displayed on their flags and painted sides, a small group of four equally distinctive guards posting watch over them.

"SS," the soldier offered his sympathy.

"I can see!" Thiele snapped, conscious how his fingers were suddenly cold, rigid.

"I can see," he whispered, his fingers gripping the binoculars, staring back over his shoulder, desperately searching for the Hauptmann and his wagen. But the cloud of dust was gone. It had been gone awhile. That made no sense. If Reineke hugged the side of the cliffs and crawled, eyes thoroughly trained would still see something.

Ears no longer dulled by civilization would still hear something.

And if Thiele closed his eyes and concentrated, he would hear the distant hum of the wagen's engine. When he opened his eyes, he would see the grains of sand floating through the air.

But it was clear and quiet. Thiele's chill spread along his arms. The Hauptmann did not like surprises. To the contrary, Reineke not only coveted his privacy, he insisted upon it, and trespassers into his domain were likely not to be treated politely.

"But they are German," Thiele begged, refusing to remember how the suggestion had seemed to annoy Reineke as much as any thought of Allies or French.

"You are German," Thiele reminded, as if he should have to. He stared through the field glasses at the SS. Wishing for one insane moment of his own the visitors were not German, but the enemy instead who could be dealt with swiftly without having to explain why. He turned back around, his glasses desperately searching the mountain for any sign of Reineke. But he turned the wrong way.

Inadvertently to the west, and there was nothing in the west. The road did not go to the west. Yet Thiele stood for one other moment just gazing at the horizon, the western horizon, and his thoroughly trained eyes, tired as they were, did not fail to notice the thin cloud of dust floating through the air. "Gott im Himmel," he muttered, swallowing the words and no one heard him.

"Go," he ordered the men, surprised his voice was steady. "GO!" And he went first, his ponderous thighs suddenly agile, the boulders no more threatening than the gravel under his feet.

Reineke was angry, sitting stiffly in the passenger seat of the wagen waiting for Thiele beneath the gateway to the complex. Thiele shook his head. It was no more a *gateway* than the oasis was *Eden*. The Hauptmann elevated everything around him to some fantastic level of importance for reasons known only to him. What *gateway*? After three months, it was today Thiele wanted to ask, if he had never wanted to ask before. The gateway was two broken Corinthian columns of pitted and chipped pink marble missing their capitals and cornice, standing like headless sentries, ten meters tall, frozen in the sand. That was it, nothing more. No barrier, or blockade of wire or men. Two worthless pieces of rock that when the Hauptmann was not angry the men did not dare drive around them, but through them as they should whether they were ever a gateway, part of a gateway, or what they were, the ripples of the cream sand sea eventually bleeding into a courtyard of crushed limestone, bedrock for the Emperor's villa. The ancient monstrosity towering and top-heavy as the great wall with its massive arcade protruding like a pregnant belly over a supporting colonnade where the sun struggled to shine, and its marble skin turned from comfortably cool to icy cold in the desert night. Quite unlike the courtyard where the sun shone without mercy and a man could die between dawn and dusk.

That was an idea. Thiele was not above violent thoughts, and briefly considered all options available to them. They could just leave their visitors alone, standing there. If the remaining four or five hours of sun was not enough, or the frigid night insufficient, another ten hours of sun, would definitely suffice. They would be dead by this time tomorrow. When it was over, Reineke could issue the order to pry their cooked boots from their station, burying the carrion in unmarked graves if it wasn't for one simple fact. "SS," Thiele noted quietly as he approached the wagen.

"Get in." Reineke's reply was terse, the sharp nod cold, but contained.

That should make Thiele feel better. Give him hope Reineke could be reasonable. It did not. Angry or subdued, Reineke was a man balancing on a fine wire. A high wire. Thin and tight.

Thiele attempted to keep his attention focused and straight ahead on their guests who weren't merely German, but SS. There was an unpleasant difference between the Wehrmacht and the SS, even in Thiele's mind. The SS were there for a reason. That was also on Thiele's mind. Their munitions complex however top secret it might be was a secret not only from the Allies and Free French, but also from the German bureaucratic machine that knew as much about fighting a war as Thiele knew about the Emperor Hadrian who had built this resort. The compounds were an act of desperation, some might say defiance, initiated by Rommel, and carried out by a small group of Afrika Korps officers, determined to supply the starving troops. In that way then, and only that way, they were all renegades, rebels, not only Reineke. Stealing their German munitions back from the well-fed Italians, and stockpiling them for support of Rommel's renewed push across North Afrika. And so yes, in that way also, Reineke wasn't necessarily extraordinarily overqualified to command his desert supply complex, no more than Thiele was, or any of them, but perhaps instead perfect.

Thiele's scrutiny returned to Reineke stiff and silent beside him. Perfect, Reineke would have radioed the compound when they discovered the tracks to advise and confirm any reports of unscheduled movement in the area before he issued any order.

Perfect, he would have alerted the compound of the danger he believed the movement represented whether he ultimately decided to break or close ranks, or whatever he decided to do. Including some ridiculous exercise that proved nothing, except perhaps that it took Thiele twice as long to climb down the walls into the compound than it took Reineke to drive a road that did not exist.

Thiele eyed the SS. A second road was possibly how the SS had gained access without prior announcement. The posted sentries along the wall could not possibly see everything, everywhere, not if a road also came from the west.

The same as the existence of a second road did not necessarily have to be a case of deception on Reineke's part. It could be Reineke followed the visitors' tracks, and in doing so found a second passage none of them knew anything about.

Thiele wanted to believe that more than he wanted to believe anything. He did not believe it. Reineke did not leave his men to circle the perimeter in hopes of identifying their guests. Unchallenged by his soldiers, the visitors were obviously German.

He did not leave his men to examine the perimeter and determine how and where the visitors had gained entry when there was only one way in—which apparently there wasn't. Reineke knew about the second passage, that was why he left. He not only knew about it, he obviously knew it well since he was sitting there in the wagen, waiting for Thiele to arrive. Six spent cigarettes on the ground marking how much time he had sat waiting, which had been quite a while.

Thiele drove silently through the gate of the pillars. Not around them, or into them, as he might want to do, but through them toward their visitors, only meters away. The SS making their appearance at this time was unfortunate. Thiele was a firm believer in their project, confident of success and equally confident success would stay any need for explanation to Berlin. Six months to establish the compounds and fill their bins was the plan. What could Berlin say when Rommel marched triumphantly into Cairo with the same lightning speed that first brought him to the brink of victory before he ran out of supplies? No?

No, Berlin could not say no. It could say nothing except thank you to its desert commander Rommel for his success and loyalty. Thiele looked over the throng of soldiers roused from their preoccupation with the SS and on the run for the Hauptmann approaching them. It had only been three months, the eve of December to the first week of March. An army grown from a squad of twenty to over two hundred in three short months with close to half of them in the courtyard circling the SS like hungry wolves.

Thiele glanced again at Reineke, the Hauptmann's expression unemotional and unchanged. *Your front lawn abounds with military apparatus and uniformed personnel, mein Hauptmann.* Thiele agreed silently with what he knew Reineke had to be thinking above all. *The anonymity of your compound has been compromised, not only by the SS, but also by your own men in clear violation of your strict regulations. This is why you are angry, isn't it? Isn't it?*

It added to Reineke's anger, yes. Along with the SS invasion, his men's disregard of his orders was a blow to his authority, neither of which Reineke would tolerate. Careful and diligent in shielding the depot from the invisible enemy out there in the sand Reineke's sentries patrolled the courtyard dressed as Arabs from the native camp. Thiele could see only three men in Arab robes in the foreground of the swarming, angry mob pressing forward. As they pulled closer, he spotted three more hovering uncertainly in the distance by the low walls of the dead marble gardens. That made six sentries. It should be eight. Thiele would find them. Deal with them, as he would deal with all of them, later, after the situation with the SS was resolved.

However it would be resolved. Thiele scowled, in favor of reason not kowtowing. The SS were certainly smug for men outnumbered more than fifty to one. Casually at attention, a burning cigarette in the hand of one of them, unimpressed by the jeering catcalls of the men guaranteeing the reprisal they had only threatened before as the Hauptmann's wagen rolled in and halted in front of them. Reineke rose from his seat with ease, his hands slipping behind his back, resting comfortably on his tailbone as he just looked at the four SS guards.

"Not too far," Thiele cautioned quietly. It was not worth it, and something yes, they would work out.

"Not too far," he barely whispered aloud as he alighted to hold the door open for Reineke.

"SS," Reineke commented, something disturbing in his voice, his attention on the skull and cross bone badges of the capped blond heads.

Thiele felt the hot metal of the door handle begin to scorch his fingers.

"Relieve these men of their weapons and post," Reineke instructed his waiting squad, the threat of eruption distinct, inevitable.

"Not too far!" Thiele moaned. His hand was going to stick to the metal if he did not let go, but he couldn't.

"Kill whoever refuses," Reineke ordered and the door handle turned to ice.

But they are SS! Thiele did not say as Reineke stepped down from his perch to disappear into the mansion. Behind him, Thiele heard the single satisfied click of the rifles locked and pointed. *They are SS!* He stared at the assembled firing squad, but the soldiers did not care, they were smiling. And it was out of Thiele's hands. He knew he released the door because he saw his knee come up, and he started to run, but it was already completely out of control.

Chapter Three

"Where is Erich?" Reineke demanded the appearance of his Staff Sergeant clearly not at his post. The broad stone steps of the villa disappearing two at a time under his boots, he was inside, pounding across the polished marble foyer, gilded and gaudy in its sparkling pink brilliance and fading colors of the Eastern Empire. Recognizable as an atrium, common to Rome and its territories, the once open walls and ceiling had been closed to the sky for four centuries, changing the villa's purpose from pleasure to defense, its god from Jove to Allah, waxy pillar candles caged in copper chandeliers providing an illusion of air and light. Reineke headed for the grand staircase, a lazy flow of worn marble lava that would carry him to the mezzanine and his office.

"He is in the wine cellar, Hauptmann!" tried the Korporal who rushed to meet him at the door and was roughly pushed aside.

"Get him!" Reineke ordered.

"He is!" the Korporal said.

"Get him!" Reineke insisted.

"With the prisoner!" the Korporal finished, and Reineke came to an abrupt halt.

"Prisoner?" his back arched. Everything he had been trying not to think flooding into his mind. His reign was over, finished, done, his world, his life. He knew that before he raced to the nomads' settlement. He knew it now. The visitors might be German, but the guns would be French and they would be there before morning. Two-hundred men slaughtered. Two-hundred German suicides.

"Indeed," Reineke said, and it was hardly in surrender to the French or the SS.

"Yes!" the Korporal leapt to explain, foolishly joining him on the stairs.

"Prisoner?" Reineke accused, the dangling binoculars around his neck swinging madly as he whirled.

"Yes, Hauptmann ..." the soldier startled with a step back, flushed with freckles and giddy fear.

"From where?" Reineke loomed above him.

"From?" the Korporal repeated, confused.

"Where? From where?" Reineke pounded back down to him, wrenching his bobbing glasses free, their cord catching his hat, sending it on ahead to the frightened youth, quick enough to catch it before it hit the stairs.

"From the truck, Herr Hauptmann," the Korporal stammered, "the SS!"

"Liar!" Reineke accused. He saw a car, not a truck. *One* car, not ten, and *four* guards castrating a courtyard of two hundred men!

"No, Hauptmann, I swear!" the Korporal said.

"Liar!" Reineke's hand struck his hat, knocking it from the juggler's grasp.

"Hauptmann!" Thiele appeared, bolting through the door with a jump for the stairs, pushing the Korporal out of the way.

"Verdammt!" Reineke shoved Thiele instead. "SS!" he insisted. "SS!" he fired his binoculars like a missile cutting through the air. They crashed into the wall, skidding across the floor.

Yes. Thiele caught his balance to stare at him.

"Herr Hauptmann, it was the Leutnant ..." the Korporal dared to move forward, but Reineke turned on him and he retreated.

"A prisoner!" Reineke hissed at Thiele, and he was gone. Down the stairs and off down the hall for the cellar, his heels clicking on the wood as he ran.

"What Leutnant?" Thiele seized the Korporal by the arm, propelling him toward the door.

"Faust," the soldier hastily defined. "And a Major Weiheber—SS, Herr Oberleutnant. They are SS."

"Yes!" Thiele had eyes, two of them.

"Gestapo!" the young man cried. "They are demanding the Hauptmann's arrest."

"What?" Thiele stared at him. They were heroes not traitors or anarchists. "What are you talking about? How do you know this?" he insisted. "Who even admitted them—who?" he demanded. "Where is Erich? Why isn't he here? What is this about the cellar?"

"Sergeant Erich admitted them, Herr Oberleutnant."

Thiele dropped his arm. "Erich?" he repeated. "Sergeant Erich is SS?"

"Yes," the Korporal nodded. "He was expecting them this morning, when he was expecting you—"

"Never mind!" Thiele silenced him, the details irrelevant, the facts, fact, Erich's betrayal of the operation to the SS apparently one of them. "Find them, I don't care where. Find them and bring them here—and have the courtyard cleared!" he reached for the door to fling the man outside. "Do as I tell you. Move!" he barked, and did an about face, heading for the cellar, cursing Erich. "Fool! Fool! FOOL!"

If the fool had any brains at all, he would be gone.

Except fools, do not have brains. That is why they are fools, and there were four fools in all. SS spies or agents, or simply opportunists, the ranks were riddled with them and that fact apparently applied here regardless of how scrubbed clean. They were also drunk, or drinking in premature victory. Thiele clamored down the steps of the cellar to find Reineke waiting in the doorway of the subterranean vault that like all cellars lacked the luster of its upstairs palace and was instead simply old, the air damp and stale. Silent, the Hauptmann appeared almost relaxed, comfortable in his misleading posture, his hands calm and clasped behind his back.

So, I look like the ridiculous one. Thiele bit his tongue, damming his mad dash to catch him. Erich and three other soldiers who Thiele recognized as belonging to them were on the left, near the dusty racks of wine. Absorbed in their conversation they did not notice Reineke. His words muffled in wine, Erich said something Thiele could not quite hear, but had the men laughing.

"Sergeant?" Reineke responded to the joke, announcing his presence with a single step forward.

And the private celebration died. The slurred voices silent, the full, wet lips of Staff Sergeant Erich paused in molesting his bottle of wine.

"An explanation," Reineke took a second step deeper into the intoxicating smell of machinery and fruit, "Sergeant?"

Erich glance down at his boot tops before he looked up, an insolent smile on his face. "You are late, Hauptmann," he said. "I should have been advised of your return."

"So I see," Reineke inclined his head toward the others, but they averted their eyes, less confident in their betrayal than their leader was in his.

"I see," Reineke repeated, and stepped past them into the alleyway lined with racks of wine. Bits of green glass littered the dirt floor, glittered like emeralds under the naked bulb of light powered by the generator slowly leaking gasoline. Bending down, he retrieved the discarded bottle. It was broken, severed in half, and as he rolled the neck between his fingers, the air around him seemed to grow thick, heavy. But, then, the pungent aroma of the wine was rather thick, heavy, and so it was possible the bottle had been dropped?

Indeed. The racks pressed close. The fractured body of the bottle was ragged and sharp, as if someone had intentionally struck it against something and ...

He rounded the corner, a sour sickness quickly rising in his throat. It was not what he expected. The prisoner was white, a young girl, perhaps fourteen. The blood he expected, there was blood on his men—but so much! Everywhere he looked he saw blood. The walls, the floor stained in the crying red rain. It was not what he expected, and he thought he heard a sound rather like that of a wire snapping.

"English." Thiele's voice spoke behind him. His middle class upbringing surprised by the carnage, but emotionally flat.

"Indeed," Reineke replied. At first glance, he had been unable to distinguish her from a bag of trash, least of all identify her race and political affiliation. Thiele a better soldier than him apparently, cool, and detached under pressure. Reineke stared down on the bare, bruised legs protruding from the lightweight wool skirt a filthy and bloody gray-green. She had been beaten, undoubtedly raped, and possibly dragged by the telltale friction burns on her arms and legs, a broken coil of wire still wound tightly around one of her ankles.

"No jacket," Thiele continued with his observation, and so he was guessing. Without her jacket he couldn't possibly tell what she was other than someone's child.

Reineke stared at the long twisted red braid of hair as she lay face down in the mud in an odd, deformed position, her wrists lashed with the same wire binding her ankle. "Untie her," he said, feeling Thiele's eyes shift in his direction.

"She is alive?" Thiele countered, it of some relevance apparently.

It was not. "Untie her," Reineke repeated, "or I will kill them here, now, the SS as well. Choose. The choice is yours. It is not a war against women and children."

Or old men. So Thiele had been told. He knelt, feeling her throat for a pulse. "She is alive," he announced, but Reineke was silent and Thiele obediently slid his knife from his belt to pry the wire loose.

"Indeed," Reineke said when Thiele turned her over to lay her flat. Hair clung to her battered face. Filthy strands held fast by the drying blood. Her eyes open, staring and dilated, Thiele was acutely conscious of the Hauptmann's stare bearing down.

"Call the sentries," Reineke instructed, and Thiele's head jerked up.

"Sentries?" he repeated. "For the woman?"

Reineke's stare bore into him.

"For the men?" Thiele stared back. "They are your men!"

"Now," Reineke said.

"The woman is alive!"

"Now," Reineke said, the broken bottle he held in his hand suddenly ominous, very important.

"Hauptmann ..." Thiele said.

"*Now,*" Reineke whispered, and Thiele obeyed. Hurrying away to hurry back with two sentries to find Reineke where he had left him, his hands and trousers bloody from where he had tried to wipe them clean. Thiele glanced at the prisoner. Her blouse was closed covering her naked breast, hair no longer clinging to her face.

"Pick her up," Reineke directed. One sentry shouldered his rifle pausing as Thiele's hand shot out, stopping him.

They are here for your arrest. Thiele stared silently at Reineke staring back at him. *Arrest. Do not give them a reason.* It was however a worthless argument not merely unspoken, so Thiele lost. Thwarted by the very rulebook he waggled in Reineke's face, held in check by the first commandment: The leader is always right. Reineke was the leader, not Thiele.

"Do it," Thiele muttered as if he had a say. He lowered his hand and the sentry stepped forward to lift the prisoner from the floor.

Reineke nodded satisfied. "Bring her upstairs."

"You," Thiele directed the second guard, "go with him."

"No," Reineke stopped him. "Thiele, dismiss the men."

"Hauptmann ..." Thiele said.

"*Now*," Reineke whispered. "Do it now." And Thiele walked out from the racks with a scowl.

Staff Sergeant Erich was a large man, tall, Reineke's height, and Thiele's muscular build. A Phalic by race, driving force, even-tempered and reliable, his mental abilities second only to the leadership of Reineke's high-strung Nordic man, or so the truth read.

The truth was true. Erich had apparently forgotten that. He was second to Reineke who was first and second to no one.

"Oberleutnant?" Erich reacted slightly at the dismissive wave Thiele gave to all but him. The soldiers nearly tripping each other in their haste to get out of there, and though they ran now, they would not run far. Reineke carefully selected a bottle from the racks.

"Oberleutnant?" Erich repeated.

"Shut up," Thiele muttered. "Just shut up. Keep still. Don't be an idiot, don't say a word."

"What?" Erich's frown shifted to the racks and Reineke emerging, one foot in front the other, his left hand behind his back, the bottle dangling in his right.

"Hauptmann ..." Thiele sighed, though he did not really believe Reineke would do it, anything.

"Indeed." To the contrary, Reineke's attention was on Erich who knew he would. "Sergeant?" he asked, a question that wanted no answer. Not what Erich was thinking, or why the betrayal. Reineke did not care. Erich studied the bottle in Reineke's hand. Seconds passed, twenty, then thirty, Thiele could hear the ticking of his watch, the volume seeming to increase as the time wore on.

"Hauptmann ..." Erich smiled finally, bored with the drama and

Reineke snapped violently to attention. Rage inspiring strength, Reineke was a strong man. The body, muscles of an athlete, acrobat, dancer, and Erich despite his size was driven back against the stone wall, Reineke's arm across his larynx that for all Erich tried he could not move, the bottle threatening his gut, Reineke's leg slammed between his promising to crush his pelvis and groin.

"Will I?" Reineke's head tipped in the slow, erotic movement of a snake. Taunting and teasing, watching the pulsating throb of the Erich's jugular vein, the sweat Erich tried to ignore, beading on his forehead, tickling the tip of his nose, it was not hot in there, it was cool, almost cold. "Indeed," Reineke assured, "a man would."

"Hauptmann ..." Erich said.

"Beg!" The bottle smashed into the wall, Erich's eyes straining in their sockets to stare at the jagged glass. "Like she did," Reineke encouraged. "Say, *don't. Please.*"

"Do it!" Thiele insisted behind him. "Do what he says!"

"Don't ..." Erich agreed, but the words were lost, his gasp sharp and unbelieving as the glass slashed his cheek, blood bubbling out from the torn flap of meat.

Reineke released the bottle. It fell, shattering into pieces at Erich's feet. "Sixteen," he advised Erich down on his knees, searching for the bottle with a confused grope.

"*Six*-teen," Reineke stressed, promoting the woman from a fourteen year old child to a young woman based solely on the development of her naked breast, like two small buds he could cradle or crush with his hand. She was half his size, half his age, and helpless under the brooding power of his Sergeant Erich.

"You are dead," Reineke promised Erich, and was gone.

"Leave him alone," Thiele threatened the sentry taking a step toward Erich. "Get out of here. Leave!" he ordered, and the soldier gratefully obeyed.

"Idiot," Thiele cursed Erich. "Sergeant!" he scattered the glass with a determined kick, and Erich's head snapped up.

"You are a fool," Thiele assured him. "Fool! Radio for our patrol to return and put yourself on report." And he was gone, after Reineke.

Chapter Four

Reineke stalked across the foyer. "Find the Holy Man!" He ordered the small army of men crowded in the front hall to search the complex for the toddling old priest. "If he is not with the children, send one of the women—" Reineke's attack abruptly changed direction, noticing the girl deposited awkwardly on a wooden bench meant as a decoration, not to be used as a litter for the dead.

"I said to pick her up," he charged the sentry. "Bring her upstairs, not fling her in a corner!"

"Yes, Herr Hauptmann!" the soldier jumped to snatch up the prisoner and stand there trying to decide exactly where the Hauptmann meant by upstairs.

"And, I said," Reineke turned back on the others, "to find the Holy Man. Do it!"

"But he is here, Hauptmann," he was told. "Already in the compound."

"Then get him," Reineke insisted, not sure why, or when, it had become necessary to repeat himself. "Get him!"

"But he is!"

"GET HIM!" Reineke screamed and the soldiers fled, Reineke sputtering after them, "Misfits!"

No. No, they were not misfits. They were startled perhaps by the arrival of the SS, worried as to what it meant, confused in what to do without their leader, so, tell them. Thiele stood at Reineke's elbow. Give them orders, not temperament. "Hauptmann ..." he said.

"Bring the girl to the library," Reineke ignored Thiele for the sentry apparently still struggling with confusion.

"Hauptmann!" Thiele's request immediately flared to a warning.

"Indeed. She belongs where I put her," Reineke corrected.

"Not in your office!"

His office. His library. Sanctuary. A magnificent gallery, largest of the vault arcades, the finest the villa had to offer, spanning almost the entire width of the northern façade it was the villa's pregnant belly as Thiele called it. Reineke's ability to walk on air. Perhaps. It was a porch, a portico atop the colonnade, whose purpose was more than likely a private shrine for the owner's convenience. Originally open on three sides, it too, like the atrium, had been enclosed. Clay walls and heavy wooden doors divided its interior into three compartments. Paned glass French windows installed along its front and sides opened onto an exterior balcony where the hand and footprints of the Emperor Hadrian lay on its original rail and floor. The other two compartments his quarters, and a small apartment kept maintained for guests. It seemed perfectly reasonable to Reineke to order the prisoner remanded to the gallery's vacant apartment. She was their guest.

"My office, Thiele," he agreed, where he, like the Italian dictator Mussolini, could pretend to be Hadrian, Lord and ruler of this withered and once-auspicious retreat. "If it will help you, look upon her as yet another ornament for my office."

With that, Thiele expected him to turn with a flourish for the grand stairs, on the heels of his clumsy sentry, but he didn't. He walked to the front door to stand, impatiently glaring outside.

"Hauptmann ..." Thiele was again at his side.

Reineke sighed, heavily and tired. "Indeed, if I had a gun, Thiele, I would shoot you."

If? Thiele's eyes dropped to Reineke's belt missing its pistol and holster, Reineke waiting when he looked up.

"I threw it away, Thiele," he agreed. "I had my reasons."

"What reasons?" Thiele demanded.

That would depend, Reineke supposed, if he were as concerned for the nomads as he claimed to be, or only for himself. It was both. His concern naturally extended from the vulnerable natives to his munitions and men, something to do with being German and not being a traitor, merely schizophrenic. Yes, that was what he was, schizophrenic. Reineke knew this, realized, and decided it. And since he had now decided, he knew it was hopeless. He was hopeless.

whether or not Thiele continued to believe he could somehow be miraculously cured by this desert vacation. "Pick a reason that satisfies you, Thiele," he offered, "and go away. You are dismissed."

Thiele had no intentions of leaving. "Hauptmann—"

"The penalty is the same for insubordination as it is for treason," Reineke reminded him. "That is not only my rule."

No, it was the law. "They are here for your arrest," Thiele snapped. "Their reasons I can only guess!"

Reineke looked at him. They were here because of the munitions compound, even Reineke in his insanity, knew that. "Arrest," he scoffed. "Indeed. Who is here for *our* arrest, Thiele? The SS? Do as I say. Today is no different than any other."

It could not be more different. "Hauptmann, I think ..." Thiele nodded.

"Do not!" Reineke stopped him, his hand raised calling halt. "All right? Do not. I do not want you to think. There is nothing for you to think about."

"It is you who is not thinking," Thiele insisted, "and you have to. Listen to me!" he grabbed Reineke's arm. "There are two SS officers here. Gestapo. Berlin has sent them. They must have sent them. You have to think, Hauptmann. Think!"

"Indeed." Reineke shrugged free, reaching in his pocket for a cigarette. "I do not care—"

"Are you out of your mind?" Thiele was in his face, snatching the cigarette out of his hand.

"Not about Berlin!" Reineke angrily shoved him away. "Anything it thinks or wants, least of all its SS! You are dismissed. Do not make me tell you again!"

Except Thiele did not want to leave. He wanted Reineke to leave, come away from the door and his vigil for the Holy Man, but Reineke was staring again outside, impatiently waiting for the priest to appear, and Thiele pushed past him for the shaded heat of the porch.

The courtyard was clear and quiet, the vehicles and uniformed soldiers gone, order restored. The security of the villa returned to Reineke's costumed Arabs, two of them were on patrol now, high-powered rifles easily accessible under their loose robes, heads and faces wrapped in layers of white gauze, protection from the sun and recognition as Reineke was unwilling to risk healthy tans and patent black hair as being sufficient in passing inspection even at a distance. This close it did not matter. Any unauthorized person would already be dead.

Or those were the orders. To date they had not yet needed to enforce the orders, not even today. The SS, while unexpected, were not unauthorized. There was another Arab-soldier on the porch. More alert than his comrades and rising from his slump against one of the columns in response to Thiele's presence. Thiele's response was crisp, a nod, and roll of his eyes. He disagreed with the need for the masquerade, finding it more of a game than a trick to fool or deceive anyone. A form of entertainment concocted by the Hauptmann to amuse the troops, rejection of the boredom they all struggled with aboard the lonely oasis so deep within the Sahara seas.

This particular soldier was good however, taking his role seriously, imitating the sly slink of the Arab ferret to perfection as he moved away from Thiele for the end of the porch.

"Du ..." Thiele called him, only interested in ordering the patrols halted for now. The SS were likely sufficiently entertained for one day. If not, Thiele was.

The soldier had a different idea. He took off, straight for the banister with a vaulting leap over it.

"Halt!" Thiele recovered with a shout and rush for the stairs to give chase.

"Thiele!" Reineke's harsh bark interjected and Thiele whipped around.

"Dismissed?" he hissed. "Dismiss them! What is the matter with you? Get them out of here!"

"That is enough," Reineke warned.

"Enough?" Thiele spat, and was up and down the steps, spinning in his tirade. "That was an Arab, and you are telling me, enough? You call for your Holy Man, and you are telling me, enough? I saw you!" he assured, only he did not have a chance to say where. A crack across his face from the back of Reineke's hand sent his head reeling.

"Enough!" Reineke seized Thiele by his jacket lapels, catching him as he stumbled, struggled to keep from toppling backwards down the stairs, and when Thiele looked up the Hauptmann looked possessed, eyes on fire in his face. Thiele had never seen him so crazed. "Leave now or I will kill you, do you understand. Kill, not reprimand!"

The hall clock chimed the half hour. It was four-thirty. The Hauptmann remained outside, positioned on the steps, waiting and watching for the Holy Man. Thiele's chin was wiped clean of the light trickle of blood, his shirt neatly straightened, having sacrificed only one button, his hat set securely back on his head. Reineke's hat lay on the floor, its proud eagle at an odd angle.

Thiele studied the hat, ignoring the sentry who, for some suicidal reason of his own, was back downstairs with the prisoner sprawled back on the bench. Perhaps they had never left. Thiele vaguely remembered they had, but he could be wrong.

"Herr Oberleutnant ..." the sentry petitioned for Thiele's attention.

"So you are a misfit," Thiele agreed, retrieving Reineke's hat to revive its crumbled peak, laying it to rest on the newel post. "You have your orders."

"Yes, but the doors are open."

"Doors?" Thiele said absently.

"The library doors, Herr Oberleutnant," the sentry whined. "They are open."

Instead of locked and under guard. "SS?" Thiele guessed.

"Yes," the sentry assured.

"Of course." Thiele remembered his orders to have the SS officers located and brought there for the audience they seemed to want so badly they came there to have it. Two of them, Thiele understood. Two officers, four men, six SS in total. Six was not enough. There had to be more of them out there, a platoon at least under the Leutnant's command, and who knew how many under Herr Major, possibly a hundred or more. There were certainly more than that north in the Italian stronghold Sebha. But Thiele was not thinking as far north as Sebha. He was thinking of a small village, not too far from the complex, only a few hours no more. Their village where their Colonel Schönfeld was scheduled to arrive from Algiers to supervise the first major shipment between compounds, theirs, and the struggling next in line. A village Reineke controlled, a second compound he wanted just as he wanted Sebha, not only for her munitions she could give him, but her power, position, and size. It would never happen. It did not work that way in the modern world where the SS controlled the cities and towns worth having, either openly, or through their puppeteers. They were under siege. The SS was not there to punish. They were there to take. The Hauptmann should be flattered how after three short months his compound could be so valuable as to be stolen from him.

Back outside the dreaded Holy Man was still not yet in sight.

"Have the girl placed in the apartment," Reineke clarified his earlier instructions, his office no more appropriate as a morgue than the hall. Thiele did not take the ring of keys offered. The prisoner could not go into the apartment and neither could the Holy Man. They would have to pass through the library, and the SS blocked their way.

"Do as I tell you," Reineke snapped.

But, "SS," was all Thiele said, and he stepped aside, allowing Reineke to run.

For the moment, Reineke's temper was confined to the pounding of his boots claiming the stairs. Enraged, he still remembered to collect his hat, and the pounding came to an abrupt halt when he reached the library doors.

Parade rest. Thiele watched Reineke assume his pose of confidence and control, feet spaced and hands behind his back. One SS officer was in the library, a Leutnant, Thiele's age, standing at the helm of Reineke's compound, loitering at Reineke's desk stationed on the raised landing, in front of the wall of French windows.

Faust. Thiele recalled the Korporal mentioning the name. He was ugly, SS Leutnant Faust, fat and fleshy, with thick lips and a broad face squatting on a short fat neck. Thiele thought of a turtle first and then a python. A turtle wanting to be a python was probably closest. Thiele was not intimidated, his own confidence intact.

"Ah, Hauptmann Reineke," the turtle closed the book he was reading with a crisp slap, his smile contrived and misleading. "I am

SS Leutnant Günther Faust. My colleague and I thought perhaps you and I should meet first ... *Sooooo* ..." he swayed toward them, down the short steps of the landing. "I have been waiting to do that."

"Waiting," Thiele sneered; he could not help it. The SS was not *waiting* for anyone. Faust had been brought there, ordered to appear. Thiele knew this. He had ordered it. He caught himself though with a quick look at Reineke whose anger appeared briefly displaced by his amusement for Thiele's bold display of ill temper. The Leutnant Faust did not share in Reineke's pleasure, but was shocked by the affront. Thiele shrugged. He wasn't necessarily brash, he was just truthful, and no more a fan of the SS than any of them.

Especially this one, Thiele eyed Faust, some fat man with some ridiculous order for the Hauptmann's arrest. For what? The compound? What compound? Thiele could play games, too. He also outranked this Leutnant, whether Thiele was merely Wehrmacht, and this one elite SS. "You have orders," Thiele took a step forward, hand outstretched. "I want to see those orders ..."

"Open the apartment, Thiele." Reineke interrupted, pressing his ring of keys into Thiele's hand.

"Hauptmann ..." Thiele stared at them.

"Do it now," Reineke advised, Faust's eyes following Thiele's sharp steps across the room before revolving back to Reineke with a smile.

"You have an excellent library here, Herr Hauptmann," he congratulated.

A meaningless observation, irrelevant. He had questions, this Faust, but no evidence to support them. If he had evidence, he would not have the courage to be there. Lies, he had whatever courage he thought he needed. Reineke smiled under his deadpan expression. The SS knew nothing and were afraid, struggling to regain ground, ill prepared for the resistance by his men even in his absence.

"There are some old—some very rare manuscripts."

The SS worked hard at showing its ignorance in its effort to show culture and class. Reineke had a library that rivaled Alexandria, the secrets of mankind fragile as silk and turning to dust on their shelves. *BANG!* The lacquered brass handle of the apartment door interrupted that time, striking the plastered clay wall, disturbing the fresco buried underneath. A sound like something scurrying as a few chips crumbled and fell. Thiele did not apologize. Wrenching the key from the lock, he retired against the molding his arms folded and face sullen.

"Oberleutnant," Faust acknowledged before returning again to Reineke. "But then we are not here to discuss books, are we?" his porous, fleshy hand extended in greeting went ignored.

"I see," Faust said, concerned by such behavior, and certainly most perplexed. "Yes, well, very well then, may I?" he waved at an available side chair, its baroque design as oddly out of place as the French windows. "Yes? No?

"Very well then, Hauptmann," he sighed when Reineke did not answer, "obviously, there are far more important matters to discuss than your squandering seditious literature ...

"Munitions, for one," his smile broadened, teeth flat and white in his pudgy face. "It would make matters much simpler if you would see to cooperate. Once these tiresome matters are finished, we are then free to discuss your position on any issue of your choosing ...

"Unless you would rather begin, Hauptmann?" he wondered. "Yes? No? Hauptmann," he sighed again, "am I boring you?"

"Boring me, Leutnant?" Reineke replied, and Thiele's hands tightened their hold on his jacket, the fat of Leutnant Faust beginning to redden under the Hauptmann's unwavering gaze. "Indeed." Reineke called for his sentry who responded, carrying in the prisoner, and Leutnant Faust stopped turning red. "One of your tiresome matters," Reineke agreed as the girl was paraded across the library, disappearing through the apartment door.

"Yes," Faust said, "so I see."

"Good," Reineke approved. "It is my position."

Was it? Faust looked at him. "Is it?" he said. "Really, that is most interesting, Hauptmann ..."

"Which this conversation is not," Reineke assured. "Leave my complex now. Get out."

"Out?" the abundant flesh of Faust's cheeks pinched tightly. "Hauptmann, you fail to understand—"

No, he did not. Reineke failed at nothing, including suicide. The idea of it, the risk, already having crossed his mind, he rejected it until he was ready to accept it. When he did, it would be his choice, not the SS. He called out again, that time for the guards, two more sentries quickly responding, standing on either side of him. "Remove this ..." Reineke looked Faust up and down, the uniform of the elite snug across his girdled belly. "Remove this swine from my office. If he refuses, kill him."

"Kill?" The ring of keys slipped from Thiele's hand, clattering to the floor.

"Kill?" Faust sputtered, not quite managing to take a step, the butt of a sentry's rifle responding, burying itself in his abdomen, sending him crashing to the floor.

"But he is SS!" Thiele bridged the distance to Reineke in two steps.

"Indeed," Reineke said, thoroughly unimpressed.

"You cannot do this," Thiele insisted. "Tell them to let him up or I will. I will!"

Reineke looked at him, the silence between them long. Faust's eyes closed under the sights of the sentries' guns, waiting for the click of the triggers.

"I said to let him up!" Thiele turned on the soldier nearest him, wrenching the gun painfully from his hands.

"Let him up!" Thiele insisted and a powerful kick with his boot would have dislocated a knee, except the second soldier spun, his rifle presented at Thiele's chest. Thiele stared at it.

"So that is enough, eh, Thiele?" Reineke's soft voice brought the rifle down. "Enough."

But, no. Oh, no. "No, I do not think so." A new voice entered the scene, and with the grace of a mechanical toy, Thiele turned around to the SS Major breezing through the library doors.

Chapter Five

He was fifty, Herr Major, thin and tall as the Hauptmann, but dark. *Sudetendeutscher.* Thiele guessed. A Czechoslovakian cousin of the Nordic race. This one of Hungarian or Romanian descent, the face foreign and sharply angular, creased with power and age, the hair black beneath his blue cap. Thiele stared from the cap to the uniform resplendent with medals and field gray. The medals inappropriate, the color, and uniform itself an unusual choice for the region where the khaki standard of the Afrika Korps provided comfort but also camouflage; the last thing apparently on Herr Major's mind. Thiele bit the inside of his cheek. Well dressed, the SS were from the north. Tripoli or Tunis perhaps, Berlin even, as claimed, and they were here for conquest definitely. The business attire of Herr Major complete with dangling party sword.

"We would have been introduced earlier, Hauptmann," the Major assured, his finger extended like a pointer as he strode across the floor, unmindful of the sentries quick to fix themselves to his hip pockets. "Except your men thought it best to postpone our meeting—a commendable attitude, I might add. We are second to no one in our appreciation of the soldier who knows his duty, performing it without question or complaint," he smiled, so terribly pleased with the little joke.

Thiele's teeth clamped tighter, his eyes traveling back to the breast of the jacket with its dozen medals—

No, nine. Thiele counted them quickly. The Knight's Cross with oak leaf clusters was coveted and rare, restricted to the most exceptional circumstances and men, and still nowhere near as impressive as his wound badges. Gold wound badges, two of them. Five or more wounds each, they boasted, *each.* Herr Major had been wounded in duty at least ten times, probably in two different wars.

The inside of Thiele's mouth was going to bleed, and he released the tortured flesh, staring at the man who was either extremely lucky or careless, or insane.

He was left-handed. The packaging blinded Thiele. Reineke observed the man, and he would not have expected anything less from this illegitimate peasant calling himself SS. The sword was on the wrong side. The hand he held out, the wrong one. An insult Thiele should have noticed having been born with the same affliction, and only awkwardly cured.

"Hauptmann?" Herr Major retracted his finger stained by nicotine, ending the temporary pause. His eyes bright under the influence of his drug, the face pitted with the pox of disease and age, the shoes were worn beneath their polish, the tailored wool suit with its inappropriate display, three years out of date. They had no place for him in his new Reich once established, not even in the elite SS. He was saying something about intrusion, moving past Reineke for the steps of the landing, apologizing and understanding how their unexpected appearance could account for any unorthodox behavior, the words overflowing his tongue ...

And then his foot touched the first of the three steps, the sentries separating to stand in front of him, block his way, and he hesitated for the first time, one foot up and one foot down, stood there posing in his fading finery with its pretty little pins soaked in blood.

"Oh, no, shhh, Oberleutnant," he smiled at Thiele for some reason, stepping back down. "Please do not say 'Hauptmann'. We know who he is, as we know who I am."

"Herr SS Major Hanse Weiheber of Berlin," one of the sentries provided to Reineke.

"Yes," Weiheber chuckled softly, "yes," shifting his attention to the rotund figure on the floor. "Ah, Faust," he noted. "Ah, yes, Faust." His SS Leutnant Günther Faust.

"We both have reputations, Hauptmann," Weiheber agreed with an accompanying amused shake of his head, "and neither of us, I am certain, wish to waste any more time flexing our ... celebrity ..." he paused with a savoring, fluttering look over the fine Nordic specimen. Such poise Reineke had. Beauty. A flawless figure and face.

"Mythical, really," he teased. "Man or angel, Hauptmann?" he wondered equally amused by the Oberleutnant Thiele's startled blink when surely the lieutenant must have thought it himself at some point, some time.

"Man or angel," Weiheber mused, producing a pair of rimless spectacles, perching them on the bridge of his nose for a closer, clearer look.

"Michael, Hauptmann?" he smiled. "Or is it the Archangel Gabriele you prefer?"

Neither. Thiele knew. It was Lucifer. The most beautiful of all. Those were not the eyes of an angel watching Herr Major. "Hauptmann ..." he attempted to claim Reineke's attention, but was ignored.

"Either way you have succeeded in your humiliation, Hauptmann," Weiheber assured Reineke, "of my ... well, somewhat *wanting* specimen," he agreed. "Won't you now take pity on him and allow him to get up? After all, he can't *go*, Hauptmann," he reminded, "unless you let him. He can't leave and let the men talk."

Never. Thiele knew, and he blushed in embarrassment for the Leutnant, a frightened turtle on his back.

"Up, Faust," Weiheber encouraged. "Get up, Faust," he waggled his finger, waved his hand.

"Hauptmann ..." Thiele tried again and was ignored.

Weiheber sighed. "Now, we can't all be heroes, Hauptmann, can we?" he said. "Try as we might, as much as we may want to. There is only one Göring, one Richthofen. One *Rommel*," his tongue brushed his lip.

And one king. "Get up," Reineke instructed Faust.

"Thank you," Weiheber beamed. "Really, thank you very much, Hauptmann. You see how easy that was?"

"And get out," Reineke directed Weiheber.

Weiheber chuckled again at the sentries with their rifles, one of them tapping his arm. "How possessive you are of your little sandbox," he agreed. "I was told I would find you possessive. As a matter of fact, Hauptmann," he winked, "I have been told a great many things—"

"Fire," Reineke ordered, and the guards obeyed. Two-dozen

bullets hammered into the ceiling over the Major's head, showering him and the room with chips of plaster and white dust as they penetrated the mosaic panels, ricocheting off the marble arches, scoring angry black furrows across the face of the dome, and six more sentries armed with machine guns barreled into the library. Reineke stood in front of the dumbfounded SS, his steel-toed boot toeing the powder until he found a chunk to his liking. Retrieving it, he held it out. "A piece of my sandbox," he offered. "Now get out, or they will cut you in half."

"Swine!" Weiheber lunged faster than Thiele could stop him. It was only the second time in his life Reineke had ever struck anything with his bare hand; Thiele had been the first, outside on the steps. Weiheber he hit with his fist. It was unsatisfying and hurt, angering him more. His knuckles immediately bruised and swelling, cut by the defiant eyeglasses as he caught Weiheber's face flush, and Weiheber was down on his back in the dust, his spectacles shattered, Reineke reaching to rip the cross from his throat, the silk ribbon unraveling as he tore it free.

"Filth!" Reineke spit and flung the medal in the dust.

"Swine!" Weiheber screamed. "Insolent swine!"

"Drop it!" Thiele barked. His pistol drawn and pointed before Weiheber could finish groping for his. "You are not a fool," Thiele warned, the sentries looming threateningly behind him. "Drop it or die!"

"I see!" Weiheber said.

"Do you?" Thiele doubted it. He yanked Weiheber's pistol away, emptying the clip. "He is letting you leave, can you see that? They want to kill you, can you see that?" Thiele could. It was in their eyes. The puppets laughing, happy, unmistakably proud.

"Now, get out of here," Thiele tossed the gun back to Weiheber, "or I will give the order. Get out of here!" he screamed. "Leave!" They did.

Thiele intended to keep watch from the library balcony overlooking the courtyard until the last of the Major's dust settled onto the road. The arrival of the Holy Man changed that, the dwarfed brown figure appearing on a toddling run across the blistering stones for the villa.

"Du sau!" Thiele angrily released his watch over the SS to meet the priest on the grand staircase.

The door of the villa whisked open by the Korporal, the sentries stood at stiff, respectful attention for the Algerian Jesuit priest whom Reineke had cried out for in the desert as if invoking some god.

He was no god. His fat body crippled and dwarfed from birth and age. His misshapen brown face flushed and perspiring, he cursed Thiele in words Thiele could not understand, daring the German lieutenant to block his way, try to stop him, as he boldly hoisted himself up the stairs.

Thiele did not stop him, not because he did not dare because he did dare, and would suffer Reineke's wrath for having dared. It was just oddly, for a moment as Thiele stood on the stairs the priest sputtering in his French, "Out of my way, pig! Out! Go!" he wanted the Holy Man there. Someone, something to bring the Hauptmann under control, a potion, a spell, Thiele did not care. Then the priest could return to his village and children, and they could return to their munitions and war.

Chapter Six

Reineke was in the apartment, the smallest of the three suites of the arcaded gallery, overlooking the eastern courtyard from its wall of installed French windows and narrow stone balcony. Reserved for visiting officers or guests of distinction, there had never been any, and was only on loan now. His sentries he sent to help in the search for the missing Holy Man and a basin of water. They were going to need water.

The prisoner lay prone on the bed, mangled, but still alive, her eyes unchanged from the cellar, wide, open, and unseeing. Her chest was moving though, unevenly as she gasped and strangled on her breath, and so she would die soon, choked on the blood covering her. Reineke studied her irritably, curious whose face lay beneath the beating she took. She was extremely young, barely sixteen, and so unless the Allies also engaged their youth in military service, he failed to see what possible threat she could be to anyone. It did not make sense, none of this. He needed to relax and think. Relax so he could think and it would make sense. Think until it did make sense. Her clothes were from the north like the SS pigs who brought her there. She was possibly new to the North Afrikan arena with her woolen suit. A recent transplant or implant with no intention of staying long.

Either that or her luggage had been lost. Such an idiotic thought to cross his mind. It was the heat of the room. The sudden silence around him for which he should be thankful, but was not.

Who are you? He bore down on the bed, looming over her. The helpless, almost peaceful expression she wore, ridiculing his silent interrogation. A fleeting chill of embarrassment passed over him. Why? He was uncertain, and pushed it away. His interest was natural. To be expected. This deep in the desert? Three hundred kilometers from the nearest hint of European civilization, and even then it was Italian, not Allied. *Who are your people*? He persisted, annoyed by her clothing that did resemble a uniform. Without its jacket, though, he could not be certain if the issue was English or French. This could be traced to the Holy Man. It was absolutely the work of the Holy Man. Some hapless band of gypsies with some sad story—yet another band of gypsies with the same sad story the Holy Man never tired of telling. *Where are your people*? He demanded, as if he did not know. Lost in the desert, as she was lost. Lost, and probably dead. *What are you doing here*?

He stepped back from her in disgust, her smell so much worse in the heat of the room. This close to her, she made him nauseous, her body reeking of urine, teeth thick with bile. "Mademoiselle?" he attempted to penetrate those ragged last breaths she took, looking for information and trying French first, and then English. "Mademoiselle, can you hear me?"

She could in fact. With a snap, her eyes turned on him, their swollen pupils staring up at him. She said something, possibly a word, but he could not understand her, not even what language.

"Mademoiselle?" he requested impatiently. "Try to speak slowly. You have been injured, severely. There is a priest on the way for you to make peace with God."

She said something again in a hoarse dry whisper, moving as if she was trying to sit up, and so he stepped closer, leaned over her to hear her and she attacked him. So fast, she was up, clawing at his shirt, knocking his hat from his head and pulling at his hair, her heels digging into the bed, trying to run, the sting of her broken nails slicing across his cheek as he struggled to untangle himself without hurting her more.

"No!" she hissed, her words English and perfectly clear. "No!" She was going to vomit. He watched her start to heave, the heaves bringing up bile and that he did not want to see. His only intention was to stop her. In her fright, she was going to fall off the bed. But those claws came at him again, and he hesitated, her hair the easiest thing to grab. That filthy knotted braid of dark red hair ...

There was a *pop* as he snatched it. A neat *POP* like a cork released from a bottle. In midair, she stopped, dropping to her knees and Reineke brought his hand away sticky with blood.

"Mademoiselle?" he said, quite perplexed.

Death tried again to take her. A series of violent, spastic convulsions attacked her that she attempted to fight and failed. Her eyes rolling up into her head, she fell over backwards, a thin trickle of blood slowly seeping out from the back of her head staining the sheets as she lay there gasping. Shocked, Reineke yanked her practically back to her feet, desperate to find the wound he had caused, but the blood suddenly gushed, and he panicked, almost dropping her on the floor as he clamped his hand over the gash to staunch the flow, her body dangling over his arm like some bizarre rag doll.

"Mon Dieu!" the Holy Man Pierre exclaimed horrified from the doorway. "Raise her head, mon capitaine, not her feet! Quickly!"

Pierre pushed his way into the room, Thiele catching a pointed elbow in his side as the priest shoved past him to snatch the towel away from the sentry returning with the basin of water.

"Sit down, mon capitaine, sit down," Pierre's arthritic claw fastened itself around Reineke's wrist. "It is all right. You do not have to let her go, just sit down!"

Reineke stared at him. His eyes wide like a frightened child himself. "Are you deaf?" Pierre insisted with a sharp crack on his arm, rousing him awake. "Sit down!"

Reineke obeyed, the girl securely cradled on his lap.

"Good!" Pierre approved, surveying the situation quickly. "We will need water. Very hot water, very cold, and these, more of these," he bounced the towel in Thiele's face. Thiele ignored him, and Pierre angrily turned on Reineke for help. "Tell him what to do," he insisted. "Do not just sit there. What is one towel, eh, idiot?"

"Do as he says." Reineke snapped in German at Thiele, annoyed, the black eyes of the Holy Man brightening happy with the support. "He wants towels. Bring him towels, cloth, anything. You can see the girl is bleeding!"

"Thank you, mon capitaine," Pierre beamed, not forgetting to curse Thiele. "The stupid German Lieutenant listens only to the German capitaine, even though he knows what I ask, is what mon capitaine wants. And!" he shook his crooked finger in Reineke's face, "what you want is many things. Pay attention so you can tell those clowns out there what we need."

Thiele did not stay to hear the orders rapidly translated from French to German. He left it to the sentries crowding the doorway. Moving across the library, he was in Reineke's chambers and back out with more towels, though he was too late to prevent the last of the guards from leaving.

Arschloch! Thiele damned the wily Algerian priest condemned to spending eternity in Hell for some crime against the Holy Empire of Rome. Outspoken in his hatred of Mussolini and the German occupation he was lucky either of them did not kill him.

Rather than indulge him, which the Hauptmann did. Thiele glared at Reineke, talking to the Algerian in his French. Thiele did not speak or understand French, and so he was also condemned, reduced to interpreting the priest's gesturing hands and anxious excitement he could see in Reineke's face.

It was not excitement. Reineke did not know what he felt, only that it was not excitement. The appearance of the Holy Man startled him as much as the prisoner had, especially since he had expected to find the Holy Man dead, the host of his orphan flock along with him, Diana, the village matriarch, dangling beside her sons in the courtyard, not this. He continued not to expect this. Some child alone and on her own hundreds of kilometers from any European settlement? How could he be expected to expect this? *Relax!* Reineke ordered himself sternly. The explanation was reasonable. It was war. The explanation lay with the Holy Man. Reineke knew it if he knew nothing else.

"You see, mon capitaine?" Pierre explained as Reineke sat on the bed, clutching the girl to his chest, the towel clamped tightly to her head. "The blood is stopping already. Pressure, oui, pressure, that is the answer. Head up, feet down."

"That is what I was trying to do," Reineke insisted. "I have no idea what happened, none. She slipped. That is what happened. She slipped."

"Of course," Pierre had no doubt of the good intentions behind the circus act. "I did not think you were trying to dance."

Dance. This priest would be in Hell before him. "Watch how you joke," Reineke suggested coldly. "She is dead."

"Possibly, oui, probably," Pierre agreed. "If not now, very soon. She has been poisoned, drugged. Henbane, nightshade. An overdose. Her heart is very erratic."

"Drugged?" Reineke said.

"Truth serum," Pierre nodded. "It dilates the eyes."

"Indeed," Reineke stared down on the child in his lap. "Who could she possibly be that the SS would drug her?"

"Or bring her here," Pierre pointed out, and Reineke's head jerked up to eye him. "I do not know, do you?"

"Yes, " Reineke assured. "This is not me, it is you."

"No, it is not," Pierre denied. "A few more minutes and I will wipe her face so we can perhaps see for ourselves who she is, no?"

"Yes," Reineke said. "Of course, yes—indeed, why do you think I sent for you?" he snapped. "This is why. She is why. Why are you even asking me?" he demanded. "Just do what you do and be done."

"I am," Pierre handed him a fresh towel to hold in place while he quickly rinsed the first in the basin. "The head bleeds very much, mon capitaine. That is not always bad, it can be good, a natural way of cleansing."

Good? Reineke stared at the water bleaching the towel pale pink, a slick of blood sticking to the sides of the basin. His stomach turned, sick as he had felt in the cellar. "I did not do this," he repeated. "Good, or bad, I had nothing to do with any of this."

"Oui, Pontius Pilate," Pierre agreed. "You do not have to explain to me."

Reineke glared at him. "I am innocent," he assured. "I tried to help her. Certainly not hurt her in anyway. She was going to fall. I pulled her hair to stop her from falling, but the braid was stuck like glue." He stared at the saturated bed sheets. "Glue." And just like glue, it gave way.

"Oui, I know," Pierre vigorously attacked the woman's face. "An accident. For a ballerina, mon capitaine is such a klutz—"

"Gently!" Reineke slapped his hand away. "What is wrong with you? You are not polishing some boot!"

"She is dead," Pierre reminded, "soon to be."

"Gently!" Reineke insisted.

"All right, gently," Pierre shrugged. "You worry about your reputation at the oddest times, mon capitaine, in the oddest ways. Gently, it will not come clean, but, you are the master, I am only the slave, have it your way."

His way? Indeed. Reineke should be so lucky and the Holy Man so inclined. He had no control over this priest, none. Try as he might, as much as he might want to, he was not the master and the Holy Man hardly some slave. "Indeed," Reineke said coldly. "My reputation is above reproach."

"For this sort of thing," Pierre agreed, "oui."

"For all things," Reineke assured, "in all ways, every way."

"It is an all right one," Pierre granted, "yes."

All right. It would be better if he wore a different uniform, such as Allied, or best of all, French, instead of the one he did wear.

"Not French," Pierre said.

"What?" Reineke said aloud.

"She is not French," Pierre said.

No, she was English according to Thiele. Reineke studied her skirt.

"Is she German?" Pierre asked.

German? Of course, she was not German. Reineke could not actually know that, any more than Thiele could know who she was, but he did know it. "She is injured," Reineke replied. "She has been injured—enough, I would think, regardless of who she is."

"Oui, mon capitaine is a patron saint of kindness," Pierre agreed. "He does not have to defend himself. It is good, because she is lucky. Oui, very lucky," he acknowledged, sympathetically. "The man with her not so lucky, no, his ears filled with blood."

Man? Reineke had not heard anything about any man. "What man? Indeed," he was incredulous. "You attended to some man first?"

"I did not attend to any man," Pierre corrected, "I buried him. It was his head, like Mademoiselle, but much worse. The skull crushed. Bones like spikes sticking out through the flesh—"

"All right!" Reineke silenced him. Accounts and lectures on

German pigs could wait. "The man can wait. We will discuss the man later. Tend to this one now. Focus your energies on this one—and do not!" he grabbed that deadly paw, "scour her. Wash her. If it takes ten minutes, it takes ten minutes. Your spies can wait to give you their report!"

"Are you sure?" Pierre asked and Reineke sighed. No. No, of course he was not sure, not of anything. Clearly, obviously, he was unsure of everything, including the reasons for the apparent murders of some man and child on his doorstep, only that once the SS were done with her, they threw her like a bone to his dogs.

"What happened?" Reineke insisted. "What went wrong? Where are the rest of them? Her family? People?" This priest could not tell him there were only two of them. There were never only two of them. By this point, if Reineke counted them, they had to outnumber his men. "Be assured she has told the SS whatever they wanted to hear. You must tell me now what happened. I cannot help you, if you do not tell me!"

Pierre scoffed. "Mon capitaine, we can talk about whatever you want, now or later, and it will change nothing. This has nothing to do with Pierre. The SS would be dead if it did, and they are not. You think not, think again. Pierre is as afraid of the SS as he is of you, and he is not afraid of either. Think about that."

Think. Where had Reineke heard that before? Though they were on different sides in this war Thiele and the Holy Man had more in common then they realized. "Indeed," Reineke closed his eyes. "I have not had time to think."

"So think now. Does mon capitaine really think if I had known about this child, I would have waited?"

No. No, of course, he did not think that. He just did not know where the priest was. He could not understand why he was not there. "Where were you?" Reineke insisted. "You were not in the village, and you were not here, where were you? I went to the village," he assured before the priest could lie, "and no one was there. The people were alone."

"Did you go to the children?" Pierre asked. "No, of course you did not," he agreed as Reineke reacted. "Mon capitaine would never frighten them more than they are frightened already. And that is where they were," he said, "that is where they are. To protect them, of course. Reassure them for when the SS walked among them—which, of course they did not," he assured. "Mon capitaine's men are not too smart, but they are not stupid. The SS went nowhere except here, the villa. If they tried, the men lined up," he gestured, "stopped them."

"You were not at the children," Reineke said. "I sent the men to the children to find you."

"No, I was in the gardens," Pierre agreed, "because I knew nothing about her. You, on the other hand, can wait until the crack of doom. How would I know she is why you called for me?"

"Why did you not know?" Reineke asked.

"Pardon?" Pierre said.

"Why did you not know anything about her?" Reineke repeated. "Why do you not?"

"Because I do not," Pierre said simply. "I know nothing about this at all. Not who they are or why, and I was too busy burying the first victim of your police to find out for you."

That was not an answer. A flimsy excuse for a priest who knew everything, *claimed*, to know everything, and now when it was under his nose? "They are not my police," Reineke corrected. "I have nothing to do with the police—indeed!" he snapped, temper rising. "You know *that*. When have I ever had anything to do with the police? Do not be insane."

"Mon capitaine, I have known you three months," Pierre reminded. "Hitler has been here a year, Mussolini, twenty. You could be them, or you could be you. In time we will see."

"Never," Reineke insisted. "Never."

"I know," Pierre grinned. "Because they are pigs, dogs. You believe that, and so I believe you. I just like to hear you say it."

"Indeed," Reineke shook his head. Dizzy, he felt no less than dizzy whenever he was around this priest, nothing to do with some prisoner, the heat, or the smell, but simply the priest alone. "Talk to me about this man you buried," he requested, a safer subject far more important.

"So soon?" the priest laughed, his eyes wicked and sly, sliding to the side and the hovering presence of Thiele, remembering him even if Reineke had forgotten. "Later comes quickly even for you. Less than a breath, what is no, is suddenly yes. Something perhaps though you have forgotten about?"

Reineke had forgotten nothing, least of all about Thiele. It was simply ridiculous to suggest his interest in the affair did not extend beyond the melodrama of some child dead or dying on his lap. "Yes, now," he said. "*Now.* Talk to me. A white one? Mufti, as they call them?"

"Mufti is not what they call them," Pierre said. "Mufti is civilian clothes, not a civilian man. The word you are looking for is wog. Their word for Arab is wog, yes, wog."

"Just tell me!" Reineke demanded. "Their skin white or brown? And their clothes, what about their clothes? Could you recognize them?"

"White," Pierre shrugged, "and only one. One man and this child. I do not know anything about their clothes. They are similar, I guess, but not the same, no, definitely not. So, who she is? Who knows? There is a belief the man could be American. Oui, an officer," he nodded and Thiele's unfortunate scuff of his boot as he bristled at the one word *Américain* that he could understand had Reineke quickly on the alert.

"Army, I think," Pierre agreed. "Oui, army, I am almost positive this is what was said."

"Later," Reineke silenced him.

"Pardon?" Pierre said.

"Later!" Reineke insisted.

"All right, later," Pierre shrugged. "Now, later, make up your mind."

Reineke had. "Go and start a fire in the stove," he directed Thiele, leaving him to scowl as he left, hating the Holy Man. "Not here, my quarters. We will need fresh kettles of hot water. Bring them when they are ready. Indeed." Reineke stared at the enemy in his lap. "A master understands what it is to be a master," he told the Holy Man smiling so shrewdly at him. "I am a master. This is the work of hoodlums, filth."

"I understand that, mon capitaine," Pierre agreed.

"So do I!" Reineke assured. "So do I."

Chapter Seven

"**S**he is very young, mon capitaine, you are right." Tongue clicking in dismay, Pierre gently patted the girl's face dry.

Yes, she was young, and not dead. This was absurd, some sort of trick. Ten minutes, twenty, and she still was not dead. Reineke's body might be hostage to the prisoner making her bed on his chest and lap, but his mind was not and his thoughts continued to race, unable to settle, focus on one thing at a time. He returned to scrutinizing the girl, cruel bruises and a freckled suntan emerging from under the washed blood, the thin marks of a chain pulled from her neck. He briefly wondered what the chain could have been, its purpose, but then decided he did not want to know. The less he knew, the more he could decide what he wanted to be the truth rather than the Holy Man deciding with his glib tongue and honest heart. Politician, philosopher, caretaker, priest, the Holy Man could be any and was all of them. Thiele was not the only one who did not trust the deceptive brown beggar neither did Reineke. If he ever had, he did not now he could not now, not with the SS, Allies, and whoever else roaming around, alive, dead, or somewhere in between.

"Indeed, this is ridiculous," he accused finally. "How long can it possibly take to bathe some child and give her your last rites?"

Pierre looked up, but Reineke was already ordering him to silence. "Never mind. Just do what you are doing. Continue," he waved, "doing what you are doing."

Pierre disobeyed of course, speaking even though he had been warned. "Would it be easier for mon capitaine to talk about the man again?"

What did that even mean *would it be easier*? What Reineke might find *easier* was not the point. The point was it was taking too long. "Thiele will be back any moment," Reineke reminded. "I ask you again, if this has anything to do with the village, you must tell me now."

"What village is this?" Pierre requested.

What village did he *think*? The Arab, the native, the nomad, the settlement where Reineke had remanded the civilian population and even that was not far enough, not then and certainly not now—obviously not now. He was too generous, too reasonable, compassion teetering on the brink of treason and giving aid and shelter to the enemy. Thiele was right. And where had it brought him, what had it gotten him, other than this? "Your native village," he assured. "Or is that too fantastic to even think?"

"It is paranoia, possibly," Pierre agreed. "I do not know about fantastic, but paranoia, oui, perhaps. You are as annoying as a fly, mon capitaine. Six times, I have told you it has nothing to do with Pierre, but still you insist. So, paranoia, oui. You are paranoid."

Paranoid. Paranoia was unreasonable panic or fear, imaginary persecution from imaginary persons or things. The village was neither, but far too real, much like its priest. Strength in his bent posture, gifted with intelligence, blessed with education, and training, cursed and defrocked, crippled from age, birth, or beatings to whittle away his sins and other earthly delights, the limbs twisted and broken and healed as they were, but still a master. Once master of the desert oasis, father to countless orphans from babies to adolescents, one quarter of the oasis's population, half of Reineke's native façade as young as or younger than the girl on his lap.

"Indeed," Reineke said. The answer had to be the village. There was no other reasonable or even plausible explanation. The first weeks of Reineke's occupation had been a constant battle between him and the Holy Man. The comical Algerian spitting his resistance loudly to the all mighty German with his demands, refusing to surrender what Reineke called the villa and Pierre called the children's home. The random adult population, the Holy Man had insisted were unaffiliated with his orphanage. A scattered band of nomads simply visiting the oasis for its water before moving on—which they would continue to do whether the Holy Man had the power to stop them or not, which he also refused to do.

"*And as far as you!*" the unyielding priest had assured, picking up a glass paperweight from off the desk where he had once sat reading stories to his illiterate brood, heaving it at Reineke, striking him in the chest. "The next is a bullet!" he promised if Reineke insisted upon staying even the night, the German Captain, nor his troop, alive to leave in the morning.

Reineke had stayed, unafraid of some priest fearful for his children. The screaming group of them gathered up with their priest and the nomads and marched to the desolate western sector of the oasis and its tomb of ruins, and in the morning, despite the heavy ring of guards, the heads of two goats hung in the courtyard, their bloody carcasses thrown on the steps of the portico in warning. Reineke ordered the heads cut down, the carcasses cleaned and cooked for dinner, and come the second morning there were two more goat heads hung in the courtyard, but no carcasses; the children had to eat, too.

Reineke was convinced the natives would consume the whole of their livestock by the end of the week if the nonsense did not stop. He tried reason. Threats of punishment and even death when reason failed, vowing to kill them all, which he did not, but instead, agreed to a compromise and it was Thiele's turn to explode. You do not compromise with the enemy!

But Reineke refused to listen, severing the children from the nomad tribe and returning them and their priest to the main ground, remanded to a private area of their own. The nomads remained in the west, the borders of the oasis the boundary of their prison, and Reineke would know if they attempted to stray, because he would count them if necessary. It was settled and it worked, for two weeks. Thiele was not surprised when the arguments started again, only this time he was excluded, first by the language, no longer in French and explained in German, but in French and not explained at all. Then suddenly, the feud moved away from the villa, out of Thiele's sight and hearing all together. But he knew the fight continued, until one day, as before, some agreement was reached, a pact made, the terms of the contract known only by its two authors. Confounded, Thiele had no choice but to watch, eventually, begrudgingly, admitting to the treaty's success as the Hauptmann emerged from the drama focused and concentrating on the complex, the rapid and thorough organization helping much to soothe the concerns of his uncertain First Officer.

Impressed, Thiele's apprehensions faded, convincing himself, he was capable of balancing Reineke's high-pitched emotions with logic and cooler heads, and the two officers were becoming ...

Friends?

The Holy Man did not leave. Not the villa or the main grounds but was as free as Reineke to wander where he wanted, walk where he wished. Thiele attempted to overlook the relationship, ignoring it at first, but it was becoming difficult as the two opposing authority figures also continued to talk. The private conversations now quiet, increasing in frequency and length as the days and weeks passed on. The bond between the Hauptmann and the Holy Man was not something Thiele could understand, least of all solve, and manacled him with its strength. The Jesuit monk was a private possession and at the top of Reineke's strict list of rules and regulations was Rule One: No one interfered with the Holy Man.

Not even you? Thiele stood in the doorway in the minutes before Reineke ordered him to leave, watching the meek and submissive Hauptmann obediently sitting in his enemy's blood, the prisoner cradled on his lap. It was disturbing to see, disturbing to think how the hands controlling the puppet strings might not necessarily be Reineke's.

What did he offer you? What did he promise? Eternal life? Divinity? Thiele was at a loss. Reineke was not even Catholic, he was Lutheran. A heretic by the monk's Roman measure, child of the demon Beëlzebub, spawn of the anti-Christ, Lucifer ...

Who was leaving, they were leaving finally. The Hauptmann shifted in his seat and Thiele's tight lips parted, a cool breath of relief escaping to be cut short. Thiele stiffened, bristling when he realized they were not leaving. In disbelief, he watched the Holy Man tip the woman's head away from Reineke to allow him to adjust to a more comfortable position before he took her back into his arms.

"Go and start a fire in the stove, Thiele," Reineke directed him. "Not here, my quarters. We will need fresh kettles of hot water. Bring them to us when they are ready."

"Mon capitaine?" Pierre's voice roused Reineke from his thoughts.

Yes, he was listening. Paranoia, indeed. That was the taunt of the sibyl Diana. Her harsh threats and promises of annihilation issued in concert with the Holy Man's schemes of redemption. Reineke had yet to decide which of the two of them was worse, which of the two he could trust least, knew best, but he had a good idea. "I saw two in the courtyard," he assured, hardly paranoid, simply not blind. "Thiele saw them. Hanuk on the steps—"

"The dentist and the lawyer," Pierre interrupted, "yes."

The dentist and the lawyer. Somewhere, somehow, if only in his mind, Reineke held the belief he was the commander of a munitions complex, and in control. That this was a munitions complex—a *German* munitions complex despite appearances to the contrary, of which he was at least partially to blame.

"Indeed," Reineke said. He was not responsible. Perhaps in some small way that did not count, such as the inspired scheme of an Arab façade, but that was the extent of it. That was the limit. The dentist and the lawyer, he did not know. Not which was which or who was who. The doctor among them, yes, the doctor among them he knew. The doctor he dealt with when needing to deal with things, occasionally talked to on subjects other than the neuroses of Diana or the Holy Man they conspired to apply to him. And the doctor among them would never have been so ... what? Stupid? Brazen? Bold? The doctor among them was clearly not there, but elsewhere, leaving the dentist and lawyer to fend for themselves however inept they were, which apparently they were.

"Defense, of course, mon capitaine," Pierre was claiming as the reason behind the native infiltration of his camp. "Interest, and, yes, defense."

"Suicide," Reineke assured.

"Not really," Pierre denied, "there were only a few SS. Six, I heard, six, I saw. Four men and some fat lieutenant, and uglier Major with the syphilis face and the Devil's hand—you have seen him?" he verified. "When you see him, you will understand."

Reineke had seen him, and his face and hand were irrelevant. Six SS did not travel the desert alone. There were more of them. "Suicide," Reineke assured. "If their interest was defense, they would have killed the SS in the desert before they arrived." He failed to understand why they did not kill them, only that the dentist and the lawyer were not the only ones who were inept when his own squad also let them live. "They wanted the prisoners the SS brought. They are from the village, stop lying."

"If they wanted the prisoners, mon capitaine," Pierre countered, "they could have taken them in the desert and killed the SS."

That was Reineke's argument. That was what he was saying. "Why then?" Reineke insisted since they agreed. "Why come and look and do nothing?"

"I do not know," Pierre said. "Perhaps to see who they were? Understand why they are here?"

"Why?" Reineke maintained.

"Why do you want to know?" Pierre smiled.

He did not. Were he to tell the truth, he did not care. Not why or who they were, but he would have killed them in the desert without question, without a doubt, the SS, and the strangers they brought with them.

Or perhaps not the strangers they brought with them. Reineke glanced down on the girl in his lap. He would not have killed them until he was certain, unless he was sure. Unsure, he probably would have called for counsel with the Holy Man, Diana and her sons, the dentist and the lawyer and the doctor among them.

"Talk to me about the SS," Reineke instructed. "Did you see them arrive? I know you did, and if this is some sort of trick to auction me to regain control—"

"Has mon capitaine lost control?" Pierre asked surprised.

Only of his mind. But that was so long ago Reineke had not only forgotten when, he had forgotten why. "Talk to me," he warned, "or I will destroy the village and bury what is left of it in the sand like the Romans did Carthage."

"Salt," Pierre corrected him, a threat, not just a history lesson behind his words, a promise, reminder, portent. "Carthage was buried in salt and the sand was born, a curse upon anyone who attempted to rebuild her."

Reineke looked at him.

Pierre shrugged. "I, as a priest, of course, do not believe it such things. Curses, sand, salt, it does not matter, Carthage survives, and you will never live to bury anyone. Two hundred men, two thousand, many more have tried, all have failed and so will you."

"Did you see the SS arrive?" Reineke repeated his question.

Of course, Pierre had seen them. Knowing something was wrong before he had seen them when he had first noticed Erich and the two sentries who should be in the gun towers arguing outside. "You always tell me who are where," he reminded unnecessarily, "so I know because I do not speak German." Or so he claimed. No more than Thiele, or any of Reineke's men, spoke French. Those who had were gone, less so they could not speak to the Holy Man but so he could not speak to them.

"From the hill I saw them." Pierre reported in detail how he climbed the mountain despite his crooked, bowed legs to watch them arrive, his head swaying sadly for the murdered child in Reineke's lap. "It is my fault, for when I see how they are SS, I went to the village, oui, naturally, and it is hours before I am here. Had I not done this? It would never be like this, no, never. This is terrible, mon capitaine, terrible. She is not of the village, I swear. Nothing to do with the village, or anywhere for hundreds of miles, I would know. A white woman like this? I would know."

"She could be Scandinavian," Reineke agreed absently, eyeing her and thinking of the lawyer so blond like him, a ghostly white in his sea of brown brothers. "Polish even perhaps."

"Pardon?" Pierre said.

"Nothing," Reineke shook his head. "A thought, that is all. She is clearly European." He touched her stained auburn hair wondering what color it was when it was clean, the texture coarse or soft. Her skin was freckled from the sun, or just from chance.

"Like Martin, yes," Pierre smiled. "I did not realize you knew."

That the lawyer was Polish? Or that he was Martin? Of course, Reineke knew. He knew everything. John was the dentist, a burly man, darker hair like his mother, with stone-blue eyes. "You were saying something about Erich. Sergeant Erich," Reineke reminded.

Only that Erich had been outside, and that he knew. "Oui, mon capitaine, he knew." Pierre told him. "You know this for yourself by now. He is the traitor, the betrayer, not Pierre and his children. Had

I not come down the long way, the American might not have died until later like this one, or perhaps not at all. It is hard to know," he admitted. "Only that if they lived, it is possible we might know more."

Such as who? If not why? And therefore from where? Instead, it all died with him, there on the ground in the middle of the compound. "What?" Reineke said.

"His head, mon capitaine," Pierre said. "The butt of a gun, sometimes it kills, not only the bullets. Boots, perhaps, but I do not think so. Too severe, too much. His head was crushed, beaten until his brains lay in the dust."

"Of the courtyard?" Reineke hissed. "He died in the courtyard?"

"I saw him, and so I know," Pierre nodded. "I buried him, and so I know. He was dead. The blood fresh and red."

And his men did nothing. The SS killed some man in the middle of the courtyard and his men did nothing.

"They were angry, mon capitaine," Pierre offered as if reading his mind. "If that is what you mean."

Angry. Reineke could hear the catcalls in the courtyard when he arrived, two hundred cowards in men's dress, peasants hurtling angry barbs at the king SS, but daring to do nothing.

"They sent for your sergent," Pierre nodded, "the small one who watches your supplies?"

"Linke," Reineke replied. "Sergeant Linke."

"And he was extremely angry," Pierre assured. "Arguing and fighting with your Erich and his SS, because he knows how the people could riot—which they will not, mon capitaine," he quickly promised. "I swear. There will be no trouble in the village. I will talk to the people. They already know it is not you."

It was not him and he would talk to the people himself. He did not need the Holy Man, or Linke. He waved Linke and his loyalty aside. "You should have sent for me; *you* knew I was en route. The dentist or the lawyer come for me, not Sergeant Linke!"

"I did," Pierre said. "I told John 'check that fancy watch of yours and see where mon capitaine is. He could be dead himself'. I did not see Hanuk and so I thought they had sent him to meet you on the sea." He hesitated.

"What?" Reineke insisted. "*What?*"

"Nothing. I was thinking perhaps there was another person." Pierre shook his head at the remnants of clothes the prisoner wore, discolored and stiff as her hair. "Oui, I am positive, at least one more. This is too much blood, much too much and too long. It was the same with the man. She has been in these clothes for days. This much blood from either of them and both would be dead before now, and so another person, at least one more, at some time before."

And from some other place other than there.

"A grave perhaps." Pierre offered, able to see bodies lying in some mass grave. "But why bring two here?"

Reineke had no idea. "An airplane," he said suddenly.

"Pardon?" Pierre said.

"Indeed, airplane," Reineke assured. "They went down in an airplane. They could have been there for days. There could be more bodies at the crash site. A plane!" he stressed.

"Oui," Pierre nodded, "I understand. That is very good, mon capitaine. Very possible. But what about the SS? Where were they? Just there? Just found them?"

Possibly. "Indeed," Reineke said. Erich's betrayal was far reaching if the Allied were around, and it would be Erich, not some Allied prisoner, who swung from a rope in the courtyard. Trouble or no trouble in the nomad village, Reineke would turn his dogs loose on Erich in a second. "I will take care of the SS."

"Oui," Pierre grinned. "It is why I like you. You know how to be the boss. That is good because unlike you, Diana does not threaten, but kills. Turn her dogs loose, you can be sure, and that includes, mon capitaine, on you."

They would have to catch him first and like the SS, probably not like the taste very much if they did.

"If Diana were here," Pierre was continuing. "She is not. Too bad because Pierre is a priest, not a doctor, but we will see what we can do. Will you stay, mon capitaine, will you help?"

Stay? Reineke looked up.

"It is deep," Pierre nodded. "I will need to close it."

Close it? Reineke stared at the assembled stack of medical supplies; he had not heard the soldiers return, Thiele in the doorway with his basin and steaming kettle of water. "Stay?" he repeated. And do what? What was this priest talking about? He could not stay!

"Mon capitaine?" Pierre said.

"Dismissed," Reineke released the guard, Thiele setting his kettle down and leaving with them. Surgical needles and thread in the ready hands of a priest not something he wanted to understand.

"Mon capitaine?" Sometime later, the Holy Man Pierre stopped Reineke before he left. "It will be all right," he believed, optimistic about the prisoner's chance for survival. "She is young, but she is strong. The young are always strong."

That was not good news.

"Mon capitaine?" the priest said curiously, when Reineke did not respond.

"It is nothing," Reineke replied. "Continue."

"Thank you." Pierre smiled, and Reineke stepped into his office, glad to breathe the fresh air of the library.

Thiele was waiting, and would demand to talk. Reineke did not want to talk. Thiele was too honest, applying pressure without diplomacy and flattery. He fumbled in his breast pocket, searching for a cigarette, but the pack was blood soaked; there would be no way to avoid the confrontation and he laughed. A short, hollow laugh as he walked toward Thiele tossing him a fresh pack. The long awaited nicotine satisfied only his lungs and he laughed lightly again, watching his bloodied hand as it moved back and forth in front of his face.

"Your men need a lesson in discipline, Thiele," he proposed with an eerie smile.

Discipline? Thiele preferred to pretend he had no idea what Reineke meant.

Reineke nodded. "Would I, or would I not?" he agreed. "Slit Erich's throat, or merely cut his cheek? Which were you thinking? What? A man would have killed him."

He was brooding about the SS Major, remembering what was said. The teasing, the taunt implying he was something different than a man, something less. He wasn't, and right now Thiele couldn't care less. "A sane man would have done neither," he retorted.

"Which I am not," Reineke agreed. "I think ..." he watched his hand. "Yes," he decided. "I think I will bathe, Thiele." He walked away.

"Hauptmann!" Thiele came alive and Reineke stopped.

"Yes, Thiele?" he said as if he did not know.

"The woman cannot stay where she is."

Indeed. The woman was a child, not a woman. Perhaps slightly older than sixteen as the Holy Man had proposed, and simply small, extremely small, *la petite mademoiselle,* Reineke believed the Holy Man had said if once, six times, like it was a name. And *la petite mademoiselle* was, and remained a child, in Reineke's opinion whether she was sixteen or what she was, if only because her persecutors could not have been any better a judge of her age than he was, any less interested in her age than he was.

"Indeed," Reineke said. "The girl is currently occupying the apartment, not my office. I would have thought that would have been of some consolation to you."

"The woman is a prisoner," Thiele reminded harshly, hardly consoled, and Reineke turned around to him.

"You are observant, Thiele," he agreed, waiting expectantly.

"A prisoner of the SS," Thiele assured.

"Indeed." Reineke mocked, not to be disappointed, and two small patches of color brightened on Thiele's cheeks.

"They are the SS," he insisted.

"So you have said," Reineke tossed his cigarette to the floor, grinding it under his boot, "repeatedly."

"For all it has mattered to you!" Thiele snapped as Reineke turned his back on him again.

Mattered to him? Why? Because they were SS? Reineke fell into a thoughtful pose, studying the scorched ceiling above his head. His father was SS, a Colonel living lavishly in Berlin, the cancers eating away at him as stubborn and ruthless as he was, refusing to die.

"I suspect my father may have something to do with our predicament, Thiele," he replied. "Though, admittedly, by this time, I would have expected him to be too tired, too old, and too dead, to trouble me."

"What?" Thiele said.

A reasonable challenge. Reineke's father could have nothing to do with any of this. That was fantasy, infantile and thoroughly unrealistic. It was the munitions, of course, what else? Not only him, their entire effort had been betrayed by Erich to the SS.

"Indeed," Reineke's head came down from his observation of the ceiling. "This is a munitions compound, Thiele," he reminded coldly, "not a Stalag. It is my compound. I have a thousand tons of ammunition. That is what matters to me. Not the SS and not some child."

"And what are you going to do with her?" Thiele insisted.

Do with her? Reineke could not answer that question. He stared at the cracks in the worn marble floor smeared with the soot of his cigarette. He had absolutely no idea what he was going to do with her. Hopefully, she would die. Quietly, though, in the middle of the night, and everything would take care of itself. He did not take prisoners, ever. The implications of that rule unnerved him for the first time. *Never.* The word hung suspended, deadly, a thousand voices alive inside his head, their curses, and screams so loud he knew even if he screamed he could never drown them out.

But there were reasons! He tried anyway. *Legitimate reasons*! Prisoners brought problems, questions, the obvious complications of unwanted guests. He could not risk either. He had no desire to extend a welcome to either. It remained, as always, so much simpler just to ...

His stomach turned, his mouth dry and tasting foul. The Holy Man said she would live; he wanted her to die. "The Holy Man could be wrong, Thiele," he wished, though he doubted it. "He still could be wrong." He had been wrong, was wrong about the Amerikaner. The man would have indeed died.

But, quietly, though! Reineke insisted to the floor. *Not in the compound. In the middle of the compound, MY compound!*

But this is different? It whispered back. *Is this different*?

Of course, it was different. "I do not know, Thiele," Reineke charged him, "but perhaps you can enlighten me. Do you think Allied scouts take their children along with them on their missions, or perhaps you think she is a scout herself?"

Thiele had no idea.

No, of course he did not. Thiele had so far managed to avoid fighting his war, satisfied to quote its rules he knew so well. "What would you like me to do, Thiele?" Reineke insisted. "What do your rules say? Hang her in the courtyard? Would you like her to die in the courtyard? In the middle of the courtyard like the American?"

"What American???" Thiele jumped, wanting to know.

"Indeed!" Reineke said.

"What American?" Thiele insisted.

"It is a fact, Thiele," Reineke said coldly. "The only fact you need to know."

Was it? "And can your Holy Man also tell you why the SS are here?" Thiele demanded. "The reason, *cause* for your arrest?"

He was talking about the village. That was ridiculous. After considering the nomads initially himself as the source of interest, Reineke had since decided it was ridiculous, at least from the perspective of the SS. The SS were there for the complex, to claim it and take it for themselves. No one knew about the village. His men barely remembered it was there.

"Indeed," Reineke said. Thiele was worried about the Holy Man, the children, complaining as usual, as in the past, and now this new one with the English skirt and torn blouse and what was left of her at only sixteen years of age. "I do not care why the SS is here," Reineke snapped. "Paris is occupied, are all her citizens dead? Are we traitors because we do not kill everyone who crosses our path?"

Thiele did not believe him. He considered Reineke wanton, his displays of compassion, kindness and diplomacy misplaced, indicative of weakness, not strength. "Hauptmann ..." Thiele said, prepared to offer him what? A pill to cure whatever ailed him?

"No!" Reineke silenced him. "There is no difference between here and Paris, Oslo or Warsaw. They have their ghettoes, I have mine. They have their whores, conscripted servants, I have mine. I care to bathe, Thiele, that is what I care to do. You may join your SS, or whatever it is you care to do!"

He stalked away. Thiele screaming, "Hauptmann!" after him like a rabid dog.

Chapter Eight

R eineke was in his quarters. His suite of two rooms and a bath, similar to the apartment with its high mosaic ceilings, towering stone columns and painted marble walls, though much larger, German under its Arab décor. Less congested by furnishings and flourishes, stark and grand, just the way he liked it.

"Indeed," he resented the reminder of how imperfect, rejecting it. He was not responsible for the world.

"Indeed, I do not care," he repeated to the haggard exhausted face waiting for him in the bathroom mirror. His flesh pinched and drawn; scratched with anger, frustration, and some frightened child's fingernails. He touched his wounded cheek, the injury cosmetic and annoying. She assaulted his vanity, insulting it, her blood soaked through his shirt to his chest, the pattern of her head outlined on his skin. The heavy, dangling gold chain and Prince's cross he had worn since he was fourteen, stained and wet as he was with her impending death.

He did not particularly want to bathe. Finding he had no pressing desire to sit in a tub of water and watch it change colors from clear to cloudy rust.

But you have already started the fire. The stove behind him reminded, the heat from the burning wood beginning to dance over his back.

"So I have." Reineke could see the little cast iron stove in the corner of the mirror. It was going to be very hot in here, very soon. Steam would cover the mirror and he would not be able to see himself anymore.

That might be nice. Reineke moved as far out of sight of the face in the mirror as he could until the fog rose to cover him. But the bath was too small for him to escape entirely.

"Indeed," Reineke cursed his marble prison with its gleaming tub, toilet, and sink, and a little ornate cast iron stove for heating the cool desert water. "Ingenious," he mocked. His predecessors as determined as he was to bring a sense of civility to their insufferable world. There were five such stoves in the massive building, all of them designed for their companion baths ...

"No," he shook his head. No, that was not true. There were only four stoves. One was not missing, merely relocated, given to the Holy Man for his children. There were no stoves in the smaller, outer buildings to heat their water, and he did not think it was right.

"But, I made a mistake," he admitted, confessing to the steam. He had told Thiele what he planned to do, and, oh, what an argument they had. Reineke treated to a dizzying deluge of facts and fears of the natives taking advantage. "Of whom, Thiele?" he wondered. "Whom?" Him? The complex put at risk of attack by stones and spears?

"It is a stove, Thiele," he nodded. "Over a stove, Thiele." A furnace for heating Nature's caldron so brutally cold at night. Yet Thiele was the realist, and he a dreamer.

"Or fatalist," Reineke shrugged. It amazed him how he could be both, but apparently, he was. Still, dreamer or fatalist, he did it anyway, despite Thiele's lengthy list of reasons why he should not. Just him and the Holy Man, in the middle of the night inspected the limited selection before deciding, and come morning, Thiele found his stove gone—*poof!* like magic.

And the unexpected labor of hard work. Reineke did not know much about disassembling and reassembling century-old stoves. But the Holy Man did. The Holy Man knew many things. Sixteen years he had lived in Libya, in this house with his children. It was for them he learned his things. Survival, he called it, and Reineke could not argue with him there. One would have to learn many things if they wished to survive here.

"Including how to best to survive with the occupying forces parked on your doorstep, eh, Holy Man?" he suggested. "Indeed."

He stared in the mirror, the fog uncooperative in covering the glass. Diana, matriarch of the nomads living among the ruins, was an occupying force all her own, her marble statue intact and high on its pedestal, stretching three meters tall. One hand to the heavens, one hand blessed her flock, a smile on her face, her dogs positioned and poised. But then Reineke had warned the Holy Man he would check on the settlement camp, conduct a census to ensure all remained present and accounted for, and so he had.

The Fezzan
January 1942
"She looks like you." It occurred to him as they stood there and so he said it, the sun high and hot above the brilliance of her Temple. He meant her strength possibly, her two thousand years of survival and torment, or perhaps he just felt like being fresh.

He was fresh, and just so handsome. An air of humor about him among all his other airs and sins, surprisingly poised and dignified with a devil behind those blue eyes as they say, threatening to distract her for all her years of wisdom and worldly ways. It was a good thing she knew them for what they were. Her daughter's soul beside her in case she forgot.

"Does she?" the crone looked up at the goddess with a laugh.

"No," he assured.

"You are right," she agreed, old, and soiled, and fat, her rifle automatic and pointed at his head. *"My husbands should be so lucky."*

"Husbands?" he said and she shrugged.

Indeed. *"Where did you get that?"* he inquired instead into the gun holding him hostage.

"It's standard issue," she teased.

"It is French," he said.

"You have better?" she said.

Of course. *"How long have you been here?"* he asked.

"Five thousand years," she assured and his eyes rolled.

"I meant ..." he said, speaking less of her Moses having taken some wrong turn than he was speaking of her personally.

"Oh, you mean this time around." She understood. *"Long enough. Two, three years. Since they closed the gates to Eden. Why?"*

"You speak German like a native," he said simply.

"So do you," she slyly agreed. *"And so if I kill you now, how many more will come?"*

"None," he shrugged. Alone and on his own apparently, for the first time in his life, not just at night, but during the day.

"Really?" she said. *"The bishop seems to think there are thousands."*

Bishop? *"What bishop is this?"* he frowned.

"Pierre," she said. *"You didn't know he was a bishop?"*

"I thought he was a monk."

"No, he's a bishop," she said. *"With a son your age, a little younger. They're like that. Catholics."* She shrugged. *"Latins. Men. What are you going to do?"* She took his cigarettes, lighting two and offering him one. *"Where are you from? Berlin? Do I know you? Should I?"* She eyed him. He was so German like any good officer should be. He didn't work for a living, the hands were too soft, and unless her senses deceived her, smelled almost spicy, fragrant, of incense and lilacs. *"Come on. It's not a difficult question, not even important. I just want to know."*

He hesitated. *"The Rhine."*

"That's it?" she said. *"The river? The water? Funny, you don't look like a fish to me."*

"I am Hauptmann Dieter Reineke," he said. *"You do not know me."*

"You're right," she agreed. *"I don't. I've never heard of you."* And that put them on equal footing if nothing else could. She lowered her rifle, cradling it in her arms like an infant, but still he did not chance it. She looked too serious, adept, and so she was in many ways. *"I am Anna who knew Albert. You may call me Diana since you think I look so much like her."*

"Albert." He considered the Alberts he knew. There were a few. He eyed her.

"Einstein." She blew a thin stream of smoke from her lungs. *"You know if you were young and handsome, Hauptmann, I might consider having sex with you."* And she laughed again as his eyes flew wide, a reassuring tap of her steel on his arm. *"It's all right mein Liebchen, we'll think of something else."*

And so they did.

March 8

Reineke stared at the water pump, her voice in his head. "*Prison's not so bad, Hauptmann,*" she promised whether she could support her words or not. "*You'll see. Especially since you get to live in a big beautiful house when all we have is this.*"

Outrageous, utterly absurd, he was not a prisoner he was a king. Whether or not he was a king here, should be a king, ever belonged being a king here, he was still a king. "Indeed," Reineke touched the pump. He was giving himself a headache. He needed to think about something else, anything else.

"*And the children?*" He had questioned the crone about them first, and then the priest, one of them more boastful than the other, one of them less cooperative and shy.

"*Pardon?*" the monk said from his seat where he had been ordered to appear and sat like his arms were strapped to the side; would probably claim they had been strapped to its sides.

"*The children,*" the German repeated. The band of creatures the monk claimed as his.

"*What about them?*" the monk said.

"Nothing," Reineke assured aloud. He was thinking about the pump, remembering when he had questioned the Holy Man as to how there could be such a pump in the middle of a desert he received an unwanted lesson in geography. The few existing rivers were not perennial, rarely even above ground. But under the desert, were many rivers, springs that fed the waterholes and like the Roman before them with their baths, the Arab had cleared the rubble and tapped a spring.

"*Though that is not to say,*" Pierre had also strongly advised, "*there will always be water.*" In the summer, it only trickled. And many times since he had lived there, it had not run at all. "*But!*" he assured. Beyond the villa were the wells in the west, and the baths in the east, and so he could foresee no immediate or acute problems.

"Oh, yes," Reineke nodded, talking to the pump, "no immediate or acute problems." Simply mutiny, SS, Allied prisoners alive and dead, and a thousand tons of ammunition to shield and protect. One thousand tons. Fortunately, the Holy Man who knew so many things did not know about that.

Or he pretended not to know. For now. For as long as it remained convenient for him and his children, the Holy Ghost of the unholy trinity, Pierre, Diana, and him.

"Indeed." Reineke stared at the kettle of boiling water, its mist spiraling up around the chimney. It was probably not a good idea to have two fires lit at one time. Dual columns of smoke might attract the attention of whoever else was out there.

"Such as the survivors of your mass Allied grave, Holy Man." Reineke's gaze followed the riveted stovepipe up to the ceiling. "Precautions. One should always take precautions." An excellent excuse for delaying his bath, the heat making him sick. He picked up the ladle, the flames howling as he tossed the water over them, but they lost in the end, and the ladle splashed into the kettle to stay.

"I will use you tonight," he forewarned the dry tub, sitting down on its edge. No one would see the smoke in the night.

"A great many things," he joked at the drain, his heels kicking against the side, "go unnoticed in the night—Indeed," he stood up. The dampness of the rim of the tub reminding him the seat of his pants was also wet with the prisoner's blood. He really should bathe. He looked from the kettle to the small sink with her deep inviting bowl. "Sufficient," he shrugged. The water pump belched as he grasped it, her ancient plumbing angry at being disturbed twice in such a short time, but the air abated, the water gurgling into the bowl. The scratches on his cheek stung when he touched them, and he pouted, attacking the water. The marks would be there for weeks, could be there for months, infected within days from her dirty, broken nails. He did not want scars. He had one scar on his leg and it was enough, the flesh thick and still raised after two years, a flaw where he had been flawless.

"Indeed," Reineke wiped the moisture from the mirrored glass, studying his face, wondering what the Holy Man might have in his bag of tricks to help him. He had already given him a lotion of berries and zinc to protect him from the sun, and though he was tanned, darker than he had ever been, his skin no longer cracked and bled, sucked dry by the vicious climate. If the Holy Man could manage a remedy for the sun, it was possible he could concoct a medicinal compound that would soothe, instead of irritate. Even if Thiele persisted in criticizing him, for the heady olive salve made him shine, it was still worth it. He had the skin of a woman. It seemed only fair he should be entitled to the same vanity.

"Indeed!" Laughing, Reineke dunked the cloth. The cool water felt good and he remembered his body with a glance at the tub. A cold bath? It sounded inviting. Smiling, he grasped the handle of the pump. If it proved too cold he could always get out, though he did not think he would, no, he did not think he would.

Reineke emerged from his frigid bath forty minutes later to paw roughly through his closet, searching for the perfect uniform. The elaborate style of the SS Major, frayed and out of place for the region had not impressed or escaped him. He, too, owned beautiful custom uniforms and he might decide to wear one. Two dandies entrenched in a duel? It would have made for an interesting evening had Herr Major insisted upon staying. He had not, and Reineke was almost sorry he had not for he enjoyed a good fight, the excitement and victory.

"Indeed," he assured Thiele's ever-hovering ghost hovering somewhere. "A duel to the death, Thiele. Not simply a prick of the cheek like some child's game, or scolding."

Herr Major would understand and appreciate the difference. One of those scars on his face had come from the point of a sword. Reineke should know, having seen them often enough. His father had one, a telltale cut below the apple of his cheek. It made him a man, and was the motive for their argument so many years ago when Reineke refused to stand for the same baptism of blood. At times, Reineke preferred to think he rousted his father in defense of Alexia whom the father hated, so desperate for another son to replace the one he did not like. Both reasons were probably true if Reineke needed another reason besides the simple one of hate.

"Do you know my father, Herr Major?" he wondered. Herr Oberst Reineke of the SS? A violent, sadistic man, abusive of his wife and infant daughter, cursed with fits and epileptic seizures, and a son stronger than he could ever be.

"You should know my father, Herr Major," he agreed, and would be surprised if the two had never met.

"Indeed." Reineke stared down on his uniform laid out on the bed, envisioning the Major's chest aglitter with its trinkets of gold and silver and blood. "I do not have nine medals," he admitted, though he did have a Knight's Cross, proudly worn on its narrow silk ribbon. He earned it, together with his promotion, in *France* ...

The memory started with a whisper. He did not like to think about France. He died in France, becoming some man he still did not know whether homicidal or suicidal, and either way he could not feel sorry for *France* ...

Reineke let his body fall backwards onto the bed, watching the mosaic panels of his vaulted ceiling as if watching some film. It was from France he had borrowed the idea of keeping the nomads as cover for the compound. They were being harassed, continuously harassed by an irritating band of French raiders. But his Captain did not care for they were advancing, eternally pushing onward. Oberleutnant Dieter Reineke did care, and backtracked with the squad of men under him, finding the irritating band of Frenchmen in a village not too far away. The successful nighttime raid might still have ended in a reprimand, except Reineke went in to make sure. He wanted them all ...

They took that village apart stone by stone, and what they found was not a sleepy country parish after all but a well-stocked resistance cell filled with equipment, supplies ... land mines ...

Reineke touched his thigh. There were few actual villagers, perhaps thirty, mostly children, all dead. He shut his eyes. There were children here, but no land mines. You could not have land mines with children, children ran around ...

They leveled the village as a warning, and when Reineke left the hospital, completely recuperated from the mine that had killed the soldier with him, he was a Captain with his own command and a Knight's Cross. A hero, all because he cared, and his Captain had not.

Reineke opened his eyes, the film speeding along faster. He did not like officers who did not care about their men. He cared a great deal. And now he was in North Afrika still fighting under the famed General Rommel who continued to care as much as he did.

He sat back up. Reineke held a great admiration for the General Rommel. Self-made men impressed him. Men of nothing who became men of power and dreams, usually they impressed him. Some he paid little attention to at all, still others he scorned. "You boast German supremacy, *mein Führer*?" he called out to the ugly little man whose picture disrupted the beauty of his library wall. "Rommel is your German supremacy. Not those creatures skulking around the courtyard—*MY* courtyard," he assured just so there would be no misunderstanding between them either.

"Indeed," he glanced down on the rumpled uniform he had clutched thinking it was his torn leg. He did not wear wrinkled clothing. Back in the wardrobe, he flipped over his formal suits. Some were field gray, all of them tailor-made of the finest linen, soft as cashmere. "Not wool, Thiele, not wool," he advised. "No one wears wool in this heat, not even the English." He touched his parade dress, so similar in color to the girl's skirt in the other room. She had to be from the north where it was still cool, perhaps from one of its convents or schools. He could not imagine why, or what had brought her here except an airplane. Unless the Holy Man was lying and she did belong to the village, her family dead in their mass grave.

"Indeed," Reineke chose one, its crisp white jacket and luxurious gray pants so perfect for a summer evening and a chat with the crone. "No, I do not have your medals, Herr Major," he agreed in the mirror, fastening the perfectly creased trousers, "but I have a great many reprimands. Would you like me to pin them on my chest? Hm? Are you going to threaten me with another? Have me deposed from my command not only my compound? Arrested or shot for protecting instead of killing the enemy regardless of affinity or age? Indeed!" he laughed.

The laughter was brief. His hand stopped buttoning his blouse.

He might know. The mirror nodded sympathetically.

"He cannot know!" Reineke threatened the glass with his hand. There was no way. No way! The prisoner was unrelated to the village, merely a coincidence as the Holy Man claimed.

"Stupid!" he cursed and spun around, hands jammed in his trouser pockets. It was his own fault. The Holy Man had said he would understand when he saw him. He had seen him, and he did understand. Herr Major was not at all like him. Herr Major was not stupid.

Like you. The jacket whispered from the bed.

"Indeed!" Reineke seized it, sending it sailing through the air. "Who are they?" he turned on the mirror. "Why are they here? From where?" he insisted. "Where?" But the mirror refused to tell him, it was not a crystal ball, besides he already knew. Whether from the village or the north they were undoubtedly the Allied. "Fool!" Reineke sputtered, damming himself. "Thiele is right, I am a fool."

Arrogant. The mirror corrected.

"Ha!" Reineke said. "I am a king. And you are nothing," he assured the jacket crumbled in the corner like the SS crying for its life, "filth!"

And? The jacket prodded from the corner.

"And?" Reineke stared back at it. "And what?"

But the jacket only shrugged.

"Games," Reineke marched back to his wardrobe. "Indeed. I do not have time for this."

Games. His uniforms agreed.

Reineke paused. "What?"

Games. They assured.

"Indeed," Reineke studied them, thinking. "Do you like games, Herr Major?" he eventually turned back to the jacket. "I do."

He was very good at games, playing and winning, he made sure of that.

"You should know, Herr Major," he warned, "murder is not difficult for me. To the contrary, I find it simple and easy, and satisfying. There are few vices some investigation of me would reveal, simply murder and—"

"Women?" Reineke blinked. "Indeed." That was interesting. He turned on the mirror. "What are you saying? The prisoner is not a woman. She is the village, a child. There is no difference, they are the same. I did not *take a woman away* from him, I took a woman *away from him*—never mind," he shook his head. "I know what I am saying, and it is different—and, *IF!*" he promised the jacket, "you bring another woman here in the condition you brought that one, I will take her away from you, too.

"If you bring a dog," he assured, "in that condition, I will take it away from you. That is what some 'investigation' of me will reveal."

And? The jacket waited, holding its breath.

"And I will not kill you," Reineke scooped up the jacket to toss it in the laundry pile, "not yet."

But in the end, he would, because he had to.

For the children. The mirror understood. *The children.*

"Indeed." Reineke resumed his search for the perfect uniform.

"I think this one," Hanuk's hand appeared beside his, his head tipped and midnight eyes teasing in his handsome face. The hood of his robes flung back and collar open, exposing the leather strap of an arrow quiver slung over his strong shoulders.

Chapter Nine

How long Hanuk had been there in his quarters, Reineke could only guess. Long enough and the Baron's arguments with the inanimate fixtures around him were nothing new or particularly alarming to Hanuk. It made Reineke seem somehow more human, not less, distinctly fascinating and intense, not crazed, lonely, or lost. Still, one or the other should be embarrassed, Reineke for himself, Hanuk for him. Neither of them was. Hanuk, bemused and sly, Reineke in control and in command, disapproving, tolerant, adult, suddenly Thiele, though calmer, much calmer, composed and self-possessed.

"Angry with me?" Hanuk laughed at Reineke's vexed expression for the tall young man forced by circumstances into being much older than his seventeen years, though Hanuk was still only seventeen, boyish and brash, and disarmingly charming. A lover in another world and life, a killer in this one, deadly and calculating as the savage he pretended to be.

"No, you are not angry with me." He patted Reineke on the shoulder, wandering away toward the glass windows and wandering back. "Anne sent me to tell you to come to us and we can tell you what you want to know, which we can't," he shrugged, more realistic about such things than his little sister. "Not really anything. It's just Anne being Anne, but we can probably help you find out. Today, tonight, tomorrow, just come," he requested. "You know Anne. She'll kick and scream and call me a coward and come here herself—cigarette?" he offered with a clever smile, picking Reineke's pack up off the bed.

"Indeed," Reineke surrendered, accepting the cigarette with a critical nod for the burnished chest of muscle sporting its courage and weapon of choice. "A bow and arrows? Are we cowboys and

Indians now?"

"It's quieter than a rifle," Hanuk assured. "Besides, I'm good. Very."

"Really," Reineke said. "I have a Luger on the floor of my wagen outside. If you were as good as you think you are you would not only know that, you would have it."

"Who says I don't?"

"I do. There is another in the chest," Reineke pointed, returning to the bureau to change into his uniform. "Take it and keep it. It is much better than your French ones. I will send more tonight, rifles, too, as many as I can. The men may arm, but they are not to do anything. You understand?"

"I do."

"Good. The Holy Man is in the apartment with the SS prisoner, a young girl, your age. When she is feeling better, and if you are polite, perhaps I will introduce you." he winked at Hanuk in the mirror. "Right now, I do not want you to disturb them. Understand me?"

Completely. What he said, and what he meant, but then Hanuk was German under his stained mulatto skin and sable black hair, at least half, a native of Poland and Berlin society, a distinct however distant memory. "Is she pretty?" he teased.

Not at the moment. Reineke stared at the mirror. "Small," he replied, attempting to be polite. "Anne's size. Perhaps a little larger, I do not know," he agreed briskly, wanting to change the subject. "She is a small woman, yes, young—*la petite mademoiselle*. That is what she is. You speak French. How do you communicate with the Holy Man if you do not?"

"Latin," Hanuk shrugged.

"Latin?" Reineke paused.

"And French," Hanuk laughed. "Enough to know she's no taller in French than she is in German."

Reineke ignored him, eying himself critically, the uniform standard, and nondescript, principally identical to the one he just took off. "Well, there is room for improvement, particularly if you are planning to make a career as a fashion consultant ... are you sure this one? I do not agree. I wish to make an impression."

"On whom?" Hanuk wondered.

"The world," Reineke laughed with a flick of his head for Hanuk's exotic robes worthy of a sheik. "Look who is talking, a young stallion in a sea of kindergarteners. It is all right, though," he nodded, collecting his boots and belt. "I would probably do the same; definitely. I want you to stay here. Those are your orders. Here, until I return and tell you it is safe to go."

"I can do that," Hanuk returned to the expansive stretch of French windows. "I like this room. It reminds me of home."

"Home?" Reineke stood up. "The opulence, I would understand you to mean, rather than the scenery. Or you are from a very different Berlin than the one I know."

"It would be a very different Berlin than anyone knows," Hanuk assured. "I was born in Berlin, but we lived in Khartoum, in the Sudan until I was ten. My father, like Abe's, was mixed. Sudanese, Indian, Turk. Call them anything but what they were—*English,*" he laughed. "Yet another noble officer in the British crown. After my parents' divorce, we moved home to Berlin for a short time until my mother married Hermann and we moved to Czestochowa. Poland."

He turned around, but Reineke was busy in the mirror, refusing the opportunity to comment on what he knew of his tenants' plight, the presumed death of Hanuk's mother Hannah among them. Hanuk had a feeling he would refrain. He nodded. "And then back to the Sudan, and then to here. Summers, yes," he said, "before the war, were usually split between my grandmother in Berlin, and my father's family in Kent, until my grandmother decided Berlin had become very different than the one she knew, and she called grandpa khalif for help in opening the gates of Hell for the Promised Land." He smiled. "He couldn't. He tried, or he didn't. I say he did. My grandmother says that's why she divorced him forty years ago because he was pretty but not much else, kissing the boots of the English and drinking their tea, wanting to be one of them."

"A very interesting life." Reineke agreed. "Still," he combed his hair, watching Hanuk in the mirror, "why are we having this conversation? What are you waiting for me to say?"

"Nothing in particular," Hanuk shrugged. "I'm sure you've wondered about the brown skin."

"Not really," Reineke denied. "When you say mixed, I think of your grandmother, Bohemia, and that the sun here is very hot."

"Yes," Hanuk laughed again. "Conveniently so, if not why we make such good Arabs." He winked. "Better than the ones you have out there."

"Yes," Reineke said. "Who else is here with you? I saw two in the courtyard, before I saw you."

"John and Martin," Hanuk acknowledged. "The intent was to blend in with the guards. I just wanted to get a little closer than they were willing."

"Yes," Reineke agreed. "Thiele saw them, and you. But you know that, right? Of course you do. That is why you ran, smart and foolish at the same time. The SS know Arabs, and they know German guards. You think they would not know you?"

"There are enough of us," Hanuk assured. "Yes, enough of us— why?" he teased. "You want to know specifics?"

Not necessarily. "Stay here." Reineke tossed him the pistol from the chest.

"Promise," Hanuk caught it, tucking it in the sash around his waist. "It's why I'm here. To stay and make sure everything's all right; with you," he grinned again. "Pierre, I know can take care of himself."

"And do not ..." Reineke reminded.

"Disturb them," Hanuk shook his head. "I won't. It's all right, though, I've already seen her so you don't have to worry about protecting me."

"Embarrassment," Reineke corrected diplomatically. "It is not a question of fear, or protection. I do not wish to embarrass you, or her. Since you have seen her, you understand what I am saying."

"I guess so," Hanuk shrugged with the callousness of his youth. "She's not much larger than Anne, you're right."

"Indeed," Reineke did not wish to think about it. "You said you saw her, the Holy Man says he did not."

"He didn't," Hanuk agreed. "He and Uncle John had taken the body away. I stayed behind with Uncle Martin. She was still in the truck—until they took her out, and then I saw her." He smiled. "I practically had to sit on Martin to keep him under control. It's probably a good thing Pierre did not see her."

"And the man, did you see him?" Reineke asked. "Was it an American who the SS killed in the courtyard?"

"I think so," Hanuk frowned, not thoroughly convinced. "My English is worse than my French. It said US Army on the jacket, easy enough even for me to read. But I didn't recognize the uniform. None of us did. It had a lot of patches on it, odd ones with symbols. John's the expert and his best guess has him some sort of engineer—*Army Corp of Engineers.* Something like that. Martin, as naturally, has his own ideas. Insisting it's too early for them to have any organized outfit of their own, especially out here." He winked again. "Perhaps a special detachment, like you. Rommel's no monopoly on hunger or thirst."

"Something else of value to learn," Reineke sidestepped the topic of his complex, "English. English is business, money, a language of the financial world. And money," he said, "as you know, is power; opportunity and ability. I can think of no greater assets a man can have or miss should he lose either of them."

"It's the end that matters," Hanuk echoed the mantra of the SS. "How you get there, doesn't."

"Yes," Reineke said. "I will be rich whoever wins this war. That is not greed. It is good business and common sense."

"And a Swiss bank account or two," Hanuk nodded.

Reineke laughed. "Indeed. A few Swiss bank accounts yes, of course, right next to your grandmother's."

"Well, I'm working on it," Hanuk assured. "English, and Arabic, too, though only so I can swear at them in their own language, no offense." His grin flashed.

"I am not offended," Reineke assured. "If you want to swear, swear. Refugees ... and, yes, prisoners," he granted, "are a casualty of war, not only the dead or wounded. They should be respected, assisted, whatever is the need, not ignored or mistreated ..." Even before he finished he knew he sounded like he was talking to a five year old. How, even Anne at her age would find him patronizing. He smiled. "You know what I am saying. The SS changes nothing. You know that also, or you would not be here." He nodded again at the burnished naked chest of courage and muscle. "To protect or to kill me. Anything else? Or are we finished?"

"I don't know," Hanuk said. "Are we?"

"I am thinking," Reineke agreed. "A curiosity, perhaps, but one I cannot seem to resist. Since you are the smartest—"

"No, Abe's the smartest," Hanuk assured. "As John says, the rest of us can only try."

"Since you are so willing to try," Reineke granted, "as I asked the Holy Man, is there a particular reason one of you did not first attempt to find me, before coming here?"

"You can say it," Hanuk nodded.

"What is this?" Reineke requested. "What can I say?"

"Their names," Hanuk assured. "John, Martin, Pierre. You have no trouble with Anne's or mine. It only hurts a little, and only the first time."

No. Names were personal. Acknowledgement something was personal. He called them what he called them, the dentist, the lawyer, the Holy Man. As with Thiele, and all others, he called them who they were, what they were. Not to keep them apart, or distant, himself aloof or dignified, he was naturally aloof, and as naturally dignified. They were not friends they were acquaintances, faces, and bodies in a particular point in time.

"Want to know what they call you?" Hanuk asked.

Reineke knew what they called him. Dieter, if they were young or the doctor Abraham appointed ambassador from their camp to him. Dieter, if they were Diana, though usually only to scold, otherwise it was King David to annoy him, le Metapel to entice him, the others, most frequently, the Baron, not the Hauptmann, never Herr Hauptmann that would be too painful and impossible to ask of them. *Mon capitaine,* the closest any of them dared, and that was only the Holy Man.

Reineke smiled. "What I know is that you apparently left your manners not only your silk handkerchiefs and ties when you left Berlin, spending too much time in the Sudan. You forget your position, as much as you conspire for me to forget mine, as I said, so smart and foolish at the same time."

"It is the end that matters," Hanuk's hand clapped his shoulder again in a gesture of assured friendship and trust. "If you're curious about Erich, he is in Thiele's office waiting for him. When you need me, let me know. The arrow is quick, quiet, and native," he hinted. "We can always find some bandits for you to execute should the local authorities insist upon it."

"I will keep it in mind," Reineke promised.

"Good," Hanuk said. "As far as you, you, I missed catching by this much," he demonstrated how little. "I got there as you broke away from the convoy with Thiele. But I knew you were on your way here, so I came back. Why risk frightening someone and end up getting shot?"

"And Thiele?" Reineke asked amused. "Where is Thiele?"
It was Thiele who skulked about the courtyard. The tale of Reineke versus the SS reaching the barracks of the men before Thiele did, the outcome fell short of the mob's expectations that wanted and expected more blood than some trickle from Erich's cheek. They looked forward to the show, spectators at an arena where the gladiators failed to appear. Disappointed, they settled for keeping the truck and casting the SS adrift on the sand sea without water or gasoline where they would die in sacrifice to the Hauptmann. Revenge, all they cared about; a sudden and mass outbreak of amnesia befalling them, closing ranks with Thiele firmly on the outside when Thiele pressed for information on the prisoners. Annoyed, Thiele moved on for the depot, Sergeant Linke, and the commandeered SS truck.

Idiots. Thiele denounced the group of them, unable to appreciate what they thought they would accomplish, hoped to gain by declaring war on the SS. Thiele hopped up onto the back of the truck, and pulled the canvas drapes aside. Someone <u>had</u> died. The rank odor of rotting flesh assaulted Thiele's nostrils as he looked over the interior painted with blood. The severed hand he found in a corner belonged to a man. Three of its fingers still attached, the missing two were probably there somewhere or long gone. He settled for the evidence of the hand, climbing down out of the truck with a signal for one of the mechanics working nearby.

"Yes, Oberleutnant?" the man asked, wiping his hands clean as he walked over.

"Now, where is the American?" Thiele waved his gruesome find in support.

The soldier paused.

"Well?" Thiele demanded.

"I believe he is dead, Oberleutnant," the soldier said.

"You believe," Thiele said. "Who knows?"

He still was not going to tell him. None of them were. All work had stopped, the men watching him in silence.

"Wash this truck down and move it out of the sun!" Thiele flung the severed hand at the Korporal in retort.

"Sergeant Linke is the one you should speak with, Oberleutnant." A second soldier stepped forward in defense.

"Get him!" Thiele said.

"Yes, Oberleutnant!" he exited to a chorus of jeers.

"Dismissed! Back to work!" Thiele sounded like Reineke with the barking, clipped orders, only the Korporal would never have dared bang the truck's gears as he drove away.

Thiele impatiently waited for Linke. The soldiers stubbornly slow in moving on as ordered confirmed for Thiele his suspicions of the Holy Man's involvement. Thiele's dislike of Reineke's Algerian mascot was not a secret it was unimportant. The Holy Man belonged to the Hauptmann. That alone was sufficient in ensuring no interference or comment from the men.

"Sufficient." Thiele moved to the corner of the truck yard where he could see the villa, the outline of its roof through the trees. He glanced at his watch. The thin tail of smoke rising from the chimney of Reineke's stove had dissipated into the air nearly an hour ago, and yet Reineke remained closeted inside. Disinterested apparently as his men in pursuing the issue of the SS. Satisfied the crisis was over, finished, when the SS left, leaving things to return to normal.

"How normal?" Thiele insisted. "What normal?" Things were hardly normal nor would they be. He stopped short of saying *ever again* because they would be eventually. They just were not now, or yet.

"Oberleutnant?" Sergeant Linke was behind Thiele. A small square man in his forties, Linke was another Western commoner, ordinary, a city laborer, rail yard worker, tough with a hardened liver and weatherworn skin, not a secretary like the Oberleutnant Thiele with the clean fingernails and smooth soft hands. Linke liked Thiele though, continued to like him. That had not changed. Linke just also disagreed with the Oberleutnant wanting to pursue what was over with the SS leaving and Erich's arrest. It was the SS, Erich, not the Hauptmann, or his Holy Man who needed to be stopped and so they had stopped them. It was Linke's idea to set the SS free without hope, keeping their gasoline and water. They would make it, if they were lucky, perhaps sixty, seventy kilometers, no more, and probably less. A simple order simply offered to the SS: "Leave, and die later, or stay and die now", and so the SS left, the six of them piled into the one staff car. The truck was too precious and Linke would never have let it go.

And so, they kept it, adding it to their supply. Enjoying the looks on the SS faces, the registering disbelief, apprehension in the men, cocky confidence of Herr Major, and stunned shock of his fat Leutnant, Linke wasn't sure why. They had told them, tried to tell them, warn them for several hours until the Hauptmann returned to tell them for himself. So now, they knew. And not one man there saw any SS, heard of any SS. A small squad, who, if they even existed, clearly must have died en route before reaching their destination, whatever that destination might have been, and therefore, what prisoners? Allied, American, or French, not one man there saw, or heard of any prisoners. Linke had no idea what Thiele was concerned with, or even talking about.

"All right!" Thiele interrupted Linke's creative bullshit. Linke's opinion of the SS was just that, opinion. Thiele was interested in fact. But it was the facts that were remarkably clear to Linke. Sergeant Erich had conspired with the SS to betray the Hauptmann and them. That was unacceptable and unforgivable, It was treason.

"Treason?" Thiele repeated. Could this man hear himself? They were tantamount to treason, their very existence. Coupled with the murders, yes, murders of the SS? They were not the heroes they aspired to be. Erich was the hero with his clear and indisputable loyalty. The bad made good, and the good made bad. "I do not suppose the idea of compromise occurred to you, Sergeant, once it was realized they were SS?"

"Compromise?" Linke followed orders, as did the men, and

compromise was out of the question. They did not heed Erich and would not heed Thiele now. Reineke was the Hauptmann.

"Yes ..." Thiele admitted to Linke's drawn cheeks. Reineke was the Hauptmann, Thiele his First Office, and Sergeant Linke was out of line.

"I doubt if you would find the SS interested in compromise, Oberleutnant," Linke suggested. "They were here to take or destroy not thank us."

"I think I am aware of the role of the SS," Thiele snapped, "including why they are here. That is my point. No, don't *give* them the compound. But, yes, show them around. Compromise, Sergeant. *Compromise.*"

"Show them around?" Linke frowned.

"Yes, around, Sergeant, around," Thiele said sourly. What was wrong with this man? Show them around the compound. They had nothing to hide, and everything to prove. To hell with *orders*, Thiele was talking about common sense. The SS was there, and Linke could not just snap his fingers and expect them to disappear.

"They were here for the Hauptmann's arrest," Linke assured.

That was ridiculous. Something that had happened, *because* of the men's resistance and behavior, Thiele was sure of that. "Why didn't you radio the Hauptmann?" he charged. "Killing the SS are not your *orders*, Sergeant," he assured. "Defying the SS does not *protect* us, are you mad? This *is* a munitions compound, exactly what they came to see, so show them. From one end of the oasis to the other, if that was what they wanted, who cares?" They had all been from one end of the oasis to the other ...

A shadow crossed over the sun, and Thiele shivered despite the heat. He had been from one end of the oasis to the other, but the soldiers who came after the first squad had never been, and the original men had never gone back.

The cloud moved on, and the heat beat down. Thiele removed his hat, wiping the sweat from his forehead.

"Oberleutnant," Linke suggested wisely, "don't worry about it. They're lucky all we did was take their truck. A small troop like that out in the desert?" he smiled, an unappetizing sly smile of teeth and nicotine. "Anything could happen. No one will know who or where."

"I know," Thiele corrected. "I know."

"And you'll get over it," Linke promised. "So will the SS. No radio, no water, no food."

"And three cigarettes." Someone in the background laughed, a group of them placing bets the fat one would be the first to lose his life.

"And no map," Linke assured. "They might make it to the waterholes before the water boils out if one of them has the memory of a camel, and the others can see in the dark. After that?" he was open to suggestions from the audience, but the stage was his. "They could kill and eat the fat one but at some point even he will rot. The wagen cannot run on urine, and if they decide to walk, walk where? Back here? That brave, they would have stayed.

"So, don't worry about it, Oberleutnant," he advised. "Not the munitions, the SS, Erich, or anything. It is over."

"You are relieved," Thiele retorted. "You are relieved!" he insisted, and Linke shrugged. Relieving him wasn't going to change anything, except perhaps delay the scheduled shipment they had planned for later this week. Linke was a camel, able to see in the dark, knowing the procedures and caravan routes blindfolded, and Thiele could not afford to relieve Linke of his duties. He knew this. Linke knew this.

"You are dismissed." Thiele relented, revoking the order to report and Linke smiled again with that toothy mouth of his.

"Don't," Thiele suggested. "Don't." he warned, cursing the retreating back of the sergeant, blind, deaf, as the rest of them, so self-confident and smug because of some unbroken chain of luck. *But a chain can break*! Thiele warned. And when had it even been tested? It hadn't. More time spent on collecting equipment than supplies. But now they were ready, and come Thursday they would be heading north to intercept and seize a major shipment slated for Sebha, turning it south to feed them and ultimately the fifth complex in line struggling in the southern plateaus of Algeria. It was that big, that grand. And what if they failed? It was four-hundred kilometers to Sebha, another hundred to position. Linke should be reviewing his strategies, preparing to leave, not playing games ...

No. If they failed, it would not be Linke's or the Hauptmann's fault, but Erich's, the SS whose appearance threatened the safety, security, and secret of their munitions compound—

"Damn!" Thiele hit himself in the head with the heel of his hand, remembering what he had forgotten to ask Linke. The prisoners. "Sergeant!" he broke into a trot after Linke.

"Yes, Oberleutnant?" Linke turned around.

"Where is the body of the American?" Thiele insisted. "And do not tell me you do not know what I am talking about."

Linke wasn't going to tell him that. "The Holy Man buried it in one of the gardens."

"What?" Thiele said. "Buried it?" he repeated. "You did not stop him?"

"Stop him, Oberleutnant?" Linke was puzzled.

"Yes, stop him," Thiele said sourly. "Stop him, Sergeant. Stop him." Stop him from taking the prisoner from the SS as Thiele had tried to stop Reineke and failed to the marked amusement of the SS.

"No," Linke said, and Thiele hung his head staring at the dusty toes of his boots.

"Oberleutnant ..." Linke said kindly, an older man to a young one.

"No!" Thiele's head snapped up. "No, everything is not all right. The Allied came from somewhere. Or are you prepared to tell me the SS brought them with them—from Berlin?" he barked.

Linke laughed and Thiele stared at him. "What?" Thiele insisted. "What?"

"We are all rascals, Oberleutnant," Linke assured, "even you."

"No." Thiele said finally and walked away dismayed to learn Linke's talents did not include common sense.

It was five degrees hotter inside. "Where is the Hauptmann?" Thiele asked with little enthusiasm when he returned to the villa.

"He is in your office, Oberleutnant," the Korporal reported gleefully. "He said for you to come."

Thiele was already on his way. Erich was in his office, also.

Erich was not in his office any longer. The room a pantry by comparison to the luxury of the library, cramped and crowded with a desk and innumerable wires to run the necessary assortment of telephones and radios, Reineke used the convenience of the opened drawer of a filing cabinet for a tabletop as he stood there, reading one of the personnel folders. Several others he had pulled out and discarded on the floor, the dangling ash from his cigarette threatening to ignite them. Thiele looked hesitantly around the disarray, worse than usual but that was all. "Where is Erich?" he asked.

Reineke did not look up. "In the guardhouse with the others—the wine cellar," he clarified when Thiele was silent. They did not have a guardhouse, Reineke finding them unnecessary until now, *expecting* them to be unnecessary, as he expected them to be unnecessary again.

Under the ground or above? Thiele was wondering. Buried in the dirt or simply lying on top of it? He glanced at the scraped knuckles of Reineke's hand, but they looked the same. He nodded. "There are a few areas we can use ... for a guardhouse," he clarified as Reineke slapped the folder down on his desk.

"They are to be transferred," Reineke assured. "Until they are, the wine cellar is sufficient since they seem to like it so much—we will need a new Staff Sergeant," he tossed the files on Thiele's desk. "Choose a suitable candidate, at least two. We will discuss them."

Thiele nodded again. "The body of the American is buried in one of the gardens."

"I know," Reineke said.

Of course he did. Thiele sat down to tackle the transfers first. There were five. The fifth was the Korporal from the truck yard. "Hauptmann!" he leapt up, file in hand. Reineke hadn't gone far. Thiele found him on the mezzanine, leaning over the rail watching the ashes from his cigarette trickle down to the floor below.

"The American and the English are Allies," Reineke said. "I do not think you will find the association any more mysterious than that."

"What?" Thiele said.

"You seemed to think the girl was English," Reineke prompted.

"A guess?" Thiele tried to remember when this had occurred.

"Reasonable," Reineke drew heavily on his cigarette, eying the personnel folder in Thiele's hand. "Or is that not what you wanted?"

Hardly. "Hauptmann, this soldier ..." Thiele waved the file like a cardboard flag.

"What about this soldier, Thiele?" Reineke took the file to look it over and hand it back. "I do not tolerate insubordination. I am surprised to hear you do. He is to be transferred with the others."

"Insubordination?" Thiele repeated.

"Precisely," Reineke walked away.

"Hauptmann," Thiele followed him. "It is Sergeant Linke who is insubordinate."

"Sergeant Linke was following my orders," Reineke corrected. "There is a difference."

"How do you even know any of this?" Thiele insisted.

He knew. That was the point. "You require respect and obedience from the men. I not only expect, I demand this."

"Respect?" Thiele challenged. "Sergeant Linke refused to obey superior officers, abandoning men to the desert and certain death. Members!" he gasped, "of the SS!"

"If you consider that to be a reason," Reineke surrendered, "be sure and include yourself in the transfers."

He turned for his office.

"And yourself!" Thiele bulled after him. They collided in the doorway. The Holy Man was in the library, sitting in the Hauptmann's chair, books stacked four high on the Hauptmann's desk.

Chapter Ten

"**M**on capitaine," Pierre stood up, book in hand. Seeing Thiele he put the book down, apologizing for his intrusion with a quick bend of his head looking to slip away. "I am sorry, mon capitaine, I will come back."

"No," Reineke stepped past Thiele with a glance at the apartment door. "What is it you need?"

"Nothing," Pierre assured, "you are busy. I will come back."

"You will stay," Reineke corrected, an edge to his tone, "and tell me what you need."

"Mon capitaine," Pierre looked down at the desk. "Mon capitaine," he looked back up, "I need to check something that is all."

"What?" Reineke glanced at the books. "What do you need to check?"

"It does not matter," Pierre assured, "it is not here. I thought it was, but I was wrong, and so, I will need to go."

"Where?" Reineke said. "Go where?"

"Mon capitaine," Pierre sighed, but Reineke had already snatched up the book. It was one of Diana's, an anthology of medical journals from twenty years ago. But it was obviously something she had considered valuable enough to keep at one point, and informative enough to give to the Holy Man, the priest struggling through the Germanic language he claimed not to be able to read and could, but only to a limited degree.

"The girl," Reineke flipped through the pages. "What has happened to the girl that you thought you would find in here?"

"Nothing," Pierre denied. "Mademoiselle is fine."

"You are lying," Reineke slapped the book shut. "Tell me and I will find the articles for you. Read them to you if I have to."

"No," Pierre said. "It is just that I do not know everything, and there are some things I do not know well at all."

"What things?" Reineke said. "What are the some things, the nothings you need to check?"

"Mon capitaine, please," Pierre requested.

"What things?" Reineke insisted.

"Fine," Pierre held up his hand. "Mademoiselle has been assaulted. This is not something beyond Pierre's experience. It is something I do need to check. Collect a few additional supplies you do not have here."

"Assaulted," Reineke said. "You mean the rape?"

"Yes, of course, I mean rape," Pierre took the book away from him with a huff. "There is no reason to be indelicate. These are pigs, and we know what pigs do, to her, to whomever they please. Venereal disease is epidemic in the desert, no one is immune, and few are clean. I need the recipe to ensure she is properly washed. I had it, but I cannot find it. There has been no need for a long time. May I go now, please?"

"Go," Reineke waved. "Go!" he stopped him from wasting time collecting the books. "Just, go."

"Thank you, mon capitaine." Head bent, he scurried past Thiele and out of the library.

Reineke clutched the books tightly, convinced they would take flight around him if he were to let them go. He was so hot, sweating, and then cold. The books crashed in a heap on the floor. He sat down and reached for the telephone, ordering a patrol sent after the SS.

Thiele was on top of the desk in seconds, ripping the receiver out of his hands, wrestling him for the cord. The telephone came apart, falling to the floor, its bell ringing on impact. Reineke stopped, his head tipping in curiosity as he stared at it, covered his mouth with his hand, and started to laugh.

"You are out of your mind." Thiele picked up the phone, slamming it back on the desk.

"Am I, Thiele?" he whispered. "Am I?" Was he quite, quite, insane?

"Yes!" Thiele gave up trying to put the phone back together, flinging the receiver aside. "If the prisoner is dead, there is nothing you can do about it."

"Dead?" Reineke perked up. "Indeed. What makes you think the girl is dead, Thiele? What makes you think," he could not wait to hear, "something has happened to the girl at all?"

"No?" Thiele said. "Fine! So then nothing should be the matter with you."

The matter with him? "I?" Reineke said.

"You!" Thiele assured. "Why do you want a patrol? What did he tell you? What is he telling you?" he insisted.

"The matter," Reineke said, "with me?"

They were in the sand, so hot, quiet, and the desert refused to answer him. He stood on the rocks overlooking the village, on the floor, above the dirt of the cellar, and he heard them laugh. He heard the soldiers laugh.

"The matter with me?" Reineke's fingernails dug deep into the polished wood of his desk as he straightened up. "Indeed!" he exploded, and the telephone went flying. "A child has been assaulted, raped. Here, by them, and you are asking, what is the matter with me?"

Thiele groaned, bending to retrieve the telephone.

"Leave it alone!" Reineke ordered.

"Hauptmann ..." Thiele said.

"I said to leave it!" Reineke's foot slammed into his chair sending it spinning into the French windows, crashing through the etched, beveled glass. "I am waiting for you to answer me, Thiele. I am waiting to hear something other than '*Hauptmann*' and '*SS*.' come out of your mouth."

Thiele juggled the broken cradle of the receiver, and then placed it down on the desk.

"Well?" Reineke demanded.

Thiele looked away, remembering the cool stubbornness of Linke in the truck yard; he looked back. "Linke said ..."

"I am not talking about Sergeant Linke," Reineke snapped.

Neither was Thiele, just something Linke said. "We are all rascals," Thiele nodded, "even I. And, no," he said. "I am not. I am not Linke. I cannot be Linke, or you."

"And I can?" Reineke said. "I can be any man. Sergeant Linke.

Heinrich Thiele. Whomever," he said, "they tell me to be."

"Hauptmann ..." Thiele weighed his words in his mouth.

"What?" Reineke said. "I tell you a girl has been raped and you tell me you cannot be Linke. What does that mean?"

"You fight everything," Thiele nodded. Something Thiele did not do. That was what he meant. Thiele chose his battles usually carefully, sometimes choosing not to fight but compromise, yes, instead. Reineke fought. No matter who, no matter what. If it was not his idea, his thought, will, or whim, he fought. "You rebel to rebel. This is a war—"

"A war," Reineke said.

"Yes!" Thiele snapped. "And I would assume—"

"Assume?" Reineke accused.

"Yes!" Thiele insisted. "I would assume, I would expect, I would think you would be capable of realizing—"

"How these things happen." Reineke nodded like he was quoting from some book. "That these things happen."

"Yes!" Thiele said. "It is a war, not one of your stupid games. Damn you! How long must it take for you to realize the game they play is a war out there?"

"Out there," Reineke agreed, "not here. Your things do not happen here. A child is not assaulted here, beaten, raped!"

"You don't know that it was here," Thiele stared at him. "You only know what that priest tells you!"

"There was blood on those men!"

"There was blood all over you. You!" Thiele slapped the desk disgusted. "And you just closed her blouse. You!"

"Indeed," Reineke straightened up. "Child's blouse, Thiele. *Child's* blouse."

That was a matter of opinion. She did not look particularly like a child to Thiele. He did not know what she looked like, other than the enemy. That was what she looked like. That was what he saw. "Hauptmann, I think ..." his hand ran tiredly through his hair.

"Assume, yes," Reineke mocked. "Indeed, expect."

Thiele looked at him. "Shut up," he suggested. "Just, shut-up."

"*Condone,*" Reineke had no intentions of shutting up.

"Condone?" Thiele echoed. "I am not condoning anything. I am telling you, your soldiers are men. She is a prisoner!"

"She is a child," Reineke insisted. "And they will be punished!"

"Punished?" Thiele said. "They are your men. She is the enemy, not them!"

"They are filth!"

"Hauptmann ..." Thiele said.

"Filth!" Reineke grabbed up the broken telephone determined to hammer it back into working order.

"Hauptmann!" Thiele insisted, and Reineke grabbed him, shoving him away. Thiele hit the chair, landing on it, bringing it over on top of himself as he hit the floor.

"Get up," Reineke ordered. "Get up!"

Thiele got up slowly. "That is twice," he said. "There will not be a third time." He walked to the door as if he were thinking of walking out.

"Where are you going?" Reineke insisted.

"I am leaving," Thiele assured, only his hand never reached the latch. The smooth glass paperweight found its way into Reineke's grasp and he flung it. The weighty ball whizzed over Thiele's shoulder, smashing into the door, narrowly missing his head.

"You are going nowhere," Reineke assured as Thiele stood there silently studying the chipped wood. "You are going to stay here until you learn—"

"I am leaving," Thiele interrupted. "You can call for your sentries, all two hundred of them, if you like. They can hear your outrage in the courtyard and attribute it to another one of your fits. They think you are mad, but I know you are afraid." He turned around. "You were afraid out there, and you are afraid in here. But whatever it is, you are afraid of, mein Hauptmann, take it and get rid of it out there, not here. There is a war to fight here."

"Indeed," Reineke said.

"Yes," Thiele nodded. "Yes."

"Delay the rendezvous with the convoy shipment," Reineke replied, and it was enough to rock Thiele's newly discovered strength.

"What?" Thiele said.

"Do it," Reineke instructed. "And issue a notice of radio silence.

The idea of the Kufra intrigues me."

"The Kufra?" Thiele marched back to him. "The French are in control of the Kufra."

"A reason why it intrigues me," Reineke agreed. "Perhaps the girl is French, not English or American. Perhaps a survivor of an air transport or courier off course and downed in the heat. It is irrelevant. The Kufra intrigues me. It is two weeks minimum to supply the Coast Road under the most ideal circumstances. What we gain with the depots, we lose in time. That is unacceptable."

"What are you talking about?" Thiele insisted. "We have no time for the Kufra. The convoy will be in port in a week. That's it. Our one chance to take what we can, at the docks, there is no other. After that the cargo will be on the supply trains and it will be too late. It must be the docks, the trucks must leave immediately for Sebha, and *we* must leave to meet them on the supply route, as scheduled, as *planned*. Unless you think they are going to hold the convoy, the trains, the trucks for you, timing is critical."

"I think," Reineke said, "an airstrip at the Kufra is ideal for our cause—"

"The airstrip was destroyed!" Thiele snapped.

"By the French," Reineke agreed, "one year ago. It is time to reevaluate the area and determine if the French have decided to keep her, share her with the English, or abandon her ..." He collected his chair to sit at his desk, hastily scrawling a message. "Dispatch a courier to Schönfeld ..."

"Herr Oberst is in Algiers." Thiele snatched up the note, not bothering to read it. "For that you need the radio! By the time this reaches him, he will be here—wondering why you have not left and the munitions on schedule for Sebha instead of en route here!"

"Dispatch a courier to meet him," Reineke said. "We are at radio silence. The cargo is to be intercepted as planned, at the docks. The trucks can simply camp and wait, yes, for me."

"Camp where?" Thiele insisted. "Wait where? Once they leave the coast, they are on the supply road to Sebha. An open target until they do, unless they do, and even then. They must keep moving. There is no place to camp or wait—except Sebha. If we are not there to meet it, they will destroy the convoy. Those are their orders, *your* orders. Linke must be there to meet them en route, or this is some useless exercise. *You* are the one who refused to give them the route here!"

"*You* are dismissed," Reineke said, "When I am ready to tell you more, you will know more, until that time consider it your punishment. Indeed," his eyes narrowed. "If you are fortunate, your only punishment. I am hardly afraid, Thiele, of anything. Now, get out."

Unfortunately, I am unable to accept your invitation and attend the celebration. My regards to your family and friends. Hauptmann Reineke.

Outside in the hall Thiele read the message and read it a second time. The only *celebration* he knew about was the interceptions of major shipments to the Italian forces planned for the next few months. Reineke couldn't be anticipating a delay of all of them. All of them? Thiele turned back for the library, twisting the latch open. Reineke sat on the floor in front of the French windows, the glass paperweight at his feet, his head buried, resting in the crook of his arm, one thumb absently chipping away at the peeling paint.

"Get out, Thiele," he said, knowing who it was without needing to look up.

Thiele's steel-blue eyes bore into the apartment door, cursing the prisoner, whoever she was, English, American, or Free French. "Die," he whispered, "Die!" and headed for the radio room with the order to fall silent.

Chapter Eleven

It was very late when the Holy Man returned to the library. Reineke sat in his chair at his desk, his fingers tapping his mouth, studying the small brown figure seated across from him. His throat felt dry, sour and he kept trying without success to moisten his lips with his tongue. The monk knew that. He knew everything. Did he? "I thought it was you," Reineke said finally, quietly. "I had thought the SS prisoner was you, not some child."

"I, mon capitaine?" Pierre's voice echoed in the darkness. "No, not I, mon capitaine, never. Never."

Of course not. The Holy Man was far too clever to fall prey to the SS. But when the prisoner turned out not to be the Holy Man, instead of being relieved, Reineke had no idea what to do. He rose to study the stars through the French windows. "I had to choose," he explained. "It seems I continue having to choose who the enemy is, and who it is not. You cannot know how that feels."

Of course, Pierre could know, having made such a choice himself three short months ago. But that was not important right now. "Mon capitaine ..." He moved forward on his seat of velvet cushions worn and fraying in spots, and dry. Everything in this desert was so dry, everything in the room. "You are very upset. Let me give you something."

No. His body, like his skin, was highly sensitive, easily upset, and irritated. It was not only his emotions or his moods. It was not worth the risk. "The wine will do." He returned to his desk, his tongue still feeling foreign as he drank and he tried wetting his lips again.

"As you wish," Pierre sat carefully back in his chair, watching.

"I am angry," Reineke assured, "not ill. Indeed," he studied his glass, the deep blood color of the wine, full and rich, regal, like his, "if I am ill, I have been ill since the time of my mother's womb."

"Melancholia," Pierre agreed, "not battle fatigue."

"Civilized," Reineke downed the wine. "I am civilized." He could feel his uniform pressing against his flesh, the color of his flesh, part of it, seamless. The flattering lines soft and smooth as the material, inseparable, the two of them, rather than a misfit. He was not a lost man, simply misplaced. This was not his life, his world. The monk should understand such things.

Pierre did, tried. "Nordic," he said, as if reading Reineke's mind, "not Nazi. Mon capitaine is a being, not a political ambition."

"Civilized," Reineke said with a reach for the bottle to refill his glass. "This is unacceptable to me, what has happened, the girl, the prisoners, even the American with the bones sticking out like spikes in his head. I would think it would be unacceptable to anyone. It is inconceivable to me it would not be. It is inconceivable to me," he said, "it would not be to you."

"Unacceptable, mon capitaine?" Pierre said. "Oui, of course it is. Inconceivable? Non," he shook his head. "It is not inconceivable to me."

"This is war," Reineke quoted Thiele.

"Oui," Pierre agreed. "It is war. What war looks like, what war is."

"Thiele said that," Reineke nodded with a sip of his wine.

"He is right," Pierre apologized.

"No," Reineke said. "No, he is not. War is a fight, a battle, offense, defense. In war men do not have time—"

"To rape?" Pierre injected, and Reineke looked at him over his wine. "What men are these? Of course they do. You are angry, mon capitaine, not naïve. In war, men have time to do whatever they want to do. Fight their battles the way they want to in any manner they wish."

"This is not Russia, indeed, we are not Russians," Reineke insisted harshly, having heard the tales from both sides. "I expect a soldier to conduct himself with honor. I demand a soldier conduct himself with honor."

"Nor is it Warsaw, Oslo, France," Pierre agreed, having heard those tales as well. "Whose soldiers are these you expect so much of?"

Indeed. Reineke stared into his glass. France was a fact, not a confession. He could not feel sorry about France; he would never feel sorry for France. "Indeed." The crystal cracked in his hand, blood running down like wine. He was on the balcony, the smoke from his cigarette burning his eyes, the heels of his hands pressing tightly into their watering sockets, trying to catch his breath.

He caught it and he was not at the windows, but still at his desk, staring into the unbroken glass of wine, everything else in his mind. "We are not all monsters," he repeated. "I refuse to accept we are all monsters. I refuse to accept those who are. The men responsible will be punished."

"Punished?" Pierre asked visions of a spanking in his head. "How mon capitaine?"

Executed. Shot, hanged; Reineke did not care which. He rose for the cabinet and a bottle of wine that looked less like blood. "You and Thiele are so obsessed with my weakness for compassion you forget how easy it is for me to kill."

"The men responsible are partners with the SS, mon capitaine," Pierre replied. "Do you have the authority to execute the SS?"

His authority was limitless. "Do you have a better idea?"

"I have no idea," Pierre assured. "I have concerns the SS will return, that more will come and take your complex from you and all will die. You, your men, the children, everything we have strived to protect."

"Diana's reasons for not taking care of them," Reineke nodded.

There was a pause before Pierre answered, brief, but long enough. "Is it?" he said. "That does not sound like her."

That was what he had said, but apparently, he was wrong. "I meant before," Reineke said. "The reason why she let them come, instead of killing them on the sea."

"Oh," Pierre said. "Oui, yes, of course. She would want answers, mon capitaine, just like you. Assessment of her exposure could not be gained from dead men."

No, it could not. Reineke returned to his desk with a doubtful bottle of Bordeaux. "And I am talking about the men here who are responsible, Erich, the others. I will have answers, and they will be punished. The SS are banished to the desert without water or fuel, map, or any means of contact. They will die walking in circles. That should be enough to satisfy her. If not, tell her to send the dentist and lawyer to kill them as she should have done before."

"Be assured, mon capitaine," Pierre nodded at the scarred and blackened ceiling, "what you have done is enough."

Indeed. He had already ordered the ceiling repaired, the broken glass panes of the French windows replaced, the bruised and dented wood of the library's door smoothed. The glass paperweight he could do nothing about except order it polished, which it was, and back on his desk, an interesting pattern of tiny fractures deep within. The ashtray however was filled and overflowing with ashes and cigarettes. It seemed incapable of looking any other way. He seemed incapable of not having it look that way. "It was worth it," he assured.

"Pardon?" Pierre's head tipped.

Worth it. *Worth it.* The looks on the faces of the SS who thought he was too pretty to mean what he said. More than one had made that mistake before, more than one would probably make that same mistake again. "Worth it," he assured. The cork snapped off in his hand, dry from age and improper storage. The next bottle was much more cooperative and satisfying, the cork slipping out like it had been greased. Reineke returned to his desk for the third time, finding room in the ashtray for his cigarette before he lit another. "The men responsible here will be removed, transferred and tried for failing in their orders." And therefore executed, shot. He should be satisfied; he was not. Like the SS condemned to death in the desert, mere execution was insufficient. He wanted them to know who killed them and why.

"Not a bad idea," Pierre shrugged, a demon under his pious cloak. "There are children here."

"I am thinking of the children," Reineke assured, and he was. The children, as always, were on his mind. He drank his wine.

"I know," Pierre smiled.

"And what to do," Reineke acknowledged, "should the SS return. Indeed."

"Return?" Pierre dismissed. "No, they will not return. Die in the desert as you said."

As Linke calculated. Far enough away from the complex, and far short of their encampment, wherever it was. At least a hundred kilometers, it had to be. He should have followed the tracks back to see where they were from, not forward to where he knew they were going. "The rest of them," Reineke assured. "There are not only six SS, as there are not only two Allied out there."

"What Allied is this?" Pierre verified.

The ones who did not exist. American, English, or French. The ones who came from nowhere and somehow managed to end up there. It had to be by airplane. An engineer suggested perhaps the Suez Canal. The only thing he could think of except for the Kufra. Flying in or flying out, off course and downed in the heat, extremely off course. "You are to stay here," Reineke nodded. "Here, at the villa until the girl lives or dies, then you may go."

"Of course," Pierre agreed, surprised. "Naturally, I will stay."

"I will make certain," Reineke said, "you have anything you need."

"Nothing," Pierre assured. "I need nothing. What I need I have with me."

His hands. He called them hands. Reineke knew they were wands, magic wands, moving as wands, thin as wands. "How is she?" he asked. A remarkably rude inquiry when he knew the answer he wanted to hear. "Do you know yet?"

"Still sleeping?" Pierre shrugged. "I think tomorrow she will probably wake up—alive, mon capitaine," he assured. "If she survives the drugs, she will live. The injury to her head is old, days, perhaps even weeks. Since she has lived, I think she will continue to live, the other injuries are not life threatening."

That was not the answer he wanted to hear. Dead, was the answer, continued to be the answer he wanted. She had to die, saving him the responsibility of executing her. "You said something about drugs before." Reineke sipped his wine, an image coming to mind of him trying to sneak into the apartment while the Holy Man slept and suffocating the prisoner with her pillow, laying her death to the drugs. He would never get away with it. Probably take too long to decide which pillow was appropriate for the act and by then he would be caught.

"I said something about drugs because I believe she has been drugged," Pierre agreed.

Henbane. Nightshade. "The ether could not have helped her situation." Reineke suggested, fooling no one with the proposed innocence of his remark. The Holy Man opened his mouth as if he intended to retort, but then did not. It was all right. Reineke knew what he was going to say. "I did not say I wanted to kill her," Reineke assured irritably. "I am simply saying it would be far less complicated if she died."

"Less complicated for whom, mon capitaine?"

"Us," Reineke insisted. "You, the children, and I."

"Then it is complicated," Pierre agreed, "because she may not."

Apparently. Reineke rose for the French windows and the cool night air. "Why would they drug her?" he asked. "Who could she possibly be? What could she possibly tell them, a child her age? The SS might use a child, yes, of course. But to rely on them would be foolish."

"We have children here," Pierre said.

Yes. A sea of kindergarteners armed with guns, bows and arrows, and knives. "I am not saying a child cannot know things," Reineke assured. "But what a child knows they cannot fully comprehend or is even necessarily true."

Pierre shrugged. "To keep her quiet perhaps?"

Quiet? Why? Because she was screaming? Reineke stared through the French windows.

"Who knows?" Pierre said behind him. "Why would they do anything to her other than they are soldiers, she is a woman, and this is war? It is all right though, I think ..." he looked away as he thought; Reineke could see him reflected in the glass, a frown between his black pig eyes replaced by confidence when he looked back. "Oui, I am positive the blood is not all from her. There were others."

At least one. "The American you buried in the gardens," Reineke nodded, "under the nose of the SS."

"A good guess," Pierre agreed. "They cut off his hands. I did not tell you this before, but I tell you now. They cut off his hands. They are butchers. Mademoiselle is lucky to be in one piece, not simply alive."

"The SS have been condemned," Reineke reminded. "I said I would take care of the men responsible here."

"Good," Pierre shrugged. "And I will not pray for their souls, not even to burn in Hell. Hell is too good for them. There is no place for them. Hell is for you and me, where we will live together as we do here, in harmony."

It was time to change the subject. "Who will stay with the children while you are here?" Reineke moved on to the Holy Man's assignment as nurse. "You cannot leave such a responsibility to Anne—or Hanuk," he made a point. "Obviously still a child himself. Thiele could have shot him, or any one of them. Indeed," he heard himself say, "the adults are as bad as the children they swear to protect—"

"Mon capitaine!" Pierre requested as Reineke spun around, panic on his face, realizing what he was saying, who he had to be talking about.

"No!" Reineke insisted. "What is she doing in camp, are you insane? She can see who they are—indeed!" he seethed. "Regardless of what you say, none of you can defend why the SS were even allowed to penetrate the perimeter. Why I did not find their bodies alongside their tracks! What did Diana think? I had decided the guards should pose as SS instead of Arabs to deceive your French?"

"The woman Sotma," Pierre nodded. "It is the woman Sotma who is with the children."

"I do not care what she calls herself!" Reineke insisted. "I have a thousand tons of supplies—"

"And men," Pierre agreed. "A thousand tons of supplies and men; fine," he said. "I will stay here with Mademoiselle. You can go sleep in the village to make sure your men and supplies will be here in the morning when you wake up."

Reineke looked at him.

Pierre grinned. "Keep your storm troopers quiet, eh, mon capitaine? Diana will keep hers. That is what she is doing here, of course. An assessment of her exposure. And destroy you as quickly as she could the SS. But, it is all right," he promised with a wave, "no big deal, the dentist says. A bargain you have, a bargain Diana will keep, and, oui, Pierre will keep his, too."

"I have no bargain with Diana," Reineke assured. "Any bargain she believes we have is all in her head."

"Yes, you do," Pierre nodded. "Oui, you do."

No, he did not. His bargain was with this priest, some crippled old man, and his army of orphaned children, their families long missing or dead.

January 1942
The Fezzan
"The children," the German repeated one last time. "I want to know about the children."

"Pardon?" the Algerian said. "I know nothing about the children. I do not know what you mean."

Yes he did. "The children," the German started to pace. "I want to know how many there are, exactly how many there are, and why there appears to be more since they were remanded to the settlement camp." He finished triumphantly, his fists down on his desk.

"Fifty-two," the Algerian smiled. "All Catholic."

Fifty-two. Fifty-two was the number revealed by the census, a staggering number that shocked him. However, there were at least two more. The pair with the crone who had held him captive for hours he had never seen before. One of them admittedly was not a child but a young man of perhaps eighteen. The girl was definitely a child of approximately ten. "Catholic?" If his tone sounded tired or irritable, it was at the idea of a roving band of desert Catholics.

The Algerian's smile widened until he was grinning like some clown. "Libya is a very different country, you should know. It is not like everywhere or anywhere else. There are Catholics, and there are stone men who live in caves."

"Caves?" the German echoed.

"There are caves beneath the wall," the Algerian reminded what the German had already discovered for himself.

"Those are tunnels, mine shafts and tunnels," the German huffed. Accosted by some crazed witch he was in no mood to learn of a band of desert trolls.

"Mines?" the Algerian smiled. "No, you are wrong. They are graves. This is the temple Diana of the Emperor Hadrian. The wall her citadel now holding back the sea as the sand fights to consume her. The desert it like that, it rises and spreads, and will eventually consume her, yes. Like the Great Sphinx, buried to its neck. When you get to Egypt, you will see."

The German looked at him, continued looking at him until the Algerian shrugged. "Mine, graves. Who says a grave cannot be a mine, or a mine a grave—"

"How many are there?" the German interrupted. The crone claimed hundreds, he was guessing that was not true, and was still lucky to get out of there alive. He remained uncertain as to why he had been released alive, only that it bolstered her confidence, supported her claim she was as powerful, if not more powerful than he.

"I have no idea what you are talking about," the Algerian insisted. "Some trick of the sun."

It was no trick of the sun. The sun was not armed with French guns. The pool of water, yes, he thought it was a mirage himself at first. A shimmering lake in the distance, struck by how real it looked, incredulous to find it was authentic as he approached. Clearly an imperial garden had stood here once, so peaceful and calm in her surviving beauty amidst the graveyard of marble stone. One lone goddess standing proudly in the background of the empty pedestals and ring of columns surrounding the ancient pond, one hand raised to the heavens ... in the other a gun, the steel barrel approaching his head reflected in the water cool, and crystal clear.

"*Mon capitaine*?" in the distance the Holy Man's voice attempted to penetrate from the present day, but Reineke could barely hear it.

"Dangerous?" the German sarcastically answered the Algerian's claim of the native settlement being too dangerous for the children to live. It was obviously much more dangerous than it should be, and nowhere near as dangerous as it could be if he did not get the cooperation he sought. "Talk to me," he encouraged. "Now is your chance. There is no reason for these games. I do not believe in witches, and I do not believe in trolls. What do you want from me? Tell me, and I will see what I can do."

"I can prove it," the Algerian smiled.

"Prove it?" the German said. "Prove what? How?" More dead goats hung in the courtyard? Or simply the gift of some blackened necrotic hoof waiting when Reineke woke to find the Algerian standing at the side of his bed.

"Foot, not hoof, foot," the Algerian explained as the German leapt from the sheets, gagging on the stench. "See? Here is where the toes would be ... it is all right," he reassured the German recoiling from him. "It cannot hurt you, it is dead."

"And the rest of it?" the German said hoarsely, the smell still burning and vomit aspirated into his lungs.

"Rest of it?" the Algerian sat on the rim of the tub, offering him a towel to wipe his face. "It is all right, take your time. There is no rest of it. Eaten away."

"Body," the German snapped. "Where is the body? Where have you hidden it?"

"Oh, the body is fine." The Algerian laughed, amused by the German afraid to do what? Open his cupboard? Climb back into his bed? "She is fine. The foot, no."

He stuffed the rotted limb so casually back in its sack. "The temple is too dangerous as I told you for the children to run or play. It is very beautiful, yes, but too dangerous, unsafe."

"She," the German stared at the sack.

"Oui, she," the Algerian watched him. "A little girl."

"Girl?" the German looked up. "There was a girl with the crone. This could not have happened in a day, not a day."

"Anne," the Algerian said finally with his smile on his face. "No, this is not Anne, this is Adva." he patted the sack, his smile softening a little. "Palestinian," he offered after another pause, in afterthought. "But, what does is matter, eh?" he shrugged. "It does not. There are seventy-five children here, some Catholic, some Arab."

Seventy-five. That was twenty-three more than the census had revealed, an entire third of their population unaccounted for. It did not seem possible. Where were they?

"What is wrong with you?" the Algerian inquired, a dangerous question, but he was asking it anyway with that smile on his face, thinking of the look on the face of the German, the vomit erupting from his throat when he saw the amputated limb. "What happened? Who did you think this was?" he held the sack out. "Who did she remind you of?”

“Where is Czestochowa?” the German answered finally. “I have never heard of it.”

“Poland,” the Algerian nodded. “A slaughter in Poland. There has been none worse some claim.”

“I was in France.” Was the German’s defense, forgetting perhaps the man he was talking to was French.

“Recently?” the brow of the Algerian cocked in tune with his consideration.

Of course, recently, if not a thousand times before, what did this priest expect him to say? That he went shopping, leaving the invasion to someone else? He did go shopping, check on his friends upon his arrival, Maxim turned from couture to whore. She hit him when she saw him, but then gave him a hug. He urged her to go to Vichy and she laughed, reminding him this was Paris. And who leaves Paris? No one leaves Paris, any more than they ever leave the Rhine.

“Did you tell her that?” the Algerian asked.

What? The German watched him. Tell who, what? That he spent his recuperation in Paris where the whores made him feel better about his torn leg?

“Diana,” the Algerian assured. “Moses she called herself when she first came here, but agrees how Diana is much better suited for her. Did you tell her you never heard of Czestochowa? She would believe you if you did.” his smile deepened for the German continuing to frown. “That you know nothing of Czestochowa. Too stupid a question for you to ask if it was not true, too stupid a lie to tell. It had to be true.”

“Moses,” the German repeated.

“It is the same thing,” the Algerian shrugged, his voice sounding louder for some reason, outside Reineke, not inside him. Reineke roused himself. It was today, not three months ago, and he was outside on the balcony where the air did not help.

March 9

“The woman Sotma?” Reineke answered sourly.

“Oui,” Pierre grinned. “Pretty good, eh? I like it.”

“Indeed,” Reineke said. “Any bargain *the woman Sotma* believes we have she violated when she sent her sons into my camp.”

“That was for your own protection, mon capitaine,” Pierre assured and Reineke scoffed. A moment ago, it was in the spirit of annihilation, his and his men, along with the SS.

“The SS came here without the roads,” Pierre reminded. “Roads they cannot know, and yet they came here anyway.”

“My Colonel knows the road.” Reineke walked back inside for his wine.

“Is he SS?” Pierre asked and Reineke’s eyes rolled.

“No,” he assured. “I am saying the caravan routes are not necessarily the secret you believe they are. Indeed, perhaps two-thousand years ago, but not now.” He drank his wine.

“That is because you gave them to him,” Pierre nodded.

“Of course I gave them to him,” Reineke snapped. “Yes, naturally I gave some to him. Indeed,” he said caustically, “something to do with the bargain between him and me.”

“Mon capitaine has too many bosses,” Pierre advised. “He should pick one and then we would not have problems like this.”

Gods, he meant, gods, not bosses, with this priest wanting his to be the only one. “What *problems*?” Reineke insisted. “Indeed, this is the first *problem* we have had in three months.”

“And it is a big one.” Pierre assured, disputing what the dentist had called ‘no big deal’, whatever that meant. Like Reineke, he preferred speaking with the doctor whose French he could understand. “You have a spy in your organization who reports to the SS,” he made his point about the roads. “It is the only way.”

“Erich,” Reineke walked the length of the room. “We know that, and he has been confined. Diana’s involvement is not only foolish, it is unnecessary—”

“The woman Sotma,” Pierre interrupted. “The woman Sotma is with the children.”

Reineke looked at him, and Pierre shrugged. “You were saying?”

Nothing. He was saying nothing, and the Holy Man would not listen if he did. He gave up, returning to the topic of the prisoner that for some reason seemed more pleasant. “Tomorrow you are to begin exercising the girl in the gardens. I will order a guard.”

“Pardon?” Pierre startled.

"Exercise," Reineke sat down at his desk. "You are to begin her exercise. You said she was fine."

"Not dead, yes," Pierre agreed. "But not tomorrow, mon capitaine, a few days perhaps."

"Tomorrow," Reineke assured. "I have ordered us on radio silence—"

"Is that wise?" Pierre interrupted again.

He had no idea what was wise. He was trying to think of something wise, making it up as he went along. "Indeed," Reineke downed his wine. "We are four days from the Kufra. The oasis can be the only logical explanation for the Allied."

"French," Pierre said. "Kufra belongs to Leclerc, no one else. No English has ever seen her, no American even heard of her."

"According to you," Reineke made a face.

Pierre laughed. "According to Mussolini the Italians are in control of the Fezzan. One of us is right."

Reineke did not have the time to decide which. "In any event, not German," he assured. "I have supplies coming in a few days that must be able to reach us."

"So soon again?" Pierre replied quietly.

"Food supplies," Reineke said impatiently. "Indeed, food supplies. We eat, too. You may take whatever you need."

"Thank you, mon capitaine," Pierre's head tipped.

"And you are to begin the girl's exercise in the morning," Reineke instructed. "There can be no delay. She is to be ready to return with the convoy for more suitable quarters. This is a supply depot, not a Stalag. I do not have the facilities to house prisoners of war."

"Camps," Pierre corrected. "What you have are camps not facilities, prisons where you would not send a dog to. It would kinder of you to leave Mademoiselle on the sea with the SS."

"There are no camps!" the wine bottle banged down on his desk. "Indeed, you tell me *facts* no one else has ever heard about, least of all seen!"

"That is not true," Pierre shook his head. "Two-thirds of the population of Libya interned by Mussolini in his Italian War, one-third killed, slaughtered, and the League of Nations did nothing,

nothing. One million people, nothing, and they look away again now. Oui," he assured, "continue to look away, just like you do."

No, he did not. He did not look away, and he did not look at things that were not there. Germany fought to restore its position and dignity, regain territories and lands stolen from her. Occupation of opposing governments was a necessary act to ensure cooperation, expand the borders of protection against Russia who thought it could just sweep in—what did that have to do with camps? There were no camps. "Indeed," Reineke felt the gold of the Prince's cross beneath the breast of his uniform, cool against his chest warm and perspiring. "The girl is to be ready to leave with the trucks. I am not Mussolini. This is not the Italian War."

"If you insist," Pierre shrugged.

"I do!" Reineke said.

"Fine," Pierre rose to his crippled legs. "Mademoiselle will begin her exercise in the morning, and she will be ready to leave in a few days. This will never happen," he predicted, "but that is all right, too. It gives mon capitaine a few more days to think."

He was finished thinking.

"You have a sister?" Pierre smiled.

What? Reineke eyed him. He had two sisters, the priest knew that. One whom he hated, one whom he loved. Alexia he loved. The eagerness in her fingers and fascination she had for balls, brightly colored balls, when she was just a little baby, and he was a child of fourteen, his father's brain rotted from the gases in the trenches, poised to take the Baron's throne. "You know I have a sister," Reineke assured. "Why?"

"I do," Pierre agreed. "Would you send your sister to this camp where Pierre would not send his dog?" He walked away, for the door.

"Holy Man," Reineke said.

"Yes, mon capitaine?" Pierre immediately turned around.

"You understand what I do, I do for the children," Reineke said. "You must trust and believe the decisions I make are for the best."

"We are all children, mon capitaine," he replied.

No, they were not. Children were innocent. "The girl is to be ready to leave with the trucks," Reineke repeated. "She is not Arab or French, otherwise I would consider keeping her here. Remanding her to you, not only now, but permanently. But that is not possible. The SS did not choose us by random. It would be naïve to think I could somehow trace them back to my father's wrath."

"That would be something more than naïve, mon capitaine," Pierre agreed.

Insanity, yes. Paranoia, heat stroke. Unfortunately, he simply had a headache and upset stomach from too much wine. "If the SS came from the north, the south, east, or west, they did not come without a reason or without a map. If they are here, they are everywhere, the Allied obviously as well. Indeed," Reineke said, "would you sacrifice your children in this girl's stead, sending them to this camp where you would not send your dog? Because that is what will happen and is what I will prevent—if you let me. Please let me."

"I understand your reasoning," Pierre stopped him there. "Good night, mon capitaine, sleep well."

That was unlikely, Reineke knew, and gave up on the wine before he could not sleep at all.

Chapter Twelve

The Fezzan
March 8

Joanna Lee was nineteen years old. Neither English nor American, as she lay sleeping on a strange, foreign bed. She wasn't even Joanna Lee yet. Not in her dream. In her dream she was Joanna Edwards and she was nine years old. She remembered it well that afternoon in the parlor of Grandfather's home in Cambridge. She hadn't been peeking or anything of that sort. She hadn't been doing anything in particular for that matter, except pressing her nose tightly against the window pane and drawing pictures with her breath when the auto drove up.

At first, she thought it was her mother and stepfather Henry coming home, but then the door opened and the people got out and she could see it wasn't her mother and Henry after all, but Michael with Grandfather and her stepbrother Justin, which was surprising because Justin was not supposed to be there, not that she recalled.

She would have met them at the door, but she needed to find her shoes. Claudia would scold if she did not have her shoes. She didn't seem to understand how Joanna hated them, but Joanna still took them off anyway, every chance she got. Shoes were boring. You couldn't feel anything with shoes.

No one heard her coming down. The stairs were thickly carpeted and she was barefooted, not having been able to find her shoes after all, but she really didn't think Claudia would say anything, not with Michael there to protect her and she brought along one of the dolls Michael had given her, just to make sure.

The door to Grandfather's study was almost closed, the voices coming from inside very soft, but she must have known before she even went in—children do that sometimes, they just sort of know—because she stepped ever so quietly, and, yes, that was proof she knew something because Joanna was anything but quiet.

No one heard her come in, they were all so busy with their conversation, and it did not take her long to realize how her mother and Henry would not be coming home, ever.

Never.

Her eyes were wet. In her dream, Joanna shook her head trying to shake away the tears, but she kept bumping up against something ... a pillow. Some stupid oversized pillow, soft and damp. How odd. She didn't seem to remember her eyes being wet, or any pillow.

"In fact!" Joanna snarled, she distinctly remembered hanging onto her doll as she listened, refusing to allow her eyes to be wet.

"But it was so hard!" she whispered, the pillow beginning to fade. "So very hard." They were all so upset. Poor Justin. Joanna looked at her stepbrother standing with her friend Michael asking him so many questions. Michael wanted Justin to tell her. But, Justin couldn't. Henry was his father too, and he had been a father to Justin a great deal longer than he had to her. To her he was still brand new.

So Joanna understood. The grown-up person inside of her understood about fathers, because in the dream she remembered something else. She remembered how her mother had come to tell her when she was only about seven, how her father had gone away and would not be coming back. Ever. Now they were all gone. All of them.

Joanna believed it was then her doll developed its permanent lump of stuffing as the little person she was, tried to decide if she should just back away and let them come and find her, or what she should do. She would never know because Claudia looked up from her handkerchief and saw her and the men turned around to stare at the little girl, who could only say, "Hello," in such a child's voice. Justin turned away, and Claudia ran out. No one said a word for the longest time until Michael dashed across the room, swooping her high up in the air, laughing. Only this time she didn't laugh back, which was something she always did, and Michael set her down, his handsome face pinched, and Joanna felt sorry for him, she really did, but she had to know. So, she asked him—not fresh, just curious—if she could stay, anyway? If it was all right anyway, if she stayed? And they were all there. Hugging her, patting her, reassuring ...

No, that was wrong. They were not all there. Certainly not Justin. But there was someone there she could not quite see. In her dream, Joanna's head moved around, trying to shoo the clouds away. It was all so confusing. They were beginning to talk so loud. Michael was saying, and kept saying, "*Mademoiselle?*" And that was wrong. Michael hadn't said, "*Mademoiselle?*" There hadn't been a pillow. Her eyes had not been wet, but they were. "Michael?" she whispered.

"Try to speak slowly," he answered in a voice she could barely understand, "You have been injured, severely."

Injured? Whatever did he mean? She hadn't been injured. Never in her life had she ever been injured, though people around her certainly had been killed, first her parents and then Joe.

"Joe," Joanna whispered. That was who she couldn't quite see. Of course, Joe was there. She remembered it now quite clearly. Joe had come into the house with Michael, Grandfather, and her stepbrother Justin. Really, how wrong of her not to have remembered Joe from the beginning. Claudia would never approve. Joe was her husband. She married Joe. Scolding herself severely, Joanna settled back into her dream. Her marriage to Joe was a long way off. She was still a child in her dream, and she wanted to think about Michael.

"*Michael.*" The young woman lying on the bed smiled and the dream took on a rosy glow. Michael was wonderful. So absolutely, wonderful. So much better looking than Gable, a hundred times more exciting than Flynn.

Michael had been born in the States. The isle of Brooklyn. The balls and backbone of the United States and New York, the greatest city in the world.

Michael had the most God-awful voice, and with those grating adenoid-suffering sounds, he slew all her dragons, gorged her on fairytales, and pranced his way into her heart forever.

"Oh, God, Michael," Joanna muttered, and her sweat soaked body twitched. She needed Michael now to ward off the nightmares. It always worked before. He was always there before. Even after, yes, even after they had shuttled her off to live with Grandfather, he came as often as he could.

Even when, yes, even when the war came Michael was still there.

And especially when, yes, especially when the war took Joe away.

"Oh, God, Joe!" Joanna cried, a host of demons appearing to surround her. It was unfair. So terribly unfair. They had no right!

"Go away! Go away!" she screamed, but they refused to listen, their heads starting to bob, twist, and spin. "*Noooo ... !*" she echoed as they swarmed over her, pushing her down, and they would come again, and again, even in the dream, even though it was her dream, her dream ...

"My dream!" Joanna was gasping. "My dream. It's mine. Mine. Mine, MINE!" and she tightened her grip on her doll until she strangled the life from it.

Her eyes were wet, but she didn't care, and she made a promise to fight. "I'll kill you!" she told the last of the demon faces, glad to see it was bleeding.

"I'll kill you!" she hissed, clutching at its arm, trying to fend it off, and it stopped. For one moment it stopped surprised and Joanna reached for the pillow, but it was so far away. She lunged for the pillow, but the floor was too soft, tugging at her ankles, and the demon cheated, catching her when her back was turned. It raised its hand and grabbed her hair, trying to take her head away.

The Allied

Chapter Thirteen

Cairo, Egypt
March 9, 1942

D r. Michael Delegianis MD, PhD, Abc, xyz, etc., ditched his duffel bag and hopped sprightly from the jeep. Cairo. In ten years, it was as common, sultry, steamy, as he remembered it.

"What about you, Red?" he almost looked over his shoulder and asked Red, but did not. Red was not there. He had promised her once, a decade or so ago, give or take a month or two, but it never came to be. He took her just about everywhere else though. Six weeks after the car crash that killed her mother and stepfather Henry, Michael booked the trains, boats, and bicycles, and they were off; around the world in eighty days. Swear to God. From London to Paris to Timbuktu, she in her polka dots and patent leather, he in his white bucks and Panama hat, a couple of hefty side arms strapped under his jacket. The 14-karat cheaters he wore necessary only so he could see his hand in front of his face never mind the Eiffel Tower.

He wasn't half bad though, still wasn't at thirty-seven. Still had the movie star good looks, Einstein IQ, and Jimmy Cagney swagger. Still dressed the same way, wore the same gold frames, carried the same two guns.

He wasn't much bigger than Cagney, shared the same birthright, the USA, though Michael's stork set down in Brooklyn, not Manhattan's lower east side, *"Kiss this"* his motto on St. Paddy's Day. Because when it came to rough? As in tough? As in doing a tap dance on someone's face? Dr. Michael Delegianis *Jr*, only son and progeny of Brooklyn's Mick-the-Prick rubbed out in Harlem in '38 (they were picking up his forensic evidence for a week) Mikey, as some of Michael's friends sometimes called him, would give you three guesses who'd win hands down? He had an edge, Michael, what you call an attitude. Came by it naturally. Thirteen bullets his father took to the chest, count them, thirteen. *"A baker's dozen"* the tabloids read.

"'Rumor has it my mutter done it.'" Justin quoted the sub-caption blazon underneath, losing a lot in the translation and like Michael *knew* what he said would be repeated when he wasn't even there, not even stateside at the time but home in England in jail, or it felt like jail. Thirty-three years old and if it wasn't his wife, it was everyone else still telling him what to do.

London, England
A hotel room, 1938
"'Answered the mobster's son when asked,'" Justin continued flapping his gums. His beard still black and hair practically gone, you remember Justin, unforgettable that he was, tall thin guy son of Henry begat by Scotty, it was Michael you haven't met. Hotshot, hot-blooded Italian-American with the golden yellow curls and killer blue eyes, husband to Claudia daughter of Drake buddy to the old guy now called Gramps the father of Robert father to Joe, and so forth and so on. *"'The notable Dr. Delegianis, Rhodes Scholar and Nobel laureate.'"*

"Yeah, well, I'm not a Nobel laureate," Michael assured. Not to say he couldn't be, for that matter one day might be despite a chronic battle with booze. By '38, a creeping alcoholic stiffness to that Jimmy Cagney swagger. "Shows you how much they know."

"Still wasn't too bright, Mike," Justin tossed the rag on the bed.

"Yeah, yeah." Michael also wasn't the one with the secret handshakes and decoder ring. He was just a *guy.*

Actually, Michael was a physicist, an impressive and elitist profession, respected by his peers and barkeeps alike, but that was beside the point. With or without Michael to keep him on his toes, Justin was a spy, protection of the family paramount and still weighing heavily after six years and the car accident that damn near wiped out the lot of them. The fortress Justin built in response to the IRA come calling wasn't only there for Evelyn and Joe, or the surviving tot Joanna now fifteen, but also for Michael and his growing brood what with Claudia's connection to the secret society via her old man.

"See you got a promotion," Michael nodded at England's newly commissioned Squadron Leader whether or not Justin had to curl into a fetal position to fit inside a cockpit. "Only took you what? Ten fucking years? Is that what this is about? What's the matter? Afraid I might ruin something for you?" he took a drink, but only to clear his head. "What the fuck time is it anyway?"

"Noon," Justin said. "Down to business. Want to do something about this or not? Your father, I mean."

Michael looked at him; he couldn't be serious. "You serious?"

"No," Justin assured. "Asking if you are."

"Nah," Michael said after a while. "His racket, not mine, never in the racket. Just talk, you know that, small talk." He found his coat and hat. "Come on, let's ditch this place, I've got a funeral to get to."

Justin and Joe went with him because that's what friends do whether one of them was a spy, another a schoolteacher, and the other a louse, which Michael admittedly was. But he still felt bad about his father getting nailed on some street just like Justin felt about the passing of his old man, and Joe felt about his, until Joe kicked the can himself leaving Joanna once again in Michael's hands.

Cairo

March 9

"To the left as you go in ... a few doors down ... you can't miss it," claimed the friendly tour guide with the Groucho Marx eyebrows and yesterday's lunch fermenting on the dashboard of his cab, interrupting Michael's personal and private heartache of misplacing the pint-sized kid he nicknamed Red. He refused to acknowledge Joanna was *lost*. He refused to admit she was *dead*.

"That easy?" Michael cocked a brow beneath his sunshades protecting his hangover from the sun.

"Easy as pie," the Brit assured.

"Righto," Michael dug in his pockets. "Ta-ta, toodle-oo, whoop-de-do, va fa'n cul—what's the damage? Can you handle a fin?"

"Sure can," the cabbie laughed, and drove away with Michael's change.

"Fuck you, too," Michael flipped him the one-finger salute and lifted his duffel, toting it up the steps, stopping at the sign that promised "Joint Divisional Headquarters" **TEMPORARY** stamped through it in glossy black.

"Ya got that right," Michael assured, now that *Over There* was right here, not that you'd know it by the sign.

"'XIII Corps'" Michael read.

"'XXX Corps'" OK, he was getting the drift.

"'New Zealand Division, Second New Zealand Division', Charge of the frigging Light Brigade," Michael nodded. "Yeah, OK, whoever you can think of, except for us." But he went on inside anyway because why the hell not?

"I'll tell you why not," Michael figured out presently when to the left and a few doors down said MEN on a slip of cardboard instead of Office of Squadron Leader Justin Charles.

"Yeah, well, why the hell not?" he shrugged, gave Justin the bird, wherever he might be, "Here's looking at you," and went inside to do his duty, straighten his tie, and give his suit a wipe. He changed glasses while he was in there, too, from dark to light, only it failed to make the place look any cleaner.

"You know, I've seen subways better than this," Michael swaggered back out, scraping a host of pathological specimens from the sole of his shoe. "Hey, buddy!" he called for what appeared to be a Redcoat on the horizon. "Yeah, you. Wait up!

"Wait!" he hollered. "Yeah, screw you, too," he thumbed his nose at the soldier who gave him a blank look and kept on going where he was going, which was exactly the way Michael just came.

"I mean," Michael said, "what the hell gives here, anyway?

"I mean," Michael said, "who won the frigging war, anyway?" He just wanted to know. "The Big One. The one back in ... what the heck was it?" he scratched his frontal lobe. "1783? Yeah, that's the one.

"And!" Michael said, "Who won the fucking rematch after that? 1812, if you follow my drift?"

Which if anyone did, or did not, it did not matter since there wasn't anyone around to care. On the third swing past the toilets, Michael's duffel bag ended up against the wall with Michael's head on it and his legs stretched out across the floor. For a large building, it was largely empty, but there were a number of doors all over the place, and odds were someone was going to have to go in or come out of one of them sooner or later. Hard of hearing, failing eyesight, it wasn't as if they could lose Michael in the woodwork. But if they failed to notice the great White Hunter sleeping off a good one in the middle of the hall, they'd notice him soon enough when he tripped them and they fell down—

"Hello!" Michael said to the pair of knees carefully stepping over his. There was no way he'd trip that. He scrambled to his feet, pushing his hat up and off to the back of his head so she would be sure and get a load of just how lucky her day was.

"Your lucky day, sweetheart," he growled. "Your lucky day."

"Yes?" she said, not that she was necessarily agreeing with him, merely acknowledging the whistle blown up her skirt.

Oh, yes, yes, yes, yes! Michael perused her up and down. "I'm looking for Major Charles—Major Justin Charles—Seen him lately, around?"

"I'm sorry?" she said, which made sense if one knew Justin like Michael knew Justin, which Michael did.

In the meantime.

Oh, no, don't be sorry. Don't EVER be sorry. Michael quickly vetoed that idea, because if someone had something to be sorry for, this lady did not. We're talking Jean Harlow, Veronica Lake, and Mrs. Clark Gable, Carole Lombard, all rolled into one sweet perky package sealed with pencil-thin brows, cherry-bomb lips, blue eyes, and bottled blonde hair, but that was all right. What worked, worked, and this kid, from the tip of her stacked heels to the top shelf of her padded brassiere, worked.

"Squadron Leader," Michael apologized with a lick of his lips, "keep forgetting where I am. But, look, strike that, OK? Forget Chuckles. I'm Michael Delegianis—*Dr.* Michael Delegianis," he wowed her in her tracks and had her hand, "Alumnus of Oxford, Cambridge, Johns Hopkins, and Yale."

"How do you do?" she agreed, though unaware she was scheduled for a physical.

Michael did just fine. So did she apparently from the feel of that pulse. "Eighty," he congratulated her, "on the nose. I'll bet there's nothing wrong with those lungs either, can tell from here."

"Yes, thank you," she appreciated the information however aware the last thing he was ogling about her chest was her lung capacity. "Doctor," she smiled politely while carefully measuring the distance between her knee and his degree.

"Michael," Michael offered, really an informal sort of guy.

"I'm sorry?" she paused.

"Michael," Michael nodded. "My friends call me Michael. Just Michael—the ones registering an IQ that is," he tipped her off. "The rest of them are meatballs, but there's no reason to get into that. Especially," he crossed his heart and hoped to spend the night, "since my past is behind me, swear, two, three feet at least."

"I see," she said.

"That's a start," Michael approved, because so could he. There was nothing wrong with his eyes, positively nothing wrong with them to the power 10, which was the approximate magnification of his baby-blues on her side of his Coke-bottle lenses.

"Yes ..." she said, for some reason thinking of Carroll's Cheshire cat rather than Kipling's white anything despite her being British and his dusty white safari suit that at least suggested he might consider himself some great hunter. "However, Squadron Leader Charles ..." she turned to point him back across the Atlantic where he quite obviously belonged.

"Who?" Michael said.

"Squadron Leader Charles?" she offered. "Your friend?"

"My friend?" Michael said, and she nodded. "Oh, yeah, sure!" he remembered. "Justin. Hell of a guy. Know him?"

"No," she hadn't had the privilege or the pain.

"That's good," Michael assured. "Save yourself a bundle on aspirin."

"I'm sorry?" she said.

"Not important," Michael promised. "Sure you've got better things to do."

"Oh, yes," she agreed with a polite tap of his wrist. "So, if you wouldn't mind, please?"

"What?" Michael said. "Oh," he noticed.

"Yes," so did she. "So, really, if you wouldn't mind, please?"

"Yeah, hey, sorry, about that," he gave her back her hand.

"Quite all right. However, Squadron Leader Charles ..." she turned to point him back to Mars, if she could somehow manage it.

"But, you see," Michael said, interrupted, actually, "you are terribly attractive."

"I'm sorry?" she paused again.

"Positively, terribly attractive," he nodded.

"Thank you," she smiled. "However, Squadron Leader Charles ..."

"Who?" Michael said.

"Squadron Leader Charles," she said, a little firmer that time. "I'm sorry, Doctor, but what did you say your name was again?"

"Mike," Michael nodded. "Short for Michael. But, it's OK. I got it; figured it out. You're talking about Justin, right?"

"Actually ..." she believed he was the one talking about someone named Justin.

"Known each other since diapers," Michael disclosed. "Odds are he still wears them, but hey, who cares?"

No one she knew.

"So back to the low down," Michael said. "Fifty bucks says I can talk you into dinner before lunch."

"Fifty bucks," she repeated, though not because she thought the price was extraordinarily high or low.

"Make it pounds," Michael helped her out.

"I see," she said. "Well, yes, actually, Doctor ..." she found she found herself between the proverbial rock and his hard place where no doubt dozens had found themselves before, "you really are quite handsome yourself."

"Oh, yeah?" Michael said.

"Oh, yes, positively, awfully handsome," she nodded.

"Yeah?" Michael said.

"Positively awful," she assured.

"Right," Michael pointed, getting her drift. "Back to Justin."

"Yes, please. You will find Squadron Leader Charles upstairs."

"What?" Michael said.

"The office of Squadron Leader Charles is upstairs," she nodded.

"Upstairs?" Michael looked around. "What stairs?"

"These stairs," she pointed down at the steps they were standing on.

"Oh!" Michael said, "*these* stairs."

"Yes," she nodded.

"Yeah, well, you see," Michael confided, "I'm lost."

"I beg your pardon?" she startled, being as they were only fifty feet from the front door.

"What I mean is," Michael said, "I was lost. Several times. Look, let me tell you something, kid, in case you haven't noticed, there are an awful lot of doors around here, all over the place."

"There are more upstairs," she imagined.

"I'm sure there are," Michael agreed. "Probably hundreds. So, I don't suppose you would be willing to drop whatever you're doing and help me out? Screw King and country, I am definitely something you owe yourself."

"No," she assured.

Funny, she didn't look like a nun. But hey, win some, lose some, break even every so often when you've been at it as long as he had, and he'd been at it a long, long time. "Yeah, well, thanks anyway," he said. "It's been very nice chatting with you, Miss ... ah, Miss?"

"Assistant Section Officer, WAAF," she smiled, just in case he missed the RAF eagle stiffly pinned to that padded brassiere.

"Yeah, right, *sieg heil* to you, too," Michael forwent the curtsy and stuck with the salute. "It's still been what you call nice ..."

"Not at all. Upstairs, and to the left," she pointed right. "You'll have no trouble."

"Excuse me?" Michael said.

"To the left," she nodded. "The office of Squadron Leader Charles is upstairs and to the left, just a few doors down."

"Of course it is," Michael agreed. "Right next to the can."

"I beg your pardon?" she said.

"The toilet," Michael assured. "Look, honey, I've been in there six times, and if Chuck has his own stall, I didn't see it."

"Oh," she said. "Yes, well ..."

"Not worth the wrinkle cream," Michael stopped her. "I'll figure it out."

"Oh, yes," she was certain he would.

"Good-bye then," he tipped his hat.

"Good day," she said, and beat it out of there as fast as she could in her heels.

Oh, yes! Michael grinned, watching the knees wiggle away. *Oh, yes, yes, yes ...*

Wrong. Upstairs and to the right, then left, was a desk.

Oh, no! Michael stared at the sergeant who stood up and kept going. *Oh, no, no, no, no, no.*

"Why, hi, I'm Dr. Delegianis!" Michael explained brightly to one of the nipples eyeing him from the naked breast of meat coated with a copper-colored carpet of fuzz. "Dr. Michael Delegianis. I'm here to see Major Charles. Major Justin Charles of the RAF. I have with me letters of introduction ... official letters ..." he fumbled in his jacket pocket, pulling out a stick of gum. "All official—would you like them?"

"That I would," the you-ain't-never-seen-a-fellow-quite-the-likes-of-me-before assured with a Belfast drawl.

That's what you think! Michael corrected the seven-foot primate with the wiry orange pipe curls hanging down past his shoulders like some mutant Tarzan of the Apes. *I've been to the zoo.*

Out loud he said, "Say no more!" slapping an envelope down and deciding to throw in for some stupid reason, "Hey, you're Irish!" as the big guy took the papers, and Michael looked down at the desk plate that read *John James Joseph Neil Reynolds* in Kelly green. "I thought you guys were neutral. I'm Italian. American, of course."

"Of course," the freak agreed like he even knew the world was round.

"Oh?" Michael looked him up, up, and back down. "Well, then, hey, can I?"

"No." He was flatly told.

"No?" Michael said.

"No," the eighth wonder of the world shook his curls, causing a down draft that nearly blew Michael's hat off his head.

Now, see here. Michael glared at the envelope stuffed back in his hand. "Hey!" he sputtered. "See here!"

"Now, what would you be wantin' with Charlie, anyway, Doc?"

Johnny James Jack Joe Jim chuckled with a slobber, bending his back and replanting the whole of his entire arse on that one little chair. "Can you tell ol' Nellie that?"

"Can I—can I—what?" Michael said. "Huh?"

"Charlie," Nellie cooed, like just being ugly wasn't enough.

Charlie? Michael wrinkled his nose and screwed up his eyes trying to figure out who in the name of Darwin was Charlie. "Who the hell is Charlie?" Two hundred and twenty-plus IQ, Mikey didn't have a clue.

"You tell me," the fossil smiled.

He was trying to. *Justin*? Dr. Michael Delegianis stared at Mighty Neil Joe Young. Now, Michael had known Justin thirty years, and there was no way in hell anyone would ever call Justin, Charlie. "Look!" Michael said, diplomatically. "Fuck you and the mammoth you rode in on. The papers say I've got a right to speak with Justin ... and, I've not only got a right," Michael leaned over the desk, looking the bastard dead in the eye, easy enough to do when he was sitting down. "I'm gonna do it. Read 'em and weep, OK?" he shoved the envelope forward. "Read 'em and weep. They're signed, you seedless cantaloupe, by the goddamn fucking President of the United States, as in Franklin DR."

"Now, Nellie can't tell you what they say, Doc," Nellie advised.

"Excuse me?" Michael said.

"That he can't." Nellie did not lie, but left it up to Michael's imagination just what it was he meant.

Try common sense. "You can't read?" Michael said. "What the hell are you saying, you can't fucking read? Fine!" he picked up the phone, cramming it under the hairball's nose. "Then raise your leg and fart three times and get somebody out here who can, or do I have to split an atom to get some attention around here?"

"Charlie is busy," Nellie was comfortable right where he sat.

"Well, tell him to get fucking unbusy," Michael nodded. "Mikey's been here over an hour. Got it? Get on the horn and tell him Mikey is hot, he's bothered, and Chuckles will find out if that's a pistol in my pocket the hard way unless he's out here on the count of one. Got that? On the count of one."

"Aw, now, easy, Doc," Nellie said. "Didn't anyone say we

wouldn't be telling him about you. Didn't none of us say we wouldn't be doing that."

"We?" Michael snarled. "We, who? The only apparition I see here is you."

"We," Nellie nodded, and Michael grabbed the desk as the floorboards rolled and quaked under his feet, peaking at around a 3.6 magnitude.

"Oh, hello!" Michael said to Tweedledum or Tweedledee appearing to belly his way down the hall and block Michael's path.

"Bobby," Nellie mentioned as Michael stared at the monstrous navel holding him at bay, "Doc here is wantin' to see Charlie."

"Is he now?" the whale of a Welshman drawled from deep inside a herniated testicle, and that did it.

"Oh, for—look, pie face," Michael barked at Nellie, "just show him the fucking papers, OK? Just show him the goddamn fucking papers!"

"Easy now, Doc," Nellie continued to smile as the one named Bobby took Michael's papers to have a look over them himself, "we will be telling him, we will ..." he looked to Bobby for verification of what the papers did say.

"Let him pass, Nel," Bobby folded the envelope neatly between the fat of his forefingers and thumbs.

"You don't say?" Nellie smiled.

"Yeah, he do say," Michael nodded, "he do say."

"Well, now, then, find Nellie's boy for him, won't you?" Nellie requested. "And tell him we've got a guest."

"Yeah, fetch him," Michael nodded after the medicine ball rolling away, "fetch him!"

"Aye, he will, Bobby will," Nellie grew once more from the seat of his chair. "If you, Doc, would come this way ... right this way ..."

"You got it!" Michael did his strut down the hall.

"This way, Doc," Nellie directed. "Right this way ..."

"You know it!" Michael assured, and got the door himself.

Now, you know Justin had always been a man of simple tastes, but that room had one lousy piece of furniture in it, one lousy piece, a lousy fucking chair.

"Oh, hello, again!" Michael said to the fat guy as Nellie gave him a hand slamming him inside.

"Hello!" Michael said to a third freak with a pasty face and skeletal paw leaning over to help him off with his jacket with a wink of his ice-blue eye.

"Bend over, and say, ah!"

"Huh?" Michael said.

"Do what the lieutenant says, Doc," Bobby nodded, while Nellie folded those red hairy arms of his and said, "Drop 'em."

"You got it!" Dr. Michael Delegianis ditched his trousers while meanwhile ...

The Fezzan

March 9

Hand over hand they dissected the goose, fingers ripping its flesh from the bone. The wine spilled, drunk in huge satisfying gulps.

"*You are so very attractive,*" Reineke whispered to the woman seated across from him at the table, enjoying her cool lips devouring the fruit.

"*Do that to me,*" he requested, and she smiled. "*Do that to me,*" he implored, and could feel himself fill.

She ignored him, blonde after blonde, dripping gold gowns, cajoled flooding the room. The candles burned and the flowers bloomed. He stood up to cross to the table, but the floor was crowded and two gunners blocked his way.

"*But, you are so very attractive,*" he protested to the woman, watching himself take off his shirt and sit down.

"*Do that to me,*" he coaxed as she eased around the table, bringing her peach with her.

"*Do that to me,*" he spread his legs and touched her thigh.

Someone laughed and she crushed the fruit on his chest. He was surprised, but she whispered, "*You want it anyway,*" as she smeared the pulp over his breast, up his neck and down, its juice becoming butter, its oils teasing, but then glass, mutilating, and she whispered as he touched the blood, "*But, you want it anyway. Won't you want it, anyway?*"

"*Indeed!*" he grasped her.

"*Oh, no, mon capitaine!*" Pierre sat in the middle of the table. "*It is too dangerous! Please, mon capitaine, please, I beg you!"*

"*But I want,*" he pouted, looking for the woman who was gone, so far away.

"*I want!*" he insisted, and back she came, back across the floor she walked, so small, thin, then fat, and she was bleeding.

"*No, mon capitaine,*" Pierre pleaded "*No!*"

"*Indeed, I want!*" Reineke said, staring at her face, she was older, but then so was he.

"*Remember?*" she whispered and had a new peach. "*Do you remember?*"

"*Nine,*" he said the number and she tipped a smile.

"*But you want it, anyway,*" she bit the fruit, chewing tiny bites. "Won't you want it, anyway?"

"*Indeed. Do that to me!*" he tore the gown from her shoulders.

"*Do that to me,*" he moaned, her teeth sinking into his throat as he had her on the table, ignoring Pierre vomiting blood, his stomach exploding as he died. "*Promise! Promise!*"

"*I promise,*" she whispered, matching his violent thrusts, her nails shredding his back, the blood mingling with the wine.

"Hauptmann."

Reineke woke up with a jump, the sheets damp with sweat. The last thing he remembered he had been falling and someone called his name.

"Hauptmann?" The Korporal was bedside, coffee ready. It was 6:30, a mistake to go to sleep even for such a short time.

"I will need a uniform," Reineke answered, not bothering to sit up. "The smallest one you can find."

"Yes, Herr Hauptmann," he nodded and disappeared, leaving the coffee behind.

Reineke stared from the cup to the French windows and daylight almost an hour old. Deciding to ignore it, he rolled over onto his stomach, rearranging his pillows, wondering how long it would take them to realize the Hauptmann had decided to retire—

The photographs were still in the bed. Hanuk's gift waiting for him under the sheet.

"Damn you," he muttered at the soiled faces captured in terror, and could smell the fire behind them, burning.

"*Mon capitaine it is not necessary!*" He heard Pierre say so many times, but Pierre was wrong, and Reineke was dressed and gone, the pictures locked in his hand.

Chapter Fourteen

An arid cemetery of gardens surrounded the villa. A marble wasteland of the erotic and exotic reduced to barren basins of dust and stone broiling in the sun, lifeless as the ghostly tomb markers of past aristocrats and slaves. The truck yard and supply bins occupying the eastern range, to the south and west, a maze of walls threaded their way undisturbed across stone plains bordered by an orchard of cypress, palm, and olive trees strangling each other in their quest for survival. It was the line between the two worlds of the German Reineke and the Holy Man Pierre. A barrier of snarled tree limbs reinforced with fences strung with barbed wire, flimsy in many ways as the verbal agreement between them. But still, no one from either side would think to enter the tangled grove. The children had no reason, any soldier shot on sight. Even the Holy Man never came along the gardens, though he continued to walk them from time to time during his visits.

As had Reineke spent time inspecting them, particularly in the early days. Intrigued by the variety of tomb markers and the opportunity for private thought, he walked them less often now, preferring to disappear completely, sometimes for hours at a time. The unnecessary and useless fences of twisted barbed wire he had ordered built to satisfy Thiele. No secret passage or pathway in and out of the woods, the dense overgrowth was much too difficult for the aged Holy Man before the installation of the German's blockade. Reineke tried it once just to see how hard it really would be. It wasn't difficult, not for him, if he didn't mind the scrapes and scratches from the unforgiving and unyielding olive trees, cruel as the wire. He did mind them, common sense and vanity colliding and equal for once.

Virtually inaccessible then via the gardens to all but an advancing army eager to display its might, the children's area was reasonably accessible from the northern courtyard, through the gateway, across the sand, a laborious walk in the sun, perhaps five minutes by wagen. Reineke took one of the wagens, calling out for Anne as he arrived in the market square, center of the children's world. The protected area nearly as large as the compound, it was more tropical and lively. Remnants of the town's forum still evident with its surviving rows of shops, comfortable and safe in the crumbling foothills of several large buildings, the apartments and houses had all but collapsed. Their remains choking the avenues and streets, there was no egress in or out of the forum except from the direction of the Emperor's villa.

"Dieter!" the thin, young girl with dusty brown skin, looked up from her seat on the edge of the well with the approach of the wagen. Her long raven hair flying like great black wings as she raced to greet him, the sturdy ankle-high boots she wore were heavy and large for her eleven year old legs bare and free under the ragged hem of her skirt. The little general of the crowd of babies and school children, Anne was not the romance of her brother Hanuk, but an odd mixture of awkwardness, strength, and dirt. Reineke her hero in a world she could not possibly understand at her age. "Did Hanuk give you my message?" she verified excitedly, wanting it to be true, but also wanting Reineke to have come to them on his own without having to be told.

"Indeed. What do you know about these?" Reineke withdrew the photographs from his pocket. "No, they are not for you," he stopped her from taking them or even seeing them. "If you know what they are, you do not have to look at them, correct? If you do not know, you just say 'Dieter, I have no idea what you are talking about.'"

She did know, of course, there with her uncles when the pictures were taken. "They're Diana's." Anne pushed her hair out from her eyes, tucking it behind her ears with a sigh. "From her to you. Some silly reminder, I guess, I don't know. I do know Hanuk is such a coward to listen to her. It's all right, just ignore them, I'll talk to her."

"Where is she?" Reineke asked. "I know she is here. Tell me."

"The temple," Anne nodded. "She said she would be back, in hospital at nine for rounds." Nine was too long. "Come." Reineke took her by the hand, escorting her to his wagen. "You will be my agent."

"Aren't I always?" she laughed, hopping up to stand in the seat.

"Yes." Reineke pulled her down to sit like the proper young lady she was rather than the boy she pretended to be. "And as always, you are to sit. How many times do I have to tell you this?"

"Oh, please!" she stole his hat, scrambling to stand back up on the seat, and hang over the windshield. "We'll just pretend I'm you."

He returned from the temple at eleven o'clock without Anne. By eleven-thirty he stood over the opened grave of what had once been an American Army Colonel of advancing years, mutilated prior to being killed by a crushing blow to the head as the Holy Man had reported, the hands severed for some reason, and brains exposed. Making note of the patches identifying the officer as an engineer, and the significant amount of blood that seemed to support the Holy Man's proposal of at least a third person, Reineke's examination of the corpse was otherwise unrevealing. No nausea or guilt like he had experienced when finding the girl, this had been a man, a willing participant in his game of war. He turned to Linke. "Where is the hand Thiele found? Unless it is one of his, there is another body somewhere."

"No other body, Hauptmann." Linke presented him with a burlap sack he ordered dug from its hole two meters away.

It was that of a young adult male, white. Reineke examined the hand but could tell nothing more than that from it, other than the cut severing it was clean like those of the Colonel's suggesting a sharp, quick, force such as Herr Major's sword.

"Arabs," Linke proposed and Reineke looked at him. The sergeant shrugged. "That's what most would think."

"Yes," Reineke agreed. If they were oblivious to the involvement of the SS and just happened to find the grave, which no one would. "Burn it. Everything." He dropped the hand back in its sack and left the gravesite for the villa, arriving in time to hear the screams coming from the opened French windows above, and he flew to answer the Holy Man's howls for help.

"Michael," Joanna whispered.

"*Shhh, Mademoiselle, c'est tout exact,*" Pierre promised how everything would be fine, soothing her florid swollen face with a cool wet cloth as she tossed and turned, threatening to wake up.

Joanna could feel a cloth on her face like when she was a child. Michael determined to wipe the fever away before she suffered a brain hemorrhage or seizure, or something equally lurid and frightening. She would eventually wake up at noon, a harsh coughing spell rousing her to a state of semi-consciousness, the room stifling hot and out of focus.

"*Shhh,* vous êtes en sécurité, *Mademoiselle,*" Michael reassured from somewhere close by, repeating his promise of safety with a gentle stroke of her head.

French? Joanna struggled to understand the words in the gloom surrounding her. Why on earth was Michael talking in French? She tried to ask him, but could barely see him, little more than a shadow leaning over her, her throat burning when she tried to talk. "Don't," she said. "No, don't touch my head."

"*Oui,*" he agreed sympathetically with her flinch of pain. "*Mais il passera. Dans tandis que votre tête se dégagera et ne blessera pas tellement.*"

No, it would not be fine. Joanna didn't know why he seemed to think her head would be fine when it hurt so much. "Don't," she repeated, "Michael, please don't touch my head," she insisted, sensing his silent huff of impatience, feeling his hands firmly push her back down, something soft laying on top of her that quickly seemed to wind itself around her legs as she tried to sit up.

"*Ici, Mademoiselle, laissez-moi vous aider,*" Pierre offered to help, eager to assist her, and Joanna felt hands again as they grasped her, strong and tight around her shoulders and arms, but it was his hood that frightened her. This enormous dark brown hood floating down to envelop her, swallow her up inside. She screamed, her hand striking the edge of something hard, a bottle falling over; she heard a bottle fall over and saw the bright, white bundles of what looked like table linens, fluffy white table linens stacked neatly in a row.

"*Je suis Monsignor Pierre Beausoleil. Vous êtes tout fait en sécurité, Mademoiselle, n'ayez pas peur.*"

Michael introduced himself as a Monsignor, saying again how she was safe as Joanna stared at the bandages trying to figure out what they were. She frowned. A Monsignor was a priest, something like a priest. She gave up studying the bandages to eye the hood. It wasn't Michael, but a fat brown face with wrinkles appearing from inside to peer back at her. So old, so horribly and hideously old, he did not look much like a priest either, his long clawed hand coming toward her gnarled and twisted like the roots of some old tree. She hit him, her fist catching him on the chin, fighting and screaming as he tried to stop her and she tried to kick her way free of whatever it was that had wrapped itself around her legs.

"Mon Dieu," Pierre grunted in pain as her foot found his stomach. He shouted for the guards he did not want to call, and who did not want the responsibility of answering the uproar they could not pretend they did not hear. Wrong if they did answer, wrong if they did not, it was not always easy to forecast the Hauptmann's position and this was the Holy Man. They answered, and their sudden appearance in the apartment made the situation even worse. It was Reineke who bolted in from the library to subdue the riot, untangle the screaming naked prisoner caught and twisted in the sheets, the Holy Man too old and fat to do much more than try and keep her from falling on the floor.

"Mon capitaine!" Pierre breathed gratefully righting himself, fumbling to straighten the bandage she had tried to rip from her head as Reineke grabbed Joanna, forcing her down, holding her tightly.

"Fix it later!" Reineke insisted, the girl staring up at him in terror, damming him over and over until Pierre's needle put her back to sleep.

"Well?" Reineke turned around from studying the courtyard through the French windows with Pierre's appearance in the library.

"She is a fighter," Pierre was shattered and apologetic. "I am sorry, I did not know. I did not realize she would be so upset."

"That is not sufficient," Reineke assured, "when it is your duty to know." He marched out onto the balcony where he managed to smoke almost an entire cigarette before the Holy Man interrupted.

"Mon capitaine!" Pierre announced his arrival with a pointing finger, "it is exactly as I told you. I did not realize Mademoiselle would be so excited. Forgive, please, but Pierre, unlike you, is not God. Oui, I understand your embarrassment ..."

Embarrassment? What was there for him to be embarrassed about? "Indeed," Reineke snapped, "What are you talking about?"

Pierre thought about it. "I do not know," he shrugged. "But it is still your fault. You come in—and do not think I do not thank you for this, because I do," he assured. "Mademoiselle is a little mademoiselle, but she is a mighty one, and I thank you for the rescue.

"But!" he reprimanded, "Mademoiselle is also awake today, and when she sees you she is going to scream. She is going to fight, cry, spit—"

"She was already screaming," Reineke said, "which is why I came in there!"

"Oh," Pierre said. "Oui, this is true, isn't it?" he frowned, thinking about that, too. "Well," he decided, "it is still your fault."

Of course it was.

"Hopeless, mon capitaine, hopeless," Pierre stalked back into the library where Reineke found him, slumped in a chair, exhausted with despair.

"What is hopeless?" Reineke asked coldly. "Other than I am German, and you are French?"

"Everything," Pierre nodded. "Her room is her sanctuary. I her friend, savior from whatever devils she does or does not remember— that would be you," he pointed, "and this," he gestured around the room "I did not want Mademoiselle to know anything about this or you, until she is much stronger."

"And it is my fault she does," Reineke said coldly.

""Well, it is not my fault," Pierre assured. "I did not do any of this to her."

Neither did he. "If you cannot control the prisoner," Reineke sat down at his desk, "I will find someone who can."

Pierre sneered. "Such as who? Your Thiele, perhaps? Or maybe your Gestapo to finish their job? Ach, poo, I spit on all of them!" he spit on the floor. "Live for them to die."

Reineke was not impressed. "Such as Diana," he assured. The Holy Man should know how her suggestions of what to do with the girl were as cold and unfeeling as Reineke's. It must be the German in them, as she so often said. The two of them finding themselves in agreement with each other more often than one might think, or possibly prefer.

"Her, too," Pierre waved Diana and her threats aside, too. "If I want to protect Mademoiselle from the knowledge of you, I certainly want her to know nothing of Diana."

"That would be wise," Reineke agreed.

"Ach, wise," Pierre dismissed, "you give yourself too much credit, the two of you. You are extraneous, meaningless. And, so we try again," he nodded. "We do, and, in a few weeks, you will see. Pierre and Mademoiselle will be best friends. I her salvation, her life raft. She will reach for it, cling to it, and yes, survive because she has to, because she wants to. It is how the mind works," he smiled at Reineke. "You know this, yes?"

He knew more than that. "The girl is leaving with the trucks."

"That is what you think," Pierre said.

That was what he knew. "What she trusts, believes in, or clings to, is irrelevant."

"Again what you think," Pierre agreed, "but it is all right. Mon capitaine has many more important things to concern himself with. Mademoiselle is English, as he has suspected."

"Indeed." Reineke sat up straight, the threat of the Kufra looming. "How do you know this?"

"How?" Pierre said. "Simple. Her voice. You did not hear it?"

"I heard her scream," Reineke agreed, "little else."

"The dead can hear her scream," Pierre assured. "So you will leave her treatment to Pierre and stay away. One nightmare is enough. You do not need to frighten her anymore."

"How do you know she is British?" Reineke insisted.

"English," Pierre corrected. "I said English. But British could be more accurate, you could be right. I am right when I say when she speaks, it is in English whether she is of Britannia, or from one of her colonies since this is Africa and she is here."

"Indeed. *Amerika* is one of her colonies." Reineke was on his feet, at the French windows, the smell of smoke in the air from the fire out in the truck yard. "The man with her was an American."

"If you say he was," Pierre shrugged. "Mon capitaine, to exhume a body from its sacred ground is against God's law, blasphemy. And it is God you will answer to for your actions, not Pierre."

"My answer would be the same," Reineke lit a cigarette, "we cannot have it here. Particularly since you are right, there was at least one other person, also a man. Thiele found a severed hand in the truck. It did not belong to the American. There is another body somewhere."

"Which Mon capitaine can find, as he could find six more," Pierre agreed. "Perhaps this is something he should do. Track them down and burn them all if he thinks that will somehow relieve him of their significance and stench."

"Significance?" Reineke said.

Pierre smiled. "Perhaps. Perhaps not. Perhaps, mon capitaine," he proposed, withdrawing a thin silver chain from the deep folds of his robes, "the SS are not as clever as they think they are whether they are trying to be clever, or are just stupid as I think.

"I question which it is," he nodded as Reineke took the chain, "yes, naturally. I question who lost this and why? For what purpose?"

"Where did you get this?" Reineke fingered the tarnished chain with its two metal identification tags, identical to each other and unfamiliar other than knowing they were not British.

"The pocket of her skirt," Pierre said, his answer suspect in that it was so simple. To tell the truth would be to tell how Hanuk found the chain in the sand outside, apprehension in the eyes of his uncles when he showed it to them, or perhaps it was just surprise. Pierre was unsure which, but took the chain away from them anyway to bury it with her. Immune to his interrogation, the sons of Diana were not immune to him, but lived because he lived, safe in the bowels of the Arab world alongside their German benefactor. "I believe they are what the American calls the 'dog tag', no?"

"I do not know," Reineke absently circled Pierre's chair. "You would have to ask Diana. The American had no identification. But this is an identification tag, clearly, yes, of some form." He was almost afraid to look, but did and the girl's name had no particular celebrity of which he was aware. It was simple like the tin chain she had worn around her neck. "Johanna Lee." He pronounced it wrong, inserting an *h* where there was none. It was not intentional, just Germanic like he.

"Oui," the priest said in his French. "And the rank mon capitaine reads is one commonly of a nurse. See?" he pointed out, in case Reineke had missed it. "'Lee, Joanna Lieutenant'. A nurse. Oui, mon capitaine, a neutral."

"Neutrality is not a guarantee," Reineke threw the chain at him. "She is too young to be a nurse. Some clerk perhaps, some intern— or some lie," he loomed over him. "Indeed. You claim you found them in the pocket of her skirt. How do I know that is true, or that it is even hers?"

"You don't," Pierre did not lie then. "And Mademoiselle is possibly more or less important than her dog tags ... that are not dog tags," he dangled the chain temptingly with a sly smile. "Identification tags with no identification number? Mon capitaine is either tired, or he is blind."

Reineke snatched the chain back to finger its thin metal tags not quite as flexible as they should be. "Silver," he nodded slowly. A jeweler by trade perhaps, or just rich and familiar with the precious metals, their oils, their touch, feel, now that he was giving them the attention they deserved.

"Oui," Pierre said. "And this is odd, no? Who would give such a strange piece of jewelry to a young woman?"

"Interesting," Reineke had to admit.

"Dangerous," Pierre corrected, and Reineke treated him with a thoughtful eye.

"Why?" Reineke asked.

Pierre shrugged again. "She is a woman, mon capitaine. A woman in North Africa and she is not a nurse? Perhaps a driver then? But it is the native who drives the officers here. To bring the English would be unlikely."

"She was with the American," Reineke reminded. "You claim these are their tags."

"Perhaps," Pierre admitted. "I know very little about them."

Only that they called their identification tags, dog tags. Reineke did not know much more, if he knew that. Until today, he was probably less interested in knowing anything about them than the Holy Man was. "I am no fan of the American," Reineke assured, "whatever you are conspiring."

Pierre blinked. "They are your enemy, mon capitaine, as much as the English. What could I be conspiring?"

Reineke ignored him, studying the tags, cautious about making any final decision. "A school girl, perhaps. Student of some sort. She was in uniform."

"Remnants of a uniform," Pierre agreed, "oui. A mess."

Yes. "Perhaps you are right in that she lives here." Reineke sat back in his chair. "Algeria. Cairo. There are Europeans."

"Oui, I am European," Pierre said.

So was he. "A family member," Reineke dangled the chain, still studying it. "The man was not young."

"No," Pierre said. "But?"

"It still does not explain," Reineke assured, "why they were brought here unless they were close by. There is nothing for hundreds of kilometers of which we are aware. If there is no Allied encampment, it had to be a plane crash and the SS just there, in the vicinity, perhaps even shot them down. The American would intrigue them. They would interrogate him. Bring them here, why not since they were coming here." He smiled thinly. "You see I can think, and that much of the mystery is really not too mysterious at all."

Pierre nodded. "It also does not stop someone from looking for her. The daughter of someone, the sister, lover, friend, it does not matter. She is a woman, and they will come looking for her. A woman, mon capitaine, always belongs to someone."

Unless they were dead also.

"What did Diana say?" Pierre asked, more than mere curiosity for his reason.

Diana? The same that she said about the SS. Leave it alone. Wait and see, lay low, play dead. "Do nothing," Reineke replied, "and send the girl away with the trucks if she survives."

"That does not sound like Diana," Pierre shook his head.

No. No, lying in wait would be much more accurate as she had laid in wait for him. Three weeks, it was three weeks before he had even known of her existence, nine weeks since he had. "Never mind about Diana," Reineke said. "What do you want to do?"

"I?" the priest feigned surprise. "I thought it had been decided. Mademoiselle is to be moved with the trucks."

From her obvious condition that would be weeks from now, the Holy Man had also been right about that. "I am talking about her people," Reineke said, "collectively, as a whole."

"Yes, of course," Pierre said. "This Allied encampment mon capitaine believes is out there alongside his SS. I do not know. Perhaps mon capitaine should consider checking with his sources to confirm what he already believes is true."

"You are my source," Reineke whispered unintentionally, it just coming out that way.

"Oui," Pierre agreed. "And with time, I can find anything."

Of that, Reineke had little doubt.

"Good," Pierre smiled. "Is that what you want?"

He should say yes. At the very least, it would be a test of the Holy Man's claimed power over this desert and its inhabitants, friend or foe. "I have to think," Reineke replied. "There is a little time as you suggest. The girl is far too ill to be moved yet. Perhaps the next delivery."

"As you wish," Pierre inclined his head, biting back the smirk Reineke could see on his lips.

"Stop laughing," Reineke suggested. "I am not kind or weak. It has nothing to do with compassion. If there are more of them out there I want to know. I will know," he assured. "Indeed. You are right. A woman always belongs to someone, especially one as young as that."

Chapter Fifteen

Cambridge
1940

Joanna Lee belonged to Justin Charles, Evelyn Lee, and Michael Delegianis in precisely that order. At sixteen years Justin's junior, as his stepsister, Joanna had been Justin's legal ward since the death of her mother and his father a decade ago. Her arranged marriage at seventeen to Joseph Lee, twice her age at the time, was a practice steeped in antiquity, still widely accepted by the xenophobic upper classes. A convenient and practical solution for Justin serving his interests and the families of continued safety and security. Joe, with his conciliatory nature, and limited involvement in the spy game, was the natural choice of predecessor to Evelyn, Joanna's current principal caregiver. Justin and Joe had known each other all their lives, united in their friendship, and their families' historical ties. Evelyn, Joe's grandfather and surviving patriarch of the collective family born out of grief and need following the fatal car accident was getting on.

Born Christmas Day, 1864, Evelyn was sixty-seven years old at the time of the accident. Eight years later, with few signs of slowing down, Evelyn had thus far managed to shoulder much of Joanna's actual daily care. Claudia, initially interested in extending herself for Henry's orphaned stepdaughter, ended up having several more children of her own and with that understandably little time. Justin, normally not one to shirk from responsibility, was nevertheless far too busy making his mark a hemisphere away in South Africa, his cold reserve not untouched by the tragedy that befell the families already too small to survive many more generations. To the contrary, Evelyn knew Justin as he had known Justin's father Henry, and his grandfather Scotty before him, and the wound was deep and raw. Justin blaming himself for what happened as much as he blamed the Irish, convinced the culprits were Irish, Henry's death just a point to be made to him. In his own way, seeking to ensure it never would happen again. Justin's way was to separate, move halfway around the world, except for financial support of his stepsister, only a rare visit with the family once a year or so.

Evelyn's way was to become involved. He didn't give a damn about the money. He had money, plenty of it. They had a tot on their hands. Uprooted from her own world, Australia, more than halfway across the planet, and dropped down in their laps at not but nine years of age. She didn't need a pocketbook; she needed love, a family. That left Evelyn, old, and fresh out of family himself, except for Joe, and with Mike there for entertainment, Joe to take care of the formal aspects of her education, Evelyn was free to collect and give the love he had too often held in reserve. Surprising no one more so than himself with how much love he had. She was his granddaughter. He anointed her that, and declared her that long before she married his grandson Joe. As much a part of him as if he'd given birth to her himself, and was she a hellcat, not some timid little mouse as one might first think or suspect given the size of her, but a tornado, with a backbone and spirit stronger than his. She brought life to the house, noise to its too-quiet hallways, always involved in some mischief or another, wild and untamed as that country of hers. She made Evelyn young, think young, be young, realize what he had missed with Robert, and again with Joe, understand what he had been afraid of all his life, and that was life, to live life rather than just try to own and rule it. So, quite, while she might belong to Justin in the legal sense, whom she actually belonged to was Evelyn and he'd dare anyone, including Justin, to suggest otherwise.

Justin was not about to. Certainly not go toe-to-toe with the old man over something so trivial particularly when Evelyn's involvement with Joanna was also the ideal solution in what to do with Evelyn. How to provide for him, satisfy, occupy, and pacify him in his waning years, give him something to do. Regardless though of Evelyn or his good intentions, of which Justin had no doubts or complaints, there remained the fact that Joanna's care and protection would extend beyond her childhood, and Evelyn was not going to live forever. Irresponsible, Michael was out of the question for anything but entertainment—Justin quickly stepped back from the initial Claudia as surrogate mother notion once he thought it over. That left only Joe to pick up the reins in Justin's absence, offering the solid, stable influence Justin believed Joanna needed beyond the luxury and attention piled on her by the old man.

Spoiled her silly, is what Evelyn did, unmindful of what might be good for her. A burgeoning felon at nine, headstrong, careless, and carefree, Joanna was a veritable anarchist at seventeen, one of Michael's *Dead End Kids,* all boy. Which was fine, except not only was Joanna not raised in a New York tenement, she was not a boy. A boy, Justin could not only knock the chip off his shoulder, he could knock his head off, if the need arose, with one swift sock to the chin. If Joe and Evelyn had their hands full, which from time to time they did, Justin's usual even and reserved temperament would be no match for her, had he been around, and so it was probably a good thing he wasn't. However, Justin's remedy of moving Joe forward in rank with Evelyn's advancing years was destined to be almost as short-lived as Henry's marriage when Joe and his plane exploded into a fireball over London in December 1940. The papers said the North Sea. They were also off by a day or two, but that was not only all right, it was intentional. Justin did not like facts down on paper for others to read. Lest anyone forget, public record also listed Joanna as long dead, killed in the car accident alongside her parents. It might have been kinder had it been true. At only age eighteen, orphan Joanna Lee found herself a widow, back with Evelyn. Claudia there to offer advice, Michael parked on the doorstep to rescue her from the two of them, because let's face it, for all Joanna belonged to Justin and the old man Lee, Joanna did not belong to anyone except to Michael.

Cambridge

1940

Joanna really did not need rescuing from Grandfather, what they all called Evelyn, except for Justin and Claudia, and even Michael who shortened Grandfather to Gramps. Claudia on the other hand? Oh, yes, Joanna definitely could stand being rescued from Claudia.

Without ever knowing why, or with any interest in ever knowing why, Joanna did know she and Claudia did not get on together very well. That was something Michael could relate to. He and Claudia did not get on together very well, either. Claudia Delegianis, nee Drake, was a shrew, a rigid and demanding woman under her bridge socials and afternoon teas, a saintly witch with soft hands and razor tongue, discriminating and discriminatory. Michael was not sure why he married her in the first place and did not divorce her when he had the chance and only one kid instead of four—or was it five by then? All girls. Michael lost count of how many kids he had after a while. The same as it did not matter after a while. Michael's way, like Justin's, was to separate, move away from what he did not like, go out for some air and make his way back eventually to check in on how life was going with Red, what he called Joanna and no one else did.

But then she was his kid. The one he wanted. Whether or not Michael ever wanted any kid for that matter, which if he did, it would be Joanna with her freckled face and electric red hair. A pint-sized package of what Gramps called spirit and Justin looked down on as criminal. Michael had the same sort of spirit. He just did not have it in him to live up to Justin's idea of self-discipline or even consider a reason why he should. Even though back in the days when Michael was a child he already had more brains than anyone knew what to do with. There was nothing he could not do, nothing too hard, or impossible. He was a real-life progeny, Renaissance man, with an inflated IQ and ego to match. So maybe that was the reason Michael seemed to make a career out of misbehavior, nowhere to go except down.

Or maybe he was just a drunk. A monkey on his back. Talents and gifts second to alcohol. Whichever, Michael was happy being Michael, and that would never change. The fact that Michael could afford to be Michael probably made him worse, a fist full of dollars in his pockets, at his fingertips, with plenty more of it in the bank. However ill gotten, Michael could never spend what he was worth in the six lifetimes he tried to crowd into one. Independently wealthy and set for life, all thanks to his father who made a killing during Prohibition like a few other respectable American millionaires.

Not that respectability was something Michael's father ever quite achieved. No, he was a villain 'till the day he died. An Italian stone mason with a fourth grade education, few prospects, and a wife and son underfoot. A dead-end street, dead-end kid except times and things change. On the flipside of life, Michael's side, the increasing popularity of the Anti-Saloon League offered a boon to the underworld in the pre-Prohibition era. From there the rest was American and Michael's history. Not quite ten years old himself when he set sail the wrong way past the Statue of Liberty, shipped home to Europe and the best in education. A brief stint on the continent proper, by spring, Michael was in England, the first of several schools behind him, two wide-eyed chumps by the names of Justin and Joseph hanging onto his shirttails and every word. From prep boys to frat brothers, the three of them thick as thieves, Michael their ticket to adventure, Justin and Joe, Michael's ticket into the annals of society that had eluded his father. Who cared that it was British? Not Michael, not then. Married Claudia Drake when he was twenty even though she was ten years older than he was, she was pretty and classy and looked good on his arm. Two schools and three years later they had a kid, Andrea. Might have worked out better between Claudia and him over the long haul had Andrea been a boy, but she wasn't, and it didn't, and who knew really. Michael settled for Andrea instead of Andy, calling her Annie after one of his early mentors, Dr. Anna Kassim Haas. A physicist and pioneer in radiation and modern cancer therapy, one hag of a dowager, face like a mule, tough as nails under her diamonds and furs, with a brain and ego big and bright as his.

Oh, Michael liked Annie, and she liked him, even though he was about as far removed from being another Schweitzer, and she was banging the old guy Lee behind wife Martha's back. Michael was close with a few of Anna's sons, too, John, in particular. Michael went to Yale with John, stayed in touch over the years, though not recently. The last Michael knew, around the time everyone was leaving, John decided to go home to Germany. Probably not the brightest thing he ever did considering he was a Jew, and since Michael had not heard from John that probably more of less settled that.

Four years after Andrea was born, Michael filed for a legal

separation from Claudia, the first of his medical degrees hanging by where it still hung, rather lopsided somewhere in a corner of the old man's home in Cambridge. Justin put the kibosh on the filing and read Michael the riot act for taking things public and Michael blew town. Six months on the prowl Michael was back home in England for Henry and Elizabeth's wedding where he met the love of his life. Rumor in the servants' quarters and the looks across the dinner table hinted it was Elizabeth, Joanna's mother, a perky little piece from down under, practically half Henry's age. Rumor was wrong. Joanna intoxicated Michael. Six months later her parents were dead and they had been inseparable ever since. He was her best friend, her sidekick, her confidante. His idea of getting her involved with the ATS, England's *Auxiliary Territorial Services a* week after Joe died, and Justin finished barking orders from his side of the globe, was harmless enough, Evelyn supposed. He couldn't help though being a bit concerned about the London part of the equation and the shock it might hold for Joanna who, contrary to Justin's concerns and Michael's influence, had led an extremely sheltered life.

Cambridge

1941

"I'll put her in a bunker," Michael promised with fingers and knees crossed. "I'll build one around her, like this place, tailor made." Every frigging gizmo known to man tucked behind those oaken walls, including an escape hatch and tunnel to Never-Ever Land. Hard to believe Justin, a man who still believed in the rack and chastity belts, also believed in things like television and rockets to the moon. Justin was Justin, or Chuck, as Michael called him, though only to break his stones, and Michael had given up on trying to "understand" Justin around the same time Justin had given up on trying to "understand" him. Gramps, on the other hand, was just Gramps, inclined with Michael, as he was with Justin, and had been with Joe, to let them have their fun. They were boys, after all, or by that point, men.

Maybe Michael was. Justin, Michael maintained was some sort of cross between the missing link and an autocrat, and Joe? That was a whole other story Michael did not like to talk about. Joe though was dead, Justin, his usual elsewhere, and Michael, who probably could put a rocket on the moon, was averse to the sort of plumbing hidden behind Evelyn's walls.

Michael was averse to living his life surrounded by listening devices, cameras, and plain-clothes dicks who followed him everywhere. Even the cook Maria was in on it, a DP from the Franco War. Michael wondered how often she had to sit on the old guy's lap to keep that visa of hers current. "Are we cleared for takeoff, or do you want to run this around the block a few more times?"

Evelyn chuckled as he always chuckled about Michael, yes, he did. The first of his stray cats, as Justin called Mike, not maliciously, just a matter-of-fact. It wasn't Michael's intentions, or his devotion, for that matter, sworn protection of Joanna, Evelyn doubted, not in the least. He knew Michael. Knew him well. Appreciated and understood him. He was a Yank, in the first place, an American. Couldn't be expected to think the same thoughts, abide by the same rules as the rest of them. But he was a goodhearted lad underneath it all. He tried to hide it, of course, but he was a decent man, yes, Evelyn did believe that. "Yes, well, believe that's my point," Evelyn assured. "London's ground zero in England's war."

"She'll be with me," Michael insisted, that much true anyway. "I'll stay for the goddamn duration. Fucking enlist, if you want me to."

Evelyn chuckled harder, so hard one would think he was Santa Claus instead of some old cold-hearted dick. "Enlist, my boy? Think more than a few people might have something to say about that," he winked. After all, Michael wasn't a doctor, not really, now was he? Not the kind who took temperatures, delivered babies, or set broken arms. No, Michael was a physicist, an atomic scientist theorizing about the relativity of bombs. "So, we'll see," Evelyn nodded, "yes, we'll see."

"Yeah, we will," Michael promised, and tried to take Joanna out of the house that very same night. Fell and broke his ankle under the blind of the spotlights as the two of them climbed out over the roof, of all things. Spent three months in a plaster cast, another six months lobbying his cause before Evelyn finally gave in. But only because Evelyn doubted if Joanna would take well to finding herself confined in some office once the novelty of London wore off. Evelyn gave it a week, and two months later, much to his surprise, she was still there, beginning to blossom even, develop a little poise and self-confidence. Something she has always been a little shy about, same as Mike, and just like Mike, exactly like him, hid her light under a barrel, covering it up with bravado. Evelyn knew that, he did. Born before the days of electricity, Christmas Day, 1864, by seventy-seven and 1941, Evelyn Lee knew a lot.

London

1941

Except that, Joanna wasn't hunkered down in a bunker below the streets of London. She started out in one, but as the old man predicted, she was quickly bored and threatening suicide if Michael did not show her all the exciting times he had promised her. The constant threat of bombings wasn't exciting enough apparently, or the idea of spending the night in the tube. Both were, of course, but something, anything had to be better than spending every day cooped up in a steel box staring at filing drawers.

"Filing," Michael corrected, looking fairly silly with toilet paper stuck on his chin. "You're supposed to be doing something with them, Red, not just staring at them. You know, like A-B-C?"

"Well, I want to do something else," Joanna absently ran her finger through her name she drew with his shaving cream.

"Such as?" Michael couldn't wait to hear.

"Well, I don't know," Joanna said, "maybe I could be an air raid warden."

"Uh, huh," Michael said. "Maybe I could slit my throat."

"I'm serious, Michael," she said.

So was he, at least about the chance of it happening. "Fine. We'll make it simple. No. That's N.O., nada, nano, incorrectamundo, nein. I don't care if they land here in droves. It's nix on the idea of you walking around with a bullhorn. Give me a break, kid. My head aches enough. Think of something else."

"But I can't," Joanna groaned.

"Yeah, you can. Come on." He threw on his jacket and shirt, in the correct order, he might add. "Give me a ride over to the office and we'll figure something out."

"A what?" Joanna said.

"A ride." He stuffed her behind the steering wheel of his car. "Drive. Make it the station. Westminster. I think it's still there."

"Oh, but I can't," Joanna panicked at the very thought never mind the part about how she could barely reach the pedals.

"Sure you can. Go up here and take a left."

"No, I mean the car," Joanna nodded. "I can't drive the car, Michael. I don't know how."

"Well, imagine that," Michael whistled with a wicked, evil laugh. "I think we might have thought of something already."

"Think of something else," Joanna nodded. "Really, Michael, think of something else."

"Drive." Michael pulled the throttle and cranked the key, and so she drove. Propped up on the cushion of his wadded up raincoat so her feet could reach the pedals, she lurched her way down the street, for the most part managing not to hit anything too important. Michael promising as they finally pulled up to the curb Joanna swore she'd never reach they would try it again as soon as her knees stopped shaking and he stopped praying, and so they did. Again and again, every day, until the time Michael had to return unexpectedly to the States.

London
December 1941
"Well, that's it," Michael snapped the paper open. "That's what the ruckus is all about. They just sunk the *Arizona*, kid. We're in it now."

"What?" Joanna said.

"Not the state, the ship," Michael nodded. "Pearl Harbor. The Japanese bombed Pearl Harbor. We were there, remember?"

"Arizona?" Joanna frowned over his shoulder like she couldn't see the headline from the moon.

"Hawaii," Michael assured. "You don't remember, do you?"

"Oh," Joanna said. "Well, yes. Of course I remember."

"We were there a week," Michael said.

"Michael, I remember," she assured.

"Yeah, I know," he said, "you were nine. Well, now you're nineteen, and it's a date when I get back. Screw the Japs. They can have Fresno ... yeah, Fresno," he moved on to the funny papers. "Ever tell you about the week I spent in Fresno?"

"Back?" Joanna bellowed in his ear.

"New York," Michael promised once his head cleared. "I'd take you with me but it's not only the Pacific where the sailing's kind of rough. It's OK. Couple three weeks will go by just like that. I'll be back before you know I was gone."

"But, Michael!" she whined.

"Wanna go home to Gramps?" he threatened. Which, of course Joanna did not want to go home. Once having gotten her feet wet she rather liked it outside in the real world.

"But what do I do?" Joanna insisted. "Honestly, Michael, what do I do? I'm all alone."

"Easy enough," Michael assured, easy enough for him to say. For her, she was back inside, hunkered down below the streets of London with only the files to keep her company. Worse, because she not only had to stay there during the day, but at night, living and sleeping in a small windowless room with two other people she barely knew. Michael told her to pretend it was college or camp. Joanna could pretend it was the moon and she wouldn't be any less depressed.

"You're in the army now, kid," Michael straightened her up from her slump. "Chin up, shoulders back, chest covered, and legs crossed."

"ATS," Joanna corrected. "I'm in the ATS. I'm not a child, Michael."

Tell him about it. She was a pretty girl. Woman, he hated to admit, and it was starting to give him the creeps. "Look, Red," he reminded, "there's a lot of creeps out there. I should know. I'm the king of them. El duce. Capisce?"

"Michael ..." Joanna sighed.

"The answer is yes," he threatened.

"Fine," Joanna said. "Yes. What about Hawaii?"

"Huh?" Michael said.

"You said you'd take me to Hawaii."

"I said that?"

"Yes," she assured.

"Well, I don't know when I said that," Michael shook his head.

"But you've seen the news the same as I have, Hawaii's been attacked. *Nnnnroooow! Rata-ta-tat, ack-ack-ack!* Probably should give it awhile, at least until the smoke clears."

"Yesterday," Joanna assured. "You said it yesterday when you were reading the paper."

Yesterday. He barely remembered breakfast. "If you say," he shrugged.

"I do," Joanna assured, "and I want to go to Hawaii to see the *Lusitania* or I am not going in there."

"What?" Michael said.

"You promised!" she stomped her foot.

"How the fuck old was that newspaper?" Michael frowned. "The *Lusitania* was thirty years ago, kid, Ireland."

"Michael!" she said.

"OK, fine!" he swore. "We'll go to Hawaii and see the *Lusitania*. Might be a little tough to work out, but not to worry, I'll figure something out."

"Thank you!" she said.

"Don't mention it. Or this," he reminded, "to anyone. Gramps will have my scalp."

"I'll remember," Joanna assured.

"Good," he smiled with a comforting pat of her shoulder. "Couple three weeks, Red, I swear. I'll be back before you know I'm gone."

Joanna knew it the first night. By the end of the week, she was even considering calling Grandfather to come and bail her out. Definitely, something Michael would find extremely disappointing when she had faithfully promised him she would never tell Grandfather how he had left her, for which Grandfather would surely kill him.

Grandfather wouldn't kill him. Joanna knew that. That was just Michael being Michael. But it didn't make it any easier knowing that, particularly since who might kill Michael, of course, was Justin. Her stepbrother Justin. Ol' eagle-eyed, owl-eyed Justin, there, whether he was ever there or not, which he seldom was, thank God.

Joanna had no foundation for her belief or fear of Justin. In fact, she remembered Grandfather scolding Michael for telling her Justin's secret identity as the boogeyman. She was apprehensive around Justin though for some reason, uncomfortable and self-conscious as if she had been caught in some dastardly unforgivable lie.

She decided to find Michael, call him, speak to him, just to hear his voice. In one way, it did not work out because she was quickly (if not mysteriously, if she thought about it, which she did not), hauled into her manager's office for a severe dressing down and harsh reminder to remember her place. Her place? Joanna knew her place quite well because for all her manager's caterwauling in another way it worked out fine because Michael called her. Full of apologies for his unavoidable and unexpected delay he had Joanna paroled from the filing room and she started driving again for a friend of Michael's, an American engineer by the name and rank of Colonel Mahlon McDowell on assignment to London from Michael's States. It wasn't perfect, the Colonel wasn't Michael, but it was all right, particularly since she was no longer inside. Joanna enjoyed driving and she drove the Colonel all over England until nearing the end of February when he needed to go to Cairo and decided to take her with him.

Joanna fell in love before the plane finished landing. This was Michael's Cairo, Michael's Egypt, Michael's pyramids, and Michael's desert Nile. It was en route to Justin's Tobruk where the accident occurred just outside the Siwa Oasis at the border of Libya. It really was her fault. She was driving too fast for the road, and when the tires skidded onto the rough shoulder, she couldn't bring the jeep back under control. The tires exploded and the world flipped upside down.

Siwa Oasis, Egypt
February 1942
It wasn't the road that ruptured the softened rubber tires of the jeep. The explosion happened first, the crack of a bullet from a sniper's rifle. Joanna remembers waking up among a great many rocks, the jeep on its side, the wheels spinning crazily. She could see the Colonel standing not too far away, but the pain racking her head danced in the sunlight, whisking him out of sight, and so she tried to move to find him, but today the rocks moved with her and she saw they all had guns.

She could understand only part of the speech. Vaguely familiar with German, the voice of the man doing most of the talking seemed different somehow, and the Colonel's aide Paul was lying so close to her, he was distracting.

"Paul?" Joanna shook his arm, trying to wake him. "Paul?"

"Hierher!" The man talking reaching down and Paul's head bounced over to her, landing in her lap. She has no clear recollection of what happened after that, remembering only at some point they all left, she and the Colonel and the men. The last she saw of Paul he was sitting in the driver's seat of the jeep. His arms lashed to the steering wheel to keep him propped up straight, his head bobbing in the wind like some bizarre pedestrian crossing as it hung suspended from the antenna wire, his blue eyes watching her as she walked toward a truck and climbed inside.

Chapter Sixteen

Cairo
March 9, 1942

There was nothing palatial or even neat about the office of England's Squadron Leader Justin Charles. Housed in an oversized government building built sixty-odd years ago in the flavor of Islam, the room was large and overcrowded with weary steel boxes and card board files. In compliment to the plaster walls papered with maps, a discolored series of Venetian blinds hung on the windows facing the street, bright sunlight and heat filling the room with a soiled yellow glow.

The dirt, blinds, and decorative stains of age and seeping lime were there in December when Justin arrived from South Africa by way of Tobruk. The boxes were an accumulation of new and ones he had brought with him, dropping them down in a heap, and dropping himself at a desk to begin to work. He was working now, contrary apparently to a few of his staff.

"Nel!" Justin flung the report he was reading aside, pushed away from his desk and stalked across the floor. "Find that stupid Mick and tell him to get in here now!" he yanked the door open with a bellow at his startled secretary, a moment ago polishing her nails without a care in the world.

"Aye, sir!" she jumped up, ran her stocking, came close to breaking her neck on the regulation stilts she was wearing, and gave up attempting to screw the cap back on her cuticle varnish, or whatever the devil it was she had in her hand.

Justin peered at her, his hard black eyes piercing and round like a cruel fierce owl's in his sun-blackened face—or a wolf, actually. He looked more like a wolf. A skull and face straight from Hell with large sunken eye-sockets and skin stretched tightly over his pronounced features, the apples of his cheeks two hard lumps, shining and ruddy beneath his blackened tan.

A bearded wolf, actually. She eyed the heavy black bush of oily curls blanketing his jaw and chin in striking contrast to his massive dome head glistening with sweat and fairly bald. The few hairs left, black as the beard, though straighter except for the curl at their ends, not a hint of grey in their shining soiled strands. She grimaced. He wasn't old despite his leathery appearance. The hairs that had fallen out had just given up early, burnt, more than likely, to a crisp, given the ebony color of him.

Definitely, a wolf, she decided. Foul and savage, his breath reeking as he loomed over her, the only thing missing was the chest hair. She flushed, embarrassed to even be thinking about such things, but she was if only because she was staring dead at it. Not some burly bush of unkempt curls as one might rightfully expect him to have given the hefty beard and hint of a highland burr behind his slow gentleman's speech. But, no, more like his head, his chest was also nearly bald. Just a thin strip of hair, like a black line slicing straight down the middle, parting him in half. Her flushed deepened. He looked like a wolf, all right, thin and starving as one with his concave abdomen and boned breast ribbed with sinewy muscle. Two tiny teats, round, hard, cold, and black as his eyes, another pair of eyes staring at her. Daresay if she stared back at them, or him, long enough she'd see the veritable outline of his heart, thin as he was. She did not stare, not any longer than she could help it. In all, it was really much more than she needed to know, and certainly far more obvious than it ought to be, but only because he didn't button his shirt. He never buttoned his shirt. Any more than he wore too much of anything when it came to clothes other than some unsightly pair of groin-high shorts that for the sake of common decency, and her certain relief, while they might not be any cleaner than his unclean shirt, their buttons, quite unlike his shirt, were at least closed.

Oh, she disliked this man, really she did, immensely, finding him crude, coarse, and outlandish, to say the least. Embarrassed for him even if he seemed to be quite comfortable and detached, most of all from any reaction he might cause appearing near-naked in public. Never in her life had she found herself confronted with the option of either ogling a man's groin, or desperately trying to ignore it. Both virtually near impossible not to do considering his height, for that matter the length of his long naked legs, and the fact she was sitting down, or had been moments before his assault. The rumpled, threadbare crotch of his shorts appearing quite literally eye level in front of her shouting at her to get off her duff, or something to that effect. In all, sufficient to say, the reason why she got up off her duff, immediately jumped up, and if it wasn't for his astounding height and despite the fact, she did wear heels, rather high ones even though she wasn't a short woman, but average in height, damn near slammed her head off his chin. Fortunately, at six–foot five and a half inches tall before the thick soles of his over-sized boots, his chin remained quite safely out of reach and harm's way.

Oh, she loathed this man, really she did, despised him, utterly, most of the time, anyway. For some reason some of the time, he seemed to want to fascinate her. Not intentionally on his part, of course, but solely and inexplicably on hers despite the fact he was oblivious to her. Quite oblivious. Quite.

"Yes, well, who the devil are you?" Justin demanded, unable to see for himself under all her paint and hair dye, and actually expecting to find Joe sitting there. A different Joe than his deceased friend Joseph Lee, but a fellow named Joe just the same. One who practically lived there, didn't he?

At least recently. Justin eyed the blonde who damned near killed herself and him while she was at it, springing up in front of him like some grinning Jack-in-the-box. A blousy piece of common goods more so even than the last one who had sat there on her starched behind before he ordered her tossed out. He was surprised possibly though, just a touch, rare as an occasion as that might be, but only by the fact there seemed to be no end in sight to them. In three months there had to be at least nine of them he had ordered on their way and out of his. Needing some personal assistant like he needed … well, buttons on his shirt. This was the RAF, after all, SIS, for that matter MI6, the grandfather, godfather, of them all.

"Cain, sir," she nodded hastily with her bobbing blonde head.

"Assistant Section Officer Laura Cain. Your ... well, secretary," she acknowledged as she had upon occasion. Not that it meant anything to him, which it obviously did not if after nearly three months he was still asking her who she was. And, no, she wouldn't say Joe *lived* there. She lived there, or rather sat there at her desk.

"Yes, well," Justin tore her bottle of glue out of her hand for some reason. She really had no idea why he did that, proceeding to fling it in the dustbin, "explains the typing."

"Yes, well ..." Actually, Laura could explain her rather limited typing skills as she studied her dustbin. It was simply that she hated typing. She had no interest in typing, any more than she had any interest in being a nurse. Unfortunately, those were the two positions usually available to her as a female officer of the RAF being as the male officers had yet to allow their female constituents to fly their stupid airplanes, which was her interest.

This, of course, she did not say. Any more than she commented on his personal hygiene, or lack thereof, or inquired into when he last had a square meal. He really was so thin. So rugged and weather-beaten thin. She could count every rib, map the outline of his beating heart ... which, of course, she didn't. She straightened up, briskly. He was her Commanding Officer, after all, and beyond that, he was a man. An ardent, if not career, she suspected, daresay goose-stepping member of his boys-only club who did things like tear bottles of glue from their secretary's unsuspecting hands for reasons known only to them.

"Yes, well, go on," Justin waved, now that the amenities were out of the way.

"Yes, well ..." Laura also did not ask him how he would like her to "go on" in what direction, through him, over her desk, or over her typewriter? No, she just stood there with glue on her hands, a run in her stocking and scrape on her knee where she had slammed it into the desk, saying things like, "Yes, well," and having no idea where to go on from there.

"Yes, well, you know who he is, don't you?" Justin insisted, confident she must have a brain somewhere under that bleached cloud surrounding her head. If not a list in the mess she called a desk, explaining who was who, and who was not.

"Oh, yes." Yes, Laura knew who "Nel" was. Rather the same as she knew her desk was spotless. But then that probably had something to do with her spending much more time in the canteen than at her assigned post, but only because she wasn't allowed to sit, stay, or do any work whatsoever, certainly not there. To the contrary, he was correct in his belief he had relieved her of her duties and post at least a dozen times in the last two and a half months, for whatever reason. Rather like the glue, she suspected.

As for Sergeant Reynolds, or Nel, as the group called him. A man, who, yes, apart from being truly gargantuan in height and size, it was rather hard not to know who Sergeant Reynolds was. He was a Mick, the same as she was. Only to where Sergeant Reynolds was Protestant and ardently loyal to the Crown, she was Catholic and reasonably loyal to the Crown. Even though at the moment she was seriously contemplating tendering her resignation and joining the IRA as an assassin. Interestingly enough, and by sheer coincidence, the chosen career of two or more of her six brothers.

"Yes, well, he's around here somewhere." Justin withdrew his head back into his shell and slammed his office door shut, leaving her free to breathe a sigh of relief.

It was more annoyance than relief. "Oh, for goodness sake," Laura glared down on her torn stocking. Such luxuries were frightfully difficult to come by and now utterly destroyed, the ladder quickly spreading down her leg to her ankle as she stepped carefully, testing the stability of her shoe. "What a horrible man." Really, what a thoroughly despicable and vulgar man, she had to say, thinking of another vulgar man she had only just recently met. A doctor. An American doctor who claimed, no less, to be a friend of this one, Squadron Leader Justin Charles. Something Laura no longer doubted, if she had ever doubted it, but believed ardently they were best friends. Mates, as her kind would say, chums.

"Sergeant!" Laura did breathe a little in relief a few moments later, but only because she had forgotten completely about Sergeant Nel until connecting with him not too far down the hall. It was at the water cooler where she pranced to wet the corner of her handkerchief and wipe the smear of blood staining her knee as best she could. She looked up and there he was, his massive presence and frame filling the hall.

"Not to worry, little lady," Nellie winked his wink, smiled his smile, sauntering on down the hall and inside Charlie's office to see what all the fuss was about.

"Well, of course, I'm not worried," Laura assured, hardly worried, or even aware of what there might be to be worried about, other than the war. But even there she was extremely limited, if not outright restricted from worrying too much about it, and certainly barred, as mentioned, in doing anything personally about it.

Shortly after Sergeant Nellie Reynolds came and left, *Joe*, or rather, Private Joe DeSapio also happened by to announce he was "Just going in to see the Maj," with an apologetic look down on her knee as she sat there practicing her typing on a blank piece of paper set rather crooked in the carriage of her machine.

"Here, let me get that for you," Joe offered, handy with all of that kind of stuff.

"Squadron Leader," Laura smiled while Joe straightened her paper. For that matter, straightened up her desk to make sure she had enough room should some actual work ever be forthcoming, and finishing with a short instruction course on how to work the levers so the paper wouldn't get stuck the next time. Something Laura already knew. But she liked Joe, she did. She liked most of them. Joe, in particular, Bobby, the older, heavyset man, definitely. Even the disconcerting Sergeant Nellie who frequently came around, most recently with a young lieutenant whose name she did not know, and did not trouble her, as in not cause her any sort of personal alarm.

Joe was a bit odd, but then, quite honestly, they were all odd. Eccentric, Laura preferred to consider the lot of them somewhat more kindly, and certainly none of them more odd or eccentric, or outright bizarre than their Squadron Leader Justin Charles, who was not only vulgar, but a snob. Oh, yes, she knew that as well as she knew her own name, disdainful, disapproving, and disagreeable. The paper jammed. "Quite," Laura said harshly, aloud.

"Huh?" Joe said.

"Nothing," Laura assured. "Nothing at all." Back to Joe who was a Yank quite unlike the rest of the small group who passed through the corridor doors to visit Squadron Leader Charles on a frequent daily basis, but that did not matter. The significance of Joe being a Yank was limited perhaps to explaining why he said things 0586526158like "Maj" or "Major" rather than "Squad" or "Squad Le" in a shortened form of "Squadron Leader", both of which would be utterly absurd. It was a different language, American English. Not simply a dialect, but a different language entirely, and here to think how she had always presumed being English it was therefore the same one.

"Yeah, well, I think we've got it now," Joe assured as he popped the typewriter carriage back in.

"Yes," Laura agreed while he moved on to confirm the working status of the rest of her equipment to ensure she hadn't accidentally done something like dismantle her telephone in her confused female state. He was saying something along those lines now. Not about English, but about the ease or simplicity of "Maj" or "Major" versus "Squadron Leader", citing a few German ranks in example of what he meant, as well as his own name. A grin flashing through his handsome face, that was quite handsome, strikingly so with strong lines and chiseled cheekbones, a thick blue-black crop of wavy hair complementing his rugged and muscular American physique. At twenty-six, Joe was the same age she was, though oddly, as odd as anything else when it came to gender or sex, twenty-six somehow seemed so much younger on a man than it did on a woman. At twenty-six, Laura could be, or should be what, Joe's mother? To where at twenty-six Joe could be who, her younger brother? Tall, zestful, and robust, Joe was really extremely handsome in a primal, near animal sort of way, regrettably not at all her type.

"Rank," Laura pleasantly corrected Joe's use of the word "term". "It really is a rank, not a term."

"Yeah, I know it's a rank," Joe said. "That's what I'm saying ...

"I mean ..." he said, drawing it out long and thinking about it. "OK, like Sarge," he nodded, meaning Nellie. Nellie was Sarge, Bobby just Bobby, and that other freak they hired, just some freak. "I could see myself out in the field, yelling 'Yo, *Unterfeldwebel!*'" he let out a yell. "Hey, yo, *Unterfeldwebel!*" he hollered with a wave. "I mean, if I was German," Joe explained. "And instead of, you know, Sarge."

"No, I understand," Laura nodded.

"Yeah," Joe said, certain she did. "I'd end up with half my head blown off before I even got his rank out ...

"Or, um ..." Joe said backtracking fast from the gruesome details. Not sure why he felt like he had to throw them in there other than to scare her half to death, which he wasn't trying to do. "My name, OK?" he settled on. "Like my name," he nodded. "It's Joe, or it's Guiseppe—which is what it really is," he assured with a laugh. "Honest. Swear to God. We're talking first generation American. I'm first generation American. I remember the boat," he nodded, remembering it. "I do. I remember the boat ...

"So, um ..." he wrapped it up, because after all he had to get in there before the Maj came out here and grabbed him ... Joe didn't know, by the belt or something. His hair maybe since he didn't wear a shirt buttoned or unbuttoned. Nah, he didn't bother. In the first place, it was hot. Real hot. Like 106 degrees or something in there and that was with the fans, the hair on his chest heavy and hot enough to wear without adding another layer on top of it. In the second place? He didn't bother, nah, didn't feel like it.

"Which is easier?" he asked, talking about his name. "Joe or Guiseppe? You tell me."

"Joe," Laura nodded.

"It sure is." Joe laughed honestly, rising to give her back her seat with a point down on her wounded knee. "I can get you whatever you need, seriously, however many you want."

"How much?" Laura hesitated, slightly surprised by the offer, though not to suggest she wasn't grateful, or short on funds, for that matter that she found his naked sweating chest disconcerting or particularly attractive, which she did not, and it was not, either. To the contrary, for such a noticeably attractive young man, Joe's chest was possibly the least attractive, most noticeable aspect about him. The curly black hair wet, almost slick, and bronzed skin decorated with some of the most amazing and unattractive tattoos of snakes and hearts carved neatly with a razor blade or knife and painted India blue.

"Um ... you mean like dollars?" Joe verified, aware of the subtle differences in their language.

"Or pounds," Laura nodded. "Yes, I suppose I mean that."

"Whatever." Joe considered a fair asking price, though not seriously. "I don't know," he grinned. "Free sound OK?"

Free. "How much?" Laura repeated a little more firmly than the first time. Not to suggest she didn't believe him, or to clarify what he meant exactly by free, which she highly doubted if he meant anything in particular at all, other than what he said, but just to ask.

There was a pause before he answered, or at least a moment of silence before his grin spread again followed by another genuine laugh. "Nah, that ain't my style," he assured, catching her drift, which, of course, he would catch it. I mean, she was a dame, and he was a guy, and he could mean a lot, we're talking *a lot* by free.

Still, he found it a little disappointing she didn't know it wasn't his style. Not that she knew him all that much, but she knew him well enough to know while he might not be a rocket scientist like some of the guys around there, he wasn't stupid, nah, far from it. The same as it wasn't like she was out of his league or something, because she wasn't, but she was out of his reach, definitely. He didn't stand a chance. Everybody knew that—him and Bobby at least. The Sarge probably didn't, but the Sarge was a different kind of guy, and who the hell knew or cared what the rest of the freaks had to say. He and Bobby knew that was the point. The same as he knew, this lady, if she had eyes for anyone, never mind who might have eyes for her, which was plenty, she had eyes for one guy only, and that was the Maj. Written all over her face, like they say. This lady was in love, we're talking *in love* with the Maj. To the point she was walking into walls, and falling over chairs, the proof right there in her wrecked stockings with the run down to her ankle and creeping up toward her thigh.

Oh, yeah. Joe eyed those legs that were sturdy and healthy like the rest of her. She definitely had it for the Maj. With the high heeled shoes and short skirt that was really short and equally tight, molding her rear like the padded brassiere molded her chest into a high proud shelf crowned by her cocky little hat atop her perfectly coiffed blonde hair. All proof the lady did not have a life beyond this place, but spent her nights working on ways to get the Maj to notice her, and *that* not only made the Maj particularly thoughtless and unkind since he didn't notice anything, it also made him pretty damn blind.

Or a fag, Joe shrugged. Yeah, maybe he was a fag. It didn't matter to Joe if the Major was because he liked the guy, would, still, and did like the guy the same as the rest of them did, a lot.

"What I will tell you is this," he pointed with his grin while Laura stood there paralyzed, almost too afraid to move. Though Joe would bet she was a lot less frightened of him making some kind of pass at her, than she was scared to death of the Maj unexpectedly walking out and thinking what? Exactly that. Oh, yeah, exactly that. "As much as you need them," which she did need them, what was she going to wear, socks in her high-heeled shoes? "With legs like that, you deserve them."

"I'll take that as a compliment," Laura nodded.

"Good," Joe approved.

"And ... I don't know," Laura said, "two? Two pair?"

"Two?" Joe's face screwed up into a frown. Can you imagine prostituting yourself for two pairs of silk stockings? He didn't think so.

"I don't know, six?" Laura said, really wanting to get back to her desk, even if she only sat at it.

"Make it an even dozen." Joe left it and her there, the door closing on the Major's mumble and his explanation, "Yeah, I'm here, just making sure everything's off ..."

"Oh, for goodness' sake," Laura sat down at her desk. A short time passing before she realized exactly what Joe had meant by everything being off, but only because it crossed her mind as she sat at her typewriter, the carriage and paper immediately binding, almost as if deliberately. She stared at it, and the more she stared ...

"*Everything's off* ..." Joe's words seemed to echo as Laura's glance strayed to the intercom not quite daring to touch it to find out if it was working, more out of fear of finding out it wasn't ...

"Oh, for goodness sake," Laura said annoyed, flipping the intercom on, boldly snatching up the telephone. It was disconnected. No response when she clicked it, just dead.

"Or off," she repeated what Joe had said. "*Just making sure everything's off.*' Well now." Laura sat at her desk as she had often sat there over the last near three months, wondering what to do. Since discharging her hadn't worked, her dear and good friend Colonel Jim Peterson having taken care of that, there was nothing else for them to do except break everything around her, Joe, her friend, who was apparently not her friend at all, in on the game as well.

Laura did not mention it though when Joe came out after not being in there very long and left with a reassuring wave he would not forget, meant what he said about the twelve pairs of silk stockings.

"Oh, yes," Laura smiled. Meaning what she said, or thought, about grown men resorting to such childish pranks as sabotaging her typewriter and telephone simply because they did not want her there, and had to accept her being there if only because those higher up than them, put her there.

The American doctor from downstairs came by next, recognizing her as she recognized him, he with a scowl on his face, she as thoroughly disinterested as she had been before. Bobby was with him but only as far as the door, a brief pleasant nod for her as he left, "How's it going, luv?"

"Oh, fine," Laura replied, "just fine." Shortly thereafter, however it wasn't fine at all, far from it. But she was getting ahead of herself, far too far ahead of herself. Before the arrival of the doctor and the mayhem that quickly followed, there had been Joe who went in and out, and before him, Sergeant Nellie Reynolds.

Chapter Seventeen

"What the devil is this?" Justin turned around from his wall of maps with a wave of Nellie's latest field report.

"What it says," Nellie replied easily, confident Joe had accurately written down what he told him.

"It says the damn depot has disappeared," Justin assured. "We've spent a month to come away empty handed."

"Does it now?" Nellie chuckled, not remembering putting it exactly that way, but if Joe said that's what he said, it must be.

"Is it there?" Justin cut to the bottom line.

"No," Nellie shook his head, "it ain't. It was, but it isn't, and, so, disappeared? Aye." he guessed that was true since it was gone, like the other one before it.

It wasn't there to begin with. No more than the one reported last month had been there. Not there now and not there before. One month. An entire month wasted. Justin tossed the report on his desk and lit his pipe, the stench quickly adding to the flavor of the room.

Nellie waited, continuing with his easy smile, his hands folded on his tight stomach, unperturbed. Charlie's tantrums were always brief, his blood rising only when he thought he was wrong, and at thirty-five, Justin was seldom wrong. Seasoned and hardened, he was exactly what he looked like. Tough, rough, menacing, cold and calculating, power supported by education, background, and twenty years training and experience in England's elite SIS largely spent in the field whether it was a jungle, Belfast, or the concrete suburbs of Johannesburg, South Africa. He had his fair share of critics and an equal number of fans. Neither meant anything to him. With few failures and an impressive list of successes, Justin enjoyed what did mean something to him. Respect for him and his family name. He was a man who followed through, and most importantly, came through. Criticisms usually only having to do with his methods, which could be brutal, appear brutal and unnecessary to the ignorant, innocent, or ill informed. The lot of them apparently forgetting that by the veritable nature of his profession he was always involved in some conflict or another, this latest one, otherwise known as a world war. His specialty was coups. *"French for terrorism,"* he once said. Accurate in that he was a licensed killer, terrorizing groups, countries, and men, his passions poker and getting the job done, a league of experts on his private roll call to help him do that.

Justin ogled Nellie his Red Ace for thirteen of those twenty years. He relied on Nellie to do more than guard the gates of Hell and keep the occasional dissident in place. Fearsome and fearless, the giant Irishman was crafty, intuitive, and lethal as he looked. Up for any job, Justin passed his way. Except this one, apparently, when it counted most. Justin did not buy it. By the smug look on Nellie's granite face, Nel didn't buy it either. Something else was wrong, and it had nothing to do with Nellie. Something more than a reliable report of two depots on the far side of Libya's map, both now as reliably reported to have disappeared. Who then? What? Justin's gut told him he was not going to like the answer even if he did not know it yet. He would. He had the means, the power, and the men.

A few men anyway. Justin straightened up out of his temper to make a note. He had a handful of men who could spend a little more time figuring out what was wrong, since ferreting out depots wasn't the only thing on the agenda. No, that would be the war. Currently, a desperate situation inflamed by the Pacific and the increasing strain it was putting on the British forces already overburdened. If that wasn't enough, the sudden entry of the Yanks into the mix proved sufficient in coaxing the enigmatic Charles out from protecting England's interests in the south, for the north in December '41. British interests in Cairo deciding Justin could do his directing better from behind a desk in an office instead of a tent, handing him a command that included a division of the army's Long Range Desert Troops. They must have gotten him confused with some other fellow. Justin might be a director, but he was no desk officer. King Charles to his peers, he was *sir* to his men whether they

called him *Maj, Boss, or Bwana,* or whatever they called him, code
name *Charlie* to the current list of bastards trying to shut him down.
No one ever had, and neither would Rommel and his crew.

Immunity assured, with authorization to use his own methods,
Justin packed his boxes, taking Nellie and the equally irreplaceable
Bobby Roberts with him to Egypt. En route, he stopped by Tobruk,
Libya, the last of England's Saharan strongholds, to pick up Peter
O'Brannigan alighting from his airplane with an IRA twinkle in his
eye and Eire's Coat of Arms on his beret. His consecutive life
sentences commuted once again to life with Justin Charles.

North Africa

December 1941

"Oh, now, have faith, lad, have faith," Pete cajoled Justin's somber
expression, pressing a bottle of his special rum into Justin's hand as
a personal and holiday greeting. "If I ain't going to give my Emerald
Isle to you, I sure as hell ain't going to give it to no Jerry. We'll work
it out, lad, we will. Win, is what I'm saying. You have Peter's word
and support on that." And just to prove it, Pete got the car door for
him. "Where to?"

Cairo. Midnight, Christmas Eve, 1941. The needed African
foothold a coup, brazen in its simplicity of surrounding the palace
with tanks and telling the Fascist Prime Minister to get out, the flag
of Britannia quickly straightened neat and tidy overhead.

"Interested?" Justin asked. "Now that the job's been done?"

"Oh, the job isn't done, lad," Pete disputed. "The job, you might
say, has just begun."

"Get in." Justin took the driver's side for himself, still a maniac
behind the wheel, still trying to prove how his father's death could
not have happened the way everyone but him knew it had, and that
was by accident. But Pete was Irish, a firm believer in the little people
who he counted on to get him to Cairo alive. Bobby was old and
accustomed to Justin, and knew they'd make it, and as far as Nel?

Pete looked over the vision of all that was wrong and yet to be
right in the United Kingdom of English rule with that orange hair of
Nel's the crown and color of his wretched protestant soul. Larger
than life, the fellow was, physically and by deeds in a world wanting

and needing its heroes. He was no hero, though, that ol' Nellie fellow of Justin's. He was some freak of nature, morally wanting and reprehensible and damn ugly at almost seven-feet and three-hundred pounds. Even his head was two times the size of Pete's, with his eyes small and crystalline green and too close together, the skull sloped, and brain compressed, pressed tightly into some abnormal shape crushed down into the bridge of his nose.

"You still alive, lad?" Pete gave Nellie a different smile than the one he had given Justin. "Thought for sure one of those natives would have gone and eaten you by now." His tongue touched his lip like he might want to, but Nellie was too stupid to think of something clever to say back. Nellie was too stupid to do most anything except what Justin told him to do, and that was usually kill, and who couldn't do that? Pete had more notches on his belt than Nellie could ever hope to have. Peter O'Brannigan was a mass murderer, that's what they told him, tried, found, and convicted him of being criminally insane, had to be close to twenty years ago. All sorts of innocent men, women, and children, Pete, and the likes of him, had maimed and slaughtered over some six-hundred years of misbehavior otherwise known as the Irish-English dispute. England's infamous Broadmoor prison his home in between times hanging with Justin.

Maybe so. Pete would be the first one to admit that, and move right on to doing it again however much trouble he found himself in. Incorrigible, that's what he was. A career insurgent, ardent anarchist, worst of the criminal element, making his bed and somehow managing to live long enough to lie in it.

"Aye, and you, too," Pete gave up trying to get a rise out of Nellie to riddle Bobby. "Feed a damn village with the belly you have on you." He turned around to behave himself after that, sticking to business, which was what he was there for, not to make enemies or go away friends. It was war, after all, not some popularity, or beauty contest. Pete's eye flitted over Justin. Looked the same, he did, Henry's little boy Justinian with his saturnine features. Been a few years since they'd seen each other, but Justin looked the same, sun-burnt to a crisp with an expression that could either be exhaustion or surprise with those big, penetrating black eyes overwhelming his face. Be a doll if he somehow managed to be cute, too. He wasn't, and so he was more or less stuck with being a prick. Mean and tough as Pete for all his fine upbringing, not fooling anybody with his gentleman's drawl, least of all Pete. "Must be something if they called you up," he agreed, hunting for specific information.

"War," Justin assured.

"Oh, right," Pete scoffed. "Got yourself on some one's list, sounds like it to me if they stuck you out here. Don't no one give a damn what happens here, rightfully so." He looked around. Bleak, it was. Bleak and empty, and hotter than hell, he seemed to recall. "Got to head home if you're looking for a war, mate. Less action here than your local."

"Volunteered, actually," Justin said.

"Well, that I believe," Pete agreed. "You're a bastard, aren't you? Not going to find anyone out here but bastards." he looked around again. "Couldn't have picked a worse damn place on the earth to make a stand, could they now? Must know something we don't."

"Oil," Justin said.

"Suez, you mean," Pete nodded. "Aye. Heard the rumor. Take the Suez, you can forget about those oil fields, is right."

"Yes, well, it's no rumor," Justin grunted. "Take the Suez, you can forget about most things. It's the supply route."

"Still ours?" Pete checked.

"For now," Justin agreed.

Pete nodded. "Heard another rumor you might find interesting. Our girl Jewels is back inside. Two years solid for violating her probation, and not but a call away from you getting her out."

"Oh?" Justin said. "What do I need her for?"

Pete looked at him, a lot said in the look, but that was all right because Justin just looked back at Pete, a lot said in his look as well.

"She's a pilot, lad." Pete kept the conversation clean and polite, smiling his discolored smile of a life of poverty and crime, the wall of his winking right eye slightly weakened by one too many fights, but handsome just the same in his manly Irish way. He looked like he lived, saucy and sassy, and worldly-wise, tall, but not too tall, strong, but lanky, his eyes blue and hair a true red. A man. That's what Pete looked like, a man. His features kind of craggy with a few lines, some deeper than others especially around the eyes. "Don't have too many of those lollygagging around with nothing to do, and so she might come in handy, experienced as she is."

"Might at that," Justin considered, and put a call into Kenya as soon as they pulled in to set up shop in the shadows of the great pyramids and Sphinx, deep in the belly of what had to be one of the filthiest cities in the world. Big, and loud, and unimaginably overcrowded, dangerous even during the day. Her alleys and causeways permeated with the smells of intrigue, sex, and double-dealings flourishing beneath her celebrated Egyptian glory commingled with the modern. Even had a Metro movie theater, faded posters of Gable and Crawford immortalized in soiled peeling layers of celluloid skin.

"Yes, well, think that would be more the citadel," Justin commented on Pete's colorful take on the neighborhood.

"Casbah," Pete corrected. A strange world it was. Evil. Bad Mojo like some of those sub-Saharan tribes. Roof dwellers scurrying like monkeys overhead. Come out of there alive, come out of anywhere. "Remember that?" he sighed fondly. "Had ourselves a time there, didn't we?"

"Yes, well, a Casbah is a citadel." Justin had the last word as he was rightfully entitled and accustomed to, and got the office door for himself, only to stop dead still in disbelief, possibly for the first time in his life.

Cairo
December 1941
"Yes, well, who the devil are you?" Justin insisted, quick to notice the dyed stacked blonde racing him to his throne, but only because of his observational skills and training.

"Your secretary, sir," she smiled prettily, her face as Irish as Pete's under all her modern plucking and cosmetics, "Assistant Section Officer Laura Cain."

Oh, well, now, Pete noted to himself how unless his eyes and memory deceived him, to be more honest and accurate it would have to be Assistant Section Office Laura *McShane* Cain whether or not she considered scrubbing her face morally clean. Of the McShane Cains, most notably Ian, eldest of a rough band of illegitimate half-breeds born of Ireland's soulful Mary Margaret, and England's sweet-talking Johnny Cain with the holes in his pockets and big ideas. Ian, who shunned him and his father's name, slated to go down in municipal history as the fellow who killed Justin's distinguished daddy and got away with it. No more evidence to hang Ian McShane or any of his brothers than what already existed in the chronicles of the English-Irish dispute, no matter how hard Justin pushed the issue, which he didn't after the first round or two. Out of respect, responsibility, and duty to the Crown, and a few other reasons, not exactly publicly known such as there being as much evidence to suggest the assassination of Sir Henry Charles, MP, had been an insider job by a group of disgruntled Fascists annoyed at the prospect of being exposed.

Still, it was an interesting quirk of fate, born of fate or some malevolent sprite that found the sister of the man accused of killing the father of another together in the same room. A reasonable explanation sure to be forthcoming, Pete settled for the sprite that drew McShane's baby sister all grown up and not half bad, to that very room, and the tumultuous childhood that pinned the prideful RAF emblem on the spit-and-polish jacket of the fine upstanding young lass. The pin as bright and shining as she was, brand spanking new.

A bit of a surprise, the uniform, yes, it was. To Hell with Justin, Pete couldn't have been more surprised to see Cain's sister dressed in England's finery than he was to see her. Justin, on the other hand, had apparently stopped his investigation with Ian and three of his score of brothers old enough to be taken seriously at the time, never moving on to meet the rest of the family, or he was just better at deadpan than Pete would have guessed.

It was the latter, Pete decided. Justin didn't have the faintest idea who this bird was any more than she had any idea about him. No one was that good at keeping their reserve not even a Brit, and definitely not a Mick, half though she might be on her mother's side.

"Yes, well ..." Justin mumbled something unpleasant for such a well-brought up gent, while the lass busied herself apologizing for the sorry state of the office a few of the boys had likewise seen to overthrowing on their way to taking the palace back.

"I'm sorry?" Laura requested, not quite catching what it was the Squadron Leader said, and rightfully, as noted, for the sake of her Catholic upbringing, she should not have.

"Out, luv," Bobby translated for her, catching her up gently by the arm to show her the door.

"Out?" Laura repeated, still not quite sure what was meant.

"Out," Bobby clarified, handing her, her shoulder bag along with her cards, passing her off to be escorted down the hall and out of the war.

"Right ..." Pete eyed the attractive bint leaving in a confused fluster, but he refrained from saying anything about her heritage or family tree. It would eventually come to light without any help from him. He did know and believe that. Not much else to look at though now that she was gone, his attention returned to the small group that counting him currently totaled four, and would soon become five with the promised release and arrival of the earthy and lovely Julia Jones.

Right now though, they were only four and close to two hundred years' experience among them. With Justin the youngest, though one would never know it by his balding double-dome, Pete was next at forty-five, grey starting to work its way through his shaved strawberry curls. After that came Nellie at just over fifty, and Bobby Roberts, Justin's lifelong mentor and guru, no less than sixty-five, the brains Nellie didn't have, slow moving and morbidly obese, his breath shallow and frequent in the dry desert heat that would kill him likely. Make him miserable if it didn't. Succeed, where in sixty-five years all else and all others had failed, but Bobby insisted on being a part, postponing his coming and due retirement to help the lad out one last time. Stupid, in Pete's opinion, who knew demolition as well as the son of a Welsh miner, the world Bobby had been born into. Pete knew no fear, the same as Nellie, the African continent like the back of his hand. Pete knew a lot, except his place, a long-standing point of contention between him and Justin who otherwise got along fairly well despite their marked political differences.

Pete's place this go-round would be the same as every other, in the field. Number Two to Justin's Nellie, and Number Three to his Bobby Roberts.

Nellie would also spend half his time or so in the field. Bobby, no. Bobby's place was at Justin's side when Justin needed him, down in the dungeon when Justin did not, playing with his guns. Pete did not care either way what either of them did. He was his own man, had his own mind, excusing himself when Justin handed out the commissions of sergeant to Bobby and Nellie to find the whisky, since he also knew where it was.

The same as he knew who the drinker was in the crowd, and the one not above indulging in a little India hemp every now and then. It brought a personal sense of satisfaction to Pete to be so close to who should be his enemy. To be privy to the man and what some might consider his dark side, potentially damaging to Justin's public and personal reputation.

Justin and Pete were neither enemies nor friends, in the strict sense of the words. What they were, should Justin ever think about it long enough to label it or them, which he did not, was probably closest to associates. Something Justin was with most people, certainly his men, except for Bobby. Bobby Roberts was probably closest to being a friend of Justin's, and Bobby Roberts, never mind Justin, could tell Pete a thing or two about Justin regardless of what Pete might believe or think he understood or knew. Including Pete must be thinking of some other fellow insofar as Justin being the sort to wonder or worry about what society's reaction might be to the revelation of his occasional indulgences. Bobby did not think so. To the devil with Pete, Justin was a man, and men do what men do. Pete's gassy jabber and his declining to play along by not accepting an appointment of rank put Bobby on the alert. An early reminder of Pete's potential for misbehavior.

Bobby was right, of course, about Pete's potential, but he was also wrong where it counted most. While it might seem odd to some, sending a lifer, confirmed and committed IRA to boot, into the field, Justin was not about to worry about it, above all, second guess himself. Pete was not going to stage a jailbreak, escape for parts or plains unknown. The ties that bound Pete and Justin, and hence the earth, were neatly encapsulated in Pete's opening words, *"If I ain't going to give my Emerald Isle to you, I sure as hell ain't going to give it to no Jerry."* Ditto when it came to England who, might one day eventually lose Ireland to Ireland, but Justin would be damned if he'd lose it or any part of the British Isles to Germany. That was not only a fact it was a simple matter of world politics and history. Pro-German sentiment, vogue among England's young, bored, or elite in the 20's and 30's, with the war, vanished with any remnants driven deep underground.

In neutral Ireland, however, it not only thrived, but also openly succeeded in driving an irremediable wedge between the Irish rebels already divided since before the 20's. Pete was Old IRA, pro-treaty, and fiercely anti-Blueshirts, positions that within the extraordinarily muddied Irish situation, found Pete and Justin at each other's side. Squared off against mutual opponents, they were equals in Pete's mind, partners, if they never quite achieved the distinction of friends. So, no, Pete wasn't going anywhere, least of all back to jail. Might indulge in a little sass every now and then, succumb to the irresistible temptation to occasionally stick it to them, seduced by the desire and intent of being and remaining his own man, but he was not about to go back to jail until he had to.

"Wouldn't be a war without you," Pete raised his glass rather than bow his head, chance offending the patron saints of the *Dáil Éireann* by accepting Justin's RAF pin.

"Yes, well," Justin grunted, so it wouldn't be. Something goes balls-up though, even once, and Pete was out, or rather back in. Justin did not care why. He had fifty pounds that said none of them, himself included, was going to get out of this go-round alive. Fifty pounds more salary a month for each month they did. Didn't matter who they were, what their rank was whether real or otherwise.

Neither Nellie nor Bobby was commissioned in any branch of service, or convicts, though Nellie, in a civilized world, was certainly a candidate for Broadmoor. Pete was wrong about the assignment of rank being window dressing in an attempt to fit in with the regular crowd that ruled Cairo. The point and purpose was to install an order of hierarchy for the field personnel soon to follow. If there was an unusual choice or action in Justin's future, it would probably be the addition of a Yank. Giuseppe "Joe" DeSapio. A truck mechanic and avid short-wave radio hobbyist who was a convict, or criminal, of a particularly elite status. A cop-killer from the streets of Brooklyn, at large, and on the run, and who apparently thought he'd beat the gallows by enlisting in the army.

Fair to say Joe wouldn't have made the first cut if it wasn't for Pete's intervention, what with Justin akin to being a copper himself, simply for the world. Pete liked Joe and his story immediately, finding the concept of volunteering for Uncle Sam to escape the electric chair interesting whether or not Joe's theory of self-rehabilitation and redemption worked, which it did not, not even close. No more than his attempted jumping ship worked. Wanted dead or alive, Joe landed alive in Cairo, just not again where he wanted, jail. Two hours away from being shipped out permanently when Pete happened upon him after thumbing through the assortment of resumes passed his way.

"What about this one?" Pete handed Justin the report, the folder thin but wicked as they come what with the fellow widowing some decent and hardworking policeman's wife.

"Yes, well, decent and hardworking sounds like a pipe dream." Justin concurred with the notion finding a municipal foot soldier who wasn't on someone's payroll alongside the one he was supposed to be on was unlikely. As far as the civic-minded killer: "What about him?" Justin took the bait.

"Dead man walking," Pete winked. "Personally, I find they're usually the most cooperative, myself a shining example."

"Yes, well, I'm looking for more than ghoulies." Justin scanned the sheet that placed the enlistee's story among the top ten stupidest he had ever read. "He's a damn Yank."

"He's got skills." Pete played defense council for the wayward American colonist, understanding how their little revolution might have come about. "Says right there he was an automobile mechanic before he took to a life of murder and crime."

"Yes, well, actually it says," Justin read, interested now that he did, but only because he was a gambler at heart, "that motor shop was a cover for a betting operation he ran over his short wave."

Pete smiled. "Say that like it was illegal."

"Apparently so there," Justin handed the log back. "All right. See what he's got, and we'll take it from there."

"Ain't you the charitable one," Pete praised. "Go straight to Heaven, surely you will. Be there alone, but you'll go there."

"Doubt it," Justin neglected to clarify which, the part about going to Heaven, or the part about being there alone.

A month after picking Joe for his first radio and gizmo extraordinaire, Justin wasn't any closer to finding whom he referred to as his second "gun". That would be a fellow to complement Pete. An invaluable asset to any man's army or squad, and not that they weren't out there, because they were. They just weren't going to waste them by bringing them here. Pete seemed apparently right about that. Those who hadn't already written off North Africa apparently seemed hard put to remember it was there. Justin kept looking though believing in the inevitable as well as patience paying off. Another month and his crew had expanded to close to a hundred with most of them answering to Nellie before answering to him. Something else that didn't set well with Pete, as Justin continued not to care what did or didn't set well with anyone. His interest was solely the North African war, no less than winning it despite the odds. Pete would have his chance at stardom at some point, some time, particularly since Justin still couldn't find his coveted "gun". Until told otherwise, however, the primary duty of Justin's private task force was to assist in the collection of information, rather than doing some actual job themselves.

That is, all but one. Jean Paul Dumont. For the first time in his thirteen-year history with Charlie, Nellie found himself sharing the position of Justin's right hand not with Bobby, or Pete, but with the French. The reason Nellie found himself in that position was because Justin was not about to share his position as King. Intimately involved with the Free French long before Justin's arrival in Cairo, Jean Paul Dumont lived in Algeria, the pulse of French resistance. A twenty-one year old corporal left without an army with the fall of France, the entrepreneurial Dumont founded his own intelligence organization with associates numbering into the thousands.

A particularly useful contact for Justin keenly interested in keeping a close eye on Vichy, Jean Paul maintained sole power and control over his side of the line, including deciding what and when to hit, or if there should be a hit at all.

Justin did not like that part of the arrangement any better than Nellie did. Jean Paul's "side of the line" arguably stretched from the western border of Libya, deep into the Great and small Atlas mountains of Algeria, north to Tunisia, and south to the ancient Tamanrasset region where Jean Paul left the protection of the southern Sahara to the fabled forces of Leclerc.

General Leclerc, whether Jean Paul actually knew him, or was just blowing smoke, was no fable. To where de Gaulle fought the war from the comfort of London radio, Leclerc's arse was on the line. Few knew his real name, or his background, for reasons as many as they were irrelevant. Leclerc's commitment to the fight in North Africa and from there the liberation of Paris was indisputable and unsurpassed. His mistrust of the British to a degree innate, to another acquired, nevertheless set aside for the greater good, rather like Pete and his Irish Nationalism. England should be so lucky as to come up with her own version of Leclerc, particularly since Germany had come up with its Rommel.

Despite Leclerc or de Gaulle, French and British relations in North Africa were not good, barely civil. Justin was there to make use of what he could, not strain them further by dismissing one of France's loyal and hardworking sons, at least openly. Privately, valuable though Jean Paul might be, he was not immune from Justin, or his scrutiny.

Around the end of January, Justin finally managed to come up with the linguistic expert he was also looking for, Lieutenant Jeff Mulrooney, British Army. A young fellow, about Joe's age who spoke something like thirty different dialects and languages—Pete didn't know—including the big three: French, German, and Italian, what got Mulrooney his commission, Pete believed that, because it sure wasn't for any other reason, not that Pete could see. When Mulrooney finally showed up about a month later, Pete did not like him and did not want him, whether or not he could read and write hieroglyphics. Mulrooney was nervous, chewed his nails, and "liked it the Catholic way" as Pete called it, referring, with all due respect, to the time-honored method of birth control among the heterosexual faithful. Specific to Mulrooney, Pete meant he was a sodomite, homosexual. Pete, who had spent at least half of the last twenty years in jail, objected to men who "liked it the Catholic way" versus those who made do.

Justin probably objected too on the basis of some moral principle should he take moral principles into consideration, which he did not. Mulrooney, when he finally showed up, was a fair, somewhat nervous young man, who, yes, had a tendency to bite his thumbnail, at least park it between his lower teeth during moments of thoughtful consideration before responding with hopefully the right answer to the questions put to him by the intimidating Squadron Leader Charles.

And so, Mulrooney had a tell. Joe had a tell. A tendency to swipe his hand across the back of his neck when trying not to say something he wanted to say. There was nothing unusual about that. A lot of people had tells, certainly most men. It meant something, of course, always did. Stood for something. Compensated. Occasionally for nerves or some other failing.

"Yes, well, we can't all be perfect." Justin sat back in his chair and lit his pipe, getting down to what he was inclined to consider. Such as field experience, which Mulrooney unabashedly had none. In fact, he was almost entirely inexperienced, six months at best, which, yes, might set someone to wondering what in hell he had been doing the first two years of the war.

"Trying to grow a beard," Bobby muttered something to that effect, in reference to how Mulrooney looked even younger than he was. Justin checked the top sheet. He was twenty-four and unmarried.

Twenty-four was probably older than most fellows on the front lines regardless of how "young" it was. His age was fine and went in the *For* column opposite the lack of experience in the *Against*. Not married was mandatory, non-negotiable, whether or not Mulrooney could read and translate the Rosetta Stone or whatever it was Pete had said. Justin less considerate of widowing some poor week-old bride than the simple reality his casualty figures for first time recruits was somewhere in the neighborhood of 93-94 percent. The fellow wasn't coming back, in other words, hadn't a chance. And, so, yes, Justin supposed if he cared to acknowledge it, consideration of some widowed bride did figure into the equation.

So did experience. With two checks in the *For* column, not having any was a life-sized handicap to overcome. Some sort of Cabaret spiritualist who talked to the dead in a plethora of tongues, one look at Mulrooney explained his lack of experience despite being two years deep into the war. He hadn't made the cut, whether he had tried or not. He had, according to his sheet, and promptly failed. Spent time like the rest of his artistic crowd entertaining the troops until someone in the audience realized the "act" included a fellow who could speak in tongues, and the rules changed.

The army's rules perhaps, but not necessarily Justin's. Shy of Pete's exaggeration of thirty languages or dialects, Mulrooney did speak two Arabic dialects, and six languages fluently including the big three. Arabic, admittedly was interesting, useful since Justin's tongue was limited and five years rusty, almost as bad as Pete's.

What figured more was Mulrooney failing the army's physical, and therefore stood about a cat's chance in Hell in measuring up to Justin's strict requirements, which were the desert's requirements, survival for something more than an hour. Meeting the height well enough at six-feet, Mulrooney had to be two stone shy of the minimum weight and just too damn white. The desert would consume him first time out.

Had damn near consumed him his first time in. Justin considered the sunburned face sitting at attention in front of him, the pasty pale skin red, blistered, and painfully raw.

"Aye, well, he's a decent shot," Bobby shifted in his fat, adding that to the *For* vote likely only because he wanted to see how long it would take Pete to vomit outright.

"Which Peter is about to," Pete assured. "God love me, the only damn company's he's toured with is the bloody burlesque crowd. He's an entertainer—pardon me, *artiste!*" his finger jammed down on the file. "It says so right there. *Troupe performer.* It doesn't say that? *Troupe performer?*"

"Yes, well, I believe they meant troop performer," Justin said, "as in performing for the troops. Quite all right, same thing. And, all right," he decided, "we'll give it a go. See how it goes. Can always put him with Nel, I suppose, if too many of the fellows take offense."

Bobby eyed him. "You sure?"

"How the devil do I know?" Justin said. "Ask Pete. He's the one insisting he's a sodomite."

"He is," Pete assured.

"Then it ought to be all right," Justin agreed since so was Nel.

"All right, I'll get on it," Bobby hoisted himself to his feet to begin their check on the fellow's background. "Got a few things he can do in the meantime, not too much harm to anybody."

"Got quite a lot he can do," Justin assured, "for that matter, eat. While you're at it get a bit more information on why he failed his physical. According to this he should have passed. Damn near did pass," he grunted, meaning theirs. "Nothing here three squares a day can't cure."

"Aye, well, that's not why he failed, lad," Bobby hinted, apparently secretly agreeing with Pete, though he'd never let it be known.

"Yes, well, believe we took care of that," Justin handed the file off to Bobby.

"I don't want him," Pete said.

"Be a few weeks before you have him," Justin assured. "If he's that good, I might keep him here."

"Your prerogative," Pete supported.

"Yes," Justin said.

Joe was the one who nicknamed Jeff, Hollywood. Nel, who abbreviated it to Holly, though usually called him, *boy*, as he did with most others. Pete had the dubious honor of being right, Bobby, the dubious honor of being wrong, at least in finding nothing remarkable in Jeff's background, at least not right off. As far as Jeff? Yes, well, Jeff was not only as good with languages as his file claimed, he had the distinct honor of being the first mistake Justin had made in years— or was he?

"Bobby," Justin said after Pete had left, "Make sure you get a bit more on this knack he apparently has with languages. Won't go as far as saying it's unheard of, but it is unusual."

"He's a knack," Bobby shrugged.

"Yes." Justin read that.

"Uses it in his act," Bobby said. "You know, talking to the dead."

"Yes." Why Justin stopped reading. "Didn't make the infantry, but it's a guaranteed ticket to Bletchley and the lot of us. Think it's possible we've got ourselves a mole. Make sure you find the connection."

Bobby scoffed. "Oh, right, lad, who doesn't know that? Got Jerry written all over him."

"Just find it, if it's there," Justin said.

"Will," Bobby promised. "Will at that."

That was the lot of them, except Jean Paul also employed personal bodyguards, which Justin did not do. The Germans and presiding Vichy government had known of Jean Paul a long time, and Jean Paul was not sitting in an office in Cairo, the Eighth Army surrounding him, he was sitting in a hut somewhere in the Algerian Atlas Mountains.

Chapter Eighteen

Cairo
March 6

"Where?" Thirty-seven year old SS Hauptmann Eric Danzig of the Propaganda Ministry sat up straight in his disguise to turn around and stare thoughtfully at his wall full of maps. A large, gregarious man with a misleadingly glib style Eric looked and felt somewhat ridiculous in his Arab robes complete with sandaled feet, but what worked, worked, and for some reason dressing like an overweight Lawrence worked. "Really ..." Eric nodded along. "You don't say ..."

Oh, but, twenty-four year old Lieutenant Jeff Mulrooney aka Hollywood aka SS Oberleutnant Peter Reiss did say with a bat of his baby blues and tip of his tow-blond head, a line of raggedy teeth fixed in a pasty smile.

Horse manure. And they would get to that, yes. Right now though: "Yes, well, I suppose we'll have to find out more about this, won't we?" Eric picked up the telephone at his side to discuss with his superiors, so they could discuss with their superiors, this rumored link between something called the British Long Range Desert Troops and some French Resistance Group headed by a man code name Charlies? Eric was lost already, and disinterested either way, none of this having anything to do with him as far as he could see.

"Charlie!" the lieutenant stopped filing his nails to snap. "And it is not rumor. Charles commands an array of forces, an array."

Big even. Impressive, if it extended from Algeria to the Western Desert and Cairo, Eric would go along with that. "Beg your pardon," Eric begged his superior's pardon with a wave at the lieutenant to keep his thin-lipped trap shut, "make that *Charly*. Yes, of course I understand ..." And, of course, Eric did understand how the identity of Charlie took precedence over the already identified Jean Paul Dumont.

"Who?" Eric frowned, but continued along, agreeing with complete and utter confidence, a contorted expression, and a shrug. "Oh, yes. I am thoroughly confident photographs can and will be quickly secured of this ... one moment ..." he grabbed a piece of paper and a pen, hastily scribbling down, "Major Justin Charles ... Believed to be potential candidate ...

"Well," Eric straightened up, beaming into the telephone, "I rather doubt if we didn't believe Charles to be a potential candidate we would be wasting our time trying to take a picture of him—I'll get a picture of him!" Eric promised faithfully, extending the receiver to arm's length, and even that wasn't far enough, "if I have to take it myself." With that, he hung up the telephone to sit back and stare somewhat blindly at the almanac of photographs and facts presented to him by this Peter Reiss, a Russian, no less. A Russian operant engaged as a spy for the German SS while spying on the English, and of course the French. It was a complicated world, extremely. Occasionally too complex.

"I have photographs of Charles," the Russian's squeaky and irritating little voice penetrated Eric's heavy masculine thoughts.

"I know that," Eric assured being as he was currently looking at them right?

"Right," Eric massaged the aching temples of his tired brow with his thumbs. He did not like the Russians, as most of his kind did not. There was no reason why he should like them. He especially did not like this one sitting impatiently across the table from him. A man, Eric dared to call Jeff, wrapped up in his long girly figure and fine artistic hands, fixed in self-absorption. Disconcerting for a less confident man than himself Eric would suspect, there was a reason why these he-she types were not only discouraged by the new Reich, but openly shunned and shot.

Eric straightened up again (not really but at least he didn't appear to be falling asleep), acknowledging the Russian's intolerant expression with his own counterfeit smile, alluding to how underneath it all he might be as contemptible as this grappling wannabe, striving for a world that wasn't his. Wealth and riches, Eric would personally settle for, and after that, wine, women, and song. Eric was exactly who this Russian was underneath it all. They all were. Liars, if they said they weren't.

"Let me try putting it this way, Lieutenant Mulrooney ..." Eric nodded, a haughty opening statement, timeless and well worn.

"Reiss. Peter Reiss." Jeff interrupted coldly, not particularly liking his employers, the Allied, or the Axis, any more than they liked him, especially this one. Danzig. Eric Danzig. An arrogant German who thought he was more than what he was, which was nothing. Jeff eyed Eric, hunger in his thoughts. He was there for a reason. Desperation some might say, anxious to regain property stolen from him by these Germans, or just revenge. He could taste the pleasure of death in his mouth, and he would get Eric Danzig, the same as he would get the thieves, after he was done with him, after there was no need. His head cocked, not like a girl's, more like a serpent or snake waiting to spring. Danzig seemed to be oblivious to his fate, more interested in his own voice.

Eric was interested in only his own voice for reasons other than he was German, and the lieutenant was not. Eric could barely understand the Russian Reiss calling himself Jeff today. Barely follow him, when he could understand him. Reiss's syntax, while better than most, remained inevitably punctuated with awkwardness, struggling through the nuances of his adopted language of his adopted land that separated the native-born from the imposter.

Eric smiled. He smiled when he couldn't understand Jeff, and he smiled when he could. He smiled because he always smiled. The same as he never meant his smile, certainly not now. Why would he? His difficulty with the Russian's speech, his overall disinterest in being treated to a lecture on British intelligence efforts to rout out and trample Germans where and when they found them, taking a back seat to being simply agog at this Russian who seemed to think Eric should be interested enough to be willing to pay for the information.

"Or whatever your name is," Eric agreed. "Let me see if I have this right. I wouldn't be here, you wouldn't be here, if it wasn't for the fact ..." Eric checked the wordy and rambling report, searching for *the* name among all the names listed, certain there had to be someone in particular responsible for his detour other than this Russian with his high hopes and pipe dreams.

"Weiheber," the Russian informed him with a sneer. Herr SS Major Hanse Weiheber, big and bad and stereotypical as they came, even his skin was unclean. The flesh, dark, pitted and taunt in a Goebbels-like way. But then they made them that way if they weren't, didn't they? *Picked* them on occasion apparently with this Weiheber who appeared to be some sort of Czech implant, one of Himmler's clowns. Eric was of the Ministry, and therefore one of Goebbels'.

Now, *that* could prove to be a problem, yes, it could. Prophetic even and certainly as good a reason as any as to why Eric's immediate and direct superiors felt an hour or two dialoguing with some Russian comrade could not hurt. They did not get along Herr Goebbels of the Ministry, and Herr Himmler of the SS. Something far less publically known than Hitler's invasion of Russia ...

Well, perhaps something *somewhat* less publically known, Eric acknowledged. At the very least, something not talked about. Loudly, anyway. Whichever, and so what? So, Herr Goebbels and Herr Himmler did not get along, but were instead entrenched and preoccupied with stealing each other's thunder, with Goebbels currently odd man out of Hitler's divine favor. This was *news?* To whom was this news? Certainly not to Eric who knew regardless of who might be in or out now that would soon, if not surely change.

Oh, yes, *that* Eric knew for a fact, regardless of who else knew what, or thought they did, including some Major Weiheber. Eric had never heard of Weiheber. He had no idea who Weiheber was, or thought he might be, other than by way of his dossier. A sizable packet handed to Eric when he stepped off his plane, reasonably expecting to step onto another, only to be ushered away and eventually here to meet with some *Russian,* and buy, of all things, *buy* whatever the little Soviet seemed to think he had to sell. "And he is not my Major, he is my contact, like you," the Russian was saying whether true or false. "Old, and still much to prove."

Eric looked up. He didn't do anything. He just looked at the prickly little twig he could snap in two with a flick of his broad meaty hand.

"Well?" Jeff said impatiently.

"He has something to prove, you mean. To Berlin," Eric smiled. "Yes," Eric had spotted it finally, two or three paragraphs down. SS Major Hanse Weiheber lately of Berlin, and Eric was no more, and couldn't be any less interested now than he was before, so therefore, remember it? Probably not. But then Eric was *the* Berlin connection to the five top-secret German munitions complexes buried in the bowels of the Sahara and elsewhere. Algeria, Eric believed. Three were reportedly in Algeria, two in Libya, the closest almost two thousand kilometers from the front lines. That sounded like a lot to Eric, but he had been reassured how it wasn't in the grand scheme of things, and they were—the complexes—*extremely* interesting to Herr Goebbels screw Himmler and his boys.

"It's called politics, Lieutenant," Eric enlightened Jeff to Weiheber's scheme. "Let's, for the moment, anyway, forget politics, and try to stick to the facts."

And Eric's fact-finding mission to rout out the facts surrounding the five secret munitions complexes—*unauthorized* would probably be a better description since munitions complexes were seldom secret for very long, their munitions complexes, or anyone else's, though they were usually authorized, which these five were not. No, they were tantamount to a rebellion, possibly even treason, sedition at the very least, if one wanted to be hardnosed about it, which the Ministry did not, not necessarily. An unusual situation, admittedly, and time, of course, would ultimately tell, and time for the moment, was on Eric's side. His assignment, much like the installations, was also secret, if not extraordinarily sensitive. Early reports suggested the instigator could very well turn out to be General Rommel. Field Marshal-to-be Erwin Rommel, his name appearing (however invisibly) on the bottom line. His fingerprints smeared over every page. And Rommel, in case this Russian was unaware, was something of a National Institution to Germany, and therefore sensitive? Oh, ha, ha, *sensitive,* Eric supposed could be the operative word for his mission and subsequent how-best-to-handle the rebellious going's on within the ranks of the German rear services of North Afrika and keep the proverbial egg off the faces of the Axis, not the Allied, who, right now, Eric personally didn't give two pfennig about.

The SS was how, and not some random blitzkrieging outfit to go in boots kicking and guns blazing, but the Propaganda Ministry historically proven in its ability to sell anything to anyone, including itself.

Case in point. Eric looked around the sweating room, a veritable oven, veritable. It escaped him, truly, what conquering this place, for that matter Siberia, had to do with ruling the world. "How did you say all of this was connected again, Lieutenant?" he verified, still having trouble with Jeff's speech whether he could understand what he said or not. "I mean, other than the war?

"I mean, Lieutenant," he turned back with his smile for Jeff, "specifically connected, specifically to me aka Germany. Talk. Make it quick and keep it short."

"It isn't, wasn't," Jeff assured, alluding to how it might be now? "You have your Major Weiheber to thank for that."

Meaningless, utterly, the Russian was clearly playing some game. Eric nodded. "Is that English accent for real?" he wondered, a natural question, but Jeff just looked at him, and Eric continued to smile back. "Make that short, quick, and to the point."

"Fine," Jeff shrugged. "I give Charles to you or you to Charles. Which is it?"

"Which," Eric glanced down on the paper mountain sprawled in front of him. "Well, that," he agreed, "is elementary. However, Lieutenant, I believe you need to understand irrespective of the Ministry having no intentions of being sold to the Allies it's not to be construed as an offer to *buy* anything from you regardless of what some ... *Major Weiheber*, may have led you to believe. Is that clear, Lieutenant?" he smiled, "Or would you like me to repeat it? Clarify perhaps?

"I mean, Lieutenant," he continued to smile, "hypothetically, of course, but, if for example, you were to die from a sudden bullet hole, I would have all of this, the Ministry would be safe, and you would have nothing. Unless I'm missing something. Am I missing something, Lieutenant? What am I missing?" he asked.

"*Weiheber,*" Jeff assured.

"Weiheber," Eric digested. "Are you saying, Lieutenant ..." he inquired when it just sort of lay there undigested, "Himmler—

pardon me, *Weiheber,* is poised to sell the Ministry to the Allies? That is absurd, Lieutenant, utterly absurd, politics aside."

Jeff shrugged.

"Fine," Eric agreed, "have it your way—not forgetting, of course," he said, "hypothetically, I could always torture you to make you talk."

"Weiheber is there," Jeff leaned forward—loomed, actually, leered, suddenly, with a lick of his lips either literally or he just seemed to lick his lips. Eric almost recoiled, but did not. The Russian was good, he'd give him that much. A real confidence artist, sizing up his audience identifying their weaknesses and playing on them, using them to his advantage. "At your complex."

"What complex?" Eric didn't move a muscle, didn't flinch, but pitched the ball right back at him.

Jeff's head tipped. "Fine," he said, "let him destroy them, it doesn't matter to me, that's up to you. I was employed to secure something for him. He took it, and I want it back. I want you to get it for me, or, yes," he promised, "I will give your complexes to the Allies."

"Funny," Eric smiled, "to think I thought you were going to say something more like how you tried to sell him something he either took without paying, or didn't take, and in either case you're looking to sell me something. You're an information specialist, Lieutenant, let's be honest with one another. You buy and sell information. Is that closer, Lieutenant?" he asked, sure that it was. Particularly since he wasn't sure there was such a thing as a quadruple agent. That would seem a bit overdone.

"Weiheber is Gestapo," Jeff sneered. *"Gestapo."* A dated term, defunct. Apparently these Russians were not only behind the 8-ball, they were a few years behind the times. "He isn't just anyone, he is Gestapo."

Eric smiled. "I trust you mean SS, Lieutenant, SA, SD. We are one, after all. All for one, and naturally, one for all ..." he fingered the paper mountain, not for any particular reason, only because it was there. "Not good enough, Lieutenant. I want to know what you wanted to sell Weiheber. What he took, or didn't take, whichever the case may be."

"Better idea," Jeff countered, "you worry about what he wants—*Rommel*. Now," he said, "do we have a deal? Or would you like me to clarify it for *you*, Hauptmann? You give me what I want, I give you what you want ... and Weiheber?" he dismissed. "He's yours. Free of charge."

Eric smiled. "The crux of my point, Lieutenant—*Rommel,*" he clarified. "Forgetting how astounded I might be that you seem to think we would acknowledge the existence of some *rumored* complex, General Rommel is precisely what separates Herr Goebbels from the pack."

"Oh?" Jeff said.

"Definitely," Eric assured. "Setting aside General Rommel's celebrity status among the general populous, if the whole truth be known, he actually isn't well liked by most of the *General* population who consider him to be something of an upstart. Interestingly enough, and certainly, under the circumstances you propose, quite apropos. A rogue in hero's clothing," he smiled, "independent. You seem shocked, Lieutenant, I don't know why. Surely, it stands to reason if Herr Himmler has heard these rumors of complexes, if Herr Goebbels is who Herr Goebbels is, and I can assure you he is, the Ministry has no doubt heard the rumors as well.

"It doesn't mean they're true," Eric shook his head, "No, it does not mean that at all. What it does do is illustrate the basic difference between your Herr Himmler, and mein Herr Goebbels who understands exactly what your Herr Himmler has apparently chosen to forget—and that would be a sincere appreciation of who likes General Rommel most of all—Hitler," he promised. "So enough with the idle threats, Lieutenant, about—"

"Charles," Jeff interjected.

"Yes, well, definitely enough of that," Eric's eyes rolled. "Really, Lieutenant, you and what army are going to get anywhere near—"

"Your complexes," Jeff assured.

"The nearest shithole!" Eric snapped. "You're not only suicidal, Lieutenant, you're nuts if you really think the Ministry is about to back off for fear of you handing anyone over to anyone whether it's Himmler, some Weiheber—or this man!" he snatched up one of the photographs of the so-called Charles. "Or this one!" he snatched up one of the shots of someone named Nellie. "Or any other of your Allied chums!"

"No," Jeff said.

"No," Eric agreed. "because you can't, Lieutenant. Not because you wouldn't, or naturally shouldn't since you're not working for them, but are working for me ..." he ogled the picture of the serious and emaciated Charles with the receding hairline and bulging eyes. "Consumption?" Eric hazarded what was a reasonable guess. "Cancer? Death?"

Jeff sneered. "Are you a doctor?"

"Car salesman," Eric grinned. "Used cars. The Propaganda Ministry a simple matter of evolution ... and since we're on the subject ..." he poured himself a bourbon from the bottle on the desk, "I should take a moment to clarify the Ministry's position on any threat of Allied ... well, Allied threat," he waved. "Call it what you like. We don't care. No, we don't," he downed the bourbon with a shake of his head. "They're supposed to try and find us. Hound, harass, rout out and destroy us, and we are supposed to do exactly the same thing to them. It's the name of the game, and the game is war.

"On the other hand," Eric said, "you can be assured, Lieutenant, as well as assure anyone you care to, the Ministry does care very much about the suggestion our army would have the audacity to steal and keep our munitions for ourselves rather than give them all away to the Italians as we have been instructed to do. The Italians are our allies. They are our friends.

"They are stupid, incompetent oafs," Eric shrugged, knowing that as well, "who will never win this war I don't care what new Caesar sits on their throne.

"But, regardless, Lieutenant," he nodded at Jeff, "we are to supply them. Nurture, spoon-feed, and diaper them throughout their fight, which is our fight—though only Hitler knows how that happened," he admitted. "Whether or not we have enough for ourselves is irrelevant."

"And that order doesn't come from me, Lieutenant," he continued to nod emphatically at Jeff, "it comes from Berlin. We are to win this war Berlin's way, even if we lose. To dare to do anything else is treason, and the traitors will pay with their lives."

"Oberleutnant," Jeff stuck in, crossing and uncrossing his legs in an expression of boredom, "Herr SS Oberleutnant Peter Reiss. Lieutenant Mulrooney is dead. I know. I killed him. I needed his papers, and I needed his name."

"Painfully," Eric smiled, thinking of his Luger tucked safely under his robes, the warm sweating leather of its holster tickling the saturated hairs of his barrel chest. He was not a violent man by nature, but he could learn to be, yes, he could. The choice was there, the choice just that, a choice, and it was all his. Fortunately, for the Russian, it not only seemed a waste of a precious bullet, it also seemed a waste of time. Eric returned to the subject of the compounds. "Unless, of course it is determined Rommel is behind this novel idea of keeping a bullet or two," he said. "No, we won't hang General Rommel," he shook his head in certainty, "I can assure you. We'll kiss his ass as we always do, and wish him Godspeed … And, that, Lieutenant," he winked, "is no propaganda.

"Now …" he folded his hands across the almanac of facts and faces, the moist celluloid immediately gluing itself to his sticky wet arms, proving what he said about the Propaganda Ministry's ability to sell anything, even this place. "Unless you have something significant, or even relevant to add, which clearly you don't, I suggest you leave the way you came in, considering this to be your lucky day. Arrivederci, auf wiedersehen, adieu."

"Herr Major Weiheber is at your complex," Jeff replied. "You may not want him to be there, you can *deny* anything you please. He is there to destroy them and he has something that belongs to me. If he does not return it, I will do what I need to do, including giving your complexes to Charles. It is up to you."

"Lucky as in you get to live," Eric smiled back. "You're going to have to do better than that. Proof would go a long way, evidence. So far I've heard and seen none."

"Yes," Jeff knew. He was something like a minute or two away from being shot. "You have a great deal of faith in these walls, Captain. Personally, I wouldn't chance it. Why don't you break my neck instead?"

"I wouldn't say it's faith in the walls, Lieutenant." Eric rose to check his reflection in the soiled window panes of this average two-story mud building sandwiched between dozens of others not far from the hub of commerce, high-life, and intrigue, to see what he could do about his appearance that was about as believable as the B-films they cranked out by the hundreds. But then this was also a very naïve world, pathetically so, not just suddenly so extraordinarily complex. He smiled. "More faith in the neighborhood. The clock is ticking, Lieutenant, you either give it up—all of it, or get out while you still can—leaving, of course, Charles," Eric nodded. "Yes, you can leave the binder behind. I wouldn't want to appear unappreciative of all your hard work."

"He has the daughter of an Italian nuclear physicist with him," Jeff said, and Eric quite literally almost put his own eye out as he repaired his sweat-soggy grease paint. "If she dies, I would think the chances of finding the physicist would be more difficult than they already are.

"But then," he smiled as Eric stared at him, "I also wouldn't want the Ministry to think I lack appreciation of the interest in developing atomic power—before the Allies," he said, "and, yes," he shrugged, "before Russia, if you insist. But only if we have a deal." he assured. "So, I don't know, " he said as Eric stumbled back to the table, "do we?"

Eric did not stumble, he walked. Poured another bourbon and was perfectly fine now that his eye had stopped watering and the feeling had returned to his fingers and toes. "Ah!" he even extolled happily after downing his drink. "So for all my bluster I'm actually intrigued."

"It's a one-time opportunity," Jeff forewarned him. "Here while I am here, gone when I am gone."

"Just get on with it," Eric suggested.

"Fine," Jeff shrugged. "Charles is Charlie. Some sort of code for his fingerprints. You know this already. Your superiors confirmed it for you."

So they had. "Not Charles. The hell with Charles. That I can read." He wouldn't, but that was beside the point. He would keep the almanac and give it to someone else to read, someone much better with those sorts of details than he was. "And cut to the point, Lieutenant," he sat down with a wave for the mess littering his desk.

"What would you consider proof?" Jeff confirmed.

"Oh, I don't know," Eric said. "I'll know it when I hear it, how's that?" he tapped his watch. "Time, Lieutenant. One-two-three-*Go*."

Jeff shrugged again. "The American intrigued Weiheber—I knew the American would," he assured. "I needed the girl to get to Charles. He took the girl even though he knew that." He sat back. "The girl is the daughter of the physicist."

"Yes," Eric agreed, "you said that."

Jeff sat forward again. "Weiheber does not know what he has."

"Six to one, half a dozen to the other," Eric cautioned. "It's entirely possible he does know—or why he took her."

"No," Jeff shook his head. "No. Weiheber is a cocaine addict. A drunken old man," he indicated Eric's bourbon with his chin. "He appeared obsessed only with the complexes instead of what he was there for. *I* tracked the girl from Europe to Africa. Her itinerary Tobruk, and then Gibraltar to the United States—"

"Of America," Eric interjected. "Explains the American engineer. Interesting ... and, continue, please," he encouraged Jeff who had stopped. "Continue."

"Their contact was Charles, some British Intelligence officer named Charles."

"Who you promised Weiheber," Eric nodded, "as you promised him ... this *American* ..."

"Gave," Jeff assured. "I gave Weiheber the American. I needed the girl to get Charles. To find him."

"You have Charles," Eric indicated his desk.

"Now," Jeff agreed. "Not then. I had to find another way to get to him and I did. Mulrooney. So, do we have a deal, Hauptmann?"

"For me to assist you in securing an atomic scientist for Stalin—which apparently no one has regardless of who else they may or may not have?" Eric checked. "Well, I don't know, Lieutenant, let me think about that." He stood up and started collecting up the Russian's collection of faces and facts.

"What are you doing?" Jeff scowled.

"Me?" Eric smiled. "I'm leaving."

"Are you crazy?" Jeff leapt to his feet, his fist striking the desk.

Crazy? No. Eric smoked, drank, and ate a bit more than he

should upon occasion, but, no, he wasn't crazy. "Lieutenant ..." he said. "Well, Lieutenant ..." he said, picking up the particularly unflattering black and white glossy of the unsavory looking Charles. "In the first place, British, I'll grant you, and therefore enemy, as in foe, but honestly, Lieutenant," he whipped the picture around for Jeff to see, "if this is the picture of an intelligence officer, then boy is the Axis in for one hell of a surprise."

"What?" Jeff said.

"A joke, Lieutenant," Eric assured, his tongue firmly planted in his cheek. "He's ugly, Lieutenant," he helped Jeff out. "Extremely. Physically defective. It's elementary the spiritual, moral, and intellectual abilities therefore are, and must be, equally flawed ... Herr Goebbels, of course," he dropped the photograph down, "an exception to the rule. Herr Goebbels is an artist, and, well, we all know how artists are ..."

"You're missing the point!" Jeff insisted.

No, Eric wasn't. "You want Weiheber ... or rather this girl with him ..."

"*Daughter,*" Jeff assured. "Daughter of an atomic scientist. Yes, I want her. She is the hostage to secure the physicist. Either that or you pay for the physicist now. I have not done all of this work for nothing."

"Now we're getting to the crux of things," Eric smiled. "To do that you need my help as Weiheber is apparently at these ... *complexes*," he waved, "you think we have."

"You do," Jeff assured.

"Perhaps," Eric smiled. "In exchange I get to keep our complexes, and also Charles as a booby-prize. Do I have that right?"

"If you believe in National heroes," Jeff agreed. "That they are heroes, not upstarts, yes, you have it right."

"The Rommel card," Eric pointed.

"The Rommel card," Jeff assured.

"What if I want it all, Lieutenant?" Eric wondered. "What's to stop me? Especially since I appear to already have it all. The complexes, Weiheber, the girl ... even Charles whom you just gave me. I'll just ship the girl to Berlin. No doubt there are a few experts there who can coax her father out of hiding. What do I need you for?"

"Charles thinks the French can tell him about your depots," Jeff said.

"The French?" Eric said.

"Jean Paul Dumont," Jeff nodded at the telephone.

"Oh," Eric said. "Right ... *Dumont*." And here to think he was just about to say: "What the hell are you talking about?" Instead, he smiled, "Oh, well, they can't tell him."

"Are you so sure about that?" Jeff challenged with a cocky swish of his head.

"I'm positive," Eric grinned. "But then the Germans can't tell me about my munitions depots. They're a secret even from us. Now, if you will excuse me," he picked the binder up with a friendly pat. "I have a plane to catch."

"Yes," Jeff sneered, "for your complexes and your national heroes. You should know, Captain, he killed his First Officer six months ago, two others before him. He has a lifetime of defying authority, including his father's, who he deposed at fourteen. I wouldn't expect an honor guard to greet you, if I were you."

"Weiheber?" Eric guessed, though not to suggest he was impressed.

"You tell me," Jeff smiled, a soulless satanic leer.

"Weiheber," Eric nodded. "Sounds demonic, you're right. Definitely not something anyone would ever associate with the SS. We will have to set him straight."

Always it was something funny. Jeff eyed the comedian. "Are you sure you're SS?"

"Oh, yes," Eric crossed his cold though beating heart. "Are you sure you are?"

"Yes," Jeff assured.

"Bullshit," Eric whispered. "You're nothing, and you will always be nothing, I don't care whose clothes you wear. But that's all right," Eric nodded, "yes, it is. You say you have my 16th Army surrounded at Staraya, and it will only be a matter of time, one million-five casualties the first six months of the war. I say, in your Siberian dreams. By summer, your mother Russia will be utterly destroyed."

"According to you," Jeff said. "We'll see which one of us is right. Personally, I think the one with the scientist stands a better chance than the one with the daughter." He turned to walk out, Eric's foot catching him sharply on the sole of his behind as he turned, knocking him flat.

"I mean, Lieutenant," Eric crouched down so Jeff could see him eye to eye, his Luger out and pointed at Jeff's chest, "you do not seriously think anyone is going to buy into your single-handed ability to make or break one of the greatest heroes Germany has ever known unless we see things your way? Do you? Do you really? Because let me repeat, you and what army, Lieutenant? You and what army?"

"The 8th," Jeff smiled. "Who will win the war London's way even if they lose. So far they haven't. The offer is Charles, Captain. Charles for Weiheber. Before you say no again, remember your complexes and whose signature appears on the bottom line."

Eric was remembering the complexes. "What Himmler calls impertinence on the part of the Afrika Korps, the Ministry is quite prepared to call ingenious—providing of course, it is Rommel," he clarified, "and this plan to ensure sufficient supplies for his annual march across the desert for the gates of Alexandria works, which we sincerely hope it does. After all, it will be his second try. And if Napoleon could do it, Alexander, quite obviously, and a Caesar or two without the advantages of empty guns and cardboard tanks, then we really don't have much of an excuse for our failure, now, do we?"

"I don't know," Jeff said. "Do you?"

"That would be ingenious, as in ingenuity, Lieutenant," Eric explained, though not to suggest Stalin knew anything about that. "Strength, superiority, and last but not least, balls. We have them. Trust me when I say there are none larger. Now, tell me again how Weiheber doesn't know what he has in the girl, and how much Charles knows about the scientist ... and, yes, of course, these complexes while you're at it."

"Oh?" Jeff countered smartly, "What happened to no deal?

"I'm the one with the gun," Eric reminded.

"Yes," Jeff said, "and I'm the one offering you the opportunity to take a scientist home to Berlin, not simply ship his daughter. Fame, Captain. You like fame. I can see it in your eyes. You lust for it, after it. You're Weiheber twenty years ago. You want to be Weiheber now when you're fifty, or do you want to be Herr Goebbels?"

"Did I forget to say tell me now?" Eric checked.

"Weiheber knows nothing," Jeff assured. "He thinks he has an American spy. The girl merely his PA—personal assistant," he explained.

"Secretary," Eric nodded, "yes, I have it. And Charles?"

"He shouldn't have wanted her," Jeff insisted, "Weiheber. He shouldn't have cared. He should have listened when I said I could use her to get to the American's British partner Charles. But he didn't listen because he's an idiot. Seeing spies, spies, everywhere."

"And Charles?" Eric encouraged.

"About the scientist?" Jeff said. "Nothing. He knows nothing. The American Colonel was the connection. Acting on behalf of the United States. They gave him introduction papers and sent him to secure assistance from Charles in getting the girl out of Europe to the United States. They never arrived in Tobruk, so, no, Charles knows nothing, not yet. Who knows if the United States will even tell him, They probably won't."

"How elating," Eric beamed. "And, of course," he said, "explains why we, not he, are called Superman ... Or at least, I am," he agreed. "Dare I ask are you sure about this, Lieutenant? You wouldn't be trying to pull a fast one on me, would you?"

"I'm positive," Jeff assured. "He knows nothing. It was all a mess. Charles wasn't even in Tobruk, he's in Cairo, and not waiting for the American Colonel or some daughter or anyone. They are a piece of paper in a file about a lost American envoy, stamped received three weeks ago."

"But you're sure the scientist is out there," Eric said.

"He is or he will be," Jeff promised. "The itinerary was Cairo to Tobruk, Gibraltar, to the United States, as I told you. The American Colonel is an engineer, Malcolm McDowell. He was traveling from Cairo to Tobruk with his aide, Paul Reid, and his driver—that's the girl. The aide is dead; I know. I'm the aide and I killed him."

"I thought it was Mulrooney you killed," Eric smiled and Jeff paused. "Continue."

"I'm Mulrooney." Jeff said.

"Ah!" Eric said. "Continue."

"The girl's papers are false. The scientist is Italian."

"And your name? I mean, his name?" Eric asked.

"I don't know," Jeff assured. "The recognition code is her assumed name: *Joanna Lee*. Remember it. *Joanna Lee*. Tobruk and Charles were dead-ends. They're out there, Hauptmann," he assured. "The contacts, and the scientist. We need the girl to find them."

"Or a girl," Eric smiled, "But we'll worry about that later. How many men does this Weiheber have with him?"

"Six or seven," Jeff shrugged. "And an officer, SS Leutnant Günther Faust.

Eric's eyes rolled. "In total, Lieutenant. He must at least have a platoon."

"Then he has a platoon," Jeff agreed. "Fine. Have it your way. I don't know. He is an envoy from Berlin out of Tunis where they all are—where *we* all are. He was supposed to be my contact. He came but he was not interested. Only in the complexes. When I could tell him nothing about them, he took the girl."

"Ah!" Eric said. "So he took what he could get."

"Do we have a deal or not, Hauptmann?" Jeff asked. "Such opportunities only come around once in a lifetime."

Eric was thinking about it, considering his Luger, and settling for a sprinkling of coins as he stood up. "Keep the change. In the meantime, Lieutenant," he said as Jeff glared, "I want you to find out precisely ... and I mean *precisely* what this *Charles* knows about the compounds. *IF* he knows anything at all, and report to me. Do you understand? *Me*. Not Russia, Mussolini, *Japan,* or anyone else who may enter your head, but *me* alone."

"And the scientist?" Jeff said.

Eric smiled, "Well, obviously if you come upon any information relative to the scientist, be sure *not* to include it in your written report. After all, we wouldn't want information like that falling into the wrong hands, now would we, Lieutenant? I'm sure you realize this "girl" could be dead, if this Weiheber is really oblivious to her value, and even then ... presuming any of this is even true. There's one way to find out—and don't worry, we will be in touch either way. True or false, Lieutenant, your story true or false, we will be in touch. In the meantime, not a word, Lieutenant, not *one* word," he stressed, "to anyone. I'm sure you understand that as well."

"Asshole," Jeff picked himself up off the floor as the door closed behind Danzig, moving on to get back to the allied side of town before Nellie started wondering where he was.

Chapter Nineteen

Cairo
March 9

Justin studied Nellie sitting there in a WWI doughboy helmet for some damn reason or another.

"What's the matter, Charlie?" Nellie drawled, his Irish brogue distorted by ten years of South African dialect having to confuse the hell out of the Yanks from Tennessee. "Can you tell ol' Nellie?"

The matter was a munitions depot Nel had reported in western Libya, south of the Tunisian border, south of the Coast Road, damn bang on the dividing line between Justin's and Jean Paul's territory. The supposed site spitting distance from Gadames, a dazzling mythical city bathed in marble on the Algerian-Libyan border few even knew was there. "If they brought them in at Bone, or Phillipeville …" Justin began slowly, watching Nellie's smile spread with the implication of Algeria.

"Quite," Justin said, "it could be Algeria, or it could be Tunis. Out of Sicily, into dock, from there, fairly straight shot to the Coast Road, straight as any."

"This ain't along the Coast, Charlie," Nellie reminded.

No, it wasn't. It was inland, and dry as a bone.

"It's not Algeria," Justin assured. "Not worth it."

"Oh, well, now," Nellie chuckled, "it's not Algeria because that's Johnnie's territory, and Johnnie would know if someone were using him as a pipeline."

Jean Paul would know that went without saying. It wasn't Algeria because it wasn't worth it whether Jerry decided to cross into Tunisia for Tunis, or just head south. South, they'd hit the mountains and the Erg. It would take them a month and they would still never make it. Crossing north from the Algerian seaports into Tunisia also wasn't worth it. More mountains and time, losing whatever they hoped to gain by taking the long way around and down to the Coast Road.

"You still got Tripoli," Nellie reminded.

Yes. Or rather Mussolini had Tripoli, shared Tripoli with Rommel, yet to lose it even once in this war that had both sides moving forward as often as they fell into retreat. After a year, they were almost back to square one with Jerry on one side and England on the other of the Gazala Line, neither moving, both fair to say recuperating, long on troops and short on ammunition and supplies, England with the added burden of what was quickly becoming a round-robin of Generals. If Rommel struck now, he'd win. For some reason he was quiet. Justin, somewhat less interested in knowing why Rommel was quiet, than in making sure he stayed that way.

He ogled Nellie through a haze of pipe smoke, pensive and undecided. If the port at Tripoli made the most sense, some depot four hundred miles west of her did not when Rommel sat hungry and waiting eight hundred miles to her east. Justin had a few threads to follow, but no pattern yet. Uncertain if there even was a pattern. Currently he had two reliable reports of depots in almost random locations, and then both of them confirmed gone, vanished, from his own men, stationed in the west to keep an eye on things. Conclusion: there were no depots. Early reports were wrong. That made Jean Paul right who insisted there were no depots, and Justin's men wrong, who insisted there were. Justin had to presume his men were right. So, where did the depots come from, why were they there, and where did they go? Justin had insufficient information to answer any of those questions and only enough information to conclude something was wrong.

"Something's wrong, Nel," Justin said.

"Not this time, Charlie," Nellie smiled easily.

Not twice, he meant. No two depots there and then suddenly both gone. "Sounds more like transfer stations than depots," Justin lit his pipe. "Large enough apparently for the fellows to think they might be looking at a depot, but ultimately since they're both gone, the installations weren't fixed, but only temporary."

"Awful lot of supplies, Charlie," Nellie said.

"Yes," Justin agreed. A transfer station of that reported size implied troop movement, of which there was none at the front lines, let alone a thousand miles to its rear. "More of those facts. There's also been no damn convoy in here in months if you care to add that to the pot. So, quite. Where the hell did they come from and where did they go?" Justin sloshed an early Scotch into his teacup and rose for his maps, his pipe clenched in his teeth.

"Algeria," Justin pinned the map at the Algeria-Libya border. Jerries moving into Algeria under Jean Paul's nose.

"Sebha," Justin pinned the map at the location of the reported Italian stronghold in central Libya. "Any deeper and they would be treading into Leclerc's territory and there's been no reports out of there, so, quite. Up from Sebha if they came out of it, down south to Sebha if they went in. There's no other choice. Let's say up for the moment and then where, since they didn't come this way ..." he scanned the map. "Algeria," he nodded. "You're right. They'd have to move into Libya to circumvent the Erg. Out of Algeria, down to Sebha, or up from Sebha into Algeria. Still doesn't explain why or where, but we'll figure it out. Jean Paul's been sloppy, that's the point, or he's covering for someone who's been sloppy or worse. Won't have it, can't. Source isn't worth it unless it's reliable, too risky otherwise, too much depending upon it, too many."

"Something's wrong, Charlie," Nellie agreed, "I can feel it in my bones."

"Then let's get back out there and find out what it is," Justin relit his pipe, sitting back down at his desk, "before Rommel renews his push for Tobruk, Cairo ... and," he nodded, "the world. Someone's out there moving supplies around we need to know the details. Jean Paul's probably been trying to rout them, clearly with limited success. We'll consider that to the situation, unless you come back to me with something different. Got that?"

"Aye," Nellie said.

"Good," Justin said. "Take Holly with you. He can use the experience, and you can use the help with the lingo. I'll let you know when everything's been set up, where you and Jean Paul will meet, and when. In the meantime, you and Holly will have a few days to check things out before I let Jean Paul in on it, so get on it now, the two of you. The usual place. Frank's not here, so he can't bring you out, but it will be Frank who picks you and Holly up."

"Aye," Nellie rose with a stretch.

"Oh, and Nel?" Justin said with a point of his pipe stem at Nellie's outdated steel bonnet. "Take that damn tin cap off your head. It's a Yank's in the first place, and the wrong damn war."

"Oh, well, now I know that, I do," Nellie's eyes raised, surveying his helmet with a chuckle. "But, you see, it's my halo. Holly gave it to me. Said without it, it was hard not to mistake me for the devil."

"Yes, well, you are the devil, Nel," Justin assured, "so take it off. The fellows already think we're nutter, no need to rub it in."

"If you say," Nellie sighed, compliant about it either way.

"Thank you," Justin said and made a note to have Bobby pull Mulrooney's file for review now of whatever Bobby had been able to come up with to date. Mulrooney was hard core if he was a mole, out of line, if he wasn't. Fraternization within the ranks was not allowed under the rulebook, and Justin, in general, ignored those who broke the rule as long as it didn't spill over into the work. His reward for his leniency was it seldom did. All of them dabbled from time to time, himself included, with the usual number of a few more serious players, Joe being one of them. It wasn't unusual for Nel to participate, more often than not, easier to handle whenever he had a boy to pal around with. Mulrooney was the current boy. Somewhat more flagrant than Justin had anticipated with his self-conscious stammer and nervous stares, Mulrooney had so far managed to keep all but the most ardent hecklers at arm's length, Nel, in the background more or less guaranteeing his success. This was flagrant though, and Justin wasn't about to jeopardize Nellie's position with the men for some fop undercover or in heat.

"Oh, and, Charlie?" Nellie mentioned as his hand touched the door. "Bobby wanted me to be sure and tell you, not to be adding to your troubles, but there's a boy by the name of Michael who's been waiting to see you. Doc Michael, he says he is, and Bobby says to tell you he can't speak for his papers, but the fingerprints do match."

Justin had stopped being surprised years ago at anything Michael might do. That apparently included showing up in Cairo in the middle of the war. He already had a note to the fact Mike had. A memo handed to him by his secretary when he walked in. Justin underscored the note he had already written on the memo. "Thank you," Justin said. "Joe will set you and Holly up with a decent pack radio. Stay close to it. Holly's all right as second radio, but I rather it was you."

"Aye," Nellie assured, and left.

"Ruddy bastard," Justin picked up the phone for Bobby.

"Got my message?" Bobby answered no humor in his voice or question.

"Got it," Justin said. "Pull Mulrooney's file and we'll look over what you've got. Seen the helmet, I take it. Out of character for Nel, completely. Fellow's a tease apparently, not quite as shy with Nel as he appears around others, a flatterer for some reason, likely his own, possibly for any number of reasons including Mata Hari. Want to know now."

"Aye, I've got it," Bobby assured. *"Anything else?"*

He meant Mike. "Yes," Justin said, "see what's out on the wire, and then we'll talk. Might be something out there of interest we should know about first."

"On it," Bobby said. *"The Doc what have you wondering about Mata Hari?"*

"Yes, well, Mulrooney's the wrong kind of blond to get anywhere near Mike," Justin said, "so no. That secretary's more his type. Told Joe earlier for you to get rid of her. Now, do it. Get her out of here," he crumbled the note into a ball. "Drown her in the damn Nile. I don't care what you do. We'll have Joe cover the room and see what Mike has to say, if anything, before we shut things down."

"All right."

"Let me know if you find anything or not before sending Mike up."

"Aye," Bobby said.

"Sons of bitches. " Justin hung up and lit his pipe, setting the damn memo ablaze while he was at it, and that took care of that.

Michael looked nervous, trying hard not to be when he walked in. That was a little surprising alongside everything else that was routine. The silk white suit, straw hat, his penchant for alcohol showing a little more on his face, tanned, with lines around his eyes, Mike was two years older than Justin, always managing to look ten years younger, not any more. Mike looked his age, yet to act it though. It had been two years or more, since they had seen each other. Justin hadn't made Joe's memorial, something to do with the war. Mike made it, of course. Flew in from Cuba, claimed to have, and probably had, so what was putting in an appearance in Cairo by comparison to making it through the bombardment of Britain? Not much. Nothing was much with Michael. Not even the war. Least of all the war until it suited his fancy, which it apparently had a month or so ago per Bobby's preliminary report, until the bottle took over.

America, Mike's home town, slow to enter the fight until Japan hadn't been quite as relaxed in coaxing its limited number of physicists back from foreign shores for the green hills of home. Two years and counting since Washington first made the call to gather 'round the flag, with Mike one of the last holdouts. But that would change. Six months at best, was Justin's guess, and Michael would be looking at becoming official government property whether he wanted to or not.

"Yeah, well, who the fuck are you supposed to be?" Michael got down to basics in his assessment of Justin. One look over Rip Van Chuckles sitting there in black face, shorts up his ass, and not much else, was all it took. "It ain't Christmas, so it's got to be Halloween."

"Yes, well, could ask the same of you … *Rocky*," Justin read over Michael's "official" letters of introduction signed by *MGM*.

"'*Angels with Dirty Faces*'," Michael pointed. "One of the best damn films Cagney's made. And try fucking *Warner Brothers*, OK? Jack and the others, what's-their-names, can never think of the other ones' names."

"Wouldn't know." Justin tossed the papers in the general direction of the rest of Michael's belongings surrounding him. "No offense to you or your Mr. Cagney."

"Hey," Michael said. "You think I don't have more? I've got more."

"Yes." No doubt, introducing Michael as *Bugs Bunny*. Another of his favorite characters, if Justin remembered correctly.

"Uh, huh," Michael said. "You mean kinda like you and Mr. Hyde?"

"Yes," Justin gave a nod toward a chair parked not too far to the right. "It's all right, Mike, have a seat. Long way to come just to say hi. Sure you're here for a reason, so let's have it. Word on the street is you're looking at twenty years to life in Leavenworth this time if they don't hang you. Something to do with the Manhattan Project being rather big to think you can just walk off."

"Yeah, well, the word is wrong," Michael kicked the chair up a little closer, but did not sit down. "I didn't walk, I ran. First, unless you consider four guys sitting around scratching their asses a project, it ain't a project, nor will it be for some time. Second, it's got about as much to do with New York as you do, and third, they're looking to make bombs, Chuck, not a better bubble gum. If I screw up and drop one of those, no one will have to tell you, you'll hear it from here."

"Yes, well, there's a way around that," Justin lit his pipe and leaned back. "Get back on the wagon."

"Wrong again," Michael eyed the pile of his stuff that looked remarkably like the stuff he had packed in his duffel bag before someone took it all out. "First I've got to be on the wagon to fall off. Second ..."

"You don't want to," Justin retrieved the Scotch and a glass from his desk, setting it down. "Ten minutes, Mike, and then it's my turn. I'm on a clock, you know."

Hey, Michael could leave now. He wasn't chained. Not to anybody or anything, not there. "That it?" he indicated the rot-gut.

"That's it," Justin said.

"You always were a cheap son-of-a-bitch," Michael dug in his pocket for a cigarette. "I suppose there's a water shortage here as well."

"Is," Justin said.

"Explains the smell," Michael poured himself a double dose though something told him he could drink the bottle and it wouldn't make life any better, or easier. "Not for nothing, but there was a river around here the last time I was in town, pretty big one. Push comes to shove, you take what you can get, know what I mean?"

"Maybe tomorrow," Justin checked his watch.

"Explains why she keeps the door shut," Michael ignored the time check, downing his Scotch with a flick of his head toward the blonde bombshell who sat outside looking suspiciously like the celluloid doll he had met downstairs. "That's a looker, by the way. Don't know how the hell you managed it, and something tells me I'll up, Chuck, if you tell me, so don't."

"Five minutes left, Mike," Justin nodded.

"Fuck you," Michael poured himself another with an eye on his duffle. "I sat around fucking nine hours waiting for you."

"Three maybe," Justin agreed. "Just about zero-nine, now. Nellie said you came in around six."

"Nellie," Michael said. "That the big one with the red hair?"

"Is," Justin acknowledged.

"Outdid yourself with him," Michael assured. "A turnip's got a bigger frontal lobe."

"Yes, well, you trawl the pubs, Mike, I trawl the jails," Justin reached for the Scotch to put it away. "Some of the fellows can be pretty rough at first. Need a crew boss, not a shoulder to cry on—"

"Cry this!" Michael drained half his drink, firing the rest at Justin followed by a pair of underwear. "Those are my fucking shorts!"

"That they are," Justin calmly plucked them from his shoulder, opting to wipe his face with one of Michael's shirts instead.

"Yeah, well, who the fuck are you to tell some geek to clean my ass with his nails?" Michael insisted. "What the hell did you think I would be carrying in there?"

"I don't know, Mike," Justin agreed, "what were you carrying in there?"

"Shit!" Michael assured. "And I should have fucking given it to him."

"Yes, well ... " Justin relit his pipe with a nod for the door where the secretary sat outside waiting to be relieved as soon as Bobby got off his duff and took care of it. "Think you could tone it down a little?"

"Tone this!" Michael grabbed his groin. "Fuck her along with you. How would you like someone's fingers rammed up your ass? You're a piece of work, Chuck, you know that? A real piece of work." He sat down with a snatch for the Scotch.

"Said cool it, Mike," Justin picked up the phone to ring Joe who answered with a laugh, knowing what the Maj wanted and it was for Bobby to get his ass upstairs and get rid of the dame.

The phone on Joe's end was a radio console, a behemoth, the size of one of the walls down in the dungeon of the building, the heart of Justin's command. Deep below ground where the air was cool, moist, and loud with the sound of jackhammers drilling into the building's granite footprint and frame, extending the bunker a hundred yards out under the street, and what would eventually be quarters for Justin and his staff when completed. A series of cell-like rooms, comfortably sized. Right now, they all lived together dormitory style in the main area about half the size of a football field. Joe was luckier than most in that he got to spend at least half of his time with his radio, walled off from the construction by a haphazard collection of doors, sound panels, and blankets when they ran out of anything else, to protect the sensitive equipment.

The dirt, dust, and noise still managed to find its way in however, as dirt, dust, and noise does, but Joe just wore a full headset so he could hear, and maintain an acceptable level of confidentiality by not having to scream. If someone wanted him, they could always call him on the radio or tap him on the shoulder. Usually it was Bobby quick to move his workshop of gadgets and guns into Joe's space. They got along fine though. Joe, happy for the company as long as he had room for his pinups and barbells, Bobby, able to tune out Joe's "need to unload" that could have Joe going on for hours before he took a breath.

Joe felt the need somewhat more frequently than Bobby might secretly appreciate, but they still got along fine. Even Justin occasionally wandered down from his office to visit their homey little setup to eye the pinups and the barbells, poke over Bobby's workbench, and share a beer, which Joe usually managed to have handy. When Joe couldn't, it was because he was down to his last dime with three weeks to go because he had gambled it all away, or spent it on other necessities such as dancing and girls. Justin and Bobby were generous however, kicking in with their fair share, and in return, living vicariously through Joe enjoying his exploits as much as he enjoyed them.

"Just cost one of us half a buck," Joe's hearty laugh cackled in answer to Justin's call before Justin had a chance to say anything. That was all right because Justin wasn't anticipating on having to say much. Joe was covering the room as instructed, listening to every word, the tape running, his feet propped up on the console of the radio, a bottle of water in his hand. "Figured you'd be hollering for help before long, but Bobby says, nah ..." he winked at Bobby keeping him company, poking through his assortment of toys like an old elf, looking for something to do now that Jeff had left the roost on his first overnight outing. "You just remembered Laur and want her out of here."

"That's right, lad," Bobby nodded. "That's what I said, and it's unchanged from what I said before. He can do it himself, too, if he wants it done. Nothing wrong with that lass. Just doing her job. Should leave her alone and let her do it. Tell him I said that. Go on, tell him."

"*Yes, well,*" Justin replied in Joe's ear, keeping it simple, and presuming *Laur* was the latest secretary, "*that sounds about right.*"

"Yeah, OK, we're on it," Joe assured with a wave at Bobby to keep it down before the Maj heard him. "Or at least Bobby is. She's out of here. On his way. Five minutes tops. Consider it done."

"Aye, I'm on it," Bobby promised in chorus, not moving much, for that matter, not moving at all, just sitting there, ignoring the inevitable for as long as he could.

"So, um ..." Joe grinned into the hand receiver trying to picture Justin all stiff-lipped and dignified trying not to shrink from every other *fuck* thrown at him by some guy named Doc. "Doing OK there otherwise? Need a hand with anything else?"

"*Yes, well,*" Justin said, "*no.*"

"Suit yourself," Joe clicked off with a reminder for Bobby. "Says he wants Laur out of here."

"I know what he said," Bobby assured. "And that's four bits, please. Told you that was what he wanted, and he did. He's getting better at checking up, too. Lass didn't even make three hours today. Pretty soon he'll be meeting her at the door with a damn gun since he knows neither of us will be; he's wise to us, lad, wise to us."

"Yeah, well, don't hurry on my account," Joe tossed him the change and straightened up, sending the Maj's office to the speakers while he checked a few other channels to see what else might be going on in the world. "I'm in no hurry to see her leave. Just saying that's twice he's told you."

"Aye, and he can tell me twice more, too," Bobby groaned at Michael's colorful nasal rant filling the room at some ear-splitting decibel worse than any jackhammer. "Don't think so, lad. Shut it down. That's confidential."

"Nice try," Joe tried not to laugh as Bobby clicked off the speakers. "But you cleared the place out, remember? Nobody here but us chickens, so don't worry about it. I'm on a schedule here, too, you know. Got work to do."

"Got more work if I break it," Bobby threatened. "Sorry, lad, but what you've got to do is to sit there and listen for however long it takes. Nothing else you have to do you can't do later."

"You mean like getting rid of Laur?" Joe grinned.

"I'll escort the lass out of here when I get around to it," Bobby assured. "Not my arse or me you have to worry about. Fifty laps, I'm telling you for that crack about lending him a hand with the Doc. Four bits says you're looking at fifty laps, and then only if he's feeling generous."

"Nah, twenty-five," Joe said, "maybe, at most. He's got a sense of humor, and besides, it's hot out there."

"Aye, well, you keep dreaming," Bobby said.

"Yeah, he is a pistol, isn't he?" Joe agreed.

"Who?" Bobby said. "The Doc? Right. Pistol," he sputtered. "More like a pain in the arse is what he is. Always has been."

"Oh, yeah?" Joe said. "Why? You know him?"

"No," Bobby was happy to say, and could have lived without meeting him now. "Of him, of course. And right about him, I can tell you, Justin is."

"Nah, he's harmless," Joe promised. "Grew up with guys like that, you know? Six to every street corner. Oh, yeah," if he closed his eyes right now between the dust and the smells and the Doc in the background he couldn't tell he wasn't home. "Just kind of surprising the Maj knows him."

"Oh?" Bobby said. "Why so?"

"I don't know," Joe shrugged. "Just kind of surprising that's all."

"Well, he knows us, lad," Bobby nodded, "remember that. He's not some snob, if that's what you're saying."

"No," Joe said. "Saying it's kind of surprising. Guys like that, kind of low on class—what?" he asked. "You saying we don't have class?"

"No, I'm saying," Bobby tapped on the console, "pay attention to what you're supposed to be doing. Fellow's not harmless, capable of anything."

"Yeah, well, school's out," Joe nodded, "remember? And I passed, long ago. Been covering the room—what, like a month, right? Got to be a month, at least. Listening to some jerk for an hour as some sort of final exam isn't going to change that. Because ... yeah, OK, the guy's a jerk," he agreed, "calling himself *Bugs Bunny*, and, yeah, yakking about bombs like a show off. He's a big mouth. Thinks he should be bigger than he is. I'm telling you," he said, "I know these guys, grew up with them. Wouldn't want to be in a bar with him, heck no, apt to find myself in trouble, picking up daisies because he decided to mouth off to the wrong guy." He settled back in his seat listening and paying attention like he was told to do. "The Maj is a big boy, he can handle him. If he can't, well then, heck, probably I should be in there with him, right? Instead of sitting here listening, keeping an *ear* on things." Joe was quiet for a few seconds. "Yeah, OK," he said finally, "I surrender, what is this crap about bombs? He serious?"

"No," Bobby passed it off. "Just checking the boundaries. See how far he can go. It's all right. Justin can take care of himself, you're right. What he can't do, is pick his family. No one can."

"Huh?" Joe said.

"That's his family, lad. Doesn't share it with many. Doesn't share it at all," Bobby acknowledged. "Be stupid if he did. Still likes an ear kept on things, though. Usually it's me sitting there ... Aye, always it's me," he agreed. "Right now it's you, though, and it's about as confidential as it can get. Remember that, lad. Don't remember, and he will kill you. Trust me, he will kill you."

"Get out of town," Joe stared at the console. "That's his family?"

"Aye," Bobby chuckled slightly at Joe sitting there at a loss for words for a change, possibly for the first time in his life. "Well, don't take it to heart, lad," he said. "Relax. Clearly, he trusts you. That's the point. I'm getting old, lad, can't sit there like I used to—especially through that ballyhoo," his eyes rolled. "Needs someone who can, when he needs them. Not often, I can assure you. Once in a blue moon, if that—lad," he clouted Joe's arm. "You still with us? Not going to have to talk with him about it, if that's what you're worried about. He doesn't talk to anyone save for me, if there's something he feels he needs to talk about, rare unto itself."

"Huh?" Joe's head turned to him.

Bobby smiled. "Saying you're not going to have to talk with Justin, lad."

"What?" Joe said. "No," he shook his head, "I wasn't thinking that—I mean, heck, guy wants to talk, let him talk. I'm just saying— wow," he whistled at the console, "the Maj's family. Wouldn't have thought that."

"Oh?" Bobby said.

"Well, no," Joe said. "I don't know."

"Not what you expected," Bobby nodded.

"Heck no."

"Aye," Bobby nodded. "It's all right. That's it, though."

"No kidding," Joe said. "What is he? I mean," he said as Bobby looked at him. "He sounds like ... I don't know, *me*? You know, American."

"Oh," Bobby said. "Well, aye, he is. Italian, I believe. Like you."

"Yeah, well, that figures," Joe scoffed with a laugh. "Christ, I probably did see him on a street corner. What's he look like?"

"What?" Bobby was frowning slightly, stretching for the second headset. "Oh, I don't know what he looks like, lad. Looks like what he sounds like ..."

"No, that's OK, I got it," Joe got the headset for him. "I'm cool though, don't worry about it. Mum's the word."

"No, I know that, lad, I know," Bobby agreed. "Just a little curious myself, have to admit. Hope nothing's happened to any of them," he frowned again slightly as the Doc came in clear.

"Oh, yeah?" Joe grinned. "You mean there's more of them?"

"Well, not of him," Bobby assured. "God help me. Only one of him. But there's a few of them, aye, a few ..." he was still frowning. "Old fellow is whom I'm thinking about. Got to be ... oh, I don't know, seventy? Eighty? Not his old man," he advised. "No, Justin's old man is dead. Mother as well. They'll get into that, aye," he nodded. "You'll here that. The Doc'll be bringing that up before long if he hasn't already."

"Um ... no," Joe said. "No, I don't think so."

"Aye, well, pay attention, lad," Bobby reminded. "That's even more the point."

"Yeah, I am. I am. I got it. It's OK. Go on. Get Laur out of here. I'll probably still be here when you get back; oh, yeah," he grinned at the Doc going on and on. "Definitely will be here. I need help, I'll holler, and if the Maj needs me, well, I'll hear him."

"I'm going, I'm going," Bobby said. "Justin can take care of that, too, if he really wanted to. Get that Peterson on the blower and tell him right out instead of leaving you and me to do his dirty work. Lad's a coward. You should know that if you haven't figured it out. Damn coward when it comes to the ladies. Like they're going to bite him or something. Take his head off and hand it back to him ..." The Doc was talking about something now that sounded like trouble, definitely sounded like trouble.

Chapter Twenty

"It's called security, Mike." Justin hung up the phone after saying a fat lot of nothing, which meant either the place was wired, or he liked to pretend it was. "Some of us care about that. Bobby and Nel don't know you—or *Rocky Sullivan*," he granted, "from Adam."

"Bobby, huh?" Michael would bet his mother's uncle he was being broadcasted live and in stereo over a loud speaker somewhere. "That the fat one with the same first and last name?"

"Yes," Justin said between puffs on his pipe-load of camel manure. "And, quite, I outdid myself with Bobby, also."

"Wrong," Michael said. "You outdid yourself with the blue-haired fairy."

Justin glanced at the door, seeming to remember Peterson's latest Mistress of Public Relations was a blonde.

"Fairy," Michael helped him out, "being the operative word."

"Oh," Justin said. "Yes. Jeff. Yes, well, Jeff ..." he said.

"Is a fucking faggot," Michael assured. "He's a fucking faggot."

Meaning a homosexual, not a ball of meat. Justin understood without having to ring Joe for a translation. "Your point?" he asked, but only because Joseph Lee had been homosexual. Though that hadn't stopped Joe from giving his life for his country, any more than it had precluded him from being Justin's or Michael's friend for thirty years, though Justin suspected it was occasionally to Michael's chagrin.

"Nothing," Michael's nervousness seemed to increase, lighting a cigarette with the one he was smoking. "Got a few of them where I come from, too."

"Yes, well, if that's it ..." Justin reached for the Scotch, on the alert that time, but Michael's glass was dry. "Your ten minutes are up, Mike."

"No, that's not it!" Michael was up with a snap and a grab for the bottle, slamming it down on the desk. "Keep your fucking shirt on!" He got up to walk around a while, critique the joint while he smoked his cigarette. He didn't like the place, of course, any more than he liked the fellows. Justin let Michael go on another ten minutes or so of a lot of jabber and not much else, until he had to call it quits.

"Mike ... " Justin said.

"Look!" Michael turned around. "I've got a headline that reads a friend of mine's been missing for a couple of days ..."

Whoa. Down in the dungeon Joe blinked at Bobby. "Think we've got something here?"

"Aye ... maybe," Bobby nodded, "maybe ..." listening intently like you couldn't hear the Doc across the room through the headphones. "Put one of those corks you're always talking about in your mouth, and get me that report."

"Um ... report ..." Joe looked around.

"The one I pulled on him, lad," Bobby said. "Third file, top drawer, it's right there; *Michael Delegianis.* Dr. Michael Delegianis."

"Um ... yup, got it!" Joe was already up and rummaging through the drawers, finding it under *A,* rather than *D,* since Bobby being Bobby just stuck it in the front where he could find it. "A for asshole!"

"Just give it to me," Bobby insisted.

"Ya got it!" Joe shoved it in his hand, leaning over his shoulder, helping him dissect it. "But there's nothing here, unless you're going to tell me it's in code or something."

"Said cork it, lad," Bobby reminded, trying to read three pages in Olympic time. "If someone else has gone missing from that project of his we'd know."

"Project?" Joe said.

"Project," Bobby was up and heading for the Telex faster than Joe had ever seen him move. "That Manhattan business's no joke, lad, no joke, wish it was."

"Huh?" Joe said. "Oh, yeah, right, got it, got it," he remembered what the Doc had said. "And, I didn't think it was a joke ..." Joe snatched up his headset because, wow, *hello!* One of them really should be listening. "Thought it was ... don't know ... like a dame, or something. Him just trying to be clever. You know, 'Manhattan project'? Heck, was thinking of using it myself ..."

"Atomic bombs," Bobby nodded, typing away. "What, he's talking about, lad, atomic-powered bombs," he assured Joe suddenly gone quiet again. "It's what he is. A physicist."

"Yeah, I got it," Joe assured, his headset clapped to his ear. "Talking about some Colonel ... fuck!" he snapped his fingers in excitement, dropped the headset, hit the speakers so they could listen, and headed back to the cabinets. "I know where that is!"

"Lad!" Bobby reminded as Michael blared out into the room.

"It's OK," Joe assured, "there's no one here remember ... there's a report. I saw the frigging report, a couple of weeks ago ... fuck!" he kicked the drawer closed, yanking open another, as Bobby glanced at the console. "Goddamn Jeff ..."

"Jeff?" Bobby's head snapped up.

"Yeah, I had him helping me ..." Joe nodded.

"Who says?" Bobby demanded.

"I sez," Joe assured. "It's OK, don't sweat it. Nothing important. Just the routine crap that comes in—Christ!" he slammed that drawer closed, too, hunting through a third. "If the Maj just let Laur do her goddamn job ... if I explained the goddamn system to Jeff a hundred times ..."

"Lad!" Bobby insisted.

"I got it, I got it!" Joe yanked it out. "Siwa, February 21st ... what I fucking tell you, huh?" he said, handing it over. "What I fucking tell you?"

"Eighteenth, actually," Bobby scanned it, and it was pretty basic, though he wouldn't go as far as calling it routine. It still wasn't much though, save for them being Americans. "On or about."

"Yeah," Joe nodded, "yeah. So, um ... what's this about bombs?" he took a breath. Christ, he was so hepped up, he was almost gasping. "You on the level?"

"Don't know what you mean, 'on the level'," Bobby started typing again. "No bomb out there, if that's what you're worried about."

"No, I know that," Joe assured. "Hell, yeah, heck I know that. I'm just saying what's going on? What do you think is going on?"

"Seeing if we can find out," Bobby nodded. "What's that fellow's name again?"

"Um ... McDowell," Joe read. "Yeah, McDowell. Two *L*'s. Want me to do that?"

"I got it," Bobby assured. "I got it."

"Not that that means anything to you," Michael drank his drink.

"Should it?" Justin sat back easily in his chair waiting for the bomb to drop, hopefully not on them.

Michael ignored him, staring into space. "I mean it's like I was sitting in Manhattan, see ..."

New York USA
February 1942
"Mike ..." Lucky Seven pried himself away from the lady in the blue dress to answer the telephone before it tolled its final bell. "Mike!" he hollered like the neighborhood he was raised in instead of the uptown Park Avenue digs he was living in now with the linen shades and white deco charm.

"Keep your shirt on." Michael emerged from the can. A place he always seemed to be going into or coming out of at a crucial moment in his life. "I'm trying to take a fucking leak. Can't a guy take a fucking leak without someone yelling fire?"

"It's England," Lucky extended the phone.

"England?" Michael stared at the receiver. "New or old?" Though he knew, yeah, he knew which it was. The same as he knew who and why, and, Jesus fucking Christ what had she gotten herself into now?

"I don't know," Lucky shrugged, which was why he was called *Lucky* since he didn't have a brain in his head.

"Give me the frigging phone," Michael grabbed it. "And get her the hell out of here, what do you think this is? A motel?"

"We're going to dinner," Lucky reminded.

"Yeah, *we're* going to dinner," Michael nodded. "Nix on the Queen of Washington Heights—hello?" he answered the call.

"Oh, well, now, not trying to rain on anyone's parade," the old man Gramps chuckled in between bites of static and Michael's heart sank.

"Nah, it's not raining," Michael dragged the phone over to the bar, looking for a little fortification, his brain working overtime on what to say, what not to say, how to get out of this one with his hide. "Kind of late for you though, isn't it?" he checked his watch that appeared to have stopped in sync with his heart. "Like two o'clock?"

"*About,*" Evelyn agreed. "*Yes, just about.*"

"Yeah, well, before you read me the riot act for being here and not there," Michael decided to go for broke, but only because he was caught without a prayer. "I can explain ..."

"*Oh, no.*" Evelyn laughed so hard Michael thought the old guy would pop a vessel, convinced Gramps had popped one with the next breath he took. "*No, not necessary, not at all. I understand, yes, that I do. I understand completely. Called, as a matter-of-fact, to tell you that. Did. That I did.*"

"Oh, yeah?" Michael stopped beating the daylights out of his martini to check under the bar for a pipe bomb complete with fuse. "What, have you been hitting the sauce? Got the place wired to explode? Or have you figured out we're at war?" Not personally, of course, but Gramps knew what he meant.

Did. That Evelyn did. "*Well, now that's the point, isn't it?*" he agreed. "*And that's all right, is. Not going to say I told you so. No, not going to say that.*"

"Um ... " Michael wiped his chin. "Yeah, OK, what's the point? Said like three things. Sauce, bomb, war. Which is the point? You listening, Gramps? We've got kind of a bad connection on this end, or you do. I'm not following you."

"*You just give Joanna my love,*" Evelyn suggested, "*and go out to that dinner of yours. After all,*" he said, "*that is the point, now, isn't it? Yes, that it is,*" he assured. "*Get out. Test her wings, live a little. And,*" he said, while Michael tried to figure out just what the hell he was talking about, "*coming up on a rather ... well, don't want to say special,*" he clarified. "*Nothing special about it. But, it is an anniversary, call it what you will. Ten years. Yes, that it is, ten years.*"

"Huh?" Michael said.

"*So you and Joanna just go to that dinner of yours,*" Evelyn said again, and that time it registered, at least what he said. "*Don't let me keep you.*"

"Joanna?" Michael stared at the telephone.

"*She there?*" Evelyn asked a touch wistfully, missing her, of course he did, especially now that she was six-thousand miles away, not just off in London where if he missed her too much he could just get in the car and drive to see her for himself. The States? Yes, well, the States was something else entirely, even for him, what with the war. Hard enough to get a damn call through, yes, that it was, difficult enough.

"Joanna?" Michael repeated, his heart—fuck pound, it was hammering like a snare drum in his chest. "What? You forget you dialed zero or something? I'm in New York, Gramps."

"*Yes, well, you be sure to tell her everything's fine, it's fine,*" Evelyn said, nodded actually, on his end.

"Yeah, it's great," Michael agreed impatiently. "Whoa. Talk to me, Gramps, I'm losing you over here. Where ... wow," he cleared his head, untying his tongue while he was at it. "Where the fuck else would she be?"

"*Exactly,*" Evelyn chuckled and Michael almost passed out, he did, almost collapsed, his elbow missing the edge of the bar as he sat down, the telephone more or less frozen in his hand.

"*And I would have rung sooner ...*" the old man was saying, "*But, well, not easy even for me nowadays and I didn't want to be a bother, after all, she is with you ...*"

"She's in the can," Michael shook his head not quite sure why he said that or where he even came up with it. "She went downstairs for ice cream, we're having a fucking heat wave. I mean ... whoa," he didn't know what he meant, or even where to begin.

"*So see you?*" Evelyn checked in his own way, subtly, just when she might be coming back? "*In a few more weeks?*"

"Why?" Michael said, barely. "Why, how long has it—FUCK!" he caught himself, trying again evenly. "How the fuck long has it been since we've seen you? An hour? Couple of days? A week? A fucking month of Sundays? Gramps!" he said, trying to wrack his brains and figure out when the last time it was he had talked to Joanna— yesterday. He was sure it had been yesterday. Maybe the day before.

"*You just go to that dinner of yours,*" Evelyn reassured one last time, and Ma Bell took care of the rest.

"Fuck," Michael sat there with the telephone dangling in his hand. "I mean, fuck!" he slammed it down to pick it up dial furiously and slam it down again.

That was two weeks ago, count them, almost three and Michael could still see Lucky and his round-eyed broad staring at him like nobody ever misplaced a kid before in their life. Like nobody ever got up in the morning and didn't have somebody they had when they went to bed the night before.

Cairo
March 9
"Mahlon," Michael said dully to Justin almost three weeks later in Cairo after combing the goddamn planet for Joanna and coming up short every time. "You have the fucking report, Chuck," he reminded.

"Did you read the goddamn report?" he asked. "Mahlon McDowell. Colonel. USA."

"Yes ..." Justin recalled hearing something about a Yank Colonel now that Michael filled in a few details. "That's a couple of weeks ago, Mike, at least. Doubt if he's MIA. They brought his driver in."

"Aide," Michael said. "Paul Reid was his aide."

"Wouldn't know," Justin apologized. "Sorry, didn't realize you knew him."

"Kind of," Michael said. "Sort of. He's an engineer."

"Yes," Justin assumed he'd be something like that, though one shouldn't ever assume. Weren't many Yanks here yet who weren't engineers or geologists, swelling the ranks of those already looking for the oil everyone knew had to be out there. "Bit out of your line of work, isn't it?"

"League," Michael said. "Bit out of my league. Career. Big time. Like you."

"Heavy water then," Justin agreed. Those experiments also pretty much standard nowadays, too, North Africa no exception to the rule. "Still, if what you're doing out here is looking for answers, I can see what I can find out, though I suspect you'll find it's pretty cut and dried—"

"Red's missing," Michael interjected, and downstairs Joe's head snapped up from reading the Telex. "Red. You know, Joanna? Your

sister? She was with him. I'm pretty sure she was with him ..." he
frowned while Justin just sat there his eyes set, concentrating.

"*Holy fucking shit* ..." down in the dungeon Joe broke with a
whistle and was gone, just gone, across the room and gone before
Bobby could bark at him to get on it, he was yelling, "I'm on it! I'm
on it!" Screw the elevator, he was up the stairs, all of them, breaking
the quarter mile record as he rounded the corner to grab Scarecrow
by his collar, bust through the doors, skid for Laura and get her the
hell out of there before someone said something they shouldn't say,
and she overheard them. He wasn't in time entirely, but he tried,
gave it his best.

"Christ, Chuck," Michael stared bleary-eyed back at Justin. "I don't
fucking know. She was supposed to be with him. I've been killing
myself for, yeah, weeks, trying to find out if she was still with him.
Hoping to God she wasn't or that she's not ...

"But, you see," he squinted through the tears starting to burn,
"it's kind of like this. If she's not with him, I don't know where the
hell she is because I can't find her. I cannot find her. I do not have a
clue."

Chapter Twenty-One

The Fezzan
March 9

SS Major Hanse Weiheber sat comfortably cool in his inappropriate desert attire. His fingers curled around the first of his remaining three cigarettes, his men huddled together for warmth, Faust's wet face smeared with evidence of his gluttony having consumed enough water for the six of them. They reached the first of the waterholes by starlight. Twice as long as it should have taken them if they knew the way, the petrol exhausted three hundred meters short. The mirage of a sparkling lake in the near distance, while not a lake, but a lonely puddle, also wasn't an illusion. It had water. Wet, cool, water. They fell to fate, divine intervention, an example of the enduring strength and destiny of the Reich—they got lucky, gambled, and guessed, finding their earlier tracks and retracing them slowly as they faded, swept away by the light breeze turning stiff and frigid, threatening to bury the abandoned car by dawn as the sun set.

"It makes no sense, Faust, it makes none," Weiheber gazed up into the romantic celestial lights known as *Bernice's Hair*. Three weeks ago, he was in Tunis, gazing down on her dull grey streets, watching a sleek black staff car snake its way along the cobbled stones to turn and park leisurely at the curb. Someone was in town. Someone he did not know, not then. By now, he had his file. Danzig. SS Hauptmann Eric Danzig of the Propaganda Ministry, and Weiheber couldn't be any more interested in Hauptmann Danzig than he was, extremely interested, Hauptmann Danzig second to only a few.

"What is this, Herr Major?" Faust requested.

"What?" Weiheber looked at him. "Did you say what, Faust?" What did Faust think made no sense? Who?

"Hauptmann Reineke, of course, Hauptmann Reineke. Indeed," Weiheber smiled coyly. The enigmatic Hauptmann Reineke, pretty to look at, difficult to control. Weiheber hadn't noticed too much more than that ... and yet? "There has to be, Faust," he nodded, "there has to be much more to Hauptmann Reineke."

Weiheber was a predator, an animal stalking its prey. The bungled Russian plot to lure some frightened Italian physicist from his hiding place brought Weiheber into Afrika to secure the scientist for the Reich. It was his chance for another pin for his cushion of medals, perhaps the brightest of all. His name elevated to that of Heydrich's, Himmler's prized pet.

There was no scientist, only some *child* in his place. The agent Reiss hired to infiltrate the Russians reported the operation had been so poorly managed as to allow the scientist to escape, leaving his daughter to make her way to Gibraltar with his friends.

Siwa

February 1942

"Daughter," Weiheber grasped the girl's dangling head by the chin. She was unconscious or perhaps simply pretending. Maybe or maybe not. "Really. Does this look like a daughter to you, Faust?"

"That is the report, Herr Major," Faust nodded efficiently.

"Report?" Weiheber asked amused. "Whose report, Faust? Whose report?"

The English aide was as dead as the girl pretended to be, killed as the jeep unexpectedly overturned, much to the surprise and annoyance of the Russian Reiss who muttered *"Shit,"* between his clenched teeth. Herr Colonel, an American Weiheber understood him to be, bleeding to death, trying not to, from the stump of his severed hand.

"Herr Oberleutnant," Faust glanced apprehensively at the impatient Reiss.

"Really," Weiheber smiled at Reiss. "She is English."

"So what?" Reiss retorted. "So she is English. The scientist will come whether his daughter is English, or what she is—Hierher!" he bent down and severed the aide's head, tossing it to her. "Now, talk," he threatened, grasping her hair tightly as she tried to attack him and missed to Weiheber's continued amusement. "Where is your father? Who are your contacts? Where are they?"

"Spies," Weiheber confidently assured Faust. "Spies."

"Spies, Herr Major?" Faust hesitated.

"Of course," Weiheber looked at him surprised to learn Faust could not see this for himself. "What else, Faust, what else?"

"Spies," Faust glanced at Reiss.

"Well, it is either that," Weiheber chuckled, "or the Russian's story of a scientist at hand is true. Do you see a scientist, Faust?"

"Well, no, Herr Major ..." Faust agreed.

"Perhaps both," Weiheber patted him consolingly. "Perhaps these are the contacts, Reiss seeks, eh? Have you thought of that? He follows them here while the scientist flees. A brilliant plan if it works, Faust, a brilliant plan if it works." Which, apparently it had.

"Of course," Faust sighed relieved. "Yes. That is brilliant of you, Herr Major ... but ..." he hesitated again, "Do you think the scientist will come, Herr Major, as Reiss maintains?"

For his heartwarming reunion with his *daughter* at some later place, some later date, and the last of their exodus to America? "Who knows, Faust," Weiheber shrugged. "Who knows. That is what we have Reiss for. Let him find out."

"Reiss ..." Faust glanced apprehensively again at the agent. "He is Russian, Herr Major ..." he reminded needlessly. "I do not think it is wise to leave him alone ..."

"No, but he thinks we have the daughter," Weiheber nodded. "Faust, he thinks."

"And we don't," Faust eyed him. "We really don't."

"No," Weiheber chuckled. "No. We have his contacts, Faust, perhaps, we have his spies. But, it is all right. It is all right," he reassured him consolingly again, "we will take the *daughter* with us so if Reiss strays, he won't stray far, as he works to find ... to find ..." he snapped his fingers trying to remember what it was Reiss claimed he needed to find.

"The scientist?" Faust said.

"Yes, Faust. But, no, the contacts, Faust. The contacts."

"Of course, Herr Major," Faust beamed. "Excellent. We will return to Tripoli immediately."

"Tripoli?" Weiheber looked at him.

"And wait, Herr Major," Faust nodded. "We will wait for ... *Reiss,*" he sneered at Jeff, "to finish his job."

"We will wait, Faust," Weiheber agreed, "but not in Tripoli."

"Berlin," Faust understood. "Very important," he tried not to stress too hard, "if the spies have information on the scientist, as we believe."

"Know, Faust," Weiheber nodded, "as we know."

"Yes," Faust beamed.

"And we will wait, Faust," Weiheber agreed, "in the Fezzan."

"The Fezzan?" Faust blinked. "Sebha?"

"One would think," Weiheber chuckled. "Yes, one would think that, wouldn't one?" he agreed. "But we know differently, don't we, Faust?"

The Fezzan

March 9

"Don't we?" Weiheber looked out into the frozen heat of the desert, Reiss gone, retreating to Cairo to ingratiate himself with the English Allied the American engineer had insisted were instrumental in the scientist's flight.

The same American who insisted the scientist would be there as soon as he found out his daughter was not. Reiss believed him. Weiheber did not, any more than he believed they had some *daughter* in their possession, rather than only the scientist's contacts. But it was a good enough reason, an excellent opportunity to wait, amused by the file on Danzig that arrived to help pass the time, and then not so amused the deeper Weiheber read.

It was an exaggeration perhaps to suggest Himmler had a file on everyone. Or perhaps just easier to believe it had to be an exaggeration. Either or, Herr Himmler did have files on many. From the smallest, to the greatest, and the Ministry's entrance into Afrika on the coattails of Himmler's SS, interestingly had nothing to do with some *scientist*, but with Herr General Rommel, and the reports of insurgency otherwise known as five munitions depots.

A recent conversation with a comrade in Berlin was purely coincidental. Many a luncheon had been spent with Herr SS Oberst Hans Reineke discussing the exploits of some flamboyant son long estranged. Deposed from his rightful position as Lord and heir to a vast family fortune by a plot of his own father and only son, Colonel Reineke was an embittered, angry man, ill-tempered, and in ill health. Steadfast in wishing his son's demise, he remained steadfast in denying and defying the death that would ultimately consume him as it had consumed his father.

"It is such a romantic story, Faust," Weiheber chuckled. The gas poisoned so many of them, destroying the lungs, and the brain. The latest round of seizures bringing on a stroke, leaving Herr Reineke with a paralyzed and useless right hand at only fifty-one. Politically, however, while so many of the old found themselves replaced by the new quickly on the rise, Colonel Reineke lingered on the threshold between power and extinction, feared, if never quite respected. Known to those not familiar enough, or inclined to be afraid.

His son would qualify as one of the latter. Colonel Reineke gazed at his lost empire from afar. His overbearing father long dead, the abused and terrorized wife a prisoner of her mind, and hated son currently stationed several thousand kilometers away, while he remained sentenced to his exile and Berlin, daring only to complain.

"Interesting, don't you think, Faust?" Weiheber nodded. "Interesting." He looked up this Baron Dieter Reineke whose power extended beyond ballrooms, across continents, oceans and sand, and as Reineke would later promise, he did not like what he found. Expecting the spoils and excess so typical of wealth, Baron Reineke was a decorated Panzer Captain. The 6th Army in France, the 1st Panzer Division in North Afrika. However, in less than a year after his triumphant arrival in Tripoli, Hauptmann Reineke was relieved of his command. Something to do with battle fatigue. A complete and irreversible mental breakdown, menace to himself and his men, prone to violence and bouts of amnesia, utterly insane.

Except madmen do not break down, and Reineke was a madman with three dead officers to attest to his uninhibited violence and emotional instability. The last, his First Officer, a week before Reineke was relieved and subsequently vanished, transferred to Rear

Services and oblivion. A seemingly harsh curtain call when on all three occasions Reineke had been completely absolved of the crime, the accusations an obvious conspiracy by jealous associates. Weiheber was not so sure about that. The idea of some conspiracy tried and failed three times was as foolish as Reineke thinking he could get away with a trio of murders. Weiheber discarded Danzig's file for the biography of Baron Hauptmann Dieter Reineke, studying it. The reported disagreement with the Oberleutnant Goetz was a petty contest of wills, inappropriate on Goetz's part, and unlikely to result in murder on Reineke's, particularly since as the commander Reineke was the final authority. A madman gone insane? Weiheber looked around, beyond Africa, back into the past, and such unrestrained aggression fit well with a similar portrait of Reineke painted two years earlier in France. Of a man whose hatred of the French shone in his repeated bombardment of a village long after any return fire had quieted and of his march to plant a flag.

A very frightened soldier would tell the story of the tall, blond man who could have been one of Germany's finest sons. Of the light that stayed in Reineke's eyes, though shrapnel from an exploding land mine tore an eight-inch gash in his leg. Of the laughter it triggered because his limb remained intact while the enemies lay scattered around him. The devil himself must have chosen the arm Reineke picked up from its resting place across the torso of another. It was a child. The body whole, the head nearly severed and face destroyed. He was so small, perhaps eight or nine years old. The light in Reineke's eyes died, the laughter stopped, his hands fumbling to reconnect the pieces, make it live, and the soldier would tell how Reineke started to cry when it would not. Of a German officer rocking the mutilated corpse, telling it stories while his men collected the villagers' bodies, burying them in separate graves, markers on each, and though Oberleutnant Dieter Reineke eventually fainted from the loss of blood, his men did not dare stop before finishing their task.

Weiheber closed that chapter of Reineke's journal with fingers tapping. Danzig's file was helpful in identifying his contacts in Afrika, specifically an agent Erich, successfully installed at one of the compounds. To date, Erich's diligence had proven helpful in identifying a Colonel Alfred Schönfeld as the ranking officer in charge of the project, locally. As well as five Hauptmanns under Schönfeld's command, one of whom was Erich's commanding officer, Baron Hauptmann Dieter Reineke rising like the Phoenix, up from the ashes of oblivion and the ranks of the undead, a new First Officer at his right hand, Heinrich Thiele. Oberleutnant Thiele was an officer whose otherwise spotless record should have cast him above reproach, a hero in his own right, highly decorated marksman, one of the best. Clearly, the malignancy of these anarchists had spread deeper and faster than anyone knew, their contamination and crimes far exceeding mere mutiny. Reports from the agent Erich stationed at Reineke's compound also contained an intriguing footnote about the presence of children living freely within the top secret complex. As many as seventy-five children, and one other particularly unusual and interesting individual a French priest. Hauptmann Reineke was indefensibly and undeniably a traitor. Guilty of high treason. Giving aid, and comfort to the enemies of his country and who knew what else. Weiheber intended to find out.

"Simply a question of how, Faust," Weiheber nodded. "How." This little trip south to inspect these compounds had quickly evolved into a mission, a quest with Reineke's dramatic and defiant display of temperament. The matter of some atomic scientist relegated to the background.

"What is this?" Faust was only half-listening, his voracious appetite wetted by the water but little else, leaving him starving in his fat.

"Hauptmann Reineke, Faust," Weiheber assured, "how best to approach Hauptmann Reineke. He cannot go unchallenged. It is unthinkable."

Was it? Faust scanned the lonely world of Hell, finding it colder without food or even Mussolini's ass to console him, the salty, canned meat supplement sounding delicious right about this time. "We will prevail, Herr Major," he obediently agreed, rousing himself from the pain and rumblings of his hollow stomach, denying the madness waiting to overtake them, the water simply delaying the inevitable starvation and heat. "Hauptmann Reineke's interference with the Allied spy is temporary and meaningless. We will replace her with an agent, and when the scientist comes, he will be ours."

"You should eat something, Faust," Weiheber turned to smile into the sounds and shadows of the desert, the ghostly song of the wind moaning softly in the distance. "However irritable, Hauptmann Reineke is not a man to squander his opportunities, and neither should we. There is no scientist, Faust, as there was no daughter. Spies, yes, like Hauptmann Reineke's efforts to trap us, but instead we have trapped him."

"Eat something?" Faust frowned suddenly alert to what could not possibly be the wind in the background of the darkened desert sand unless it was attached to a motor. "What is that? Who is that?" he insisted, up on his hot, tender feet, the men also rising from the shelter of their huddled mass, angry over their death sentence and willing to fight their executioners with their bare hands.

"That?" Weiheber smiled as the lazy, drifting shadows were also suddenly awake, scurrying away from hazy orbs of light piercing the blackness, bobbing and dancing two, perhaps three feet off the ground. "Propaganda Ministry," he agreed easily as what was clearly a staff car come into view. Simply not a black one as it had been in Tunis, but desert beige with a canvas top, a standard transport vehicle carrying six men traveling alongside.

"Propaganda Ministry?" Faust gaped. "What would they be doing out here?"

"I do not know, Faust," Weiheber said. "What would they be doing anywhere ... other than their job." He raised his hands in polite surrender to the approaching victors. "Do it, Faust," he encouraged Faust to strike the traditional pose of defeat while their men stood poised in a ridiculous looking line of defense, admittedly confused themselves. "Do it, or die. For if you think he is not out there, you are wrong."

"He?" Faust raised his hands.

"Hauptmann Reineke," Weiheber assured as the car stopped, the large smiling face of an unfamiliar Korps officer filling the side window frame in friendly greeting. "Of course, Faust. Who else?"

Chapter Twenty-Two

"Ah!" Eric concurred with his driver's startled *"What the!"* as the orphaned group of Himmler's henchmen loomed suddenly in the beams of the headlights. "What *have* we here?"

"SS," the driver nodded, apparently a man with his own droll sense of humor, recognizing the stained, dusty uniforms.

"Yes, one can see that, can't one?" Eric agreed with what one could see without too much difficulty. The tried and true blue suit of the apparent ranking banana a dead giveaway to more than just its wearer's affiliation, but also his state of mind, questionable, yes, it was, right off the bat. A *lu-lu*-lulu standing like a flag out in the middle of the sand, either that or a man who was extremely, *extremely* lost. Those were the only two choices in Eric's opinion, apart from the one of who the lunatic had to be. A name crossed his mind. Weiheber. A man on his way to investigate compounds. Herr SS Major Hanse Weiheber. Eric put two and two together and came up with zero. Apparently, the Russian Reiss had told something of the truth after all, about the man's drug use or his mental state, or perhaps both.

"But that's all right," Eric beamed, though not in a manner of condoning mental illness or drug use among the elite. His gilded fatness Herr Goering, the obvious exception to those two rules as Goebbels and Hitler were to the rules of Aryan good looks.

"That's quite all right," Eric nodded, definitely in the manner of condoning the SS in general and as a whole. "After all," he smiled at his driver, "we're SS." Their telltale and random tattoos (it would be an exaggeration to suggest all SS sported a tattoo) neatly tucked and hidden away beneath their underwear. Their Wehrmacht costumes just that, costumes, as Eric's Arab garb of a few days ago had been, deceptively authentic and comfortably thin. During the day, that is, not at night. In the night, wrapped up in goat hair or some greatcoat of cotton duck, Eric froze, as he was freezing now. So the blue-suited clown perhaps had the remnants of a brain after all. Much more so than what might be apparent at first glance, particularly since during the heat of the day he could always take the jacket off.

"Shall I stop?" Eric's driver asked.

"Versus what?" Eric wondered back. "Mowing them down or passing them by?"

"Fine," the driver sighed.

"Thank you," Eric presumed his chauffeur understood which course of action was fine. "After all, it would be the courteous thing to do."

They stopped, and Eric grit his teeth, smiling into the wind and the extraordinarily cooperative group of Supermen posed in surrender, their faces as unfamiliar to him, as his was to them.

"How long have you been out here?" Eric inquired gaily, seeing no vehicle or otherwise obvious mode of transportation, for that matter any Allies, French or otherwise, and poo-pooing the idea of Weiheber and his troop having to prostrate themselves for mercy with a wave.

"Eight hours," the fat Leutnant sighed like it was a lifetime, but took Eric at his word he was friend, not foe, lowering his pudgy white hands.

Au contraire, it was apparently equivalent to a lifetime for one. "Kill them now or die yourself." Herr Blue Suit with strudel for brains jammed his mealy, scarred face in Eric's window frame, his breath thick with cigarettes, his eyes glittering, definitely in need of a fix. The aforementioned "them" the dope fiend referred to, Eric assumed as he regrouped from the assault and stench, the apparently valueless squad currently staring at their commander like Weiheber had three heads instead of none. "It would be his orders."

"Whose orders?" Eric replied more out of reflex than interest.

"Hauptmann Reineke," the Leutnant sighed again.

"Oh," Eric said. The identification meaningless and not worth pursuing, he smiled. "Well, I am Hauptmann Danzig, and these are my men—who take orders from me," he assured with a sigh himself and reach for the blue-suited arm. "Just get in the car," he encouraged roughly, before he hauled Herr Fruitcake through the window. Something Eric possibly would have done, not simply could have done, if it wasn't for the Leutnant's quick thinking grab for the door.

"Good God, man, it's freezing out there," Eric nodded. "There's more than enough room for everyone. If not, we'll—*make some!*" Eric barked at his men not exactly shoving each other out of the way to make room for their brothers piling into and on the kübelwagen and staff car without having to be asked twice. All eventually seeing their way to cutting out the comedy routine and cooperating, and Eric settled back satisfied.

"There, now isn't that better?" he proposed as Herr Major's dutiful servant carefully propped his master up on the cushioned leather seat next to Eric. "And all without having to kill even one."

"Do you have petrol?" the Leutnant asked as he climbed into the front seat to hang over the back of it like an anxious child.

"Ah ... yes ... yes ..." Eric believed they must have; they were moving, right? Right. "Enough," he agreed. "*Just* enough," he assured, "for ourselves. So let's not even bother with that."

"That?" the Leutnant said.

"The attempted hijacking of a Wehrmacht vehicle," Eric assured, "Italian though it may be. Before you even think about it, let me take a moment to clarify that would be *SS* Hauptmann Eric Danzig. As in I would be, *SS* Hauptmann Eric Danzig," Eric clarified to the numbed nut sitting aside him. "Don't let my uniform, or my style ..." his smile slid over his tongue, "mislead you ...

"As far as your squad," Eric waved. "The one I am not inclined to shoot ..." he eyed Weiheber's uniform, noticeably dirtier than the others and certainly appearing that he had recently butchered someone or something. Possibly explaining those missing two or three men (the Russian had said about six or seven and there were only four), possibly in battle, possibly for lunch. Either way, it appeared someone or something had fought back, attempted to anyway, since one of Weiheber's eyes looked blackened beneath its stain of dust and sweat. His cheek swollen and lip definitely cracked. *C'est la vie.* Eric shrugged since he also noticed there appeared to be no evidence, or should Eric say remnants, of any American or child.

"Do I really think what is widespread, Faust?" the wasted addict interrupted his euphoria and Eric to ask (or answer) a question that had not been asked by anyone. "The political independence among the leaders and troops of North Afrika? I think ..." he rested his head prepared to elaborate, or fall asleep.

"Clearly?" Eric countered with a grin, and Herr Poppy's head snapped up to eye him. "Herr ... ?" Eric inquired, though honestly wondering less about Weiheber personally than wondering where he had come from, out here in the middle of nowhere. What had happened to his car or camel or plane, unless he had walked? Eric really did not think Weiheber walked, but that was just his opinion.

"SS Major Hanse Weiheber," the Leutnant disclosed, identifying himself as SS Leutnant Günther Faust.

"Ah," Eric smiled. "Who else? Else, indeed?"

"Really," the Leutnant was fat but quick. "Do we know you?"

"Not at all. Just acknowledging the introduction, that's all," Eric assured.

Weiheber nodded, breathing after a few moments of necessary silence to remember not only who but where he was, and he was close, in the ballpark more or less. "Hauptmann Reineke is a decorated officer. A bright, however brief shining star ..." he eyed the notebook at Eric's side, good for light reading, what could Eric say? "You know," he waved for Eric's understanding. "One of those thousands who came out of France. You have read the report?"

"Ah ... this?" Eric touched the binder. "No, I'm sorry. This is a report on someone else ... the life, times, and history of someone else, I should say. Somewhat dense and lengthy."

"He's very good." Weiheber's attempted wave tired quickly, waggling his fingers, calling the binder to him.

"Hauptmann Reineke?" Eric held onto the almanac. "In what regard?"

"Reiss. The notebook, Hauptmann, give me the notebook."

"Oh," Eric said. "Oh, yes, of course," he smiled. "I was just thinking that myself, actually ..." he said, naturally thinking nothing of the sort, while definitely thinking of taking the Russian up on his offer to exchange Weiheber for Charles.

"You know him?" Weiheber asked.

"Who?" Eric said.

"Reiss," Faust huffed, fussy little thing under all that blubber wasn't he? "SS Oberleutnant Reiss."

"Oh," Eric smiled. "Well ..." he said with a gesture for the notebook, "indirectly, through his work."

"Mine, Hauptmann," Weiheber nodded, "Mine." he fell back again, exhausted.

"Of course it is," Eric grinned. "I mean ... well, how could some *Russian* possibly manage to be that good? On his own? Clearly, he not only had to have substantial help, but also realistically had to have acquired it from someone such as yourself ...

"No, I understand," Eric nodded, lying of course, but confident so was Weiheber. "Where it came from, and even what it is," he smiled at Weiheber frowning. "Yes?"

"Hauptmann ...?" Weiheber was all the way back there, trying to place, or possibly remember Eric's name.

"Danzig," Eric assured. "SS Hauptmann Eric Danzig, born in Hamburg, late of Berlin, wife Ingrid, parents Otto and Emilie, both deceased."

Weiheber nodded. "Reiss is mine, Hauptmann," he closed the notebook. "I do not know what that is. Some book. Faust, give him back his book. Foolish to waste your time reading, Hauptmann, when there is so much work to be done."

"Very foolish," Faust chimed in, stretching to take the almanac and hand it to Eric. "Few men are given a second chance. You should know this, Hauptmann."

"Ah ... ?" Eric said.

"It is all right," Weiheber dismissed with another sleepy waggle of his wrist. "It is all right, Faust. When Hauptmann Danzig fails in locating Herr Oberst Schönfeld ..."

"Alfred?" Eric blinked, not that there couldn't possibly be another one.

"You know him?" Faust gaped.

"Ah ... yes," Eric nodded. "Yes, I do. If it's the same one. Including where he is," he grinned, though not with any desire to show Faust or his superior Weiheber up. No, the latter already a has-been, Eric had quickly deduced, rather than a never-was what with that gilded breast of company dues matted with someone's hair and skin. A physically large man himself once, perhaps, not only tall. Foreign, Eric noticed, possibly a true Hun, with his dark complexion and almond eyes. It was interesting to Eric how as time went by the elite Waffen SS became increasingly foreign—twenty-six, twenty-seven percent? Dutch. Flemish. Norwegian. Even American and French, and certainly Soviet.

"Let's cut to the chase ..." Eric offered a cigarette as a substitute pacifier to cocaine, himself more of a confirmed and old-fashioned drunkard, and so personally he wouldn't know.

"Yes, thank you," Faust snatched hungrily at the pack. "You are sure of this?"

"Well, if I'm not, it's too late now," Eric agreed with a flick of his head for the match Faust struck against the heel of his boot. "Or did you mean Alfred's hideaway ... pardon me, command?" he smiled at Weiheber. "Yes, I'm quite sure I know where Alfred is. About a hundred kilometers ... or roughly a liter and a half," Eric reached with a sigh for his bourbon he had tucked under the seat.

"Of petrol?" Faust expressed concern.

"Of alcohol," Eric qualified. "It's late, I'm tired, and we all have our vices ... and limits," he rubbed his stiff and aching neck, raw from the sun, flies, and heat, and it hadn't even been a week. "This is not a road. I don't care if we call it a road, it is not a road by the stretch of even our imagination."

"The siphoning of the petrol was more than deliberate, Hauptmann," Weiheber assured, though again what he meant exactly by that, Eric could not guess. "Presuming the command post to be in a different direction than the water, he knew the choice would be the water, assuming an impossible walk."

"Ah," Eric said, "I believe I get it—part of it, anyway. So you do, or you did have a car. Which explains, yes," he acknowledged to Faust, "you inquiring into my petrol supply. Interesting."

"Interesting?" Weiheber cocked an ear.

"Elementary," Eric shrugged. "After all, you did have to come from somewhere by some means. Sebha would make the most sense, a plane. There's so few of you ... or is it possibly so few of you left?" Eric eyed Weiheber. That breast again. Bloody and emblazoned with all those medals. "Did something happen, Herr Major? Is there possibly something of which I and my men should be made aware? Something out there with guns or big teeth?"

"Hauptmann Reineke," Weiheber nodded.

Right. "Back to Alfred," Eric proposed.

"Yes," Faust agreed. "What is your report?"

"Ah ... report?" Eric said.

Faust huffed. "You said you have identified him, the location of his command."

"Something like that," Eric agreed. "Yes, I said something like that."

"And?" Faust insisted.

"And what?" Eric said.

"Is this some sort of game, Hauptmann?" Faust snapped. "You will take us there immediately."

"Or what?" Eric smiled. "You will give me to Charles instead of giving him to me? Sorry, but you should know, I turned that invitation down the first time."

They both looked at him, Weiheber raising a brow to study him. "It's all right," Eric waved them back to their respective corners. "I didn't believe it then, and I don't believe it now.

"No, gentlemen," he shook his head, "I have my own *theory* if one will, on the point, purpose, and *truth* of your charade, never mind mine. Your Reiss is a detour. Whose job the same as yours, is to locate and track Alfred—not some *Charles*, or some dissident band of French," he waved at the notebook, "but Herr Colonel Alfred Schönfeld. You set Reiss in place, hoping to delay the Ministry's arrival with all that prattle about English, French, and I don't know who else, that some of us swallowed, yes," he agreed, "or at least considered worth checking into. *I* not being one of them." He inclined forward with a serious nod. "How am I doing so far?"

"What did I tell you, eh, Faust," Weiheber returned amused. "What did I tell you? However irritable our Hauptmann Reineke may be—"

"Danzig," Eric corrected. "Herr SS Hauptmann Eric Danzig of the Propaganda Ministry—of Berlin," he clarified lest in his haze Weiheber confuse it with some other. "The Propaganda Ministry of Berlin. I'm a spy. For our side," he assured, "on our side. But then someone has to make sure we maintain a clean and orderly house, now, don't we? We do, gentlemen," he nodded at Weiheber's breast, "that we do. Your map of Bohemia reeks Heydrich, Major, I must say. *The* Heydrich. Protec*tor*." There was someone who sang soprano with his high-pitched voice and questionable pelvic region.

"That makes a little more sense than Himmler sticking his neck out quite this far," Eric agreed. "Not that it matters. I'll raise you your Heydrich or Himmler one Goebbels, and even better one *Rommel*. The invincible, undeniable Erwin J ... or is it *S*?" Eric briefly frowned. "*A*? Does he even have one? A middle name," he clarified for Weiheber, "not a party affiliation. That we know he doesn't have. Little matter, we'll keep him just the same. It's not merely a matter of privilege and therefore *known* innocence that you will find General Rommel is not involved in any of this. It is by decree he is not involved in any of this. So, hands off, and the Ministry will even spring for the ride home."

"Threats," Faust scoffed. "Do you realize who you are speaking to, Hauptmann? Do you?"

"No," Eric smiled back. "No, actually, I don't. I do know it doesn't matter. My orders come directly from Berlin. So, we can either do this the friendly way, or you can get out of the car. You wish to consider that a threat, take it up with Berlin—when you get there, Leutnant, when you get there."

"What Faust means, Hauptmann ..." Weiheber yawned, "is we find it an interesting premise the Ministry endorses these pirates and their munitions complexes, promoting them as loyalists rather than what they are. Traitors, Hauptmann. Traitors and mutineers."

"Pirates," Eric considered, as such was his job to consider such things. "Yes, that is an interesting premise, isn't it?" he agreed. "I get it though. Pirates. Sahara seas. A little obscure, but clever, useful possibly even." He scribbled it on the cover of Reiss's overblown crap.

"It confounds me," Faust shook his head.

"Well, that is only because you are not of the Propaganda Ministry," Eric assured, "where tanks are made of cardboard and bullets, jellybeans. Marketing, in other words, Leutnant, marketing. It's all in the marketing, in which truth has no role ... decidedly has no role," he popped his pencil back in his pocket and rubbed his sore and tired neck again. "Quite all right, quite unlike the ranks, I will be leaving this *Paradise* soon."

"Then you are saying the Ministry supports and agrees with these ... these ..." Weiheber sputtered.

"Pirates?" Eric offered. "I'm saying ..." his head tipped back.

"Anarchists, Hauptmann," Weiheber insisted. "Anarchists, all of them!"

"My call," Eric's head returned forward with his grin. "That's my call. Perhaps I haven't made myself clear. My orders are from Berlin. There will be a sacrificial lamb, yes, naturally, to pay for all of this. Possibly Alfred, probably Alfred," he agreed. "High enough in rank to be believable ... obscure enough not to matter, or be missed ..." he smiled again at Weiheber's breast. "You're a Czech, aren't you? That's not exactly Russian, but it's also not German, now, is it?

"No, it isn't," he assured as Faust sputtered something and Weiheber just stared at him. "Admittedly curious, though, I admit, are you completely out of your mind or merely colorblind with that sky-blue suit? This isn't Berlin or even Tripoli. It's the Sahara, the rear of the front lines. Why don't you just wear a sign that reads 'shoot me'? Because I assure you, they will, without thought, reason, and certainly without conscience or regret. No one appreciates, respects, or even *likes* the SS. They hate us. Hate us," he nodded, "fear, loathe, and despise us, albeit rightfully so. But then we're not really the elite are we, no. We're thugs. If you really want to get through this—out of it, *alive* no less, take a page from my book and lose the three-piece tattoo. The Wehrmacht rules North Afrika, trust me, it rules. *Rommel* wouldn't have it any other way."

"Are you sure ..." Faust accused.

"That I'm SS?" Eric laughed. "Oh, yes, even though you're not despite my arrogance and threats. It's less my attitude than ... well, my attitude," he dismissed. "My jokes and friendly nature, my soft, friendly hand. I believe you'll find they not only work, gentlemen, they're irresistible even at times. Like a bee to honey, a fly," he promised, "to my spider web. But then really, which of us do you really think these ... *pirates* will feel more comfortable with sharing their hopes, dreams, secrets, and schemes, even better, their *contacts* and connections? I'll give you a hint. It's definitely not *Himmler* or

Heydrich, or either of you. I'm sorry, gentlemen, but I am here to market what you are here to destroy, and I'm afraid I win. You can have Alfred, but only after I'm done with him. In the meantime ..." he picked up the notebook and set it back down in Weiheber's lap, "you may keep *Charles* as your consolation prize. If there is a Charles, I expect to hear, see, and know nothing of him. Take care of it. Put him out of business and do it quick. That's the *deal* I am willing to make. The beginning, middle, and end of it. I suggest you take it."

"What is this?" Weiheber frowned at the binder.

"A novel," Eric assured. "Not exactly *Tolstoy,* but close enough. And now that that's settled," he settled back to light a cigarette and find his bottle of courage under the seat. "What's all this about some Hauptmann Reineke? What does he have to do with any of this, other than what he's told to do?"

Chapter Twenty-Three

Cairo
March 9

Even if he tried, Justin had no particular image of Joanna in his mind. No snapshot recollection of his stepsister, tender or otherwise. What he had was a responsibility he took seriously, one he felt deeply, and an old man given a second chance to right his wrongs and prove himself worthy before he died with his head held high. "Care to try that again, Mike?" Justin said as he sat there.

"No!" Michael assured. It was hard enough the first time. "Red's missing, Chuck, bottom line. They got her, they ain't got her, who definitely doesn't have her is you or I."

"That's ridiculous, Mike," Justin said. "Joanna is with Evelyn."

"London," Michael said and Justin's eyes brightened. "Supposed to be in London, supposed to be. Gramps thinks she's in New York with me, and therein lies the problem, because she ain't neither."

"Isn't, Mike," Justin corrected, tightly. "And why isn't she? I'm waiting, Michael!" he didn't wait long, but jumped up to loom over his desk, the stem of his pipe pointed in accusation.

"Hey!" Michael could jump, too, straight up to meet Justin head-on without flinching. "Try throwing your weight around this! She's not, OK? She's just not. She's in the ATS, all right? She's a driver in the ATS. You want a confession? Fine! I confess. You got me. I surrender!"

"Damn you!" Justin exploded, and his fist almost went through the table. Downstairs, covering the radio after Joe took off to help, Bobby heard bone or wood crack. It was probably both, and Bobby wasn't concerned either way. Wouldn't be the first time, probably not the last. Justin had a mean temper when aroused. A killer's instinct, and a killer's heart, and that was all right, too. Should have killed the Doc a long time ago and be done with it the first time he showed his spots like the Old Man had dropped Teddy Drake when he started carrying on. Just dropped him in his tracks and walked away without a thought to it despite their life-long friendship. Bobby shut the radio off, smoothed the report out neat for Justin when he came for it, which he would, and waddled over to check the Telex. There wasn't anything, not yet. When it came there still wasn't much, but there would be if Justin had to turn the planet upside down and shake it out, that Bobby also knew.

"Me?" Michael said as Justin whirled away from him to try and find the paper trail in among forty million others he had laying around. "Fuck you. This is all your fault, not mine."

"Is it now?" Justin said, and the words dripping acid.

"Yeah!" Michael assured. "Look, I didn't have to fucking come here. I could have just left you sitting with your head stuck up your ass—"

"Yes, well," Justin nodded, "you certainly took your precious time—"

"Ay!" Michael said. "I took all the fucking time I needed, OK? Who kept who sitting on their frigging thumbs for nine hours—"

"I don't care, Michael!" Justin turned on him.

Yeah, well, neither did Michael. "Look, screw the fucking paperwork," he tore a week's worth out of Justin's hand. "It's not going to change anything. She's gone, all right? That's what I'm telling you, she's gone, there's nothing you can do about it, not now, not ever, and it's all your fucking fault!" he screamed again. "I mean, for Christ's sake, Justin," he whined, "you've kept her locked up for years. First with Gramps, and then with Joe, and when Joe died, where did you put her? Back it jail! She doesn't belong in jail. She belongs out doing things. Seeing things!"

"And do you think she likes what she's seeing now, Mike?" Justin wanted to know. "What she might be doing now?"

"No! And that's definitely your fault," Michael insisted. "They took her because of you, they didn't need me. They could have taken her from England, Scotland—the frigging States, if I brought her home with me. They didn't need fucking North Africa! They didn't have to wait for her to come to them. You signed that warrant long ago, buster. You and that three ring circus of yours out there. Is you, ain't you? Will you, won't you fuck with me? Yeah, well, they fucked with you, didn't they? Don't look now, but they fucked with you but good!"

And Jesus Christ, Justin must have left him standing there for another frigging hour.

"Fuck!" Michael grabbed the Scotch winging it across the room.

"I got it!" Joe slid into home plate to take over for Laura confused and up on her feet, the dead receiver of her telephone in her hand as she tried to, Joe didn't know, call the fire department or something to come and turn their hoses on the Maj and the Doc going at it pretty good behind the closed door. The two of them, loud enough to be overheard, and angry enough to be frightening, he supposed.

"I'm serious," Joe flashed his very best grin, dropping Scarecrow in front of her for her consideration and gently removing the receiver from her hand. "I've got it covered."

"Yes, of course," Laura agreed, because really what else could she say? What was she supposed to say? Squadron Leader Charles emerged from his office at that point to head off at rocket speed the direction Joe had just run.

"Excuse me." Joe whipped a ring of keys off his waistband that Laura could quite honestly say she had never noticed him carrying before, to quickly lock the office door and hence the Doc inside. A loud "Fuck!" followed by the sound of breaking glass suggested Michael may have decided to go out the window, but Joe would check that out in a moment if only because if the Doc had sprung for a dive he wouldn't be going anywhere except maybe to the infirmary. "You hungry?" he turned his grin back on Laura.

"I beg your pardon?" she said.

"Hungry," Joe shrugged, trying to nonchalantly *move, move, move* her along without actually pushing her. "Got to be lunch time or something, right?"

"Lunch time ..." Laura glanced at the wall behind him and the clock that said not quite twenty past nine.

"What I mean is ..." Joe said, but changed his mind and cut the bull crap laying it out as polite and sweet as possible. "Look, don't take this personally but I need you out of here now. Try to stall me, and I swear to Christ I'll carry you."

"Quite all right," Laura stopped him there, collected her shoulder bag and left, leaving him to blow a low appreciative whistle after her with a shake of his head.

"Out of this world," Joe said. "Definitely out of this world—yo!" his hand connected with Scarecrow paused to take in the sights. "Escort her, man, escort her. We're talking out of the building and gone. On a boat back to England. Wherever." Scarecrow left and Joe sat down to hook the phone back up and get ahold of Bobby and forewarn him the Maj was on his way. He was already there.

"Yeah, OK," Joe took a breath. "Just give him whatever he wants," he said like he had a say in the matter. "I'm here, Laur's gone, everything's covered ... yeah, him, too," he turned around to look over the door in answer to Bobby's inquiry about the Doc. "He's in there, trashing the place and talking to himself. Thought he might have tried to make a break for it, but, I can hear him—what? You telling me you can't?" his temper flashed suddenly, not at Bobby but at the idea of someone messing with his equipment. "Oh, you turned him off," he nodded. "Yeah, OK, got it, guess so. I mean, who the fuck's he gonna call? I don't think so.

"I mean," Joe sat down with a wipe of his sweating neck, "what's the deal here anyway? What's this crap about the Maj's sister? Where's that coming from? Yeah, I got it," he nodded. "I'm fine. Count on me. I'm just saying this is crazy. It's nuts."

Crazy or nuts could describe her assignment, Laura supposed, as she propped herself at a local pub for a light early brunch, a healthy splash of rye whiskey in her juice cup, Colonel James Peterson at her side, flashy and dignified in his polished brass and grey temples. Condescending, certainly, for all his sympathy and attention, as they all were when they weren't trying to out-shout each other in their profanities and general rudeness.

"Really, what a vulgar world it has become," Laura remarked as she sat there.

"Vulgar?" Jim's brow arched. A kind brow it was, older, like an uncle's or a priest's. She really was being unfair to him and she softened. "Charles?" he said.

Her softness did not last long, Laura felt herself immediately bristle at even the name. "The world," she repeated. "For that matter, the war." She looked around the public house, crowded for this hour of morning, extremely crowded, from the looks of some of them, more than a few of them had been there, or elsewhere, all night.

"It's war," Jim chuckled.

"So it is," Laura acknowledged primly with a sip of her drink. "War." A vastly different war than the one she had left behind at home. The land perhaps decimated, in some ways desecrated, but not its people, their spirit or their morals. Here it was almost primal. "Why did you say Charles?" she asked.

"No reason," he shrugged. "Don't like him much myself, but he's not the vulgar sort, wouldn't think."

No, of course he did not. But then vulgar to a man meant something sexual. To where vulgar to a woman meant vulgar. "Fine," Laura said, "we'll compromise. He's a nutter."

Jim chuckled harder. "That's on point. Makes a fine living at it, too."

"Really," Laura said. "And what sort of fine living is that?"

Jim shut up like the proverbial clam. Really, it couldn't be more obvious, and really, that was the point, wasn't it? Yes, it was. "That's the point," Laura nodded firmly.

"No, it isn't," Jim tried to claim.

"Yes, it is," Laura insisted. "It's an assignment, not a game. Of course, I've no idea what my assignment even is, other than to sit there and be made a fool of on a regular basis."

"Look, luv," he patted her hand.

"Don't call me luv," Laura requested, "and for God's sake please stop patting my hand. I'm an officer in your bloody air force and it's high time the lot of you learned not only to accept, but to respect that. I'm not a secretary—for that matter, I'm not only a pilot," she reminded him, her Irish rising. "I'm a trained and experienced cryptographer. I didn't spend six months in Buckinghamshire warming the benches."

"Yes, all right …" Jim nodded.

It was hardly all right. "And," Laura said, "I do seem to recall your saying not only what an ideal position this was for a woman of my skills, but what an ideal candidate I was, better than any other."

"Well, you are," he assured, "you are. Just takes a little time."

"Of course," Laura ignored him, "you did say woman, not officer, so I should have known right then and there, shouldn't I? Of course I should—except," she set her glass down sharply with a crisp nod of approval at the offer of a refill, "I can't even sit there and look pretty for your parade of brass flashing through, any more than I can do anything else, I'm not allowed."

"What do you want, luv?" Jim asked. "If I can do it for you, I will."

What did she want? Laura straightened up. What did he think she wanted? A transfer since an apology was certainly not in the offing. "What did you mean when you said it takes a little time?"

"He's one of those man-fellows," Jim downed his bourbon with a shrug. "You know how they are."

A man-fellow? Laura wasn't sure she knew what a man-fellow was, least of all how they were. "Oh," she sat up a little straighter as a thought crossed her mind. "Yes, well," she said briskly with a somewhat heartier drink of her tea, "daresay for all you don't know about Squadron Leader Charles, that's certainly one thing I did not know. Definitely," she shuddered. "What?" she said, but only because Jim was looking at her oddly. "Your words, not mine. I merely said he was vulgar. Who knew how so? Quite," she downed her tea, requesting another post haste.

"Oh, no, luv …" Jim started to laugh once he figured out what she was saying.

"Please don't," Laura stopped him from elaborating. "Really, it's not anything I need to know."

And not anything he was going to tell her, other than she had it wrong. "All I'm saying is he's one of those opposed to women in the services—a queen? Charles?" he couldn't laugh any harder, though he certainly did try. "He's a bit queer, all right, but not in the way you're thinking. Likes them savage, naked, and wild, if you know what I'm saying."

"To the contrary, I'm quite sure I do not know," Laura assured.

"Yes, you do," Jim patted her hand.

"Fine," Laura said. "I know what you mean. I'm twenty-six, not thirteen. Old enough," she assured the barkeep apparently puzzled about her request for a fresh cup of tea, "to know precisely what you mean. Tea, please, yes, tea. Contrary to popular belief, we're not all alcoholics ..." she scowled at Peterson, fairly gasping.

"*Charles?*" Jim said for what had to be the fourth time with a shake of his head, marveling at the notion. "Talking out of your hat with that one, luv. It's rich though. That's pretty rich. Might be tempted to spread it around myself, if I thought it'd catch on. Be the end of him it would."

Laura was not talking out of her *hat* or any other object, inanimate, or otherwise. "Yes, well, that would explain the blonde then, wouldn't it?" she pursued the wild part of things. "Rather nicely."

"Blonde?" Jim frowned.

"Or perhaps not," Laura nodded firmly with an even firmer sip from her cup. "After all, such a man's man, one can't imagine why he would want her around."

"You talking about Julia?" Jim frowned, hard put otherwise.

"Yes, well," Laura dared say she wouldn't know, and didn't know if she was talking about *Julia,* or whomever, not having been introduced.

"Didn't realize you knew her," Jim reflected curiously on that with a wrinkling of his chin. "That's a bit odd, now that is a bit odd."

"Yes, well," Laura never claimed to know her. Seen her, yes, she had seen her. Once. Only once, and rather briefly, but still long enough to know once was enough.

"Right. Well, don't be too hard on her," Jim patted her hand. "There's more to her than meets the eye."

Yes, well, there couldn't be much more to her from what Laura had seen, however briefly, rather all of her right there to be seen.

"Fairly highly skilled lass herself," Jim assured.

"Obviously," Laura concurred. "Simply a matter of what sort of skills one is talking about."

"A pilot," Jim assured. "She's a pilot, luv. So see? Just need to bide your time, you'll get your chance."

A pilot? Laura almost choked on her tea. "A pilot?" she slammed the cup down before she did choke for that matter, pour the damn tea over Jim's head.

"Luv ..." Jim groaned.

"Oh, this is too much," Laura couldn't get her purse out fast enough, the change down on the bar fast enough, or herself out the door. "This is really too much."

"Laura!" Jim caught up with her, caught her by the arm, a step or two outside. "Laura, what in bleeding hell ..."

"A pilot?" Laura turned on him so angry she could barely get the words out. "That woman is a pilot?"

"Yes," Jim said. "Fairly decent one—Laura!" he protested, but only because she walked off on him again.

"How dare you," Laura sputtered as he trotted along besides her walking as fast as she possibly could in her tight skirt and stacked high heels. "Really, how dare you, all of you." She stopped, eyeing her father's oldest and dearest friend, God rest his wretched soul.

"What do you want me to do?" Jim asked again in all seriousness and understanding. "I will, if I can. Anything."

"What in bleeding hell do you think I want?" Laura snapped. "A transfer, of course. I'm sick to death of your 'Charles' and I scarcely even know the man."

"Right. Well, that I can't do ..." Jim scratched behind his ear.

"Oh?" Laura said coldly. "Why not?"

"It's not that simple," Jim said simply. "You know that. This is Charles's problem. Thinks because he says it is, it is, and it's not."

"What's that to do with me?" Laura asked.

"It doesn't," Jim said. "You're the right one for the post. So to hell with him. Besides," he smiled, "you're rather a brick. Wouldn't have put you there if I didn't think you couldn't be a match for him. I'm right, aren't I? Of course I am. Might even come around. Stranger things have happened."

"Come around," Laura said. "Dare I ask to what?"

"Just that," Jim shrugged. "Never had a secretary before, can't see why he has to have one now. It's rot. You know it's rot, and I know it. He's an arrogant bastard. Needs to be knocked down a peg or two."

"Well, if else fails, there's always the Jerries," Laura considered only half-joking.

"Exactly," Jim chuckled. "It's nothing personal, luv. Really, you're taking this far too personally."

"I beg to differ, but it is personal," Laura corrected. "I shouldn't have to defend wanting to contribute to your bloody war effort. At least be allowed to feel I'm doing something worthwhile to the best of my limits and abilities. But instead, I'm an object of ridicule, by, of all things, and if you're telling the truth, a man who would prefer not to have a secretary. How absurd. How perfectly and utterly absurd. Quite frankly, if that's all it is, your *bizarre* Mr. Charles is the one who is taking things far too personally, with the simple answer for you to do us both a favor and let him have his way."

"Can't," Jim shook his head.

"Why not?" Laura insisted. "Surely you're not suggesting he really does have the final say in whatever game the two of you are playing."

"Clearly he doesn't," Jim smiled. "You're still there."

"Then why not?" Laura insisted. "And don't give me your rot it's not that simple."

He shut up like a clam again, and so the point remained the point. Laura stared off down the street.

"Luv ..." Jim tried. "Now, don't start crying on me, it's really not worth it, it's not. So he's a prick. All right, he's a prick. Just do your duty and leave the rest be."

"Crying on you," Laura said. Yes, well, crying, Laura could assure him was the last thing on her mind. "To the devil with you," she said. "The lot of you. If you're thinking I'll likewise come around—"

"You will," Jim nodded. "You will."

"Like some second class citizen to you ruddy beggars?" Laura looked him dead in the eyes. "The devil I will. If you know anything, James Fillmore Peterson, you know that."

Chapter Twenty-Four

"So!" Michael said when Justin finally decided to show back up to hunt up a pair of dusty knapsacks and some old rifle that hadn't seen action since the Crimean war.

"So what, Michael?" Justin emptied his desk into the knapsacks, checking the sight of his rifle on Michael's lapel.

"Put the gun down, Chuck," Michael nodded. "In the first place you never could hit the broad side of a barn."

"Yes, well, in the first place it's not a barn I'm looking at, now is it?" Justin countered.

"And in the second?" Michael thought he'd ask.

"Yes, well," in the second, it would be too easy, too damn easy. Justin set the rifle aside. "When I pull the trigger, is when you really have something to complain about."

"Ditto," Michael breathed, "save I'm the one with the balls to do it."

"Debatable," Justin said. "But that's all right, you'll do."

"Me?" Michael's head jerked up to stare at him. "You're kidding, right?"

"Do I look like I'm kidding?"

"No!" Michael snapped. "So let's can the witty repartee and get down to brass tacks. I'm here because I want to be here."

"Yes, well, you're here, Mike," Justin said, "because you have no choice and until I say otherwise. I don't give a damn what you or Roosevelt might have to say about it. That's something you should have thought about before you hired Joanna out to drive someone's car."

"I didn't hire her out, and not on your frigging career, Chuck. You can't touch me, you can't do shit."

Yes, well, the hell with his career obviously, so Justin didn't even bother mentioning it. "No, you did a favor for a friend," Justin had it down pat. "Mahlon McDowell, Colonel, USA, and his aide, Corporal Paul Reid. Of course, Reid was apparently SIS, and who knows who McDowell really was. Don't know yet, but I will."

"He's not a friend," Michael assured. "And fuck him along with everyone else. I've got one concern and that's Red."

"Yes, well, as I said, it's a little late for that." Justin laid it out for him in gory red, white, and black. "They brought part of agent Reid in, Mike, what was left of him. Whatever the beetles ate or didn't, they cut off his hands and hanged his head from the antenna wire."

"All right!" Michael shut him up. "Bottom line, what are we going to do? Got that? Do. What is the plan? If you want to drive something around the block, try a few hard and fast ideas."

Yes, well, the 'plan' Justin already knew, rather surprised Mike didn't. "I'm going to find the bastards and kill them, Mike, simple as that. Not quite sure what else anyone would expect me to do. You, Mike, are the bait to do just that. Better get packing."

And Christ if Chuck didn't leave him waiting there another frigging hour.

"Bait?" Michael said when Justin returned that time with a couple of sheets of paper in his hand to read while he lit his pipe and sat on his ass in his armchair.

"Looks like your McDowell friend ran with the Tobruk crowd," Justin pursued his own interest. "Tough lot, but that's all right. Aside from you, I've Joe and Bobby to spare. You haven't met Joe yet, but you will. He'll be along shortly."

"Lucky me," Michael agreed for some stupid reason. "Back to the fishing business. How am I bait? Apart from the obvious," he waved. "And don't even bother with that. You're not going to sell me out, Chuck. You and I both know that."

"And you know that for a fact, right, Mike?" Justin didn't look up from sucking up the words off the papers.

"Yeah!" Michael insisted. "So, talk to me. I'm trying to talk to you!"

"Yes, well, you'll probably like Joe," Justin suspected. "Same as he'll probably like you."

Either way it was another two hours before Michael met him, not that he was in a particular hurry to meet any more of Justin's friends. It was just an uncomfortable one hundred and thirty-five minutes of silence.

"I mean!" Michael said, "under the circumstances."

"Yes," Justin thought so, too.

"Right." Michael concentrated on polishing his shoes for a while. "Let's get back to fucking," he offered presently. "And speaking of fucking," he said, not that anyone was, "Ever fuck her?" he wondered with a flick of his head toward the silken legs he knew sat just outside the door.

"Who?" Justin said.

"The dame," Michael huffed. "The frigging dame who sits outside."

"Oh," Justin said. "No."

"That figures," Michael said. "Mind if I do?"

"I don't care what you do, Michael," Justin assured, and Michael shut up.

"Why not?" he opened up again seconds short of Joe.

"Why not what?" Justin said.

"Why haven't you fucked her?" Michael sputtered, not really understanding why he was bothering to talk at all.

"I don't know," Justin said. "Never thought of it, I suppose."

"That figures," Michael snorted. "You always were a queer bastard. Ever fuck Joe?"

"I don't know, Michael," Justin said, "why don't you ask him?"

Easy enough to do, considering Joe just walked in the door, however it was not the sort of question Michael wanted to ask Joe. Joe appeared to be a pleasant enough chap with a flashing, friendly smile and extended hand, and Michael could see no good reason to ruffle Joe's good nature with a question in such obvious poor taste. Besides, a darkly handsome kid of about six feet even, Joe had a waist as tight as Michael's should have been, a chest as broad as Michael's could have been, and arms bigger around than Michael's head.

"Joe," Justin introduced them, "Mike."

"Yeah, hey," Joe gave Michael's hand a hearty pump, and Michael was surprised to be listening to a voice as familiar as home.

"Jersey?" Michael frowned.

"Flatbush," Joe grinned. "You know, Brooklyn. New York."

"No kidding," Michael whistled. "Hey, I was born in Brooklyn."

"Yeah, I know," Joe's grin stayed. "The Heights. I knew your old man."

"My old man?" Michael repeated with a glance over the tattoos, but only because they were there. As in obvious. As in, the kid was half-naked. Not because he expected to see *Dad* carved next to *Mom* in a heart. "You knew my old man."

"Well, not *knew,* knew him," Joe admitted, "seen him around. It was a while ago. Couple, few years. '37, '38, something like that, before they took him out. Harlem, right? Up in Harlem?"

"Never fucking heard of you," Michael said, and that was the end of their conversation for a while.

Joe turned his attention to the crumpled typing paper he had in his hand and Justin. "This is yours, because, well, I kind of figured," he shrugged, "I might as well do something while I was sitting out there. Not exactly hard work, a monkey could do it."

"Thank you," Justin stuffed the report in his knapsack with all the others.

"Not that I mean the lady's a monkey," Joe hastened to clarify for whatever reason. "Definitely, she's not a monkey. She's ..."

"Temporary," Justin finished for him.

"Yeah, huh?" Joe laughed. "Aren't they all? That's the way it should be. Definitely the way it should be."

"Yes," Justin swung his knapsack over his shoulder. "Is that it?"

"Oh, yeah," Joe waved. "Everything's fine. Not to worry. Just saying I got rid of her. She's gone, history—not rid, rid, of her," he said, quick to clarify because Justin did sort of pause. "I mean, it's not like I killed her and buried her out in the yard. Christ, give me a break. I set it up for her to be transferred ... why?" his grin slipped in. "Having second thoughts? Thinking ... I don't know, you'll miss her?"

"No," Justin said, "but you might."

"Yeah, I might," Joe nodded. "Definitely. Too much though and I'll just go looking, know what I mean?"

"Yes, well, speaking of looking ... " Justin suggested as the phone rang.

"Bobby," Joe reached to answer it, apparently taking his secretarial duties as seriously as he took everything else. "It's OK, I got it. Pain in the ass, anyway. Reams me out for pestering him and now look who's suddenly in a hurry—what?" he said into the phone. "Turn the frigging thing back on and you won't have to ask if we're coming. Yeah, we're coming, on our way ... He's out in the yard," he explained to Justin. "That's why he's calling. Wanna talk to him?"

"Yes, actually," Justin agreed.

"Yeah, well, you're out of luck because he doesn't want to talk to you." Joe hung up the phone with a laugh, a snap of his fingers, and a point at Michael. "Yo. You're with me, let's go."

"Yes, well," Justin cleared his throat, not about to let that little business with the telephone just slide, "that'll cost you a few laps."

"I can handle it." Joe headed out, leaving Michael to look at Justin and Justin to look back at him.

"What?" Justin said.

"Nothing," Michael picked up his duffel. "Let's get on with it."

Siwa Oasis, Egypt
March 10

They got there at first light. The sun rising over the baked plains, scarred with reminders of last season's heavy fighting, life a few thousand feet away in the distance, churning away as it had for centuries. Justin stood solemn in the isolation, taking it all in. Behind him, Bobby waited, arms folded, propped against their jeep, Joe perched comfortably on the hood of his, Michael uncomfortably sharing his space with Joe's large pack radio *Christine*, his white suit, shoes, and Panama hat, dusty and dirty, his bladder on overload. "Siwa, huh?" Michael hammered his spine straight, prying himself out of the jeep to take a leak, looking out over the expanse of nothing stretched before him. Behind him a city waited, half stuck in the Stone Age, half not. Made sense to him, he supposed. Could be someone around who knew something, what's more, willing to talk, yeah, right. "Think I've seen this movie. What are we, a mile out of town? Is there some particularly special reason we just don't bite the bullet and go the whole hog instead of waiting for the guys in the shuttered car to come to us?"

"Yeah, well," Joe said, reminding Michael of a rule he probably never even heard of, "you know sometimes, Doc, a forward approach isn't necessarily the best."

"Uh, huh," Michael could have fun with that but he passed. "You mean because we're on the corner of first and the front lines? I don't know why that should concern anyone. There's four of us."

"Actually, Doc," Joe looked around, "out here the front kinda depends on what day of the week it is. Know what I mean? Not that the place hasn't seen its share of action like the rest of the world."

"Uh, huh," Michael looked up with the whine of a toy airplane overhead. On cue, another jeep appeared from nowhere, cutting across the sand on high as Lucky Lindy and his crop duster swooped into view, circling to land, and taxi maybe thirty yards before he got serious with the brakes. Justin lit his pipe, meandering to meet them.

"About time," Joe slipped off his perch with a grin for Bobby.

"Right about that," Bobby nodded tersely. "Now is not the time to try the lad's patience."

"No, it's not," Joe agreed, his knuckles cracking Michael's arm. "Yo. Put the package away. Let's go."

"Suck spaghetti," Michael said. "The crowd's forming as we speak. Think it's a little late now to be discreet, for that matter, in a hurry. It's ten-of fucking Tuesday. What happened to we'll know everything there is to know within an hour?"

"We do know," Joe assured. "Just tying up with a couple of the guys so we can do something about it."

"Guys, huh?" Michael adjusted his sunshades to ogle the jeep rolling in, Marlene Dietrich, shapely in her sweaty undershirt, sun-bleached hair, and copper tan, riding shotgun.

"Yeah, that's Jewels, Doc," Joe identified the mirage. "Julia. But, um ..." he cautioned. "Don't get any ideas. She's a lion poacher from Kenya. Takes her job seriously, in other words; know what I mean? She'll hang your hide right next to the rest of them."

"Sounds like fun to me," Michael headed for trouble.

"Yeah, right, in your dreams," Joe hitched up his pants and beat him to the draw.

"Hey, Joe, what do you know?" Julia slithered down to snake her way over and make his gun sweat a few bullets, her eyes green, voice husky, and chest breathing deeply.

"Aw, that's old, Jewels, old," Joe chuckled and probably would have squirmed a little in his shirt collar if he was wearing one. He wasn't as usual, settling instead for a disconcerted sweep of his lashes over the one semi-normal looking one of the group, if you didn't consider his oversized head. Another grizzly buzzard swung down out of the cockpit of the plane to join Chuck busy talking with some walleyed freak with a gold tooth in his mouth.

"Does it still work?" Jewels could be cold when she wanted to be, but then again, she could be real hot.

"Yeah, of course it still works," Joe's chuckle deepened, clearing his throat with a wave at the head. "Hey, Fred, how's it going?"

"It's going, lad," Fred nodded, looking rather like the cat who swallowed the canary to Joe, and so Fred had. Husband Number Two and counting for the bad lass with the good heart and generous spirit until she tired of the singularity clause of her commitment, which she would, but it still placed Fred a cut above the others, and he'd settled for that. "It's going."

"Yeah," so Joe had heard. "So, why you trying to give the guy heartburn?" he scolded Julia.

"Don't know what you mean," she was on a roll, "just because I love him, doesn't mean I can't love you ...

"Or you," she looked Michael up and down before sauntering on to see what she could do about lighting Chuck's pipe for him.

"Hey! Did you hear me say no?" Michael called after her, not too proud or shy.

"Yo!" Joe's hand cracked him in the back of the head. "Show some class. She's kidding."

"Now I know you're stupid," Michael assured. "I know a piece of fish when I see one and that is Moby fucking Dick."

"Um ..." Joe tried to hide his smile, but failed. "Blah, blah, blah. This is Fred, her old man. You know, husband?"

"And?" Michael waited for the punch line.

"And so I'm serious," Joe nodded. "Dead serious. Don't make me have to hurt you. Show some respect."

"Now you sound like my fucking wife," Michael moved on to see what he could do about helping Chuck figure out which one was the girl.

"It's water, mate," Pete hopped from the rolling jeep with his traditional offering of a bottle for Justin, this one labeled Scotch. "No cause for alarm for the safety of your gun or the mink collar draped over it."

"Yes, well, that's one way of putting it," Justin accepted the Scotch.

"Oh, what's another?" Pete unscrewed the cap of his canteen to take a drink with a laugh and a nod for the bottle. "I mean, it's water, just like this is. Bottled it personally myself not an hour ago."

"Yes, well," that much Justin had figured out before he took a swallow. "Kiss ass is another way of putting it. Quite all right, up to it or not, you're it. Nel's otherwise occupied trying to win a war."

"Oh, well, now, if I'm going to kiss an arse, I wouldn't look for it to be yours," Pete assured with a smile for Julia cozying her way into the conversation. "Am I right, or am I wrong?"

"Sounds good to me," she wrapped her lips around his canteen with reassurance for Justin. "It's water." And just to prove it she splashed a little on her throat and a few other overheated parts.

"Right," Pete took the canteen away from her. "Just been through that, luv. Let's not have the man repeating on himself."

"Been through that," Julia nodded at Justin. "Who's the porter?"

That was also one way of putting it, Justin supposed. "You mean Mike."

"If the suit fits," she shrugged, which from the looks of him it did.

"Yes, well, we'll get to that," Justin promised, more interested right now in his airplane, old, though it might be, old and painted to look like something it wasn't, which was German to the nearsighted and ill informed. "What happened?"

"Nothing," Julia said. "Hank said it sounded a little rough as I passed, I said it was just running a little hot. He took it up to see if it was him or me."

"And the verdict?" Justin asked.

"Needs oil," Hank tossed Julia the can.

"Who doesn't?" she caught it with a sharp whistle for the "boys" to give her a hand as she sashayed away.

"Right," Pete gave a whistle watching it walk away. "That's some wedding present, lads, I'm telling you. Make the Holy Lord rethink his bachelor ways." He eyed Michael muscling up, an angry look on his face. Pete wasn't too sure about him, right off. He looked like money and even more like trouble under his curls and tan. A small man in a sea of giants, even though he wasn't that small, but on the short side of average with a muscular build. Still he was apparently a little too small for his own liking from the way he moved in. The glasses lending a sense of respectability to his pretty face, the early crow's feet and tightness of the skin spelled dehydration or drink. It remained to be seen which, the same as it remained to be seen just how much and the reason. Want or need, the latter a definite problem, the former could be as well, depending again on how much. Justin was heavy with the Scotch. Pete, heavier and less fussy, satisfied with whatever tasted good, and most did. Neither of them drank when there was work to be done however, and neither of them watched the sun rise through the bottom of a glass when the work was over. Those who did were a problem.

Pete eyed Michael who looked as Italian as his name despite the blue eyes and blond hair. His skin near high-yellow like he might be mixed, it had to be the blond hair in contrast to the olive tanned damn near gold as oil since Pete doubted if Justin's family tree included some mulatto regardless of how smart this one was reputed to be.

"Is this him?" he asked Justin. "What's got your entrails in a knot? Could be somebody, I suppose, but most wouldn't think physicist, is my guess."

"Physicist?" Hank came up unexpectedly from behind, startled what with being regular army like Fred, if one considered the Black Watch and Long Range Desert Troops regular army, which they weren't. They were the ones who did the job after Justin analyzed the intelligence collected by his squad. Still, a physicist was up there all right, versus just keeping some ordinary pain in the ass on ice.

"Hey," Michael said, "it's a job. Somebody's got to do it."

Pete laughed. "Now that's a frightening thought. A real

frightening thought—what?" he said to Michael looking at him like he wanted to take somebody's head off, which Pete wouldn't suggest he try. "Got something you want to say there, or just a little indigestion?"

"Yeah," Michael said, "screw. That means scram where I'm from. Take a hike."

"Right," Pete nodded. "And I'll bet you've heard it often, too."

"Whatever," Michael turned to Justin. "Got a minute?"

"In a minute, maybe," Justin relit his pipe.

"It's all right," Pete retreated to say hello to Bobby and exchange photographs of some Yank named McDowell for those of a lass who could very well be their very own secretary Cain, some ten or so years ago.

"This him?" Pete looked over the picture of the Army Corp Engineer in his dignified getup and fun-loving expression. Getting on a little in years to change his mind and hence sides after a twenty-year career, in Pete's opinion. "Looks like an ordinary enough fellow. But then that's the whole point with these lads, isn't it? To blend in?"

"It's how they work it." Bobby was lost in his study of the worn photograph of the young lass. No doubt who she was, still stood the same way, held her head the same way, a serious look in her eyes, still had that as well.

"Sounds like the life of a coward," Pete handed him back McDowell's photograph for his scrapbook. Didn't need it, after all, what with the fellow likely dead for all his big ideas good or bad. "Right or wrong?"

"About which?" Bobby kept the picture of Laura, tucking it safe and warm, down in the pocket of his wet shirt. Pete eyed him. Soaked, Bobby was. Soaked and breathing shallow. He didn't belong out here, old and fat as he was. Seemed almost cruel of Justin to take him away from his overhead fans, and make him come, if he didn't want to. Give in to his whining, if he did want to, which Bobby probably did. Pete smiled. Knew few men who inspired that sort of loyalty. Few who'd kill themselves for you, in your stead, or just stop you from going off half-cocked doing something unlike yourself. It was one or the other, Pete knew that much as well, probably some combination of the two.

"It looks like her," Bobby was saying, "if that's what you're wondering. Could be, and probably is."

"Oh, now, I'm not wondering anything," Pete assured with a smile. "No more than I'm accusing, simply stating a fact—one I'd want to know," he pointed out. "So you either tell our boy Justin, or I will. Got enough personal problems the way I hear it, doesn't need any new ones, which that lass either is, or she isn't. Personally, I say she's not. But then I'm not so jaded as you might think. What I am is been around a while, longer even than you."

"Doubt it," Bobby disputed but only because he had close to twenty years on Pete.

"The hell I haven't," Pete assured. "Wore your damn flag for my nappy, and don't think I won't piss on it again as soon as this war business is over. Regardless, like you, I know all the devils, all the angels, and all the ones who don't give a damn about any of our crap. That would be that one," he pointed at Laura's picture, hidden away in Bobby's shirt and he could hide all he wanted to because Pete was serious; he would tell Justin if Bobby didn't. "Can't stake my life, and sure as hell won't ever stake my reputation, but what I do have on my side is my longevity, and I would have known, lad. Peter would have known if McShane's baby sister ever worked my side of the street. On that, you can stake whatever the hell you feel like."

"I'll tell him," Bobby said, and would, not because he felt pressured into doing it, but because he worried for Justin like some surrogate father. Pete could hear it in Bobby's voice when they talked over Joseph's radio. Bobby calling to tell him to make sure and bring the eye-opening photograph along with him, to where Bobby hadn't even wanted to hear about it for the last three months.

"Now, see?" Pete gave Bobby a friendly whap in the chest. "I knew you were an upright and outstanding fellow, same as me. Not at all like that Benedict McDowell. Brings shame to all his relatives his daddy left back in County Cork for the land of milk and plenty, sidling up to these Nazis the way he did, I assure you he do."

"Is that so?" Bobby said, not that he doubted Pete, or even particularly mistrusted him. He just knew him like he knew the rest of his clan, and appreciation or respect for Justin Charles, who he was, what he stood for, was unlikely. Bobby didn't give a damn about all the possible psychological reasons for Pete's exception for Justin, he just didn't believe it.

"Aye, it is so," Pete agreed, including how he and Justin together were a most unlikely cocktail. "But don't let my transgression go to your head. Liking one is not liking all of you. Peter just likes passion, that's all. Understands and appreciates it. Anytime you want to debate that, give me a call. Just make it, like I said, after the war."

Hank was thinking along similar lines, about the Yank engineer McDowell having more of a role to play in the drama other than an innocent bystander. "Anyone figure out yet what he was doing out here?" he recovered from his surprise in learning the race for the Atom bomb included the best and least likely of men.

"You tell me," Justin puffed on his pipe.

Hank scoffed. "Right. Could have saved himself a lot of time and trouble and just landed in Tobruk, if that really were his only idea. Didn't have to come all the way to Cairo and drive. But then that would have made for a different ending, now wouldn't it?" he nodded.

"That's the thinking," Justin agreed.

"Hey, whoa, wait a minute," Michael jumped in. "What are you saying? Mahlon sold Red? The fuck he did!"

Justin ignored him, walking with Hank to his jeep with a nod for Pete to quit antagonizing Bobby and put his muscle to work helping Joe and Fred with Julia's refueling. "How's the weather?"

"Little low coming in over the mountains," Hank unfolded the latest report. "She'll be fine though, unless you'd rather I took care of it."

"No, she'll be fine," Justin eyed Julia preparing to take the plane back up and once around for a test run. "Will need you and Fred to lend Pete a hand. You can head out as soon as we get these jeeps in. Have another fellow Nel out there. He's doing some reconnaissance, and after that should be heading to Jean Paul's place in about a week. That's an approximate. Nel has a new fellow with him, Jeff. A translator. He's bit inexperienced, but that's why he's with Nel. Shouldn't need your assistance with the language, but you never know. Either way, Pete will let you know." He lit his pipe.

"Whatever you need," Hank nodded. "Not thinking Jean Paul's somehow mixed up in any of this, are you?"

"Yes, well, no," Justin said. "Don't have much yet, but I doubt if it's anything to do with Jean Paul. Not that Mike's not pretty hot property, because he is."

"Aye, quite," Hank said. "That much I've got. A bloody physicist, no less."

"Yes," Justin said. "Shouldn't have overheard that, but you did, and it's not to be spread around. That includes Julia and Fred."

"Understood."

"Good. Unfortunately, for all Michael is, there's a lot more he is not. Took off for the States for a reason, and then took off from there, supposedly because of this. Might be true, might not. Something's in the works though clearly, as clearly wherever it started out, it ended up here. Need to know who, and need them all, fast as possible, and Mike can't be anywhere around, certainly not here."

"Right." Hank's eyes flitted for Joe's jeep. He was not against taking it in now and getting on with the job, not that a few minutes or even an hour would matter.

"But it's not a bad idea," Justin said. "Making use of Jean Paul," he clarified as Hank looked at him. "Since we also don't know what the problem is with Jean Paul, can't chance accidental involvement in any this, if only out of simple curiosity. Right now, Michael's a lot safer in Algeria than he is in Cairo, and I'd like to keep it that way until I know better what's going on here, damn Algeria. For the official record, Mike's a war correspondent, just moving him out for safe transport back to Gibraltar following a little trouble with his attaché. That's the story and we'll stick to it regardless of who asks. You can send a wire with reassurance to Jean Paul along with the sad news from home. Death in the family," Justin lit his pipe. "You can tell him it's my sister, just in case there's anyone out there tuning in."

"Be news if they weren't," Hank agreed.

"So it would," Justin said. "We'll see what comes of it. In the meantime, make sure Jean Paul gets the point I'm not in any mood to listen to any lip about Nel, any more than I am in a mood to entertain. I don't want or need the press underfoot, and so the correspondent is out. No action necessary. Just need a little time to make the arrangements, until then, it's hands off. If I need his help, I'll ask. Any complaints, he can send them to de Gaulle."

"Will do," Hank promised.

"Good. You can take care of that now if you will with Pete before he leaves. He'll get you the OK to send it out from Cairo. Once out there, Frank will handle general surveillance, as usual. Need anything, radio him. Pete's boss, but you're his second." Justin ogled Michael currently being held at bay by Bobby, which wasn't going to last long. Bobby didn't have the patience, and Michael, whether he believed it or not, was apt to end up shot.

"What?" Justin wandered back Michael's way, but only because Mike was definitely worthless dead.

"You about done?" Michael nodded.

"No," Justin assured. Not with throwing his weight around, telling people what to do, or with putting the blame where the blame belonged, and it was in Michael's lap. "There's no link between Joanna and I, certainly not in North Africa, unless you gave it up to your pal McDowell. The only possible link is in England, and even there he'd have to have more than just some key to an executive's toilet. You're in this, Mike, up to your neck, and I wouldn't look for Evelyn to cover your arse for you, not this time around."

"Guess again," Michael said. "Mahlon didn't do this. You're looking for a scapegoat to cover your own stinking smell, and he ain't it."

"Then it's you," Justin turned his back, climbed into the jeep, and sped away to cut Julia off at liftoff, catching her attention by crossing her flight path, the plane banging back down without damage or injury to either of them.

"That wasn't too bright, guv," Julia cut the engine and leaned out over her door to say. "Lose more than a tire that way."

"And you're going to have to do better than that," Justin countered. "Cloud cover's heavy and low over the mountains. No indication it's going to get any better by the time you're there.'"

She shrugged. "Still nothing you couldn't have said with a kiss."

"Yes, well," Justin said, "afraid you're a bit out of my league."

"Oh, right," she laughed. "Meaning, you're a bit out of mine, and it's a lie either way, but that's all right, I won't tell."

"Yes, well," Justin said, getting to back to why he was out there.

"Now we both know why you're out here," Julia purred. "You're a camel, not a monk. Something else I know."

"But won't tell," Justin suspected.

"Cross my heart," she crossed and swore.

"Yes, well," Justin said, getting back to the second reason why he was out there, his airplane. "You're a little crowded with four, but weight's fine. You'll make Malta with no problem. Put her down though, should you have to, wherever you have to. Might not look it, but Mike's a valuable piece of cargo."

"Oh?" Julia glanced toward home field. "Who says?"

"I do," Justin assured.

She smiled. "Well, in that case ... yes, sir."

"Much better," Justin approved. "You're waiting to link up with Nel, should anyone ask. Hank and Fred will be along in a day or two to bolster your crew."

"Curious more who might ask," Julia admitted. "Heard from Pete a pack of lions couldn't have done better job on the lad who was brought in from that lost convoy. No lions around here that I'm aware of so it must be the two-legged kind. Arabs or Jerry, you're thinking? Or both? Jerry would have just left him, wouldn't they? No reason to go through all of that."

"Yes, well, it's not a suicide mission, if that's what you're wondering," Justin said.

She laughed. "No, luv, just curious, like I said. Sure you've got better plans for me."

He did. "Algeria," Justin nodded. "That's where you're headed."

"Explains the mountains," Julia resumed eying home plate. "Your Michael must be hot then, too hot for Cairo. Anything else I need to know?"

"He volunteered?" Justin said.

"Oh, right," she scoffed. "Like the rest of us. But that's also all right," she teased him with her smile again. "Give that secretary of yours her cards and I'll show you how well I can type."

"Yes, well, haven't the faintest ..." Justin had to say.

"And no reason why you should," she purred. "Ugly as sin under all that paint and padding; take my word for it."

He would. "Back to Mike. He's a war correspondent. Don't worry about the details, Pete and Hank will take care of that, and Mike's got his own rather healthy repertoire should anything unexpected come up. Rather the same as he likes to think he can take care of himself. He probably can, but let's save finding out. He is hot, and too expensive to lose, so, yes, Algeria's a better choice right now than keeping him here until we know exactly what's going on. Nel will take care of anything to do with Jean Paul, and Pete will take the reins if it turns out to have anything to do with you. Nel has a fellow with him named Jeff. Bit new, and so depending on what Nel does come up with, I might pull Jeff and put him with you. Pete doesn't like him, but Pete will make do, trust you can take care of that."

"Trust Pete more than I trust you," Julia suggested, though not to rub it in. "Said something about a lady friend of yours being in that Yank's car. Can't say I'm sorry to hear the worst."

"Sounds like Pete's had a lot to say," Justin agreed. "The car was a jeep, and, yes, my sister was with them. She's dead."

"Oh," Julia flushed. "Sorry. Didn't mean to be rude, no more than Pete did, I'm sure. Just talking, you know."

"Yes," Justin said. "That's about it then, other than I'll need Fred to take your jeep in. Mind? Pete also said something about a wedding."

She laughed. "Why? Would it matter if I did?"

"Yes, well, no. On the odd chance you do though—"

"What?" Julia leaned a little further out the window of the plane.

"Yes, well," Justin kept a respectable distance and firm grip on his reserve. "Bit of a drastic measure, isn't it? This wedding of yours? After all, there's no saying I wouldn't have come around."

"There's no saying you can't now," she assured.

"True," Justin said, and left before he made good on his threat, Michael throwing his weight in front of the jeep as he rolled up.

"Let's start over," Michael suggested. "Mahlon was an engineer. You know how many frigging engineers they have out here?"

"Yes, well, the only thing you're right about, Mike, is they used

Joanna to get to me whether they intended to or not."

"I never said that," Michael's hand sliced through the air. "I said it was your fault that's what I said, which it is."

"What's the difference?" Justin asked.

"All the world!" Michael insisted. "Mahlon wasn't big enough to be given the time of day!"

"Which I am," Justin nodded. "Be careful out there, Mike, because so are you." He drove off to collect Bobby.

"Careful out fucking where?" Michael barked after him. "Chuck!"

"Ready when you are—Doc, is it?" Pete interjected jovially from behind.

"Funny, you don't look like Chuck to me." Michael turned around to find Joe standing with the grinning walleyed freak, a mission on their faces. "What the fuck is this?"

"You mean the plane?" Pete glanced fondly back at Julia waiting patiently in her cockpit, motor running. "Well, now, that, Doc, is an *Applecore* what you call an *Albacore*. Don't let her swastikas fool you, she's born and made in the UK. That paint's only to help get us to where we're going without the problems we might have otherwise."

"We'll carry you if we have to, Doc," Joe added. "Swear to Christ."

"Huh?" Michael said.

"Just get in the plane," Pete translated for him. "Make it easy on yourself."

"I'll make it a lot easier," Michael assured. "I ain't fucking going anywhere."

"Have it your way," Pete sighed, and Michael woke up three miles high.

Chapter Twenty-Five

Justin was pensive, his face deadpan when he returned to Bobby and the jeep. That was all right from Bobby's perspective, the same as it was routine, including what Justin was thinking about, less the details that would be the business at hand. The personal angle, well, that was over and done. Gone with the Doc on his airplane. Bobby believed Justin got rid of the Doc for no other reason than to keep what was personal at arm's length, far as he could keep it. Couple of thousand miles away seemed just about right. The point Justin risked his career, quite possibly his life, should anyone find out he'd done all of that being who the Doc was, apparently made no never mind to him, much as it might to someone else, Bobby among them. Bobby was mad as hell with the Doc, and even angrier with Justin for risking his neck to save Michael's. Wasn't a fair exchange, in Bobby's opinion, the hell with the damn Doc.

"Where to now?" Bobby asked with an edge to his tone Justin noticed as he lit his pipe. But then Bobby wasn't Pete who took such things as anarchism in stride, or Hank who preferred not to know. Bobby was Bobby and Justin was probably guilty of anarchy or something similar for taking it upon himself to assist Michael with his disappearing act.

Justin was probably guilty of a lot of things. In contempt of every rule and regulation in the book, including the ones no one had thought of yet, when they threw the book at him when and if Justin should be found out. It did not change anything, would not change anything. Justin was Justin, the same as Michael was Mike and so forth.

So forth and so on. Justin thought of Evelyn, how to tell him about Joanna, what to say. He could not keep that confrontation at arm's length for too long regardless of how many miles away. It did not make Justin sad to think of Evelyn. It made him what he was, and that was angry. In an odd way angrier about Michael than he was about the disappearing Jerry depots and that probably made him angriest of all. Damn, Mike. Damn him over and over again. One of those things that also never changed. Justin did not like Michael regardless of what Evelyn might like to believe about the boyhood trio who grew up to be men. They were not Evelyn, Teddy, and Scotty. They were Justin, Joseph, and Mike, and Justin could not resist thinking how it might be easier on Evelyn if Mike and Joanna went down together. Would be sad, tragic, but also poetic. Evelyn liked poetry, the sight, and smell of flowers in the spring. Justin put and kept Michael at arm's length so he wouldn't kill him. Nothing poetic about that, just plain fact.

"Want to check the town yourself or leave if for the fellows?" Bobby was asking. "Either's fine with me."

Bobby was a damn poor liar. Nothing was fine by him the same as none of this was 'fine' with Justin. Bobby had as much on his mind as Justin had on his. The fact that Bobby was fidgety clinched that. Probably thinking about Pete, whatever the business was with Pete Justin hadn't failed to notice. As far as Siwa, yes, well, there wasn't anything in the town Justin personally needed to see. He had seen it all here, from here. He considered briefly how it was no one in or from the town apparently noticed a group, large or small, of Jerries being around, but then decided the answer was rather obvious. They weren't Jerries, at least not dressed like them if they were, and even if they were the town apparently preferred not to become involved. So, no, there wasn't anything the town could tell Justin he didn't already know, which was nothing.

"Yes, well," Justin supposed he could order some arbitrary group of residents lined up and shot for complacency or conspiracy, but that would mean Bobby had to stay out in the heat that much longer instead being on his way home to his fans. "Home," he answered from the looks of Bobby with his sweat dried to wrinkles on his shirt and drying as it dripped out from under his hat. "You all right?"

"Aye." Bobby borrowed Pete's gift of water to rinse his mouth and spit. "This little bit of sweat will do me good. Maybe even drop a stone or two."

"Yes, well, as long as that's all you drop."

"Same goes for you, lad," Bobby assured. "My arse and your neck go together, last I heard."

"So they do." Justin ogled Joe taking charge of packing Christine in the plane like she was made out of china.

"Then get going," Bobby suggested, "before you find my foot up yours. Worried about the heat, a little breeze would help."

"Yes, well, I wouldn't suggest it," Justin got down to business, climbed in the jeep, hit the pedal and took off like he was flying one of his airplanes, storming the dunes like you might a beach or a barn. Difference of course being they weren't in the air, but on the ground, sand, more specifically, and so it was a bit bumpy to say the least, the sheer weight of Bobby probably all that kept him from being thrown clear. "You're in enough trouble already for that telephone business earlier. Joe's up for a few laps and you can always join him."

"Well, now, I already knew what you were going to say, now, didn't I? So why waste more time, especially since I wasn't about to listen anyway? As far as Joseph, right," Bobby scoffed. "Lad could do fifty laps before he cracked a sweat."

"The devil he can," Justin said. "Five bob says he's down and gasping at twenty-five."

"Aye, and another five for every damn lap he makes after that," Bobby nodded.

"Deal," Justin said. "Now all we have to do is figure out what to get him for his wedding."

"You mean Christine?" Bobby chuckled. "Oh, well, now, that radio's all Joseph's got now that you gave his lady love her cards."

Had he? "Might have to try that again," Justin suggested. "I've no more fired Julia than I'm sure she's fired Pete despite Joe being in the picture and that bloke she decided to marry."

"Fred," Bobby nodded. "Aye, Fred. Not going to last any more than the first one so just leave it run its course."

"Yes, well, I didn't fire her," Justin assured. "Just a reminder who the boss is and that Hank isn't going to be aboard to bail her out. Need to be able to rely on her, and her judgment."

"She's fine," Bobby nodded. "Wasn't talking about her, anyway. Was talking about your secretary. She's Joe's love, or was."

"Oh," Justin said. "Right. Sorry. Forgot about her. And, quite. I gave her, her cards. Though I wouldn't be too concerned there either, they're pretty well stocked. Bigger and better each time."

"Beg your pardon?" Bobby swallowed the water he had been prepared to spit out again.

"Quite well stocked," Justin assured.

"Right, well," Bobby shifted uncomfortably in his seat, "looks good on her, just the same."

"Yes, well," Justin said, "believe it's she looks good on him, isn't it?"

"What?" Bobby said.

"Or maybe it isn't," Justin shrugged. "What do I know?"

"That's my question," Bobby insisted. "What the devil are you talking about?"

"Believe I was talking about Joe," Justin said. "Why? What am I talking about?"

"Nothing," Bobby assured. "Not your damn business, nor mine that damn brassiere of hers. I don't give a damn if it's bigger and better each damn morning she comes in. Which it is," he admitted. "Aye, it is. Noticed that myself."

"Right," Justin said after a moment. "Yes, well, no, I wasn't talking about that. For that matter," he assured, "believe I said stocked, not stacked. Pretty damn well stocked with them," he nodded, which they were, appeared to be. "No ruddy end in sight to them, apparently. Though I can't say I'm not surprised Joe even noticed a difference between them—the ruddy girls," he clarified. "Not the damn size of the last one's bristols."

"I understand," Bobby waved.

"Well, good," Justin said.

"Though I can't say I know what the devil you're talking about now either."

"Yes, well, that makes two of us," Justin assured. "Ruddy brassiere? The devil with Joe, can't say I'm not a bit surprised at you."

"Oh?" Bobby said. "Why? No one's that damn blind, lad, not even you."

"Yes, well, it's not a point of being blind," Justin said.

"Oh?" Bobby said. "What's it a point of being?"

"How the devil do I know?" Justin said, that time impatiently. "It's a point that's all. Think you'd have more damn important things to pay attention to, that's the bloody point."

"I'm old, not dead," Bobby shrugged.

"Apparently," Justin agreed. "Still, think we can save the damn subject for another day don't you?"

"No more dead than you, lad," Bobby suggested cleverly.

"Yes, well, if you mean the secretary ..." Justin assured.

"I don't mean the secretary," Bobby shook his head. "Mean Julia."

"Oh," Justin said. "Yes, well, then you're right. I'm not dead."

Bobby nodded. "So what's your point about no end in sight to them? The secretaries," he clarified as Justin frowned. "Not Julia."

"Just that," Justin said. "There's no ruddy end of them in sight."

"Except I don't know what you mean," Bobby said. "That lass is the only secretary you've ever had."

"In what way?" Justin requested.

"What do you mean in what way?" Bobby said. "In all ways. Every way. Three months, lad, almost," he nodded. "In and out, you're right, like a damn revolving door. But I don't know what you mean about 'secretaries' is what I'm saying. There's only been one."

"No," Justin said.

"Yes," Bobby assured. "Same one, lad. Same one."

"No," Justin said.

"It's the same damn woman!" Bobby insisted. "There a day, gone the next, and back again the day after that, you're right about that. For what it's worth," he scoffed, talking largely to himself, which was fine with Justin. "Can't even tell she's ever been here at all from the state of your office. In the same damn mess since we came here."

And it would stay that way. "Now, during, and after the next one," Justin assured.

"Same one, lad," Bobby shook his head. "I'm telling you, she's the same one."

"And I'm telling you she's not," Justin assured, and he had five more bob that said one of them was right. "Check the damn personnel files, and while you're at, check your damn blood pressure and heart, because one or the other's a bit off."

"Deal," Bobby accepted.

"Deal," Justin agreed. "Now, if your preoccupation with my secretaries is satisfied, think you're ready to tell me what the business was with Pete?"

"Preoccupation?" Bobby said, and Justin looked at him.

"Aye," Bobby sighed. "And, well, I wouldn't call it preoccupation exactly."

"Oh? What would you call it, exactly? Even Julia mentioned something about them for some damn reason or another. Joe, probably. Quite," Justin decided. "And the ever increasing size of their brassieres, no doubt."

"You're talking nonsense now, lad," Bobby assured. "Same as any 'business you're referring to with Pete."

"Meaning?" Justin said.

"Now, I don't know what meaning," Bobby shifted again in his seat. "Meaning just that. Nonsense. Want to talk about something that might not be, is this business with that Doc of yours. You sure you won't find it's you they're gunning for?"

"Yes, well, it's your job to make me sure, isn't it? Fair to say at the moment I'm not sure of anything, except that Joanna is not coincidence, and that it's not over."

"Whatever *it* is," Bobby agreed. "Other than the war."

"Quite," Justin said, "other than the war. I believe it's Mike, because it has to be Mike. Do more with him than they ever could with me. Only thing they'd want to do with me is put me out of business. Don't need Joanna to try that. It's all right, though. They want Mike and I want them. So, yes, I guess Mike is right, whoever they came gunning for, who they got is me." He turned the wheel of the jeep sharply as they banged their way up onto the road where he could finally pick up speed.

"Aye," Bobby stared straight ahead. "Well, we could always beat it out of him, lad, if you think he might know something more."

"Mike? That we could," Justin agreed. "But I doubt if he does. I don't think Mike hightailed it out of England because someone was after him, save for possibly Uncle Sam. I think Washington made him an offer he couldn't refuse and he went quietly and took off the moment their backs were turned."

"You mean he's telling the truth," Bobby said.

"I mean he's telling the truth," Justin agreed. "I think Mike was on the run, cooling his heels until the heat died down, next stop Peru. Something happened though he didn't anticipate. Obviously that was Joanna. It's the North Africa part I can't quite figure. If Mike left orders, Joanna should be in one of two places, home with Evelyn or on her way to Manhattan and him. He said as much," Justin frowned. "Mike said as much."

"What?" Bobby asked.

"Actually, if someone were after Mike," Justin thought, "the last place Joanna would be is home with Evelyn or on her way to Mike, least not straight away. Too risky. Whoever McDowell turns out to be, Reid definitely appears to have been SIS."

"Aye," Bobby nodded. "Thinking they brought her here?"

"To me, you mean?" Justin said. "It's possible—Son of a bitch," he stopped the jeep.

"What?" Bobby asked.

"Too many possibilities," Justin nodded coldly, "need more facts. McDowell isn't the only one who could have been in this up to his ruddy neck. There's Reid, too. SIS he'd have access McDowell wouldn't have. Still, damn Reid's access, there's no damn link between Joanna and I. There isn't."

"Aye, there is," Bobby disagreed, "she's your sister."

"My sister is dead," Justin reminded. "Been dead ten years. No, there's one link only and it's between Joanna and Mike."

"Well, it's no coincidence, lad," Bobby said. "No one brought the lass here save to get to you. That much I believe."

"Because she talked," Justin said.

"What?" Bobby said.

"Joanna," Justin assured. "She talked to Mike's ruddy friends."

"Willingly you mean?" Bobby said.

"Or otherwise," Justin agreed tightly. "Sure at some point it wasn't exactly over tea. In the meantime, McDowell either tried to get her the hell out of there, as Mike claims ..."

"To you, you mean?"

"I mean," Justin said, "it's possible they didn't know where the hell Mike was. On the up-and-up, they had to get Joanna out of there.

On the flip side, taking Joanna would definitely work to coax Mike out of where he was."

"And that means they were privy to a lot more than you think, lad," Bobby said, "because where they brought her is here. Good reason or bad, no reason save you."

"The States," Justin shook his head. "Safe passage to the States. Into Africa and out via Gibraltar."

"Aye, well, if she were on the continent maybe," Bobby concurred. "But she weren't, according to him. Should have just taken her to Greenland."

"Except that would have been—"

"Anticipated," Bobby said it for him. "Got it. All right. So McDowell tried to throw off whoever was after them by coming here."

"Possibly," Justin said.

"And definitely failed," Bobby nodded, "what matters most."

"Or succeeded," Justin lit his pipe and shifted the jeep back into gear, taking off.

"Aye, depends on whose side he was on, you're right," Bobby concurred. "It's all right, we'll find out. Good news is, you might not be in this at all, lad, other than by way of coincidence."

Oh, Justin was definitely in it. Maybe not at the start, but definitely now. "Why Cairo?"

"Instead of Morocco?" Bobby understood. "Bit odd, but could just be more of that 'anticipated' idea. If the Jerries were waiting for them here, which apparently they were, they sure the devil had a group of them waiting in Morocco."

"Why Tobruk?" Justin asked.

"Driving? Well, that doesn't make any damn sense," Bobby agreed. "Stupid and dangerous, to say the least. That McDowell couldn't seriously have thought he was going to get the lass clear across Africa without running into a problem or two."

"He was on the run," Justin said. "No plan, he was on the damn run and making it up as he went along. You're right. That lets me out of it, since I'm here."

"And on the run he should have stayed put. Here," Bobby assured. "There's enough of us here, that's for sure. Someone would have helped him out. Should have waltzed her into the nearest brass and hollered for help. No, he was on the wrong side, lad," Bobby promised. "Of that I am convinced. He might have worked to make it look good to those who were concerned on the London side, but once here, *bam!* Just took her. No one here to stop him. Not that he was aware, which he wouldn't be if you're right there's no damn link between you and her. It's the only way it plays out, lad. It's the only way it makes even the slightest bit of sense."

"Either that or the damn family's just cursed," Justin grunted.

"Well, I wouldn't say that." Bobby shifted a little in his seat Justin noticed.

"Still not quite right," Justin said. "Don't have it quite right yet."

"Well, no," Bobby said. "Of course we don't. But that's all right. You keep thinking it through like you are and I'll do what I need to do, and we'll get it done, lad, like we always do."

"So what was all that with Pete?" Justin changed the subject since this one was about worn out.

"Nothing," Bobby said. "You do have one problem with what you are thinking, lad, you know."

"Mike," Justin agreed. "Yes, I know. Damn pinching Joanna in hopes of having Mike show up. Mike did show up, in Cairo no less, where they should have been to snatch him as he stepped off his plane."

"What do you think that means?"

"Yes, well, I'm gambling," Justin said, "it means they actually have no idea who Mike is, not only not know where he was. The closest they got was Joanna, and, quite, they needed her to move onto Mike."

"Sounds reasonable."

"Yes, well, it sounds reasonable," Justin assured, "because it's the only way it makes any damn sense, if any of this makes any sense."

"It will," Bobby nodded confidently. "It will."

So it would. "Start with the patrol who found the jeep and Reid. One of ours, wasn't it? Wasn't the Yanks."

"No, it was ours," Bobby agreed. "Second wave of them coming in from Tobruk. Jeff was with the first one, just came in a day or so before."

"Jeff?" Justin looked at him.

"I'm checking into it," Bobby assured. "I'm checking into it. Confirming everything, from the damn report to Jeff's checking in."

"Let's start with Cairo," Justin agreed.

"Aye, and it's a lot of territory," Bobby reminded, "is all I'm saying. Going to have to be a little patient. Every damn job and agenda under the sun. But we'll find the one we want, lad, we'll find it. It's how it works. Someone knows, and someone will talk. They always do."

"Yes," Justin said facetiously, "and plenty of time to sort through it all to find it. You up to it?"

"Course." Few things Bobby wasn't up to. He took the picture out of his pocket.

"What's this?" Justin asked as Bobby handed him a photograph of some Catholic girl outside her school some years back. Quite a few years back from the style of the clothes and the general quality of the print, both somewhat worse for wear.

"That business you were asking about with Pete," Bobby nodded. "And before you say anything else, coincidence, lad, remember that. Said as much yourself, such a thing does exist."

"Yes, well, what else would I say?" Justin asked.

"I don't know," Bobby shrugged. "Recognize her? Could start with that."

Recognize her. The devil with her. Recognized the fellow standing next to her like a proud father or mate. Ian McShane. That was a name out of the past, an icy road, car accident, and occupants burned alive. Evelyn swore it was the Fascists, afraid of exposure by the honorable Charles, regardless of who they got to do the job. Justin swore it was McShane regardless of who wanted the job done. "What's the point?" Justin asked.

"You being facetious for a reason?" Bobby asked.

"Could ask the same of you," Justin assured. Of course he recognized her despite ten years and her curls dyed three shades lighter and stretched into an unnatural state until they looked more like cotton batting than hair "Who is she? Daughter would be pushing it. McShane's not Pete's age, and she's got to be close to thirty. Picture's not that old."

"She's twenty-six, lad," Bobby agreed. "Sixteen in her picture."

"I asked you who she is," Justin stopped the jeep hard. "Cain was the father's name."

"His sister," Bobby sighed. "Aye, she's McShane's sister. Fifth one or so in line between that string of fellows the old man sired. Six or seven all total, wasn't it, by the time he was done?"

"Eight," Justin said, before the cow laid down and died, the widower Johnnie not far behind. Stepped in front of a streetcar, some say deliberately. Others say he was drunk on whiskey and grief, and either way it left Ian in charge at seventeen or so years of age before the authorities stepped in to break the happy brood apart. Never got them all, some retreating to their lair to regroup after a few years, others shuttled appropriately off to the children's home, a flip of the coin which lot ended up the worse for it. Still, Justin didn't seem to recall stumbling upon some teary-eyed story of some bleeding heart taking pity on one or any of them. Raising them as one of their own while the rest of her clan eked out a living as best they could. Crime, largely, two of them dead before Justin ever heard the name.

"Where's Pete fit in?" Justin handed him back the photograph and lit his pipe.

"Messenger," Bobby shrugged. "Said she was her, I said she wasn't. Said he could prove it, and I said go ahead and try."

Looked like Pete won. "And Peterson?" Justin asked.

"Now that's interesting," Bobby agreed as if the rest of it wasn't. "Went through the first war together, it seems, Jim Peterson and her old man."

"McShane's old man," Justin corrected, finding that tidbit of information somewhat interesting, Bobby was right.

"Nothing more romantic than that," Bobby nodded. "Peterson went on to make a career out of it, Cain just went home. Happens all the time."

"Deliberate, in other words," Justin said.

"Peterson putting her with you?" Bobby said. "Aye, well, obviously it's deliberate, lad. Went through the war with her old man like I just said. Doesn't mean it has anything to do with her."

"Never heard of him," Justin said, meaning James Peterson and not until three months ago.

"Right. Well, he's obviously heard of you," Bobby said.

"Quite," Justin said, "and he should have listened to what he heard. So much for him keeping that career he's worked so hard to make. You tell him that?"

"I haven't told him anything. Thought I'd leave that to you."

"Thank you," Justin said. "I'll tell him."

"Right," Bobby said. "Before you do though, just remember it's a different world. This war, aye, it's making it different, but it was different already. Different for you than it was for your father. Different for him than it was for Lee and so forth, all the way back. Not taking anything away from you. You are who you are, and you've got a lot of leverage, lad, that you do. Just saying it's different, that's all. Lots of fellows out there who don't have your lineage, but have the same leverage and then some regardless."

"Rubbish," Justin said.

"That's what I thought you'd say," Bobby sighed. "Aye, and, it's all right. Do what you want to do, since you're going to do it anyway."

So he would. "That it?"

"Well," Bobby said, "from what I've been able to gather, it's her who sought Peterson out about five or so years ago, not the other way around." He smiled suddenly, chortled, for whatever damn reason that escaped Justin. "Fancies herself the next Amelia Earhart since the first one went and disappeared. Not just Peterson you've never heard of, apparently not heard of her either; the lass I mean."

"Yes, well," there was no reason why Justin would have heard of her. He was interested in who killed his father. Ian McShane was a man, forty years old himself by this point, thirty back then. Not some tot with his thumb stuck in his mouth.

"Well, she's no tot, lad," Bobby said. "Not then and not now. She got her A-levels. Graduated a year or two behind her classmates, I'll grant you, but still she did it."

"Despite her early upbringing and a couple years off for good behavior," Justin said. "Rot."

"Now, be civil, lad," Bobby suggested, "if you can't be anything else. I happen to like her. Not too proud or ashamed to say. I've kept my eye on her, that's true. But I happen to like her, no offense to you."

"Rot," Justin just said again.

"She's RAF," Bobby reminded, clarifying the earlier reference to Earhart. "And nothing to suggest she's any idea who you are other than her assignment."

"Coincidence," Justin said.

"Innocent," Bobby assured. "On her part, I believe she is. Unless you've a mind to think it's the Blueshirts what followed you to Africa, killed your sister to finish the job they didn't quite finish ten years ago. And if you've a mind to think that," he said, "I've a mind to tell you what I think about that."

"No," Justin did not think that. He thought what he said. Jim Peterson obviously had as little respect for his own career as he did for Justin's lineage and personal feelings, and Justin would take care of that despite the damn new world on the horizon. As far as McShane's sister, it was difficult not to think she enjoyed the joke at his expense as much as her pal Peterson. If he was wrong, he did not care. Beyond that, he didn't think much, somewhat preoccupied by a hollow feeling in his stomach he was unaccustomed to and did not like. "So what is Pete's point again in bringing her to light?"

"I don't know," Bobby shrugged. "Hates the Blueshirts, he says, you know that. Point of fact, that's all. Thinking more about my reasons for not wanting him to. She's a smart one, lad," he said. "Something you might want to know before you hang her. Never graduated college, but that's also more to her credit than against. Knew she didn't have a chance of getting some diploma despite all the protests about equality and I don't know what all going on at the time. But she has her commission, and where she did graduate from is Buckinghamshire, just finished a six-month assignment as a lead cryptographer."

"So she's a smart one," Justin agreed.

"Right," Bobby smiled, "before you hang her. Now you're starting to talk sense."

Not really. Now, as well as back when, Justin didn't care much for sense, only the common sort that held McShane responsible and guilty regardless. "McShane's sister," he said.

"Innocent until proven guilty," Bobby nodded. "Which, just for the record, Pete made a point of pointing out, wanted that clear."

"Well, it's clear," Justin assured, "and contradictory, considering Pete hates McShane."

"Whatever, lad," Bobby dismissed. "Leave trying to figure out the IRA. Asking me why Pete brought her to light and per Pete his information is for your information only. It's no form of accusation, but rather believes she's as innocent as I do."

"Pete would know," Justin agreed.

"Would," Bobby assured, "that he would."

"Doesn't stop me from hanging her," Justin said. "No more than Katy, Martha, and Liz being in that car stopped McShane."

"Can't do that," Bobby shook his head. "That would be murder, lad, for all the wrong reasons."

"The devil I can't," Justin said and drove, just drove, along the heated road for Cairo, Hank close behind in Joe's jeep, Fred beside him in Pete's.

Partisans, Rogues, and Thieves (1)

Chapter Twenty-Six

Great Atlas Mountains, Algeria
March 10

By 1100 hours, Tuesday, Jean Paul Dumont received a transcript of a broadcast message they had intercepted, and was reported to have been issued by Justin in Cairo. It was Jean Paul's second urgent message of the day. Anna Haas, the Jewess he called Cassie, there since early morning to abuse him. As fast as her eldest son Abraham could fly her to Jean Paul's lair to scream about the weaknesses in Jean Paul's security network.

She wasn't the only one. The tone of Justin's message was threatening in that Justin apparently had men en route, and unclear in its references to some foreign correspondent and Justin losing his sister. The "men" had to be Reynolds for the same reason Cassie was already there: The depots. Jean Paul's delicate black face pinched with worries and concerns he should never have at his young age, but did. Had them since birth. Different ones, but trials just the same. His mother a Nigerian prostitute and slave, his father the crippled Algerian monk Pierre who bought her freedom for sixty pounds of salt. His father escaped. His mother died in Mussolini's camps during the Italian-Libyan War, where Jean Paul survived to grow up and fight for France, and watch them lose their war. He was not losing this one. Not to Hitler, or for Anna Haas. He didn't care what his father said. His father was in over his head.

"That's it?" Jean Paul demanded of his radio operator.

"Oui, mon caporal," she assured. "The signal wasn't very good."

No, and the subsequent translation into French made things worse. That much Jean Paul had figured out for himself. "Well, Justin isn't wasting his men entertaining some correspondent, and he didn't lose his sister here," he tossed the message to her, changed his mind and took it back. "Find out what this is actually about."

"The depots," she believed as Jean Paul believed. Reynolds was returning for one reason and it had nothing to do with some sister.

Jean Paul frowned at the message. He wasn't sure if Justin even had a sister. He tried to think of what else the reference could mean but couldn't think of anything. The foreign correspondent had to be Reynolds. He didn't need Anna Haas to tell him that.

"Find out," he said. "Confirm this is even from Justin. Ask them to repeat—radio Justin if you have to and tell him we've intercepted a message that has us confused—just find out. I can't argue if I don't know what I am talking about."

"Perhaps dead, mon caporal," she nodded.

"What?" Jean Paul said.

"Perhaps it is not lost, but dead," she closed her code book satisfied.

"It doesn't matter!" Jean Paul snatched the code book out of her hand, slamming it down and waving the message. "This matters. The depots are why Cassie is here. If this is Reynolds returning, do we know when? Do we know where? Do we even," he insisted, "really know why, and don't you think we should find out?"

"The depots, mon caporal," she smiled. "But it's all right. We will find out where, and we will find out when regardless of the silly English code."

"It's not so silly if we can't translate it," Jean Paul assured and left to see what he could do about winning the argument that mattered most. Anna. Anna, who wanted the depots safe and protected that Justin wanted located and destroyed. But then they were her depots, not German, mobile, temporary transfer stations, shipping supplies in, shipping them out. They only looked German for the same reasons she relied upon Jean Paul. Protection. Protection for her people traveling under Rommel's North African flag and the shroud of her beneficent le Metapel, safe passage south from the coast down into the interior and Eden. Non-interference guaranteed by Jean Paul's troops.

She was crazy. Jean Paul knew that regardless of what Justin might have figured out or guessed—which Justin apparently was onto something. Believed he was onto something worth his attention, and unfortunately, it was very much worthy of Justin's attention. Jean Paul wanted out of his arrangement with Anna for more reasons than his allegiance with Justin. What he had agreed to once had now happened ten times. If only Justin knew. There weren't two depots. There were ten, twenty, thirty, who knew how many. Jean Paul could not guess how many might actually be out there. He knew he couldn't close his eyes because when he tried all he could see was a line of German defenses, temporary or otherwise he had unwittingly helped to build and supply. Anna was like his father, believing what she wanted to believe not what was true. Eden was not Eden, and it was not innocent. It was German and out there somewhere. But taking Justin into his confidence was not the answer. If it ever had been, Jean Paul was three months too late.

Jean Paul crumbled Justin's message into a ball. He could never take Justin into his confidence, not then, not now. The people's fear, mistrust, and even hatred of the English was too great. They tolerated Jean Paul's commitment to assisting the English in their fight because they would not tolerate the rape and occupation of France and her Colonies by Hitler's Nazi. Betray their faith and trust in him as the son of some iconic monk they revered, and Jean Paul could forget it. Anna's threats of annihilation would come true. He would be ripped apart. His head sent to the English on a tray.

Jean Paul was no martyr or hero. He was a societal outcast, African, with handsome ebony skin, fine French features and bold white teeth. Apart from his name and accent, which were distinctly French, it was questionable how much of their blood he had in his veins. The closest Bobby Roberts could come to deciphering Jean Paul's background was that he was French Berber, whose pre-war history had him in bed with the Algerian Nationalists, a radical anti-French movement, increasingly popular among the disenfranchised Arab.

Cairo
January 1942
"So you're Dumont," Justin grunted, recovering from his surprise at finding some twelve year old sitting across from him.

"Yes," Jean Paul concurred without apology or embarrassment, and he was not twelve. He was twenty-one, and it was not his problem if Justin expected someone taller, older, for that matter whiter than Jean Paul was, which Jean Paul was none of those things. "And you're Charles. It's nice to put a face to the name."

"It can be," Justin sat back in his chair and lit his pipe. The face of this Resistance leader he cared about was the fact that it was radical, not the point that it was black. One who, in his present incarnation as folk hero, or whatever the devil Corporal Jean Paul Dumont was to his clan, with the invasion and fall of France had apparently decided he hated the Germans and Italians more than he hated his French half-brothers. In fact, three of Jean Paul's small round table of advisors who had made the trip with Jean Paul to Cairo, were French not just bone-white. Like their leader Dumont, deposed French army. That would be the society twins Pierre and Louis Forget, one of them an imbicile, Louis, from a war injury, both of them lieutenants, still in uniform, and almost as small and young as Dumont. Then there was a career sergeant Claude L'Heureaux whom Bobby dated to the Foreign Legion, and trenches of the First World War. L'Heureaux was dressed like Jean Paul in civilian clothes, rural, not urban. A big fellow by comparison, around the size of Pete, Justin pegged L'Heureaux as a bodyguard, and Justin would be right.

"So who was Dumont?" Justin asked.

"Come again?" Jean Paul's head tipped slightly to the side. Justin didn't say anything, but made a note the fellow not only spoke English surprisingly well despite the pronounced accent, but his choice of words indicated he had seen an American film or two, and so Jean Paul had. He had seen a few. With or without them he got what Justin was asking, what he meant. The English Charles trying to figure out just who was this Dumont that had the white boys answering to him instead of it being the other way around.

"My mother's pimp," Jean Paul smiled. He probably shouldn't have. The English did not like to think they were being ridiculed.

"She did not have a name," he offered, "not Anglicized, and so she gave me his."

"Touching," Justin sat forward in his chair, flipping through his manila folder not too obviously. A fourth member of Jean Paul's allied Algerian council who hadn't made the trip to Cairo was another Nationalist. An Egyptian woman, Moslem, Cassandra *X* as in no last name, or no known last name, or Cassie *X* as she appeared in print most often, who oversaw John Paul's extensive network of prostitutes. A fifth associate of Jean Paul's however, also a woman called Cassie for confusion's sake was where Jean's group really took a sharp left turn into the little known and under-appreciated world of Jewish Resistance. "What's this Cassie to you?"

"She prefers Cassandra, and I'm sure you know," Jean Paul assured with a gesture at the file. "You'll find her useful."

More like a pain in the arse. "Meant Haas," Justin said.

"Oh," Jean Paul said. He smiled. "Well, we don't talk about her."

For such obvious and good reasons as the hefty price on her head for consorting with and supporting known terrorists fighting their wrong and private war against the British who closed the gates of Palestine. "Make an exception," Justin closed the file.

"I can't," Jean Paul shook his head. "If you know about her, and apparently you do, you understand I can't."

Justin did more than know about her, he knew her personally. Anna Kassim "Cassie" Haas was one of Evelyn's old cronies he had met during one of his world tours some forty years ago. Entwined with Evelyn, Robert, and even Justin's father Henry with his India affairs, she was also one of Michael's pals following some stint as a visiting professor at one of his alma maters. Anna Haas was a piece of work, a fierce diva who managed in between her marriages and pregnancies to achieve renowned stature as a pioneer in modern cancer therapy. Currently she was nobody save for a nuisance, self-exiled from her native Berlin due to her misfortune of being a Jew. It was Justin's misfortune she decided to park her arse in Africa while waiting for the gates of Palestine to open for her boat people.

"We live in different worlds," Jean Paul offered.

"Yes, well," all that meant was Jean Paul lived on earth. Justin had yet to figure out what cloud Haas called home. Unable to see the world beyond her own nose, Haas's views were single-minded, unwavering and committed solely to her biblical chosen, the rest be dammed.

"It won't be a problem," Jean Paul assured.

No, it wouldn't be, not for Justin. He wasn't so sure about Haas who hated him and England almost as much as both hated her, but that was her problem. "Yes, well, it's not a problem," Justin assured, "as long as she stays out of this." Meaning his and Jean Paul's arrangement. "Get a whiff she's not, and all bets are off. She's a wanted criminal."

"So am I," Jean Paul agreed. "By the Germans," he clarified.

"Yes, well, who isn't?" Justin grunted. Still, he never thought of Anna Haas, not even in passing when Mike showed up, and Joanna turned up dead in North Africa, of all places. He probably should have, though not in any manner to imply Haas might somehow be mixed up in any of this, because she wouldn't be, definitely not anything to do with selling Mike out, whom she adored as she adored Evelyn, and therefore certainly not with murdering Evelyn's beloved granddaughter Joanna. All of that, and the fact Haas was a Jew precluded her from consideration. Had Justin thought of her it would only have been how there was a link to all of them in North Africa and it was Anna Haas. However being that it never crossed Justin's mind, at least not yet, the point was moot.

March 10

Justin should have thought of her, very true, if only in passing. Anna did hate his and his England's guts for the Palestine situation, almost as much as she hated Hitler and Germany. To where England refused, Justin could have helped them, but refused as well, and he should be the last one to denounce the concept of 'chosen', in her opinion, wearing the imperial power and attitude of his English Crown as his own. He did not like her because she refused to accept her role as second class to his first class citizen, which she would never do, unlike so many others who bowed and scraped—like O'Brannigan. Yes, Anna knew Peter O'Brannigan, too. She knew them all. Evelyn, Teddy, Henry, Robert, Martha, Katy, Liz, all of them. She danced at Henry's wedding, cried at his grave. Not so with Justin. No, to the contrary, if the young King Charles ever did topple from his throne, Anna would be right there, not to pick Justin up, but to laugh. Harder than the butchers who entombed her daughter in Poland, Hannah not her mother Anna when it came to her men.

Choosing to die by her husband's side rather than spit in his eye and leave him behind as Anna did with her latest fling, taking her grandchildren with her on her exodus, she thought to Palestine.

They did not make it, obviously, and who Justin did not know anything about being around were the boys, presuming they had more brains than their mother. They didn't, not his kind of brains. They were not only sons, they were brothers. To each other and to Hannah, the middle and only girl between Anna's four towering pillars of testosterone, intelligence, and strength with their Manhattan suites and Park Avenue addresses. Admittedly a life rather hard to abandon for the dunes of Hell, but you do what you have to do in this world, and Anna and her sons did it without guilt, apology, or looking back, just straight ahead to Israel. "Time to go home," Anna told her children like Moses told his. It was what they called her, *Moses,* not *Cassie* like Jean Paul and his French did, until more recently when they started calling her *Diana* after the Roman goddess whose Saharan temple she inhabited and controlled. Yes, Justin should have thought of her, if only in passing. She certainly thought of him and none too pleasantly.

Chapter Twenty-Seven

Great Atlas Mountains
March 10

"We are having some problems confirming the details of the transmission we intercepted," Jean Paul explained when he returned to his round table of lieutenants and Anna. "I need more time to find out what it is about."

"Oh, really?" Anna lifted a harsh brow, hardened and grey, and of little resemblance to the woman she was even five years ago, except that she was still ugly. Uglier at sixty-seven than she had been at sixty-five, or two, her iron-colored hair chopped like a man's, cooler under the wigs of the many characters she employed, her weight still heavy and large breasts staining her shirt with their sweat. "What sort of problems is this?"

"See for yourself," he handed her the message. She read it, throwing it back at him in disgust. "He is an imbecile to think you will fall for this trick. I know Justin, and I know his sister. She is home in England, diapering her dolls, not in North Africa. Isn't that right?" she challenged her son Abraham, tall and dashing in his cloak of Ishmael at forty-one. The hair black and skin browned, his medical degree home safe in his Manhattan suite, his face and flesh tattooed with the art of Arab pagans. She hated the tattoos, hated them, his life over, his career, condemned to the African wilderness and unhallowed grave. He spoke to her in her native German as much to soothe her as to annoy Jean Paul. Telling her to relax, keep still, not to tip her hand. She did not listen very well, furious over the complications of the SS, and now Justin, threatening everything she wished was only her depots. There was no separating Justin's sister Joanna from Michael, and no separating Michael from what he was.

A physicist. She had the sister Joanna brought by the SS. Michael had to be out there somewhere, alive or dead, and Justin would blanket the planet to find him to make sure one way or the other.

She returned to Jean Paul who looked surprised. "What? What's the matter with you? Did I say something you didn't expect?"

"Well, no," Jean Paul said, "perhaps a little surprised you questioned the reference to some sister rather than the foreign correspondent, which, yes, I agree with you. It is concerning, possibly an indication Reynolds is en route as you suspect." He frowned at the message. "Then Justin does have a sister."

"So?" Anna said as her son Abraham resisted the temptation to hit her over the head for opening her mouth so wide. "So I know his sister? So what?"

"Nothing," Jean Paul shook his head and sat down. "I guess you could be sympathetic?"

"Why?" she asked.

"I don't know," Jean Paul waved impatiently. "Because you could? It doesn't matter. It has nothing to do with us."

"I just said that," she agreed, "didn't I?"

Yes. So did he. He felt sorry though now that he knew it was a line in a message, not some code. He liked Justin when he met him. He liked him still. Anna, he felt sorry for, until he met her. She was not a woman who inspired pity, but was quite capable of taking care of herself. It escaped him why she remained in Africa, bent on protecting and assisting those who had escaped the Nazi, instead of returning to Europe to help those who had not.

That was a lie, actually. Jean Paul knew why Anna stayed. She stayed because she was not stupid, survived, and lived out of spite. Her power was limited to herself and her wits, her sons, and their wits. She did not believe in martyrs, fighting battles she could not win, but instead in winning those she could. She did not have a chance in Europe, here she did.

"If you want sympathy," Anna's hand flitted at Abraham, "talk to the psychiatrist. He'll give you all you want. Me, I could give two-shits."

Yes, Jean Paul got the message. "Why did you say trick?" he asked curiously.

She shrugged again. "Trap then."

"Trap," Jean Paul savored. It had to be her. French was his language. "Meaning?" he asked.

"Meaning just that," she snapped. "I know."

Jean Paul eyed her with a glance at the twins Louis and Pierre Forget and the long, thin frame of his whore Cassandra with a hook for a nose behind him. Cassandra was tense, Louis, his usual nervous, Pierre his usual deadpan. It was Cassandra who straightened up to dangle her jewelry over the wooden door they used for a table, her Egyptian breath in Anna's face. "How do you *know* anything?"

"Meaning?" Anna countered.

"Meaning this," Cassandra's fingers took the message out of Jean Paul's hand to wave it at her. "You know so much, you should be telling us instead of asking us to tell you."

Anna sneered. "You mean care, and I don't."

"She's lying," Cassandra said confidently to Jean Paul, and not so evenly to Anna. "You're lying, Jew. What do you know about this? What did you do this time for Israel?"

Jean Paul silenced Cassandra, waving her back to her post. Lying was a strong accusation, suggesting Anna might have something to do with the death of some girl was simply ludicrous regardless of how angry she was over Reynolds. "Let's not read into things," Jean Paul suggested. "Lose sight of what is important. Reynolds."

"Me?" Anna said. "Me lose sight?"

"Any of us," Jean Paul assured. "I'm sorry," he apologized, "it was confusing that you would say 'trick' or 'trap'. Let's talk—" he started to say again.

"Trick or trap," Anna interrupted him, "is what Justin does. Nothing is ever innocent, not some *sister,*" she waved, "or some *war correspondent,*" she waved again. "Trick, or trap, that is his forte. *Coup d'état.* You know what that is? Of course you do. You say you are allies. I say you wouldn't interest Justin unless there was something about you he did not like. His job is to infiltrate and destroy at any cost, you'll see. You are his means, not his partner. He wants the people kept in line, not inspired. If he tames you, he will tame them, because you will do it for him. I know," she smiled, "you're right. I do it every day, all the time."

And said it all the time, Jean Paul looked away from her again, over his small arrangement of advisors, the twins, very pro-British, like him, not partisans of Vichy control. His companion Cassandra? Loyal to no one except him. "There is no one here to divide ..." Jean Paul said carefully, turning back to Anna. "We are all on the same side."

"Oh, good," she said. "Because you forget it is you who guarantees me, not the other way around. And now because Justin speaks ..." she snatched the wire off the table to wave it like a flag. "You are suddenly frightened? Really, Jean Paul, if it is time for you to have a conscience, kill your own, not mine."

"That is enough!" Jean Paul snatched the wire away from her in frustration. "I am killing no one. If I ask questions, it is simply because I am asking you to verify information I have received—"

"About Justin," she nodded.

"About the depots!" he snapped. "And perhaps we can figure out what to do about Reynolds together. But I have to know, Cassie, what I am involved in. I have to know for a fact before this goes any further."

"Which you are asking me to explain, not verify!" she assured. "Me. Who is insane? I am a Jew. My daughter lies dead in their camps. Would I walk with the creatures killing my own? Help them? Hide them?"

"No, of course you wouldn't," Jean Paul waved. "No one is saying you are. But I have men, Cassie," he stressed, "talking about munitions depots, not supply compounds. Why are they saying this? Can you explain that to me, yes?"

"I do not have to," she refused.

"Excuse me?" Jean Paul said while Cassandra smiled satisfied behind him.

"You have an idiot by the name of Reynolds breathing down your neck," she assured. "Kill it."

"Kill it," Jean Paul repeated.

"Yes," Anna said. "Kill it, him, get rid of it."

"Actually, 'men' and 'war correspondent' are separated in the message," Abraham advised his mother who glared at him for talking out of turn. "That implies more than Reynolds are coming."

"Will you talk to her?" Jean Paul agreed with Abraham excitedly in French. "I can't kill Justin's men!"

"No?" Anna said. "Not even when they are plotting against you?"

"How?" Jean Paul insisted. "How are they plotting against me? Where is your proof for any of these accusations? Even if I agree with you Justin is not satisfied with the reports of the depots and this proves Reynolds is returning!" he waved the message which said no such thing. "We will take care of it. We will work together to take care of it. That has nothing to do with killing anyone."

She snatched the wire back to read it. Dissect it. Decipher.

"What?" Jean Paul insisted. "What is it you see in there that I cannot?"

"That's a good question. What is this?" Anna thrust the notice impatiently at Abraham. "You know Justin better than I do, you tell me. What is the meaning of his silly post script about his sister if it's not to include this one in his fishing expedition? Some sad note to a friend? I don't think so. That girl didn't come here alone. You know who she had to be with, and Justin will go where he needs to go to find him dead or alive, as would I. He will not stop at the border of Egypt. And if he comes here and finds those depots where do you think they lead? To us with his sister laying right there as well. So who is crazy to be concerned? Not me. You want to wait until Justin shows up on the doorstep? I don't. I want those depots safe."

"Yes," Abraham agreed in part. "But there are two separate issues here—"

"Oh, really?" Anna sneered. "I'm sorry, is there no girl at my compound?"

Dieter's compound, and, yes, obviously there was. "There are two issues here," Abraham said again. "The girl and the depots. Justin did not send the message to this one. They intercepted it as we did."

"And that's not intentional?" Anna said. "Justin just happened to broadcast instead of wiring this one directly?"

"Of course it's intentional," Abraham said. "Justin has dropped a fishing line to see who bites. The bait about the girl isn't meant for this one or anyone. He's stirring the pot to see what boils to the top."

"And that's not Reynolds Justin is talking about?" his mother's finger pounded down on the transcript.

Yes, Abraham believed it was, and he did not like the message at all. It was well crafted, deliberately vague on the surface, allowing the audience to read into it what they wanted to. Abraham read a lot. Justin was on the warpath. Disclosing the dead girl as his sister when for ten years, on paper for public knowledge, he had no sister, was bold. That bold, meant that angry. Men on route had to be Reynolds and his boys, the 'war', or 'foreign' correspondent Justin separated from the pack had to be whom? Possibly Mike? Abraham did not think so. Instead, who came to mind was O'Brannigan. Out loud, he said calmly to his mother, "We've been over that. Yes, it has to mean Reynolds is returning. Yes, Justin involved this one to throw a scare into him—about the depots, not the girl. In the meantime, Justin thinks the girl is dead. That's why the broadcast. Notice to whomever else intercepts. Not us. Let's leave it that way. Stick to talking about Reynolds and the depots. Do not talk about the girl."

"I want them safe!" Anna insisted. "We are between Vichy and Cairo, and Justin is out there. If they come here, kill them! Reynolds, O'Brannigan, whoever. All of them. Or I will let David off his leash and it will be over!"

It would be over all right. David was Dieter, who Jean Paul and his gang only knew as le Metapel, Anna's mysterious benefactor. She called him *David* not to say his name. There was another name she avoided saying and it was Mike. Justin wasn't the only one out there somewhere, so was Mike. Like his kid, Red, dead or alive, and yes, Justin would scour the planet to find out which, find out who, and certainly find out where. He was setting himself up as bait, taunting them, daring them. That was the message Abraham read in Justin's note. The fact Justin made sure his broadcast reached as far as Algeria confirmed Justin considered the French suspect, and that had to be the depots, not the girl or Mike. An assurance from Justin he knew things others did not think he knew, whether he actually knew them or not. Justin knew something or he would not be sending his men back.

That was how Abraham read it anyway, and he was confident he was right. The problem was his mother's point that there were depots. And this one, Jean Paul, apparently knew a lot less than he should about Justin's movements and motivation.

Abraham studied Jean Paul. Nellie Reynolds was Justin's blood hound, his Ace of Aces, but not his Ace of Spades. That was O'Brannigan, the head of Justin's death squad. Peter O'Brannigan wasn't en route because of some depot. He was en route to kill. Who? This one, Jean Paul? Justin wouldn't waste O'Brannigan on Jean Paul unless Justin knew a lot, if not everything about the depots, and if Justin did, he wouldn't need Reynolds, and even then it would be more of a revenge killing.

Maybe it was Mike, Abraham considered, and maybe it wasn't here at all, at least not Jean Paul specifically. But Algeria in general included in Justin's manhunt. Reynolds to find Mike? O'Brannigan to kill Mike if they couldn't get Mike out, or wasn't dead already? If the girl wasn't at Dieter's compound, while not completely out of the question, Abraham would say Vichy Algeria would be stretching it. It wasn't, and the facts supported one scenario. A plane en route that failed to show. Cairo to Gibraltar the route? Mike aboard, it probably had escorts across Libya, dropping off as they reached Algeria, and that was when they lost contact with the plane, forced down, shot down, or crashed.

"Jesus Christ," Abraham muttered, the odds good the story went something like that. Bottom line, Justin was out there, and that was not good. Anna had one thing on her mind, her depots, from there, Eden and Dieter. This idiot Jean Paul, had to know something more, and if he didn't, he should. Abraham turned uncharacteristically hostile and impatient on Jean Paul. "Reynolds is Justin's scout, but O'Brannigan is Justin's assassin. If it's not your neck he wants whose is it? *Le Metapel?* That's her concern. Something has to be out there, someone has to know something. She is right. You're not out here alone. Justin is too close for comfort whether it's Reynolds, or O'Brannigan, or whoever it is. Justin did not ensure the message reached Algeria for no reason. So, what happened? What caused Justin to send Reynolds back? Whatever line you are trying to sell Justin about the depots he clearly isn't buying it."

Jean Paul couldn't have played it any more convincingly in Abraham's opinion. He didn't know anything, less even than they did. Abraham sighed. It was a little late to try and pretend they didn't need Jean Paul regardless.

"We intercepted the same transmission," Abraham offered as Jean Paul stared at the wire. "That appears to be the extent of it. Justin sending Reynolds out is one thing, but O'Brannigan is another. O'Brannigan is here to kill. The question is who? Why? We assumed the death of this girl happened at home, but perhaps it didn't. Perhaps it was here, Cairo. What is the chatter over the last few weeks? Is this the first time you've heard any mention of this?"

"I don't know," Jean Paul said. "Cairo ..."

"Three-thousand kilometers," Anna shrieked in support. "Justin is not sending men three-thousand kilometers for no reason!"

"I got that!" Jean Paul assured. "And I don't know. We presumed this had to be about the depots. We were puzzled about the reference to some sister, but I don't think any of us considered ..." he surveyed the twins, but they were shaking their heads, confused as he was. "You know as much as we do. This is it, yes. The quality of the transmission was very poor—the Telex? Forget it. They're still trying to re-contact them and confirm, but so far that's it."

"The mountains," Abraham nodded. "We have the same problem."

"Yes, of course, who doesn't?" Jean Paul dismissed. "I am confused. What are you saying? Justin is investigating us for his sister's death? How? Why? What does that have to do with the depots?"

"It doesn't," Abraham assured. "It can't. It is the choice of men that is concerning—obviously concerning," his impatience returned, "especially if one of them is O'Brannigan."

"Yes," Jean Paul agreed, "that is a good question, isn't it? Especially since, I agree with your mother. Justin isn't sending men three-thousand kilometers to kill French or Jews in revenge for his sister's death—in Cairo!" he turned viciously on Anna. "What the hell is actually going on here? Palestine? What did you do?"

"Stick to Reynolds!" Abraham barked at her in reminder.

She ignored him, vehement as the Gorgon Medusa, her tongue whipping Jean Paul in counter attack. "What do you think? I am not waiting until Justin is banging on the door! I do not care about your British, or your Free French, I care about mine. Justin and his idiots are a threat to mine. Get rid of them!"

"Cassie ..." Jean Paul said.

"No!" she refused. "No, if you had done your job correctly no one would be confusing depots and supply stations—and I would not have the SS at my door!" she hissed. "Now, what do you think I should do?"

"SS?" Jean Paul stared at Abraham.

"Yes," Abraham sighed. "Yes. Somehow, the SS is also mixed into this. It's a mess, and this doesn't help," he threw the message back on the table. "Justin's fishing, maybe, maybe not. But he must think you can tell him something he wants to know otherwise this message would have never reached here. Reynolds at least has to be coming here."

"He's right," Cassandra said in Jean Paul's ear. "Why would the English be coming here except for you? They're right. The Jew is right. Kill them now, all of them, her, too. Do it!"

Jean Paul ignored her. "We'll find out," he promised Anna. "Talk to me. Calm down—both of us, yes," he agreed, "and talk so we can figure this out. Together," he stressed. "Together."

"Twice now you have told me," she fumed, "how Reynolds has been where he does not belong—"

"Yes, and we took care of it. The supply transfer is safe, the camps are both gone. I will put a stop to Reynolds, I promise you. Without killing him, I will stop him. A guarantee."

Her brow arched. "You mean my camps. You want blood, Jean Paul, le Metapel will give it to you, and it will not be mine."

Jean Paul straightened up. "I do not want blood. Is that a threat to me? Because I will tell you something, Cassie—"

No, she was telling him. "I will strike a bargain with you, Jean Paul. When I am confident, mine are safe, perhaps Justin will find he has his sister back. In one step, the SS have gone from Egypt to Eden. You are a smart man. Someone has to be supplying them with this information, the same as they are supplying Justin. Is it you?"

"No!" Jean Paul turned on Abraham. "What the hell is she saying? You have Justin's sister? Are you complete idiots?"

"Do we look like idiots to you?" Abraham said.

"Don't lie to me!" Jean Paul's fist hit the table. "I'm sick of it. No, you don't look like idiots, but apparently, you think I am some kind of fool, and I am not! You can tell me what is going on, or you can tell Justin, that is the only bargain I am willing to strike with you."

"Except they are supply stations," Anna jeered. "So what could be going on? Bullets for Rommel, or pillows for my children's heads?"

"Cassie, they are hardly pillows," Jean Paul ran his fingers through his hair. "I am asking you now about Justin's sister, I want to know what you did."

"No, they are munitions," she persisted instead. "Mine! To blow open the gates of Palestine Justin has closed."

Palestine. He knew it. "Justin did not close the gates!"

"His army did! And England is never wrong, never. Ask him!"

"Fine!" Jean Paul said. "His army closed the gates, and his army is the only one who can open them—not Justin! You kidnapped his sister?" he gaped at her. "Holding her hostage? I cannot believe this. And then you come complaining to me, asking me why he is coming here? Why the hell do you think he is coming, eh?"

"Take care of it!" she barked. "A good idea, if only to stop the French from hanging the great Jean Paul Dumont first!" She stalked out the door leaving him to stare helplessly at Abraham.

"She likes him," Abraham shrugged, sometimes wondering if his mother carried on the way she did, simply because she liked him. He lit a cigarette and sat down to think. "Le Metapel," he clarified as if he had to.

"Yes," Jean Paul agreed hollowly. "I got it." She was not alone. Just ask his father who revered and idolized him. Upheld and promoted him until he was more than just a sympathetic ear, but a legend, a god no one would dare deny, betray, or offend.

"Who else?" Abraham nodded. "The sword she can see in his hand, ready to strike, defend, whatever he needs to do. A true King. Not simply an aristocrat with a guilty conscious and Superman complex, which he is," he smiled. "Make no mistake. Superman. Immortal and invincible, just ask him."

Jean Paul looked at him tiredly, and Abraham felt almost as sorry for him as he did for Dieter. "A bad joke," Abraham apologized.

That wasn't it. "I'd rather not know," Jean Paul said. "We," he waved, meaning Cassandra, the twins, "would rather not know anything about le Metapel."

"Suit yourself," Abraham said, amiable to the blind leading the blind. It worked out better that way. "It doesn't change anything."

Of course it did. It changed everything. Confusing the lines between enemy and friend, creating a war no one could win. "Why?" Jean Paul insisted. "Why was it necessary to kill Justin's sister if this is all as innocent as you claim? Revenge for Palestine? Give me a break. Justin is not responsible for Palestine!"

"We didn't kill her," Abraham assured.

"No, of course not," Jean Paul nodded. "Your mother is just talking. She's upset and couldn't think of anything else to say. Abraham," he advised, "I really am not an idiot, and neither are you. Your mother is so concerned about being sacrificed she is willing to sacrifice anyone."

"Probably. But then it is only a supply station," Abraham supported the claim of innocence beneath the flag of the Afrika Korps. "We need it and le Metapel right now. When we don't, you'll be the first to know—or the second," he shrugged, since Dieter would be the first when his kingdom went up in smoke, the poor fool.

"A supply station with the SS at its door," Jean Paul said.

"More like the Gestapo," Abraham stood up. "Makes sense to me why she wants to end it here, now."

"And how does this end it?" Jean Paul insisted. "How does killing Justin's sister, his men, end anything? Punish, is what she wants to do. She wants to punish who she thinks is responsible."

"Which someone is," Abraham assured. "Make it Reynolds. Satisfy her. What can it hurt?"

"Us," Jean Paul said. "It can hurt us!"

"Not as much as it will hurt if Justin finds those depots," Abraham promised, "and definitely not as much if the SS finds any of us. Look," he said, "the kid's no one. She's a blind. Don't bite the hook Justin's dangling. She has nothing to do with you."

"You mean like you didn't bite it?" Jean Paul said.

"Oh, no, we bit," Abraham assured. "Hard, fast, and furious, and not about to let go."

"But why," Jean Paul insisted, "if your hands are clean."

"Ma wants to know what's going on," Abraham said simply. "No guess work. Justin is on to something. He thinks he is, anyway, and regardless of his reasons or plan, there is a link here linking all of us. You, le Metapel, the SS, AND me. The depots. So you take care of Justin's men, and we'll take care of the SS, because, well, let's face it. Regardless of anything else, nothing about the SS is coincidence. You know that. I know that. And, yes," he said, "le Metapel knows that. Their tentacles are everywhere. Even more than Justin's."

"I don't even know Reynolds or Peter O'Brannigan," Jean Paul stared dully into space.

"Lay it to Vichy," Abraham said. "In war men die, kid sisters as well. Either you do it, or we'll do it—"

"Or le Metapel," Jean Paul said sourly.

"Definitely," Abraham assured. "Without losing sleep. That altruistic nature of his extends only so far. I wouldn't look for it to include the ranks of England's 8th Army. He is still German, after all. But then, so are we," he shrugged and exited, leaving Jean Paul to stare at his trio of advisors.

"We cannot betray le Metapel for the English ..." Louis began carefully, positive Jean Paul could not seriously be thinking of taking such a risk with the loyalty of the people without which he could not survive.

"Shut up you fool!" Cassandra snapped. "We can betray whoever betrays us. It is all right," she reassured Jean Paul. "We will think of something."

"We have a day," he said. "A day. Two, if we are lucky. A week if we kill Reynolds. Another if we kill O'Brannigan. I have a headache," he sat down with a thud.

Chapter Twenty-Eight

The Fezzan
March 10

Joanna Lee was no longer sleeping. Her eyes were closed and she was lying very still, her chest rising and falling at regular intervals. Michael, you see, had taught her that. If you're going to pretend to be asleep, you have to do it right. People when they sleep breathe evenly, slowly, occasionally making strange sounds. The man, whoever he was, was in the room. Joanna knew it was a man because she seemed to remember a man, though not quite sure why. That was peculiar. Why didn't she remember? She did not know. The same if someone should ask her what she remembered about yesterday, for example, or the day before, did she remember enough to even know if she had forgotten anything? Days, weeks, people, places, things, it all seemed rather like a blackboard that had been wiped clean. Any trace of what had been written—was there any trace left? Heat. She remembered being hot for some reason, feeling hot. A stifling dry hot like one felt when they bent over an opened oven door, or the dusty plains of Queensland where she had been born.

She remembered thinking about Australia and home, about a day in the future, any day, Tuesday, why not? That if she thought about Tuesday, imagined herself there, this day would be over and she would be safe a week in the future where whatever one felt now they didn't feel anymore because it was over, finished, gone.

Not that it was, or had been a bad day. Had it? What was she thinking to even think that? Joanna did not know. Not what she was thinking, or what she was not. She felt odd, groggy, only half awake, and so not really, completely, pretending to be asleep. Just as everyone did the first thing in the morning before waking up to think anything. Before the world came into focus and dreams became dreams much to your disappointment and occasionally to your relief. She could tell she was on a bed of some sort, the mattress soft and thickly cushioned like a pillow, the sheets smooth. She could feel a hot breeze close by and an odd smell threatening to make her sneeze. That would be inconvenient, since surely the man would hear her unless he was deaf. Could he be deaf? Was it odd or just wishful thinking to wonder if he might be deaf? There was no rule saying he couldn't be deaf, if he was even really there at all.

He isn't really there, Joanna decided, shifting slightly to a position more comfortable for her back. He was a mouse, or perhaps a ghost. She had never seen a ghost, and while she might be nineteen, she still thought occasionally about them. He had to be one or the other, and she tried to listen closely to figure out which he might be, knowing she could always ask if she really had to. Muster her courage and call out, *"Who's there?"* Cry or scream if she did not like the answer. Fight, or die or just fall back to sleep. *God!* Joanna wished she was on her stomach. It would be so much simpler to pretend to be sleeping if she was on her stomach. She wouldn't have to worry if anyone was staring at her face. What if the man was staring at her face?

Let him stare, she decided. She hurt too much right now to even want to move and that was also very confusing. Why did she hurt? She had so much pain in the parts of her she could feel she could not help but realize there seemed to be parts of her she couldn't feel. Her legs for example, she could barely even find her legs, figure out where they were ... what *was* that smell? It really was awful. A harsh antiseptic filling her nose and tickling her tongue. She wouldn't be surprised to wake up and find she was in some hospital corridor— she was in hospital? That thought startled her even more than the idea of some man haunting her room. What on earth would she be doing in hospital? She didn't hurt that much, only bad enough to want to lie flat like the time when she was ten and fell out of the tree, the wind knocked out of her. Joanna tried not to open her eyes and check things out for herself. It wasn't easy being she was, by nature, a curious person. A kind of curiosity that occasionally got her into trouble ... *like the tree ...*

Joanna fell back to sleep, or she thought she might have because when she woke up it almost seemed as if she was pointing a different direction. But, no, she wasn't. She was still on her back, still inside the hot smelly fog. That fog would be there for days. She did not know that now, but it would. Sometimes less thick than others, and sometimes so thick she couldn't remember what she remembered one minute and did not another. Like the furniture. She always seemed to have trouble remembering furniture, where it was or that it was even there at all. That's what Claudia said. *"That child never pays attention. I don't know what it is."* She was better by now, of course, much better, far less rambunctious, much more mature, her nails less frequently dirty and broken, a solid steel barrette taming her wiry red hair ...

England before the War

"What if I cut it?" Joanna sighed as she flipped through the magazine of the very latest in glamour and glamorous dress, so tired of being thoroughly unglamorous and short. Horribly and thoroughly unnaturally short. It was so depressing. It wasn't like everyone around was so extraordinarily tall because they weren't. Michael certainly wasn't. But even next to Michael she seemed to disappear. Everyone having to look down to notice she was there. It really was time for a change. A desperately needed change and today was the day. It most definitely was. Why just today, this afternoon, Andrea, Michael's daughter and her best and only friend even though they were a solid four years apart, looked so pretty in her afternoon dress, long, and golden, like summer itself. It absolutely was time for a change.

"I need a change, Michael," she assured, "and I need it today." Tomorrow, of course, they would find her up on the roof where she belonged, lookout for Michael hiding out next to her, Andrea and her sisters Millicent and Heather down on the lawn taking pictures with their mother Claudia. "Michael," she insisted, "Michael, are you listening to me? I want to cut my hair, and I want to cut it today."

"Over my dead body," Michael took the magazine away.

"But it's 1937," Joanna stared in the mirror. "I'm fifteen."

"So?" Michael said.

Well, it was Claudia's point, actually, how she still looked so much like a savage. "Perhaps you're right," Joanna agreed as she turned this way and that way in the mirror. "I rather like it, actually. It's rather exciting to think of myself as—*savage,*" she shook her head just to be sure it was savage enough.

"Keep it up and we'll shave it," Michael picked up his razor to clean it, salvage what was left of it and her knees, which wasn't much, nope.

"You wouldn't," Joanna gasped.

"Oh, wouldn't I?" he countered. "You're two years into my first heart attack as it is. Christ," he shook his head at her bloody knee. "That's a hell of a hack job. I knew something was up when the buzzards started swirling overhead."

"I don't know about that," Joanna surveyed her handiwork. "I didn't do that bad."

"You did worse," he assured. "It's OK, it'll grow back."

"Grow back?" Joanna said. "But, I don't want it to grow back, Michael. That's rather the idea, isn't it?"

"The skin," Michael patted the sink. "Leg up, hold still, and pay attention because I'm only going to do this once. Hold still," he insisted. "Christ, which one of us is drunk?"

Well, she wasn't, of course, it was just the idea of holding still. Joanna wasn't very good at holding still, even worse when someone asked her to. The more they asked, the more she seemed incapable. Even by nineteen when she ought to be *years* into being mistress of Grandfather's house that had no mistress, Joanna still wasn't very good at anything she ought to be good at. She left such responsibility to Claudia who was really very good at everything from directing the cook to managing the horde of cleaning personnel ... That's what her mother had called them. "*Why, for goodness sake, Henry ...*" Joanna could hear her mother's clear, soft voice, unaffected and genuine. "*Who are all these cleaning ... personnel?*" Her ladyship Elizabeth Edwards not quite sure what else to call the overwhelming number of house staff with their military stiff backs. Henry laughed, chuckled as he always did, citing it to be as good a description as any, but then he always agreed with her mother, no matter what she said, why wouldn't he? Her mother was a beautiful woman in mind, body, and soul, slender and tall in her comfortable heels, elegant and respectable in her fine fitting suits and some saucy little hat she always wore perched to the side of her head.

Joanna remembered her mother quite vividly, the smell of her lip rouge, the touch of her hand. She remembered her father also, the first one, John, her mother saying *"John"* exactly the same way she said *"Henry"*. Kind and affectionate to them as they were to her, rarely with any sort of reproach. John was the broader of the two men, muscular, the younger of the two. Henry, a tall, dignified stick, his hair grey, and face defined with lines. A city man, to where John was an enthusiast of Nature, a fanatic for the wilds of the outback beyond their Australian ranch.

Joanna remembered the ranch, the lone tree past the fence of the corral where her father released the horses to run on the first day of spring. It was so exciting to watch, their eyes rolling and faces mad as they reared and pranced on hind legs. Too exciting, her mother would scold, for a young lady. But then her mother would be the one who decided they needed to have a fine picnic out by the tree with the ants and the birds and the leaves.

Her mother would be the one to support her daughter's claim it was a croc what got her father. He hadn't really drowned at all. Joanna stood up on the seat of her chair to reach the round wonderful looking buns in the bowl on the dining table.

"Yes, that's quite true, isn't it?" Liz thanked her daughter for the delicious roll and butter she passed forward. *"A crocodile did get John. Just in the way he would want to be gotten,"* she smiled at Henry seated across the table from her. A man she did not know well before her husband's death, but only vaguely. A look in her eyes telling him she also knew what she should not know, and it was the truth behind the life and death of Sir John Edwards. A fallen soldier in the savagery and shadows of the Outback and their ranch where he ran horses, cattle, and sheep, as opposed to Sir Henry who *"owned things"*, Liz believed was what Henry had said when she inquired into the nature of his livelihood apart from Parliament's Back Benches.

"Well, that's all right, I suppose," Liz agreed, *"if one can afford it,"* which she could. Her money, body, and soul, married to Sir John's for ten years, some old family money and John's astute mind for

business leaving her financially quite well off. But that wasn't the point. The point was she had a daughter and she was naturally curious as to what made Henry Charles think he was not only qualified, but wanting the responsibility of rearing and providing for a daughter in the midst of a financial depression. A global situation so great and dire it affected Australia and England the same as it affected the very foundations of everywhere else. The world was on its knees, ripe for an assortment of sordid troubles. Henry snorted at the idea, comfortable in the simple knowledge the world and civilization would survive as it had survived all its catastrophes before, from the wars to depressions to the famines, uprisings, rebellions, and even plagues.

"Yes," Liz recalled something about a Black Death, some four centuries past. *"Before my time, I'm afraid,"* she smiled. A subtle way of bringing to the table the fact that Henry Charles was older than she was. Quite old enough to be her father never mind her daughter's. A fact that had Henry stopping what he was saying about man, mankind, and Briton, to ask, *"See here, are you going to marry me or not?"* A proposal Liz naturally answered, *"Yes,"* though she cleared her hasty decision with Joanna while she helped her daughter straighten her bonnet and clean her dusty knees as best they could.

"After all," Liz smiled at Joanna who looked so much like her father that any less strong woman would surely break down and cry, *"we can't have Henry knowing what grubby little beggars we really are just yet."* Something which, yes, by some misguided social standards they actually were, what with preferring picnics out in the horses' corral to sipping tea any day. Still, it was something Liz rather suspected Henry wouldn't mind at all, such picnics. *"We'll save that for next week Tuesday when we sail to visit the ranch."* she nodded in appreciation to Joanna climbing up on the chair to pin her mother's hat. *"What do you think about Henry?"* she asked Joanna just about then. *"You haven't said much."*

He was nice, Joanna supposed, being only eight, and not really having thought about it. She crawled out from under the bed, still looking for her other shoe with little hope of finding it.

"Yes, he is nice, isn't he?" her mother smiled. *"Quite nice. I rather think we're going to have fun. Where's your shoe?"*

Joanna shrugged. *"I'll hop."*

"That will work," her mother agreed, *"but not on the stairs. Slide down the banister instead. After all,"* she smiled at Henry as Joanna whizzed past her, down the banister to land at his feet in the front hall, *"we can't risk breaking a leg. That wouldn't be much fun."*

"Nice hat," Henry complimented.

"Thank you," Liz accepted, and they went on to purchase Joanna's third new pair of shoes that week so they would look reasonably presentable for the Vicar who commented politely on how much Joanna looked like her mother, which was charming, but not true. Joanna did not look much like her mother at all, except for possibly in the eyes. Her eyes were like her mother's, a warm, soft, ordinary brown. Liz's flecked with intelligence and vigor. Joanna's? Liz smiled at her daughter with her restless independence exactly like her mother in that regard for all she favored her father John.

"Odd, but neither of you look like a rogue," Henry brought up the subject of Joanna's rather carefree nature later, after tea.

"Neither do you," Liz agreed. *"So that and a nickel will get you ... what is it?"* she verified.

"A cup of coffee," he smiled. *"See if any of us has made an impression on you, it's Mike."*

"Yes, well, I rather suspect Mike ..." Liz thought about the American doctor who was handsome, she supposed, she'd give him that, *"makes an impression on most people."*

"Good or bad?" Henry wondered solely out of curiosity.

"Well, both, I would think," Liz said. *"Whatever impression he's inclined to make at the time. Is he really an American gangster? I honestly couldn't decide if I was supposed to believe him or not."*

"Oh, no," Henry chuckled. *"No, Mike's a sort of chemist. Quite respectable underneath it all. Just his odd sense of humor. Don't let him trouble you."*

"Yes," Liz said. An odd sense of humor bristling with cynicism and, she would almost have to say, fierce hostility. He certainly did not seem to like his wife very much. A woman, Liz understood he had been estranged from for some time before reemerging quite out of the blue. He was a rogue, without a doubt. Not the sort of man one would think a woman of sense would be attracted to, though she was

apparently wrong since for all he did not seem to like his wife, his wife certainly appeared to like him, almost desperately. *"Trouble me how?"* she asked.

"In any way," Henry assured, leaving Michael there and inquiring naturally on his own child, since they were on the subject of children. *"What about Justin?"*

"Yes, of course," Liz smiled, thinking of the towering barnacle Henry had for a son, a young man who seemed so completely out of place around this Cambridge highbrow lot as his questionable friend Michael. No less of an adventurer than his friend Michael, she suspected, few responsibilities to tie him down, and strongly averse to acquiring any. *"Well, Justin I would rather suspect is you, isn't he?"* she said. *"Perhaps when you were somewhat younger, but definitely you."*

"No flies on you I see," Henry laughed. *"Quite all right. Might not look it just now, but he'll come around, the same as I did."*

"Come around to what?" Liz wondered. *"Seems perfectly content to me."*

"Civilization," Henry patted her hand reassuringly. *"Nothing more drastic than that."*

"Oh, yes, of course," Liz said. *"Civilization. Evening suits and evening tea rather than tweed and a beaker of Scotch. He seemed perfectly well mannered and acceptable to me."*

"You like him," Henry said.

"I do, actually," Liz agreed. *"Why? Don't you?"*

"Very much," Henry assured. *"He's a good lad. No complaints."*

"As I rather suspect he knows how to wear an evening suit," she said. *"He simply prefers not to."*

"Right again," Henry said. *"So what about you? Who are you?"*

She laughed. *"Joanna. Yes, all right, you've caught us. I'm quite like Joanna or rather she's quite like me. Rogues, ourselves, if you care to be unkind, mavericks, daughters of the Suffrage, therefore, barbarians. I'm quite sure someone along the way has said so, or they will,"* she fairly promised teasingly. *"John, for all his adventure, was really the respectable one of the group. So if you've a mind to reconsider our engagement, perhaps you should do that now, before we're announced."*

"Wouldn't dream of it," he assured, and six months later considering the grim end they came to, he rather wished he had. Bob and Martha mercifully killed on impact as the car went over the edge and the earthly world came to an end for the rest of them. Henry would have shot Liz, had he thought of it, the compartment already erupted in flames as he fought desperately in the few seconds they had to shove both Liz and Katy free. By the time, he did think of his gun, it was too late. He had already lost Liz through the opened door, the bullet jamming in the chamber, the gun dropping from his charred hand. Still who he felt sorry for most of all as peace came was that tot of hers Liz left behind to fend for herself, alone in her adventure her mother had quite innocently promised her would be fun.

"She'll be fine," Liz reassured Henry when they met along the High Road, Bob and Martha patiently waiting for Katy and them to catch up.

"How do you know that?" Henry asked, a cynic apparently even in the afterlife.

"Because I do," Liz said. *"She's my daughter, and we're rogues,"* she reminded him. *"You'll see. Joanna's quite clever, actually, quite self-reliant, she'll survive, succeed, I dare even say,"* she laughed quite proudly, *"where others less daunting would certainly fail. Largely, I suspect, because she doesn't realize she's not supposed to succeed. Never has, and hopefully never will."*

"To where apparently we're members of that less daunting group of yours," Henry grumbled, rather never dreaming he'd fail himself, and if he failed, never dreaming it would be this way; to this extent.

"Well, that's all right, too," Liz tucked her arm through his with a pat. *"After all, would you rather it be Justin?"*

"Myself, of course, naturally," Henry assured. *"Talking about you, Katy, Martha, even Bob. Not saying Evelyn, for that matter, Justin won't fare all right for himself, because of course both will."*

"Even come around," she agreed.

"What's that?" Henry said.

"Even come around," Liz smiled. *"Must have something to do with being a rogue themselves, can't ask for anything more than that."*

"The devil I can't," he corrected. *"What happened to happily ever after?"*

"We did live happily ever after," Liz nodded.

"Yes, well, wanted it to be longer then," Henry said. *"Six months? Barely got our feet wet."*

"Well, who doesn't want it to be longer?" Liz shrugged. *"Rather suspect most do, and some will."* She smiled down on the angel hovering over her daughter. An unlikely looking one, she had to admit. Though angels were apparently like that, coming in all shapes and sizes, and occasionally speaking French. *"Atta girl, Red,"* she encouraged Joanna, Michael quick to join in and drown her out with his cheer. *"Atta girl. Show them your stuff. Show them what you're made of. Fuck 'em, if they don't like it. Atta girl, atta girl, atta girl ..."*

The Fezzan

March 10

"Is Mademoiselle ready to wake up?" the man interrupted Joanna's oddly pleasant dream, his voice just above her head, and her entire body stiffened, turned into a board.

"It is after five o'clock." Joanna heard him say, the words in French and words she understood, but she kept her eyes tightly closed even when he told her his name. *Pierre.* That was right, too. *I remember you, Pierre,* she agreed, though not out loud. The only thing she said aloud was something Michael had taught her to say when she was only nine and so frightened in a sea of strangers without her mother to comfort her. Joanna Lee made her choice to cry or fight in the middle of Pierre's speech. She said, *"Fuck you."* Or roughly translated, told him to kiss her ass, go to hell.

Chapter Twenty-Nine

All of its translations were an interesting choice for the little mademoiselle who looked more to Pierre like someone's lost child than what instead? A sailor? Some prostitute in British school girl dress? Or perhaps it was simply she did not understand French and was so very much afraid?

Of course she was afraid, naturally terrified. Pierre nodded wisely. Her vulgar slang, while an odd choice, was significant in that she spoke it in English, helping him to assist in identifying her, which he wanted very much to do. He had noticed more than her fists yesterday. Her reactions to him, his voice, the awkward way in which she twisted her head, he was convinced she could understand him. To understand French suggested education, breeding. Important because he did not believe she lived here in European North Africa. Her skin under her sunburn was fair and tender, not harsh and heat browned. She was a young woman who traveled perhaps? With her husband, her family, or with her English troops? Pierre eyed her. Her fragile size and her youth were also extremely important, quite possibly the difference between her life and death. Small, she was not a child. What Pierre first suspected, he now knew from her body under its swollen black bruises. She was young, yes, but a young woman. Eighteen, nineteen years old or so he guessed, not fourteen as Reineke surmised and Pierre perhaps had been too quick to correct. The younger, the better if he hoped to convince Reineke to remand her to the children's camp where she would be safe from the soldiers until Pierre could figure out what to do. Anne, Reineke's little Anne, was eleven and no threat to him though the gun Anne carried was bigger than this English woman lying on the bed.

Pierre forgot about Reineke to concentrate on the woman, the voice he could barely hear and she could barely raise loud enough to talk. Whose English? British, Irish, Scot? He suspected Irish for the same reason Reineke considered Polish or Scandinavian. The light skin and red hair. Reineke was lying, a desperate attempt to delay the truth by pretending he had not decided what she was. Pierre was not lying. She was Allied, they both knew that, simply not whose or why. It was time to find out.

"So," Pierre teased, while Joanna stayed where she was, bravely on her back, her eyes tightly closed. "So," he primly approved, choosing the more formal Italian translation of her curse, "vai a fare nel culo? Mademoiselle proves she is not a child, but the adult. This is good. So, now, she will have no difficulty, but understand and listen when I say to her, it is time for her to get up, I have drawn for her a bath."

Joanna almost opened her eyes and Pierre knew it. She spoke French. That she could not hide and it was good. She spoke French, and he was French, and so they would get along fine. "I am sorry but we will have to speak in French, Mademoiselle," he offered apologetically. "Though I am French and can speak many languages, unfortunately, except for a few words, I do not speak English, but until recently there has been no need. Still," he said, when she continued not to respond, "for all I am sorry for, I am sorry most if Mademoiselle thinks she should perhaps sleep longer. Mademoiselle has slept long enough. It is dinner time, and she will have to eat, yes, but first, she needs to again bathe."

What he meant by her bathing again Joanna had no idea, but he obviously thought he meant something because he not only repeated it, he said it at least four more times. That was his problem. Hers was trying to find a pillow large enough to wrap around her head, covering her ears. Her hand reached out, bravely and boldly fumbling until she found one.

The sight was amusing to Pierre, offering her little protection, and proving only that she had courage enough to fight fights she did not need to win. Pierre thought again about the punches and kicks she threw yesterday. She was strong under her compact petite frame, athletically inclined, her spirit, brave and foolish at the same time. He did not have to be French any more than the men who beat and raped her were French. It was her good fortune he was.

"There is no reason for Mademoiselle to hide," he said softly. "You are quite safe. Any scars you have are only in the mind. How deep they go is up to you."

He touched her with something, it felt like a stick, and that was the trick to get her up fast. The pillow came off her head, her eyes open as she struggled to sit up, lash out at him with her fists and hoarse, harsh words she couldn't quite get out.

That was the plan, anyway. It changed the moment Joanna saw him. He was hideous. Not some disconcerting shadow she seemed to remember, a distorted figure she couldn't quite make out, but a twisted and misshapen man, hideously and horribly so like a gnome.

Why, exactly like a gnome! Joanna stared at him. Some horribly discolored gnome. Dark like a Negro, shrunken and old, and fat— round like a very fat round barrel, with a very large round brown face and two beady little black eyes peering out at her from inside some sort of hood. A brown hood. Brown as his skin and the odd looking brown sack covering him from his neck to his toes.

"Why ..." Joanna managed as she stared at him. "Why ..." she succeeded in choking out.

He smiled, leered at her in a disgustingly familiar way, his teeth old and discolored in his gums also tinged brown. "I am Père Pierre, Mademoiselle," he said. "A priest, oui, a bishop. And, oui," he granted, "to some I am a cripple, too. Washed before my seventh birthday, I was too young to endure the evil eye. Infantile paralysis," he winked, or at least Joanna thought he did. Perhaps it was her. Winking and blinking and trying to keep him in focus. "The community I was released to was the hospitality of the monks at La Trappe de Staouelli who gave me my name *Beausoleil.* Beautiful sun."

Cripple? Joanna frowned. He looked more like a midget. A fine one to talk herself, she knew that, but he looked more like a midget to her and a hundred years old at least.

Sixty-seven, perhaps. Pierre read her face, not her mind. Her height, and sixty-seven years old. Not a hundred as he might appear or the thousand Reineke feared he might actually be. A monk. Not some wizard, or a gnome, and not a Negro, simply an old, crippled French monk with a large French face darkened by age and the sun. Mademoiselle, on the other hand, was of the English upper classes despite her silent, tactless scrutiny—or should Pierre say because of it he knew this? She lived a life of privilege, wealth, and snobbery, all very clear. As clear as those bruised and loosened teeth of hers with their chipped enamel that had been cosmetically straightened, forced into place with steel and wire like his legs. "You have never heard of the monastery at La Trappe?" he smiled. "Where are you from, Mademoiselle? If it is not here, where?"

Where was a very good question. Joanna had no idea. Not where here was, or even what here was with her surroundings looming in the background of the man as unfamiliar as he was. She eyed him because he seemed closer than the room for some reason. Close enough to see him. If he was French, some kind of priest or bishop as he claimed she had no idea. She studied the massive crucifix dangling from the Rosary tucked in what looked like a black sash around his waist. She knew what a Rosary was because of Michael who had assured her they and a nickel for the streetcar would get him into Heaven, but she had never seen one so large. The long rope of dark brown beads almost touching the floor ...

The chocolate brown floor. It must be the room that made the brown so brown, almost black because everything else in the room was white. Huge white-on-white marble columns and high stone walls glistened crystal white in the sun streaming through a long row of paned glass widows with their airy white draperies dancing slowly in a warm, bright breeze.

Oh, but where was she was right. "I!" Joanna agreed in a whisper, uncertain if she was awake or still asleep after all. It was all so large, seemed all so grand. Even the furniture was white, gilded in platinum and gold. Not like home, at all. Certainly not Grandfather's with its mighty oak and mahogany halls. Or even Michael and Claudia's house built of that manufactured brick Grandfather loathed, proud, and high on its pastured hills outside Yorkshire.

But still, as fancy as Michael's house was, in some ways fantastic with its palatial baroque decor, it was far less fantastic than this. Joanna stared down on the soft, white bed, nearly as massive as the room, and swimming, simply swimming in white silk pillows. So many of them one could barely find the bed, her, or even notice the dressing table next to it ...

Joanna's head cocked, staring at the nightstand that was white like the rest of the furniture in the room. An odd green figure of a cat sat on top next to a large brass pitcher and bowl and a row of fluffy white … pillows? She couldn't quite make out what they were.

"That is not important," the fat brown barrel informed her, and she looked up at him.

"What?" she tried to say, but he picked something up, his nasty, twisted hand coming toward her, and maybe to him it wasn't important, but to her it certainly was. How awful. Really, she couldn't think of anything more awful. So much worse than realizing wherever she was, she was hardly at home, but far, far away from Michael, Grandfather, and even Claudia. That hand coming toward her held a sheet. Some kind of sheet, silk white, or just soft cotton, and when Joanna looked down to see what he was going to do with it she realized she was naked, mother naked. Not a stitch of decency or clothes.

Joanna shrieked with her hoarse, sore throat and grabbed the sheet, tucking it around herself up to her chin until she looked like one of those mummies everyone went on about, and she had yet to see.

"I am a priest, not a man, Mademoiselle," the contemptuous bastard leered at her again, exactly like that hunchback in Michael's favorite film. She swung at him and missed but he retreated, disappearing behind one of the columns, his voice still close. "Mademoiselle does not have clothes. She does not need them, she needs a bath."

Well, she certainly had them when she came in there. Joanna kicked and pushed at the suffocating mound of pillows desperate to find them before he came back. He was back, quickly reappearing and waving something that was neither brown or white, and certainly threatening. She gasped and screamed again, waving at him to stay back. He would not stay back, but advanced, sweeping unconcerned through the pillows and bedding littering the floor like landmines. "What Mademoiselle wants is not important. Today, we are going to do what Pierre wants."

Fat chance of that. Joanna tried to grab whatever it was he had in his hand, and fling it away, as far as she could. He peered at her, his beady black eyes squinting like he needed glasses. "Mademoiselle, this is a blouse, not a weapon. I am not going to strike you with it. You are going to wear it."

That's what he thought. Joanna promptly kicked whatever it was off the bed as soon as he set it down.

"Mademoiselle," he sighed. "Mademoiselle, I am sorry, but your dress has been destroyed. Though, I think, oui," he said, "even if it were not, she would not want it, no. I think, oui, I am positive, Mademoiselle has seen enough for one so young."

Seen what? Whatever could he mean? She hadn't seen anything. For that matter, could barely see anything. Joanna realized that as she peered back at him. She could see in front of her, not very well, but she could still see. But when she tried to turn her head, even just tried to look to the side, the room turned dark, her sight fading, and she swooned.

"Oui, Mademoiselle," he said for some reason as if he were agreeing with her about something, "but it will pass."

When Joanna woke up the next time, it was dark and she was clothed, wearing something that felt like a cloth dress.

"It is all right, Mademoiselle," his voice assured and she jumped. "She will wear the sahariana and not worry about her modesty, for on one so small, it will be a dress." He struck a match for the lamp. Joanna could see the dancing flame of the lantern, watching it as it came closer.

"Oui," Pierre agreed, setting the lamp down on the nightstand, the light from the flame dancing on his face. "You want me to stay back, you want your dress. But no, it has been burned."

Burned? Joanna touched the dress she was wearing. It had buttons and seemed large, but was short, like a nightshirt. A man's nightshirt.

"Oui, burned," he nodded, "in the fire."

Fire? Joanna did not remember any fire. Odd though, because she did seem to remember smoke, a thin column of smoke.

"What do you remember?" Pierre smiled at her concentration.

What did she remember? What a rude and uncomfortable question, particularly since Joanna did not know the answer.

"It is all right, Mademoiselle," he reminded as she glared at him. I am a priest, not a man. Still, you will be more comfortable like this."

Comfortable? In what way? Joanna studied the dancing light on his face. It made her stomach sick and she vomited a spicy, acidic mixture of mucus and undigested blood.

"The ether," he said. "It will pass. I am not here to frighten you, but to help. But Mademoiselle must also help. She must listen to Pierre and do exactly as he says. She has been molested, oui, molested," he nodded as she looked up at him. "Sex with a man she does not like. Your life has not been ruined by your assault, but your body has been injured. This land is a desert, wounds do not heal here, they rot. The bath is to soothe this. It is la douche. Does Mademoiselle know what that is?"

Not even what he was talking about.

"I did not think so," he nodded satisfied. "Mademoiselle is English, not French. It is all right, we will help you." Someone touched her, it wasn't him, but a nun dressed in black habit and veil.

"Come, Mademoiselle," Pierre encouraged as Joanna stared at the sister. "Embarrassment is not worth your life. Sometimes a man carries with him things that have nothing to do with the desert or an unwanted baby, but disease, infection. Une douche is no different than any other medicine to protect you from this unnecessary fate."

She was standing up. At least Joanna thought she was. Her head felt lopsided and heavy, her stomach turning with dizzying nauseating pain. She swayed like she was drunk, veering toward the columns briefly bright white in the lantern flame before returning to the shadows. They were cold when she touched them and she shivered, clutching at the stupid shirt she wore.

"Let us help you, Mademoiselle," he encouraged, "be careful, there are steps."

She could see them, but that was a lie. All she could see was she was in a loo, some sort of loo, nearly as large as the room, and rapidly shrinking in size. She sank down to the floor, next to what looked like a flat commode, resting her head on the cool marble that felt good, peaceful. From there she found herself back in bed, vomiting at least twice more as the room turned bright and hot and then back to dark and cold. The sister in black was gone and did not return, and the strange ugly man did not speak to her again except to tell her she must rest and could not eat where he had practically insisted she eat before. She wanted to complain but was just so tired. When she tried to complain he ignored her and gave her a wet cloth to suck on. At some point she decided he was a priest, French, and this was all a dream. A very bad dream, very long. Eventually, she remembered another man. Some man with a hat leaning over her. It wasn't the fat priest, and he wasn't French, and she screamed, falling back to sleep as instructed when the priest answered her call.

Chapter Thirty

The Fezzan
March 12

Joanna lay in bed wide awake and alert. A quick survey of her surroundings when she woke up confirmed the strange fat priest was not there in the room that remained unfamiliar and unchanged from its cold stone and abundance of white except for what looked like a bundle of laundry folded neatly on a chair over by the linen draped windows. How tempting the windows were, how bright the world looked beyond them, even brighter than the room. Before she could make up her mind however if she dared to have the courage to get up and look out the windows, the priest appeared through the pillars and she was down under the covers if only in an effort to escape his annoying enthusiasm.

He was undeterred by her disappearing act. "Good morning, Mademoiselle," he greeted her like some upstairs maid carrying tea. Joanna had often wondered what it would be like to have an upstairs maid bring her tea. Tea in the morning and again at night, even at noon if she wanted it. Grandfather wasn't a supporter of such nonsense, as he called it. There was no flurry of personnel to greet Joanna when she arrived to live with Grandfather, as there had been to greet her and her mother when they moved from Australia to live with Henry. There was Maria the cook, and John, Grandfather's batman, and Joe who was her tutor, as well as Grandfather's personal secretary when he needed one.

"It is good to see you are awake," the priest continued babbling. "Today we have much to do. But first ..." his voice seemed to soften, fade away but then came back, loud as before. "Mademoiselle's clothes that have been so graciously provided for her."

Joanna had absolutely no idea what he was talking about. Her clothes? The blankets came off her head and she sat up, a bit too quickly for the liking of her stomach, but that was all right. Or it should have been. She stared at the folded laundry on the bed, from it to the windows and the chair whose large cushioned seat was now empty. The clothes on the bed were not hers. Hers were green. A putrid, ugly green, awkward and unflattering, but that was beside the point. These were ... well, like something Michael might wear on one of his big game safaris.

"Dress, Mademoiselle," the priest patted the laundry with that claw of his that Joanna swore an oath to bite off the first time it came close enough, "and Pierre will be right back with her breakfast. Oui, breakfast," he promised happily, "today Mademoiselle is to eat."

He was gone, exiting out of her sight to the right. Joanna heard what sounded like the latch of a door and turned quickly, far too quickly for her head. It was a door, there on her right. It was also not white, but brown like the floor, and quite tall. Very tall. Large and heavy with a high, brass latch that looked almost too high for her to reach. Joanna wished she had turned her head sooner than she did so that she might have caught a glimpse of what was on the other side. It was unnerving not to know. But at least he was gone, not simply hiding behind the tall white columns waiting to spring. If only there was a way to lock him out, make sure he couldn't come back in. If only there was a way ...

Joanna stared at the clothing on the bed, from the clothes to the row of paned-windows and the bright world outside wondering if she dared have the courage. She did. "Trousers?" she whispered as she reached cautiously for the bundle and found a pair of trousers under the neatly folded shirt. Trousers were certainly far more comfortable than that stupid skirt she had been forced to wear with stockings that did nothing except twist and tear. Though that was not to say had she been given a fresh skirt and stockings it would have stopped her from shimmying down the sheets, rope, pole, or nearest tree to make her escape, the farthest from it. She was up, and she was out of there—planning it, anyway.

"Atta girl ... atta girl ..." Joanna invoked Michael's cheer as she got up, discovering her ankles, knees, and even her wrist up to her elbow on her right arm, were wrapped in plasters and white gauze. She *had* been in hospital, as she seemed to remember. Injured in some way. The funny priest had said something about a fire. She did not remember anything about a fire, and certainly could not take the time to worry about remembering it now. She pushed the clean shirt aside. She was already wearing some kind of shirt and could feel more plaster and bandages wound around her back and right shoulder that hurt considerably.

"*Amputation, kid,*" Michael cracked in agreement the day she fell out of the tree, "*it's the only answer.*"

"*I don't need an amputation, Michael,*" she assured him.

"*Oh, yeah?*" he said. "*Sez who?*"

"Says me," Joanna picked up the trousers. They were long and loose and threatening to fall down even though she rolled the waistband as tight as she could, and *damn!* Joanna could feel the dizziness start to swim over her. She hung on to the nightstand trying to clear her head. The floor rolling in waves under her feet as she clutched the trousers, trying to find her way to the windows, her hand stumbling along the nightstand, along the edge of the bed, and finally along the smooth slick surface of the bureau top where she came face to face with—

"My face!" Joanna gasped in the mirror. Half her face was gone, just gone, and in its place was some huge fat bandage wound around and around her head like a queer fat hat. "Michael!" she screamed, "my face!"

Joanna was in the loo so fast she could not remember how she got there. There were mirrors in the loo, she remembered them from yesterday, she must have seen herself yesterday—there were more mirrors than walls in the loo. Joanna grabbed the edge of what had to be the sink, staring at her horribly misshapen head and face. No wonder she couldn't see, the bandage did not only cover her head, it covered one of her eyes, her nose and mouth swollen under a hideous blackened purple bruise practically covering her face, neck, the whole of her body she knew if she dared to look.

"Mademoiselle should have waited for Pierre," the priest said quietly behind her.

"My face!" Joanna heard herself whine.

"Oui, I know," he sympathized. "But it will go away. It will pass. Come," he held out his hand.

Go away? Joanna's head tipped in the mirror. It was already gone.

"Come, Mademoiselle," he encouraged. "Your breakfast is here."

Joanna went with him. Why? To get away from the mirrors.

Breakfast was waiting on a silver tray with a porcelain bowl of mealy black puree and a round flat pancake of bread.

"Fool," the priest nodded as Joanna blinked.

The fool was he if he thought she was going to eat that. Joanna looked at him.

"*Fool …*" Pierre emphasized with a smile. "A type of pudding. You use the bread. See?" he dipped the bread in demonstration. "Very good, no?"

Hardly. Joanna crawled back into bed. "I'm hungry," she said. "Hungry," she repeated as he spread his hands and she sighed. "Fine. *Affamé.*"

"Very good," Pierre picked up the tray, setting it firmly on her lap.

"No," Joanna pushed it away. "Food. Not that. I can't possibly eat that. For heaven's sake," she peered at it, "it looks like someone already ate it and gave it back."

"No," he said, and Joanna's stomach turned, "No, I do not think so. This has been prepared especially for you by me."

That was his problem. "Food," Joanna insisted. "I haven't eaten and I am very hungry."

"You have a concussion, Mademoiselle," he explained. "It was decided it was best not to feed you for another day until you were awake."

"I'm fine," Joanna assured.

"I know," Pierre agreed. "Even your throat. Very improved. You are talking."

Her throat hurt almost as much as the rest of her. "Food," Joanna insisted, and to make sure he understood she shoved the tray off the bed, the heavy silver clanging like a bell when it hit the floor, the bowl rattling before it broke, and bread unscathed.

Pierre sighed. "Mademoiselle must eat."

"Food," Joanna assured.

"Oui," he nodded.

"And some water," Joanna pointed before he left. "I'm quite thirsty."

"Juice," he nodded, "sugar for your strength, and perhaps later some tea with lemon and a little honey. It is better for your stomach."

"Water," Joanna said.

"Oui," Pierre said and left.

While he was gone, Joanna debated about trying for the windows again but decided against it until she had some food in her, especially since only Heaven knew when she might be able to eat again. For a hospital, it was not only strange looking but distinctly inhospitable what with starving her to death for more than a day. She decided she wasn't sure if she was in hospital after all and decided to ask him when he returned. Until he returned, she busied herself picking at her plasters to see what this business with burns was all about. She did not feel burned and did not remember anything about being burned. However since she had never been burned except for possibly touching the stove or clothes iron when she shouldn't have, she wasn't entirely sure what being burned would feel like. Her wrists were the easiest bandages to loosen and the wounds underneath the first one were certainly ghastly looking enough to have her quickly patting the plaster back in place, not wanting to know anything more. The priest was back with another, much larger tray, one he had to push in on a wheeled cart.

"What's that?" Joanna blinked.

"Fool," Pierre set a tray down on her lap identical to the one he had set there before. "When you throw this one, Mademoiselle, we have that one," he pointed to the second shelf, "and that one," he pointed to the third and final shelf of his cart, "and many others. I think however Mademoiselle will be too tired to throw too many after a while and will eat her breakfast as she should now.

"We also have," he returned to his cart while she studied the tray on her lap, "some very nice juice. Kamar-eldin. Very good and very popular."

"Kal ... kalmar ..." Joanna stumbled over it.

"*Kamar-eldin,*" Pierre smiled. "Apricot. And then we have some tea," he nodded. "A nice mint with lemon, or perhaps another. Mon capitaine prefers tea to the kamar-eldin which he finds too sweet, and so we have many teas here, from many places. The choice is yours. India. Russia. Even your England. Would Mademoiselle like a nice hot cup of English tea?"

"Well ..." Joanna considered, since anything might be helpful with a bowl of what, she insisted, looked like smashed black beans.

"Perhaps even a sip of coffee," Pierre nodded. "Oui," he decided for her. "A very small sip of coffee with sweet cream would be nicest yet. Mon capitaine loves coffee even more than tea, and so we have many coffees here, from all over the world. Spain. France. Italy. Africa!" he laughed at some joke Joanna would not have found funny even if she knew what it was.

"You are not eating, Mademoiselle," he noticed, "and you really must."

"All right, fine!" Joanna grabbed the bowl stuffing half a spoonful of the beans in her mouth that she promptly gagged right back out they were just so awful.

"Eat, Mademoiselle," he nodded as she sent the bowl flying. "Try some bread and a little juice."

The bread was flat and practically tasteless, the juice very sweet as forewarned. "I would really like some water," she reminded.

"Perhaps tomorrow," he nodded. "Water is very harsh."

"But I can have tea," Joanna said.

"Oui," he smiled.

"Good," she said. "May I have a glass of tea with lemon and a little honey but none of those nasty tea leaves?"

He thought about that. "Mademoiselle ..." he said.

"Please just bring me a glass of water!" Joanna snapped.

"Oui, Mademoiselle," he said.

"Thank you!"

Joanna sipped her water slowly from a glass that was a heavy crystal goblet and quite beautiful if she paid any more attention to it than she had to the spoon, the tray, or the bowl. She did not. Why would she? All of Grandfather's china was china, and certainly all of

Claudia's. All their silver, silver, and all of their crystal heavy, exactly like this one.

"So you see, Mademoiselle," Pierre was busily explaining something else she hardly cared about, "it would be much better to have the water fresh from the well. This water is kept in bags, and it is warm, the taste strong. It is not so strong from the well when it is cold."

"It's perfectly fine," Joanna assured, and it was. It was wet.

Pierre shrugged. "If Mademoiselle says so."

Joanna did, and that was all she was going to say, at least about that. "Where am I?" she asked.

Pierre laughed. "A very good question, Mademoiselle. Oui, a very natural one."

"Well?" Joanna said. "Am I at that place you talked about?"

Pierre frowned. "Place, Mademoiselle?"

"You mentioned a place," Joanna assured. "I can't remember what you called it."

"Nor I," Pierre shook his head in apology. "I am sorry, but I do not recall mentioning some place."

Well if he didn't remember, she certainly couldn't. "Well?" Joanna said. "Where am I?"

"Of course," he seemed to hesitate, but then sat down in the chair by the bed.

"Well, yes, I suppose that's all right," Joanna agreed, though it was a little close. "You can clean later. I want to know where I am."

"I, Mademoiselle?" Pierre chuckled. "No, the servants will clean, Mademoiselle. That is their job. Pierre's job is to take care of you."

"Servants?" Joanna said.

"Oui," Pierre nodded. "Servants of the house."

"Oh," Joanna said. "Oh, well," she tossed off, "I knew I wasn't in hospital."

"Hospital?" Pierre said. "No, you are not in hospital. You are in a house, oui, a building. A very big, very beautiful building. Pierre's ... and, oui, mon capitaine's home," he agreed.

"It's all right," Joanna supposed. Certainly, Michael's home was far more beautiful than this. "When can I leave?"

"Leave?" Pierre chuckled. "I think Mademoiselle should think about getting stronger and well before she thinks about leaving."

"I want to leave," Joanna assured.

"Soon," he nodded. "Very soon, Mademoiselle. You have Pierre's word. It is a promise. Now," he smiled again, folding his hands exactly as a priest might Joanna noticed. "I think we should talk. God's gift of language is a wonderful gift, and since you speak French so well, there is much we will be able to talk about."

"When?" Joanna interrupted. "When can I leave?"

"Soon," he nodded, again. "Very soon. When the time comes— you will be surprised how quickly the time has come when it is here, Mademoiselle ... Lee, is it?" he winked. "Oui, it is Lee," he agreed positively before she could speak. "Joanna Lee. So young and yet a nurse?

"No, you are not a nurse," he shook his head as positively. "It is not your age or your face that tells Pierre this, it is your actions. Your curiosity with the bandages, the way you sniff with your nose. That malodor you smell, is not bowel, Mademoiselle, it is sulphur. A salve under your dressings to help you heal—"

"I haven't the faintest idea what you are talking about," Joanna interrupted again.

"No, of course you do not," Pierre understood. "You have a concussion, Mademoiselle, as I have attempted to explain to you. You have struck your head, and you must give your head time to heal."

"The car door," Joanna nodded.

"Pardon?" Pierre paused.

"The car door," Joanna assured. "I struck my head on the car door."

"Really," Pierre pondered that thoughtfully. "You remember this, Mademoiselle? That is very unusual."

Was it?

"Oh, yes, Mademoiselle," he assured. "Extremely. Do you remember anything else?"

He'd like to know that, wouldn't he? Joanna could tell by his face he would. "Everything," she promised. "I remember everything."

"Most unusual," Pierre nodded. "Most unusual."

Maybe for him. For her ... well, for her it was a lie. Joanna did not remember anything, not even why she seemed to remember a car, but she did.

"Are you English, Mademoiselle?" he was asking. "Or possibly of English descent? That is still unclear to Pierre as it is unclear exactly who you are. Do you have an uncle, or brother, or father in the army, perhaps? If not, then who could Mademoiselle Lee be other than in the army herself perhaps as her title and clothes suggest—"

"Could you bring me some more water?" The crystal goblet bounced on the floor at his feet, rolling to a stop, quite unharmed.

"Four centuries," Pierre shook his head. "Mademoiselle, you have thrown four centuries onto the floor. Are you aware of this? Do you care?"

"No!" Joanna assured.

"You are not only bold and brave, Mademoiselle, you are very reckless and spoiled," he bent over slowly to retrieve the goblet with a laugh. "A dangerous combination. It is all right though, because so is Pierre, and neither would Pierre care. A secret, Mademoiselle, between you and I," he winked. "It is possible Pierre cares even less than you."

Joanna highly doubted it. "Is it too much to ask for you to give me some water and leave me alone?"

"Alone?" he said. "To do what, Mademoiselle?"

Wouldn't he like to know. Joanna slid down under the covers, pulling them up over her shoulders as if she was cold even though she wasn't, but fairly warm as the room.

"Escape," Pierre nodded. "Yes, of course. A soldier's duty."

Joanna wouldn't know. Only that escaping was something she was going to do.

Pierre smiled. "And escape from where, Mademoiselle? Here? Why? Pierre believes you are too young to be in an army, so it isn't duty, but simply a desire to leave us. How old are you, Mademoiselle? I am merely curious. If you tell Pierre how old you are, I will tell you how old I am. Sixty-seven," he nodded, not waiting for her. "Oui, Pierre is sixty-seven years old. So, how could Mademoiselle be angry, or frightened of such a frail old man? How could Mademoiselle be angry, frightened, or refuse to talk with a priest? Do they have priests in your village where you live, Mademoiselle? Are you Catholic? Have you ever heard of the Jesuit? That is what Pierre is," he nodded. "Oui, a Jesuit missionary. I have been one for many years, and I will be one for many more ... la Trappe," he remembered. "Oui, of course. Pierre remembers now," he laughed with a shake of his head. "He told Mademoiselle about the Monastery at la Trappe. Is this the place Mademoiselle was asking about? No, you are not at the monastery, Mademoiselle, but you are some place just as nice."

"I don't care. I want to leave," Joanna nodded. "I don't ..." Well, quite honestly there was something about the place she did not like. Something about it that frightened her even if she did not know why.

"Oh, but you do care, Mademoiselle," he corrected. "You care very much as you should. I want you to listen very carefully to me. It is very important you listen to me. In a few minutes, oui, a very few minutes, you are going to have an audience with mon capitaine. I have convinced him this is very important, and I am now explaining this to you. When you meet mon capitaine you must remember not to be frightened because there is no reason for you to be frightened. Of all the things you may or may not remember," he said kindly, "if Pierre could change one thing it would be who mon capitaine is, but he cannot. You are with the Germans, Mademoiselle, I cannot lie to you. You will see how true this is for yourself when you meet mon capitaine.

"I can swear to you, Mademoiselle," he swore as Joanna stared at him, "you are safe, because you are safe. Do you know what day this is, Mademoiselle? What day it is?" he repeated when she did not answer him. "It is Thursday, the 12th of March. You have been with Pierre and mon capitaine five days, and no one has hurt you, and they will not hurt you. You have Pierre's, and oui, mon capitaine's word."

She was in a room of books, just outside her door. From the floor to the ceiling, nothing but books tucked in massive white stone and dark brown wooden cupboards lining wall after wall ...

Our father, who art in Heaven ... Joanna prayed, even though she wasn't Catholic, or particularly religious as she walked out of the darkness of the books and into the sunlight with Pierre directing her around something she knew dimly to be a scaffold.

Hallowed be thy name. Thy Kingdom come. Thy will—

"Oh, my!" Joanna stopped suddenly when the brilliant sunlight streaming in through the windows blinding her, turned around to face her, turning into a man.

"Mademoiselle?" Pierre reached for her.

"I'm fine," Joanna pushed his hand away. "I'm perfectly fine." And she was. She was startled that was all. She couldn't half see and she just did not see him at first, though now that she did?

"Oh, my," Joanna blinked, her eye opening and closing like a camera lens. "Oh, my." Why he looked exactly like Michael. He was as tall as Justin and looked exactly like Michael, how perfectly ridiculous. He could not possibly look anything like Michael, and he did not. To the contrary …

"*Sit down, Fraulein!*" the man who looked absolutely nothing like Michael while absolutely being the extreme height of Justin loomed toward her, his English awful, fairly incomprehensible, biting and clipped with a distinct and unfriendly foreign hiss.

"Over here, Mademoiselle," Pierre whispered in her ear, and Joanna found herself sitting in a chair next to Pierre, the two of them in front of a desk.

"Oh, my," Joanna stared at the overweight piece of furniture heavy on its stout short legs with savage talons gripping glassy white balls. More relics from a medieval manor, the furniture in this bright, white room was nearly all brown. Huge. Strikingly ornate with leather cushions instead of brocade satin, adorning high back chairs—

"Mademoiselle, relax," Pierre whispered in her ear.

Oh, but, Joanna couldn't. Not with some man looming over her, bearing down on her, insisting she talk while he talked at her with that harsh, nasty sounding tongue.

"I!" Joanna said.

"I am Hauptmann Reineke," he interrupted her coldly, though perhaps not quite as coldly as Joanna heard, or as abusive as his pronounced accent might suggest, and he was standing in front of what must be his side of the massive, frightening desk.

But that was not possible. Only a moment ago he was watching her from in front of the windows—

More windows. Joanna stared at the French windows that were exactly like those in the room she occupied, only these were much larger, many more of them, opened wide onto a balcony, the sun streaming in through the fine sheer draperies—

"Mademoiselle," Pierre said with a light squeeze of her hand.

Stop telling her to relax! Joanna could not possibly relax. "I!" she stammered hoarsely at the man who appeared to be waiting for her to say something, though God only knew what. "I!"

"*You*, Fräulein," she was violently advised, "are a guest." *Fine.* Joanna agreed silently. *Anything. Just sit down.*

He did not sit down.

Oh, please sit down. Joanna prayed. *Dear God, sit down.*

But he did not.

Perhaps he was incapable. Joanna stared at the straight stiff legs and high arched back with the cap on his head. She had seen that hat before. "I!" she said.

"*You*, Fräulein," She was again silenced, "are well."

The picture of health, feeling swell.

"And since you are," he advised her. And since she was currently occupying a space known as—"*There!*" his finger shot out and Joanna stared back at her room, a hundred miles away. There were a few strict and stringent rules for her to abide by, listen to, heed, honor, and obey.

"*None*," she was assured, too difficult, or strenuous as long as she did not mind the pain. She was ill—which did not make *any* sense since he just told her how well she was. And though ill, he expected her to do precisely what she was told—

"Sit back in your chair, Fräulein," Reineke ordered, "you have not been dismissed."

Except Joanna did not know she was out of her chair. All she knew was he grew taller with every word, his head higher in the air.

"The Holy Man has been given to you for guidance," Reineke continued in his notice to this appalling example of Allied frailty and German strength. "Do you understand?"

No, Joanna did not. Not one bloody word.

"I have asked you a question, Fräulein," Reineke impatiently repeated. "Do you understand me, or do you not?"

"Yes," Joanna croaked, and his head came down from the ceiling to glower at her.

"Indeed," Reineke cocked a brow. One word was not sufficient to determine either her racial background or enemy affiliation. "Beginning today," he said, carefully, watching her, "you are to be exercised." He raised his hand; Joanna had no idea why. "Your energy is returning," was his observation in contrast to the Holy Man's who maintained she was too weak to do much more than scream and cry. "I expect it to be put to a more useful purpose than the disruption of my staff. Do you understand?"

"Yes," Joanna croaked, though hardly understanding at all.

"Indeed." Again, one word was not sufficient. Reineke wanted to hear her voice, suspecting the Holy Man was in error with his presumption she was English. The voice Reineke had not heard, nor listened to had not sounded particularly English to him. The only thing it sounded was hoarse. That was understandable, considering her condition, and due to her condition, he could extend her a degree of compassion and pity. The girl was indeed small. Not much above the height of his knee. A true elf.

Another elf.

He was tired of elves.

Indeed.

"Do you have any questions, Fräulein?" Reineke asked before he sent her on her way, his voice bored and tired.

There was no answer from the elf.

"Indeed, do you have any questions, Fräulein?" he snapped, and Joanna sat up straight in her chair.

You bastard. She glared back at him. *You bloody bastard.* She watched that head of his go up in the air, and he could stick it up ...? Somewhere unpleasant, as Michael would say.

"That I have," Joanna assured, and was on her feet, seizing the edge of his desk in her savage broken claws, "where the devil am I?"

She was going to hit him. Reineke's eyes flew open. The little elf was going to attack him, leap to the top of his desk and spring.

"I asked you a question," Joanna nodded. "And don't you tell me you don't know!"

Definitely British. Of the lowest social rung. Reineke glared at

Pierre busy admiring the arm of his chair. The girl was a servant, no mystery in that. Not a nurse or some secretary, but a scullery maid, sold into servitude to the American who brought her along to scrape his boots and please his lap.

"Oh, hello in there, Captain," the girl continued her jeer, "Anybody home in there, Captain? Cat got your tongue?"

It most certainly did not. "Sit down, Fräulein," Reineke ordered with an insistent point at her chair.

"It's Frau, Captain," she taunted him. "I'll thank you to remember that."

"You will indeed thank me, Fräulein," he assured. "And you will indeed sit down—*NOW!*" he barked, and Joanna sat down quickly.

Elves! Reineke glared at Pierre. Elves, indeed. As if he needed any more elves. "Fräulein," he said.

"It's Frau, Captain," she assured, bold and brazen.

"Fräulein," he ignored her, elves notorious liars, "you are in North Afrika of the continent of Afrika under the jurisdiction of the Third Reich. Your interests, preferences and indeed, politics, are irrelevant to where mine rule. Continue to conduct yourself as your mother, and you will be treated the same. Conduct yourself as your master, and you will be treated with a similar regard. I trust that answers any question you may have."

She did not answer him.

He did not think she would.

"If there is nothing else," Reineke concluded sharply, "you may consider this interview over, you are dismissed."

"Mademoiselle," Pierre was at her side.

Over? Joanna stared at him. But that was ridiculous. He hadn't said anything, nothing at all, just something about her mother, and whatever could her mother possibly have to do with any of this?

"Mademoiselle," Pierre coaxed, but Joanna pushed his hand away.

"I remember you, Captain," she stood up, and his eyes narrowed, she watched them narrow until they were little more than slits in his glowing yellow face. "Don't think I don't. Cat got your face, Captain? Cat scratch your chin?"

"There are steps, Mademoiselle," Pierre cautioned.

"I see them!" Joanna assured, and she did. She did not remember them, but that they were there now did not surprise her.

"Fräulein."

The Captain was in front of her, holding something out to her, her silver tags. Tears welled in Joanna's eyes.

"I understand these are yours, Fräulein," he said.

That they were. Michael had given them to her for Christmas as a joke, a stupid, little joke.

"You may have them, Fräulein," his head tipped.

Joanna's chin came up. "You may have them, Captain," she corrected, "as a souvenir."

"Indeed," he said, and put them in his pocket, motioning for Pierre to take her out of there.

Joanna burst into tears on the other side of the door, choking and gasping and vomiting up what little breakfast she had eaten. When it was over, she laid there exhausted and defeated, obediently agreeing to the priest bringing her food.

"No horses," she requested as Pierre's hand touched the latch.

"Pardon?" Pierre said.

"No horses," Joanna said. "Michael's told me how they eat horses, horrid fiends they are. I don't eat horses. I can't."

"No," Pierre smiled. "No horses. A little lamb, perhaps? Does that sound nice? Even if you vomit it has more nutrients and fat that you need."

Lamb? Why, yes, sounded wonderful actually. She loved lamb. "Yes, that's fine," Joanna said. "Quite fine. I'll have the lamb."

"Very good," Pierre inclined his head and left for her lunch that would be goat, not lamb, as it had been black beans for breakfast.

Chapter Thirty-One

"Horses, indeed," Reineke was annoyed. Pierre kept diddling around the kitchen.

"Eating horses," Reineke sputtered.

Pierre laughed. "Mon capitaine, many people eat horses. It is not only the German. It was not the German who thought of eating horses first."

Germans did not eat horses. A thousand years ago perhaps, but not today that was Allied propaganda. It served the woman right to be eating goat. He hoped it made her sick, violently ill. "Horses, indeed," Reineke spit.

"Mon capitaine was listening again," Pierre clucked.

Le capitaine was not listening. Le capitaine could not help hearing. The woman's voice boomed with the power of a baritone, pounding in his brain. People not listening in Tunis could probably hear her. The daughter of someone, the wife of no one, and both of them probably gave her to the beastly Germans. "Horses, indeed," Reineke snapped. "The walls are not made of stone."

"Oui, they are," Pierre nodded. "But even at their thickest, they can be made thin when the ear is pressed against them."

Indeed. Reineke hoped Pierre ate goat and got sick. "Escape?" he demanded. "The woman plans to escape to where?"

"Who knows, mon capitaine," Pierre slapped Reineke's hand reaching for the plate Pierre was preparing for the woman. "From here for somewhere, yes, oui, obviously, perhaps even anywhere."

"Indeed," Reineke said his sharp tone for the slap. "The Kufra is less than a three-day ride."

"Ambitious, but perhaps possible," Pierre agreed. "Depending on how you ride, it could be one day or two weeks. Mademoiselle has been with us for five days. Have you had any reports of the Allied or the French in the area? No. And neither will you because it is not the Cufra."

"Indeed," Reineke said. "*Cairo* could be two weeks or one day, depending on how you ride."

"True," Pierre smiled. "But what does it matter, eh? Mon capitaine, like Mademoiselle, does not care, and when one does not care? One does not care," he shrugged. "Unless ..." he came at Reineke with a peer. "Mon capitaine has decided to care and give himself more problems?"

Le capitaine had no problems, and he did NOT care. It was simply an interesting point. One he felt he should point out. "Indeed," Reineke said. The Holy Man should be pleased. It meant he was considering believing him when he said the woman had not come from the Kufra. The Kufra, Reineke felt to be part of his backyard, regardless of how long it took, or did not take to get there, and he would not appreciate Allied beasts roaming around not eating horses.

"When did she become a woman, mon capitaine?" Pierre asked. "Rather than a girl? I am simply curious. You cannot exchange what has happened to her simply by changing her age. Rape is still not sex."

"I have no idea what you are talking about."

"Perhaps," Pierre shrugged. "But I saw your face, mon capitaine when Mademoiselle mentioned the scratches, but I would not be alarmed. I also saw Mademoiselle's face. She does not remember you. She knows she does not remember you because she knows she would. Who she is frightened of is not you, it is the uniform."

"Germans," Reineke inclined forward, "do not eat horses."

Pierre sighed. "Mon capitaine, Germans do eat horses. On the outside, many people eat horses, the same as they eat lion, elephant, monkey, or rat, and of these people are Germans.

"On the outside, mon capitaine," he said, "Germans do not live in gardens or have rendezvous to go swimming with children.

"On the outside, mon capitaine," he claimed, "the German is not mon capitaine's German. But how can Mademoiselle know this? How can anyone? How can they care? In one-hundred years perhaps, yes," he agreed. "In one-hundred years when it is over, someone might say,

'Oh. There once was a German who lived in a garden and went swimming with children'. But that is not today, mon capitaine. Today they do not know, and cannot care. And why should they? Ehiwaz, you claim for your coat-of-arms? No. Ehiwaz is an honorable and ancient symbol of defense. Your coat is not Ehiwaz; it is a swastika, a symbol of domination."

Indeed. The Holy Man probably ate horses.

"But!" Pierre could be generous too, "To help with mon capitaine's wounded pride, I think mon capitaine should know, I believe Mademoiselle has noticed how pretty he is?"

The woman had done what? "Indeed," Reineke left the goat where he had dropped it on floor.

"Oui," Pierre slapped Reineke's wrist in punishment a second time. "I saw her face when she saw you. She did not expect you, and she was very surprised. Very, very surprised," he laughed. "But that is not so strange, mon capitaine, it is simply a matter of fact. Mademoiselle does not remember mon capitaine, and mon capitaine is pretty. He is extremely pretty—

"Especially, eh?" he gave Reineke a knowing crack in the ribs with his fist. "When he is standing in the window with the sun, and he is already the color of the sun, and he makes sure you notice this because he stays in the window, he does not sit down? Glorious, mon capitaine, oh, so, glorious, oui, very, very clever. A man so glorious, how could he be evil? I noticed you did this. I did notice. But, so what, eh?" he shrugged. "Who cares? All Mademoiselle would notice is a pretty man. A horrible, oui, very pretty fiend."

Indeed. The woman noticing he was pretty was of little importance to him. Pierre saying she noticed he was pretty was probably a lie. Pierre was an elf, and this elf Reineke knew well. He was also carrying his elfin tactics over to the woman, and Reineke could sympathize with her in wanting the Holy Man to leave her alone. He was obnoxious. Deliberately sweet and coyly misleading the woman into believing there would soon be some miraculous change in her situation.

"But of course," Pierre defended himself and his tactics. "She is drawn to Pierre despite her convictions to the contrary. I am the only one there, mon capitaine. I am available to scream at or to cry with, and I must encourage her to do both for the sake of her mental health, not only her physical. I have told Mademoiselle she is safe, but she must believe she is safe. You?" he sniffed. "Who cares about you? She does not like you. You will see. By tomorrow, she will be plotting your death with I as her assistant. It will be a tempting offer, I must admit."

"Indeed," Reineke said. Pointing out the Holy Man's conniving and devious scheme was *his* point, including how it had not gone unnoticed by him. Reineke was positive, the Holy Man in his plots to glean acceptance, would get what the English called comeuppance. "You are manipulating her."

"No more than I am manipulating you," Pierre assured. "You believe she is a threat, I tell you she is not a threat, and you will see this for yourself."

"Indeed," Reineke said.

"You are jealous, mon capitaine," Pierre laughed with a waggle of his finger. "I have told you this many, many times before. You are a very jealous man. You strut your pretty face because you want Mademoiselle's acceptance and appreciation for yourself and I am taking it from you. Too bad! Learn the facts of the life you embrace. 'Beauty is in the eye of the beholder'. In the eyes of all, I am who is beautiful, not you. With you, it is just a face."

Hardly. Reineke's desire to be accepted and appreciated was not jealousy. It was nothing less than deserved, right, and fair. One hundred years from now was not sufficient for people to know there once was a German et cetera. Yesterday was not sufficient. Not all Germans ate horses. He had never eaten horses. He had lived among gardens all of his life and the mere onset of global war was, in his opinion, little cause to change. If the woman thought until her death he was a fiend then this was upon the head of the woman and her ignorance was of no importance to him. Her thinking on the whole was not important to him.

Though this would be the second time the Holy Man had alluded to how his physical appearance might be useful in persuading the woman ... from what? Attempting suicide?

Interesting. Reineke puzzled about it for a moment, but only for a moment. In fact, even thinking about it brought immediate guilt.

He could do precious little about his being pretty. It was obvious though the woman was not pretty under her bruised and swollen face. But was plain, even unattractive and therefore spared the full horror of her disfigurement. One cannot disfigure what is already ugly. It was not catastrophic what had happened to her, it was unfortunate.

And that itself was unfortunate. It would take more than a simple effort on his part to change his disinterest in women who were not pretty. His recently acquired compassion for mankind was just that, recently acquired. Only with age came wisdom, and he was not yet old. In his still youthful state, he found great difficulty extending to women the right not to be as pretty as he was even though historically speaking with the coming of age he was finding few women were as pretty as he. Even as compassionate and understanding as he knew himself to be, his ability to consider extending such a compromise to the enemy would be a true test indeed. One hundred years? They could take two. This was his garden, his swimming hole, and his children. That was his Holy Man, his apartment, and now his guest. It was not his vanity that wanted the woman to know the kindness and help extended to her came from him, not simply the Holy Man. It was his ardent respect and appreciation for the truth.

"Indeed, I am a truthful person!" Reineke snarled at Pierre. It was he who called the Holy Man. He who routed the SS. He who supplied the sutures and bandages for her head. She was sleeping in his bed, drinking his water, and eating his goat. It was not strange or bizarre for him to want her to know the bounty she stumbled upon had come from him! They could take three-hundred years! The woman probably ate horses. Anyone as vulgar as she was, probably ate horses for breakfast. He could understand any desire the Holy Man might have to punish her for her violent and abusive behavior. SHE was obnoxious. "Horses, indeed," Reineke snapped. He just might feed her horses and laugh while she—what had the Holy Man said? Something about the woman's mental state? Indeed. If she found herself in some state of nervous collapse due to him, what sort of condition would she have found herself in had he left her in the cellar, ropes around her, with not even horses to eat? Mental state.

Her mental state had nothing to do with him, but rather with her Allied associates failing to supervise some *girl* who obviously couldn't take care of herself. He maintained she was a *girl* despite her claim of marriage, something that only proved she was sexually mature, hardly chronologically.

"Michael," Reineke snarled at Pierre. "Michael, indeed." The woman had called him *Michael* in her confused and unconscious state, and he had not understood. However, he understood now, and it was an insult. This *Michael* was obviously a heathen. Enjoying the company of other heathens too busy devouring horses to even notice one of them was lost to the desert. "Who is *Michael?*" he demanded of Pierre.

"I do not know, mon capitaine," Pierre assured. "It is the first time she has mentioned the name, any name. Perhaps it is the dead American? She has not asked about him, or anyone. And so perhaps she knows, whether she remembers or not, her people are dead."

"Yes," Reineke scowled. "Obviously, yes" It was the dead American with the bones sticking out of his head. "The woman's hair is to be washed."

"Pardon?" Pierre blinked.

"The condition of the woman's hair," Reineke assured, "is disgusting. It is filthy. It is to be washed before any exercise."

"Oh," Pierre said. "Well, I do not believe she will not allow it, mon capitaine. She is very protective of her head."

"Do it!" Reineke barked.

"Oui, of course, whatever you say," Pierre shrugged.

He was staring at him again. The Holy Man was staring at him. Why NOW was he staring at him? Every time he opened his mouth, the little man did nothing except stare at him. The goat was off the floor—from where he had flung it. Its little round circle of grease was off the floor—from where he had wiped it clean. Her goat ... Her goat on the tray was cold, its fat congealed, hardly appetizing and bound to make anyone sick. You do not serve cold, congealed goat to someone who has been ill and expect it to do anything except come back at you. "That is cold," Reineke pointed in accusation.

"Oui, mon capitaine," Pierre agreed, "but it does not matter, for Mademoiselle will not eat it."

Not eat it? Then why was he giving it to her? "Why?" Reineke insisted.

"Pierre has been gone so long," Pierre shrugged, "she will be sleeping—or she will be awake," he smiled, "and will know Pierre has done other things except to find her something to eat, and she will hit him with the tray."

That woman was one of the most uncivilized persons Reineke had ever met. Offending every decent and respectable quality he had—and he had thousands—causing his perfect and glorious skin to crawl.

"One-hundred years from now," the Holy Man was saying, except Reineke had decided to leave the kitchen regardless of what he was saying, "the people who believe in the German and his gardens, will never believe in mon capitaine, never."

"Indeed!" Reineke kicked open the door of his villa to stand on her grand stairs before her magnificent courtyard and scream at the sand if he thought it would listen, except he knew it would not. He had things to do, things he should do, and did not want to do a thing about them, which was why he had called for the Holy Man, earlier, to tell him just that. He was not doing anything after lunch. He was going swimming with the children, leaving the woman the freedom to roam the upstairs halls for her exercise, unencumbered by intimidating armed personnel. However, the Holy Man who hated the war was always the first to point out there was a war, and in war, men did not find the time to do the things they liked to do. The Holy Man was wrong. There was no war, not here. Here, they were simply piling things up for when the war would start again. Let it start again. If they needed him, they would find him, swimming with the children. Ha! All his boxes and barrels of munitions were ready and stacked, his waterholes counted and still full. He remained committed to killing the soldiers who had jeopardized his compound, and he had run out of things to make rules about.

The French windows in his office and the ceiling were both under repair. An *enormous* scaffold filled the room, and did you notice? Reineke sneered at the desert. That idiot woman almost walked into it? Was she blind as well as ugly? She had the grace of one of the Holy Man's goats. Did she think he failed to notice she had little idea how to walk? Had no one ever taught this woman how to pick her feet up? She was undoubtedly a trick of the Gestapo, hardly some Allied spy or anything. He could see the Major planning his plan. Make sure all the boxes and barrels are present and accounted for.

Make sure all of the watering holes are bubbling and full. You already know he will kill the soldiers, and what could there be LEFT to make a rule about? So give him a corn for his toe, and call it a woman. No one can ignore a corn. Ha! But did they know what giving him such a corn would cause him to do? Could they have known it would cause him to blow up his ceiling, decorate his French windows with Thiele, and give the corn to his dwarf of a French priest? He doubted it. With everything done, he could stop any new things to do by placing them all on radio silence where they remained, giving him more than sufficient time to go swimming. *Ha!* On radio silence should the war begin again, no one could tell him, he could not hear them, and he would not hear them until he wanted to hear them, which he did not want to do, he wanted to go swimming!

But.

There was one thing still that should be done.

"THIELE!" Reineke shouted, surprised the man's wife sitting at home in Stuttgart did not look up from eating her solitary lunch.

Thiele listened patiently. He examined obligingly the silver dog tags thrust into his hands, agreeing they were not of a style common to Allied necklaces.

"They are ridiculous," Reineke assured. A passion for trinkets did not excuse turning precious metals into garbage.

So was Reineke's request ridiculous in Thiele's opinion. He had a thousand things he needed to do other than waste time with some ugly and offensive piece of jewelry.

"Give them to someone else," Reineke ordered. Thiele was off to the Kufra with a patrol where he would turn over every stone, sift every grain of sand until he had proof there was or was not a band of roving saboteurs, French, British, or Chinese, Reineke really did not care. The Kufra was minimally, a three-day ride going, and a three-day ride back, therefore Reineke had better not see Thiele for a week.

"A week?" Thiele gasped, he had a thousand things to do!

No, he did not. The only thing Thiele had to do was what Reineke told him to do.

But Reineke had a thousand things to do! Thiele insisted. They were conducting their first shipment of munitions to the farthest camp.

"Indeed." Reineke told Thiele five days ago they were not shipping any munitions, at least not now, not until Reineke was ready.

"Ready?" Thiele sputtered. "The war is coming!"

"It is not here yet!" Reineke snapped. He knew precisely when the war would be there, which Thiele did not, and since Thiele did not, Thiele would do what Reineke told him to do, not what he thought he should do. Come May, Thiele was scheduled for a short, personal leave. Reineke knew, come June, and for months to follow, he, personally, would have no such luxury. And since he would not have one then, he would take one now.

He needed one now.

He wanted one now.

And he would have one now!

But, he was playing into their hands! Thiele moaned.

"Indeed," Reineke raised a haughty brow. Whose hands? With what? He had nothing to play into their hands with. He played with no one's hands except his own. And his own were going to be playing with the children in the game known as swimming.

Only this, he did not tell Thiele, though he was tempted. Thiele's ideas on war were even stricter than the Holy Man's. Little did either of them know however, how many blazing battles Reineke had actually been involved in, and how, in the heat of those battles, should he, Baron Dieter Reineke, decide to put down his gun, stretch out his legs and have a cigarette, he would do precisely that, and dare the bullets whistling by to strike him.

And not one would.

Not one ever had! That was proof of something. Even inanimate objects, deadly, little lead and copper pellets were frightened of him and did not dare stop him from doing precisely what he wanted to do, when he wanted to do it.

But this again he did not tell Thiele. The only thing Thiele might have found it to be proof of was that Reineke had eaten rancid goat, and had precious little time left to decide who did what when before he died of the Holy Man's poison.

But, goat, away! Thiele away! Reineke was off, retreating inside his villa, with only one thing left to be said.

"Anyone," he vehemently informed, finding half-eaten horses was to leave them precisely where they found them.

ANYONE caught eating horses would be shot. No questions asked, reasons, or excuses accepted, end of discussion.

End of something, Thiele was sure. Upon storming away, in his heart, Thiele was convinced taking a patrol and departing just might be the best thing to happen to him. They just might find Allies swarming all over the Kufra and he might never return, never mind in a week. Thiele was not immune to puncture by deadly little pellets. Bullets did not heed him.

Chapter Thirty-Two

March 12
The Tell Atlas, East Algeria

Less the necessary stops to refuel and cool its engine, Justin's reliable Applecore made it across Libya into Algeria in just under thirty-six hours to sit there and wait, landing along the northern folds of the Atlas, Algeria's brooding mountain range. It was still winter but not cold, the air fragrant with cedar and pine under the cool shadows of dwarf palms like a line of fat-bottomed women standing there. Three and a half days, eighty-four hours—count them—since he came into Cairo, sitting around doing nothing, Michael was in a sour mood. Chuck's buddies for all their cartoon qualities were a tame lot. Ate, slept, took turns at watch and occasionally kicked a ball around, dull as housewives. Michael was angry and anxious, edgy like a kid stuck inside on a rainy day.

"Nice night, huh?" Michael solicited one particularly voluptuous tree, but she kept her opinion to herself. "Mind if I join you?" he invited himself, anyway, and Pete glanced over from where he lounged on his blanket.

"Mate ..." Pete turned from Michael to Hank who had seen to rejoining them about an hour ago by way of the Applecore's elder sister, a Swordfish, or Stringbag as they were affectionately called by Hank's lot. Hank did not fly that relic into Malta from Tobruk, though. It did not have the range, the devil with the ruddy Applecore cutting it close, or the range from Malta to there. So, Hank and Fred had to come in from Frank's place out on the Saharan Atlas, picked his Stringbag up there after catching one of the long range flyers out of Cairo to get them in quick as possible. Pete smiled. Justin was moving Hank and Fred into the ranks of his irregulars fast. He wondered how Bobby felt about that since Bobby did not like sharing with outsiders, especially the regular kind, which Hank and Fred most definitely were.

"Tree, mate," Pete spelled out in sign language for Hank when Hank looked up from playing solitaire in reply to the piece of rock Pete tossed killing Hank's Queen of Hearts dead between her eyes. "Tree. He's talking to the damn tree."

Hank looked over in time to see Joe followed by Julia emerging from walking the perimeter.

"Never mind," Pete rolled over on his blanket as Fred got up with a stretch to take his turn patrolling after giving Joe a wave, and his wife a kiss hello, and Hank returned to his solitaire as disinterested as when he first looked up.

"Ay!" Shortly thereafter, the Doc apparently decided he was bored with life and living, his swift kick catching Pete in the bony seat of his pants but only because Hank was sitting on his duff and Pete's was pointing Michael's way.

"What the hell are you looking at?" Michael sneered as Pete rolled over to prop himself up on his elbow and look the Doc over before he killed him. "I'm the one who almost broke my toe."

"Break more than that," Pete promised, "if you ever do that again."

"Save it for my mother," Michael squatted down, willing to bet like everyone else Pete had his price, and Michael was willing to meet the asking price and buy his way out of there for wherever. "Think it's time for a change—"

"Well, now, give it a minute, Doc," Pete nodded, "and it'll be as different as night and day. Algeria's one of those country's with a climate that changes as you change. What you think is snow on those branches over there, walk a few miles and it'll be flowers of peaches, apples, cherry, and pear," he smiled. "Or weren't it the weather you were wondering about?"

"Let's start over," the Doc sucked at the inside of his mouth like he was sucking on tobacco when he could probably stand a taste of something a lot stronger. This boy had a thirst on him. Pete had noticed that immediately. The Doc hadn't drunk much, and maybe he should to keep him from being so mean, the burnished apples of his cheeks tight and inflamed as his temper. Come to think of it, Pete had yet to see the Doc in anything but a bad mood, not so much as even try to smile in the face of adversity like they say one should. He had a sense of humor, or at least thought himself funny with things like the kick he gave Pete in the seat of his pants and clever double-talk, but he wasn't funny. He knew it, Pete knew it, Joe and Julia meandering their way over knew it. A flicker of apprehension in Joseph's eyes, clear annoyance in Jewel's for the Doc trying to show off. Even Hank was inspired to forego cheating himself at solitaire and get up, wandering Pete's way, nonchalantly shuffling the deck, his weight and reason shifting to Pete's side.

"Look," Michael said, "I think we both know Red being shanghaied has got about as much to do with Vichy as I do, which is nothing. So the way I see it—"

"Oh, well, now, that depends," Pete agreed easily, "on how you want to look at it—"

"Dead on!" Michael snapped. "You think I don't fucking know who I am regardless of who else does or doesn't? You think I don't know I'm out here for my health and not much else?"

"You don't look that healthy to me, Doc," Pete advised. "I've seen worse, admit I have, but I've also seen a lot better."

"And I get worse," Michael assured, "before I get better. So let's cut the crap. I want out, and I've got two big ones that say I'm up, I'm out of here. That's five-hundred each for those who are listening."

Four-hundred each if they were feeling generous and included the quiet one with the over-sized head who also showed up when Hank showed up and was around somewhere, on watch, patrolling the perimeter while his wife played house with Joe. Even Michael had to shake his head at that one, yeah, he did, but only in fond memory. "So, any takers?" Michael looked around, 'cause like he said, everyone had their price, this group hardly the exception. "Going once, going twice ..."

"For where, Doc?" Hank asked, though not to suggest he was seriously considering it, which he might be. The same as the rest of them were in the back of their minds. This fellow was a pain in the ass if he were nothing else. Trouble, not just stupid with trying to be funny.

"What do you care?" Michael countered. "I mean personally? Just out, OK? Back, how's that? Take me back to Cairo and I'll take it from there.

"I mean," Michael pled his case, and to an extent even sounded legitimate. "I've got a kid out there somewhere that until someone proves to me otherwise I say is alive. Because I'd feel it, you know?" he said, hell, what anyone in his position would say, did say. "I'd know," he assured, "whether she was or she wasn't. That's all I care about, *all* I care about. I don't care how long it takes, a month, six. Fuck, it took Noah forty fucking years to get where he was going and he had divine direction, so, screw Chuck."

"Moses, Doc," Joe chuckled, glad Pete also felt inclined to laugh even if Julia and Hank did not. "Think you mean Moses. Noah was the guy with the ark."

"Ark, huh?" Michael eyed Pete. "Little wonder it took him forty fucking years."

"Whichever," Joe's hand clapped down on Michael's shoulder in a friendly though firm gesture even though he knew the Doc didn't mean any harm with that kick in Pete's behind nah, he didn't. Joe was confident about that. The Doc was just angry, mouthing off because he was angry, probably feeling helpless, yeah, that was it. Helpless, sad, and grieving, and this just hanging around waiting would kill anyone, get under anyone's skin especially when no one was even really sure exactly what it was they were waiting for, certainly not for some kid to show up, blow in like Dorothy from Kansas. She was dead. The Doc was just having to come to terms with that, on the verge of coming to terms with it, and it wasn't easy, no, it was not. "We understand, Doc," Joe assured in his friendly way. "We do. Talk, if you want to talk—"

"Think fuck off will work?" Michael lunged for Pete and ended up with what turned out to be a load of Joe. But only because Pete was fast, Hank even faster, in a better position to put himself between the Doc and Pete since he was standing and Pete was sitting down. Joe perhaps the fastest of them all, much to his chagrin, because it was his chest hair that wound up snarled in the Doc's fist instead of the Doc's neck twisted in Pete's because there was no way in hell the Doc stood a chance to get his hands on Pete first.

"Joe!" Julia yelled, which had Pete and Hank forgetting about challenging Michael and reaching for her before she made matters worse by shooting the Doc, Joe gasping, "Whoa, Doc!" with a grab for Michael's wrist before Michael tore a few tattoos out by the roots, the pain instant, stinging and burning hot.

"Serious, Doc, let go of the hair—do it you dick-ass motherfucker!" Joe grabbed Michael by the hair on his head, "before I fucking kill you!"

"Fine!" Michael gave him back his wool. "Now fuck off before I get nasty."

"You, too, lad!" Hank advised Joe to give up the ghost before everyone ended back up in the tussle they had all just worked so hard to stop.

"Fair enough," Joe released Michael to surrender to Julia's worries that he wasn't, he didn't know, the man he was when he started out or something. "I'm fine. Serious, I'm good. Just ... wow, yeah," he noticed what she was in a sweat about and it was his blood, couple of little bright dots from where the Doc won and the hair lost, "get me some alcohol."

"For the Doc, too," Hank suggested as she headed for the medic-pack, only he meant the drinking kind.

"Aye, some of Peter's rum," Pete seconded with a smile and a wink at Michael. "Demon rum, Doc. Call it that, because that's what it is. Potent, just the way Peter likes it."

"Yeah, well, don't get your hopes up," Michael ran a hand through his mop of oily curls to make sure they were still there, which they were, like Joe's chest, missing only a few.

"What hopes are those?" Pete asked. "That it gets worse long before it gets better, because you know damn well how it does, don't you?"

"You know," Michael said but only because he felt he had to say something, wouldn't be in character if he didn't, "there's something about you I don't like."

"Oh, well, now, that's all right," Pete sat back down comfortably on his blanket, inviting the Doc to join him for that nightcap, "because there's everything about you I don't like. Not one thing," he assured Michael. "You're stupid, for one. If you weren't you'd know no one ever gets the upper hand on Peter, death wish even to try. I mean, look at me, Doc, have a good look," he smiled while he checked on the order for spirits he had placed. "How's it coming there, luv? Give Jewels a hand, won't you?" he petitioned Hank uncertain about leaving Pete and the Doc alone even for the minute it would take. "Can't have the Doc coming down with the shakes when there's no reason, none at all, Joseph will keep, he'll keep. Live even."

"Not him I'm worried about," Hank countered pointedly.

"Oh, well, I don't know why," Pete smiled at Michael sitting down, right there on the blanket across from Pete. The Doc had balls on him if he had nothing else, aye, he did. "Nothing wrong with the Doc, just like Joseph was saying, that wouldn't be wrong with any of us. Why, I remember when my old lady died ..."

"You talking about your mother?" Hank said, not to be wise, just curious since the Pete he had come to know had lots of old ladies, most he didn't even know their names.

"No, I mean yours," Pete cooed, "and a pitiful sight it was, too."

"Aye, and worth it to get away from you," Hank assured as he retreated as asked, figuring Pete had enough brains to behave even if the Doc didn't.

"No doubt about it," Pete continued to smile at Michael. "No doubt about that at all. Where was I? Oh, that's right. Look at me, Doc. I mean take a real good look," he nodded. Past Pete's bristle of whiskers starting to sprout, the same as the Doc had a few of his own, thicker and darker than Pete's reddish-blond two-day growth on his upper lip and cleft-chin adding a devilish look to his devil-may-care.

Beyond the well-worn cotton shirt no dirtier than the Doc's Italian silk, the semi-automatic strapped to his thigh ...

Jesus frigging Christ, Michael got the point. The guy had a brand burnt into his left tit never mind some pec-load of tattoos, the scarred circles of flesh visible as he bent over to borrow Michael's cigarettes and strike a match. "Yeah, what about it?" Michael said. "Think because I'm not a fan of self-mutilation I'm not as tough as you?"

"Self-mutilation?" Pete glanced down to his breast. "Why, that isn't any self-mutilation, Doc. That's a birthday present from my old man. Poor as we were at the time it was all he could afford. Had a farm, we did, long before I was born," he assured lest Michael confuse him with some country gent instead of the city born and bred fellow he was. "I never saw it, that's for sure. But we had a farm, and all my father could hope to do was burn her into my soul. You following me?" he asked, just like the Doc had asked them to follow him. "Right there should I ever chance to forget, need do nothing except look down."

"You going somewhere particular with this?" Michael checked.

"No, but you are," Pete promised, "if you ever pull a cockamamie stunt like you pulled on Joseph again, try it and see. Try it on me. Go on, grab a handful and see what happens. I don't give the King's ass who you are, save stupid like I said. Should have just stopped with asking me to get you out of here. I'd have taken you anywhere you want to go for less than half your two-thousand and take my chances on finding myself on the wrong side of Justin. It wouldn't be the first time, he'd tell you that himself, and sure as hell wouldn't be last, he'd tell you that as well."

"Let's leave Chuck and back it up to my ticket out of here," Michael suggested, "if you're serious."

"Oh, now, I was serious, Doc," Pete swore. "Take convincing to be serious again. But don't let that stop you, go on, give it your best. Convince me. The only problem I can see facing either of us is that airplane reliable as she is, isn't any help."

"Oh, yeah?" Michael said like he had wings on his back to go along with his name. "How so?"

"Oh, well, how so is that she's an airplane," Pete reminded, "not a jeep. No one's ever going to corrupt Hank. He's not us, he's RA. Black Watch. Got Justin's morals and commitment. Even Jewels isn't going to be quick to comply. Before this job she was looking at ten years—"

"I can handle it," Michael assured.

"Think so I'm sure, but she's not as easy going as she looks."

The hell she wasn't, but that was beside the point. "The plane," Michael said. "I can handle the plane."

"Really?" Pete smiled. "Is that so? You mean to say you're a pilot, Doc, on top of everything else?"

"I'm a lot of things," Michael assured.

"Are you now, Doc?" Pete smiled in the direction of Joe heading back to them on a fast trot, the Doc's nightcap in his hand. "Are you, now?"

"He serious?" Julia snatched up Pete's concoction, sloshing it into the tin beaker Hank held out.

"Pete?" Hank said. "About what? Some fellow seeing pink elephants if he doesn't have enough to drink? I don't know. Know the fellow's an arsehole, that's what I know, whether he does or doesn't need the stuff."

"No, you're right, Pete can't be serious," Julia decided. "I mean, the guv would know, wouldn't he?" she frowned at Joe. "Say something about it you would think."

"What?" Joe finished wiping his chest down with iodine. "The Doc? Nah, he's fine. Just him, you know, just him."

"All right, just him," Hank accepted. "Only problem is Pete's just Pete. Start bragging about how tough you are Pete's apt to show you how tough he is. He's not good at sitting in a foxhole. I don't care who else is or isn't. Pete's no good at it, you can see that."

"Huh?" Joe said.

"Sitting in a foxhole, lad," Hank assured. "Just sitting there waiting, pressure mounting, turns minutes into hours, after a while it even gets to the best. Pete's hardly the best. He's pressurized long before some fellow starts bandying about the size of his bollocks."

"Yatata, yatata," Joe took the bottle of Pete's rum, heading back to the Doc and Pete. "It ain't the booze, it's the Doc. That's the way he is ..."

"I'll second that," Hank snorted, offering Julia a turn at the beaker Joe left behind. "Think that lad is going to have to do better than that if he ever wants to run for President."

"Ta," Julia shook her head. "I'm fine."

"You sure?" Hank chuckled. "It'll put hair on your chest."

"Oh?" Julia laughed. "Think you're the one who's going to have to do better."

"Aye, well, I'm not good at politicking," Hank assured. "Don't even pretend to be."

"No more than Pete is at foxholes." Julia wrapped her arms around herself to calm the shivers that weren't because she was cold, but worried and wondering and not liking the feeling. "Is rather like sitting in a foxhole, isn't it? Don't suppose this waiting would go any faster if any of us knew what we were actually waiting for," she looked Hank over. "Know what I mean?"

"I do, and I can't answer you even if I could, and I can't," Hank said.

"Why?" Julia asked. "This Doc's too hot for Cairo, there's got to be a reason why he's too hot. Figure out who he is, probably figure that out as well ... only problem is I can't figure who he could be, other than a damn pain in the arse," she took the beaker from Hank, a smile on her face as it passed through her lips. "Warm the cockles, Pete's right about that. With a little luck, it will knock the Doc flat over on his. In as bad shape as Pete seems to think he is, it can't help but knock him flat."

"Think that's more it," Hank took the beaker back.

"What is?" Julia said. "Babysitting some drunk? Pete will put a bullet through his own head, never mind anyone else's."

"Or at least a pain in the arse," Hank nodded. "Think he's less hot than a pain in the arse the Major doesn't want around. I mean," he scoffed, "he seem like the sort of fellow to you, you would put your career on the line for? He doesn't to me, and I wouldn't."

"Put his career on the line?" Julia said, concerned. "The guv?"

"He's fine," Hank assured. "Think he's trying to teach that Doc a lesson that's all. Sit him out here and see how he likes it. Looking over your shoulder every five minutes, wondering who's out there, *if* anyone's out there. Which direction the damn bullet's going to come from, if it's going to come, which you know damn well it is, and if it's not, what is? Hell, if the Doc weren't a drunk when he started out, he'll be one by the time he goes home, especially if he spends much time drinking this stuff."

"Quite," Julia said. Pete's rum was as potent as he claimed, and Hank's lips, if they weren't numb they were getting a little loose. Julia watched him closely.

Hank knew she was. He smiled. "Tell you this much, luv, so you don't ruin your looks wondering, it's him who got the governor's sister mixed up in the mess she found herself in. Him who got her killed, that Doc sitting right over there. So, quite. The boss doesn't want him around, no more than I would, for the single reason he's apt to kill him never mind anyone else."

"You're lying through your damn teeth," Julia accused after watching him a little longer.

Hank laughed. "No, I'm not. Anyone come by to trouble you about him, you just send them on to Pete or me. Just tell them you don't know, but we do. Point them in our direction, and we'll take it from there. That Doc, I can promise you won't live long enough to ruin anyone's career, including his own. No one's going to have to worry about that."

"Babysitting," Julia nodded, "babysitting. Isn't that rich. I owe Justin one, I do."

"Oh, right," Hank laughed again, handing her the beaker, "Remember that and you might not be back with us so quick the next time."

"Here you go, Doc," Pete took the duty from Joe handing Michael a cup, and pouring himself a little of his dynamite. "Good as new in less than a minute, you'll see."

"Uh, huh," Michael said, "think we covered that part and had moved on."

"So we have," Pete agreed. "Doc was complaining again how he would prefer to get cracking and take care of these Jerry fellows ourselves," he explained tentatively to Joe carefully watching Michael's reaction. "Thinks he can get you interested in listening to him the same as he has me."

"Oh, yeah?" Joe grinned at Michael. "Why? 'Cause you think I'm stupid or something?"

"Yeah," Michael said, "actually. I mean, I don't suppose it's occurred to either of you zeroes that whatever scent Chuck thinks he's on is the one to get him off the track, rather than on it?"

"Oh, well, now, that would be a little strange, wouldn't it?" Pete considered the notion of being taken for a ride. "For Jerry to try and throw somebody off a track he just did his damn best to get them on?"

"Not so strange," Michael hinted, "if all they wanted to do was bust Chuck's balls. Maybe all they ever wanted was to pinch Red, slit her throat, to show Chuck he ain't the king of the mountain. Not this one."

"Now that would be a really stupid thing to do," Pete nodded at Joe nodding back.

"Too late, even," Joe agreed.

"Aye, a lot too late," Pete poured himself a little more rum with a laugh. "It's Charlie's attention they got whether it's Charlie's attention they wanted or not—not to say you don't have a point, Doc," he poured Michael a second dose, dry as the Doc's cup had been now for a while. "Doc's got a point, Joseph, he does. All this time wasted wondering if Jerry's up to finishing what he started, or what he's up to when we could just go out there and find out for ourselves."

"Yeah, you've got a point, Doc," Joe agreed, "on top of your head, and whatever scheme you're rattling around in there, just don't, OK? Don't. If we sit here two days, we sit here two days. If we sit here for ten, we sit for ten. You don't like it, I don't like it, nobody likes it, but that's the way it is. OK?"

"No!" Michael assured. "But, then, hey, unlike you, I would notice if someone puts a bullet through my brain."

"Nah, I'd notice, Doc," Joe helped himself to Michael's cigarettes, tossing Pete one as well. "Pretty sure I would—Pete might not, but I would."

"No, I'd notice, lad," Pete assured, accepting a light. "Maybe not if it were your brain, but definitely if it were mine."

"Whatever," Joe dug in his pocket for the deck of cards he happened to have. "We stay until the Maj says go, and then we go, not before."

"Maj," Pete scoffed. "Come off that Major business once and for all, can't you? He's a damn governor like Jewels says. You even know what a damn governor is, boy? Prison warden. What Justin is, and where we are, prison."

"Yeah, I know what a governor is," Joe assured. "You know what happened to the last fucking asshole who called me boy?"

"Nothing," Pete assured, "just like what's going to happen to me.

Where were we?" he helped himself to another of Michael's cigarettes to save for later. "Talking about Charlie, weren't we? And you should know, Doc how *Charlie* do mean *fool*. You know that, right? Sure you do. But if you think Justin's the fool, what do you think they are who started this?" he wondered.

"Sick bastards," Michael assured, not surprised to find it was contagious.

Pete laughed. "You do have a knack for stating the obvious, Doc that you do."

"Yeah, well, there's obvious, and then there's obvious," Michael suggested. "Know what I mean?"

"No," Peter shook his head, "can't say I do."

"Think about it," Michael stretched out, tucking his hands behind his head. "Let me know."

Pete eyed him. "Lying through your damn teeth about being able to pilot that plane, aren't you, Doc? Trying to make a fool out of Peter?"

"You tell me," Michael's perusal of the stars ended at Julia having a chit-chat with Hank, probably not about rules of some card game. He sneered. "What's she doing, taking a break?"

Pete looked over. "Jewels? Well, now, I can't say I know what you mean by that either, Doc," he advised.

"Now I know you're stupid," Michael assured. He nodded at Joe. "That goes double for you. Yeah, I can pilot a frigging plane, so do you want in, or don't you? That's what we're talking about. Me out of here, into the wide blue yonder."

"Um ..." Joe said. "No, I'm not stupid, Doc. And, yeah," he said, "you're right. Jewels is taking a break. From me."

"You mean kind of like dress rehearsal for when her old man comes back in?" Michael aimed to hit below the belt.

"Um ..." Joe said with a glance at Pete shaking his head.

"Don't do it, lad," Pete advised. "Do not. Justin will ask how the Doc got his neck broken and Peter will have to tell him, he will. But then while Peter will do most anything for you, die, even, if he's asked to, what Peter will not do is find himself back in jail for you."

"Fair enough," Joe accepted. "Yeah, Doc," he told Michael. "Yeah, actually, until Fred comes back in. You're right about that, too. Next question?"

"That's probably it," Michael said. "Just checking. After all, I wouldn't want to accidentally ruin anyone's fun by talking out of turn."

"No chance of that," Pete shook his head. "None. You've got it all wrong, anyway."

"I do, huh?"

"Aye," Pete said. "Joseph's a lifer, Doc, like I am. Who's not is Jewels. Who's certainly not is Fred. He's regular Army. And apart from Fred's the one who asked Jewels to marry him, what would you like Joseph to do? Tell the lady she can't have a life after she's paid her society dues and is out of here?"

"Is that the way it reads?" Michael verified with Joe.

"Yeah," Joe said. "That's about the size of it."

"Well," Michael said, "I've heard better, and I've heard worse."

"Knew you'd understand, Doc," Pete nodded. "Same as I'm sure you understand any momentary urge on Joseph's part to kill you. He tells me, like he says about you, it's just got something to do with him being Italian ... now is that true, Doc?" Pete just thought he'd ask since they were on the subject. "I've often wondered about that. Are you inclined to kill and not ask first just because you're Italian? Or is that just a load of what you Yanks call bullshit?"

"It's true," Michael said.

"Right," Pete smiled. "Sounds like a small man's disease to me." He stood up to hitch his pants and stretch his lanky limbs, tall enough at six-one in his boots. "About time to police that perimeter again, isn't it, Joseph?" he reminded with a tap of his watch. "Tea time's, over."

"Yeah, we're on it," Joe put away the cards. *We*, of course, meaning him and Julia, leaving Michael to hope the *perimeter* could take care of policing itself.

"What about you, Doc?" Pete asked.

"Huh?" Michael looked up.

"Want any more of this?" Pete dangled the rum before he put it away for the night. "Sure you do," he said, "same as Peter does. And then we'll take our guns out and see which one of us can hit that notch on your tree with our eyes half closed. Those the kind of games you like to play, Doc? Like they do in films? Is that what you think this is? Make-believe? Is that who you think you are with your prissy white collar and high-buttoned shoes, mouthing off about wanting to do this and going to do that? One of those gangster fellows? Like Bogart?" he poured some rum. "Or that Mick, what's his name? Cagney," he nodded. "Right, that's it. That's who Bobby says you think you are. James Cagney. How the hell old are you anyway, Doc? Forty? Shit, I'm forty-five. Been in jail half my life and still I look better than you. About time you grew up, isn't it? You'll never be a tall man, I don't care how much you pay for your shoes, but it's never too late to change, especially for something as big as this."

"Better question," Michael said, "you believe that schlock you spieled off?"

"Which schlock's that?" Pete asked, like he didn't know. "The one about Joseph and my girl Jewels? Well, now, it doesn't matter what Peter believes, now does it? Understand me, don't get me wrong. I like Fred, I do. I like Joseph. I even," he handed Michael one for the road, "could consider not hating you. But who I like most of all is Jewels.

"Aye," he shook his head, cuddling his bottle as he stood there, thinking about more than constellations. "I like Jewels. Fine lass. Mighty fine lass. Good, too, she is," he assured. "Talking about more than the services she provides. She's a bushranger—that's a bandit, Doc," he clarified. "Here in Africa that usually means poacher. Her father taught her everything she knows about her airplanes. Just playing firefighter out in the wilds of Kenya wasn't her interest, that's all," he shrugged, "can't fault her there.

"No, cannot," he shook his head. "No reason in the world to want to hurt or upset her, but then," he smiled, "she isn't doing anything a man doesn't do, and she's living in a man's world, so why not?

"Aye, why not?" he went back to hugging his bottle briefly in the moonlight thinking about things before he thought of something else. "Joseph?" he picked up his two-way.

"*Yeah?*" Joe answered on his end, sounding normal, too, except for his groan. "*What? I passed your final exam, too, didn't I? Yeah, I did. Not going to have to worry about mutiny or whatever the hell it is you're concerned the Doc might be able to talk me into.*"

"Aye, you passed," Pete assured with a wink at Michael ogling him with that mean look of his. "Remind me to talk to you about a fellow later," he said, Hank rejoining them with a frown. "Fellow by the name of Cain. Ian McShane Cain."

"Oh, yeah?" Joe said. *"Why? Something important?"*

"No," Pete said, "just remind me."

"Now, why do I know that name?" Michael asked as Pete lit a cigarette and Hank sat down to play his cards.

"Well, I don't know the answer to that, Doc," Pete assured, "haven't the faintest. McShane's IRA born and bred same as I. Neither of us has ever been to Brooklyn that I'm aware of."

"That's why I know that name," Michael said. "Go on, tell me. Tell me Chuck's plucked him out of some steel cage, and I am definitely thumbing my way out of here to have a chit-chat."

"Oh, well, now," Pete smiled. "Fellow's first got to be in a cage, doesn't he? And as allergic Pete is to steel bars, I've heard McShane's highly allergic."

"He's allergic to more than jail," Michael assured.

"Is he?" Pete said. "Well, I guess he is," he shrugged, "if you're talking about working off a sentence or two by doing a little work for the Crown. No, that's not McShane's game. But then he's not seen the light Peter has, doubt if he ever will."

"Oh, yeah?" Michael said. "And what light is this? The one where they flip the switch, or the one at the end of the rope?"

"No," Pete said, "It's the same one as I told Justin, if I don't like the idea of handing my Emerald girl over to some Brit, I sure ain't going to hand her to no German, now, am I? Fallacy, Doc, the idea of neutrals, is. Ain't no one neutral—except for maybe the Swiss," he shrugged. "But considering it takes twenty minutes to open one of those damn knives of theirs, that about explains why. But as far as anyone else? It's a fool's notion, because if you think Hitler's going to stop at that border of Erin and Blighty and not want to step over it, I've got a bridge I want to sell you."

"And after it's over?"

"Now, that is a different arrangement," Pete nodded. "Yes, it is. Justin and I are going to have to take a look at our contract should the two of us come out of this alive, that we are, and that we might. We just might." He thought about that, returning to the present with a smile for Michael, and a spray of smoke from between his teeth. "You know war is a game of poker, Doc," he said. "Took my innocence, Justin did, when he told me that, but he's right. Something less than a fool's ass thinks war's chess. To the contrary, it's all in the luck of the draw. After which," he downed the rum, "the only strategy you have is how good you gamble, how willing you are to bet your shirt if need be, and how well you bluff."

"Justin," Michael said.

"Justin," Pete assured. "Man's an addict, a veritable addict—talking about gambling, Doc, not drink or drugs like you and me," he clarified. "He's a gambler, sinister one, at that. Sure you must know that what with being such good friends and all. Bet the lot of us fifty quid apiece none of us make it out of here alive himself included, and personally, I'm on a mission to prove him wrong, same as he's on one to prove it's possible. Not saying we don't like each other," he shrugged. "Not saying we do. Got nothing to do with it, either way. Honor among thieves, that's all, honor among thieves. You've heard of that, right, Doc?" he asked. "Or did you really think one of us would sell another of us out just to give you some damn ride home?"

"Oh, yeah," Michael said, "goes something like, *'once upon a time'*. He fried his father, for Christ's sake. Chuck's! Give me a fucking break 'honor among thieves'. You're a fucking coward, that's what you are, you're yellow!"

"Who did?" Pete smiled easily. "McShane? Well, I guess you read the papers, Doc, and congratulations to you, too, considering half the world's population can't even read at all, our man Nellie among them. True," he nodded, "it's true. Though even still, even Nellie, I believe will tell you, honest fellow that he is, and being able to read it for himself or not, don't think the papers said anything about McShane being convicted of killing Justin's daddy, though I understand he was accused."

"Accused?" Michael said. "*Accused*?"

"On the other hand," Pete nodded, "I guess whether McShane did the duty himself or not, or just stood accused, who he couldn't have killed was that little baby sister of Justin's since we're running around, chasing after the ones who have killed her now ...

"Or we will be, Doc," he promised, "we will be. You might get that wish of yours after all, ever think of that? Might get that wish of yours of 'doing something about this' without having to lift your little finger to go find it, as it's apt to come to you all on its own. And then we'll see, won't we? Just which one of us is yellow like you say."

"If you're talking about Jean Paul," Hank put in, "be interesting to see if that prediction of someone coming turns out to be right. Charlie's got a stick up his arse about Jean Paul for some reason or another, and he won't be satisfied until he pulls it out. Hang Jean Paul for this, hang him for that, we wouldn't be out here unless Charlie thought there might be a reason to hang him, you're right about that."

"Now, see, Doc," Pete pointed. "There you go. Jean Paul Dumont as far as anybody knows, is Justin's right hand man, and so it's what I've been saying. My boy Justin's a sinister bastard. Could be why I like him, could be at that, could be why he likes me. Not saying either of us do, not saying either of us don't. It's up to those who believe, and those who don't."

"You do," Hank assured.

Pete laughed. "That's something else war does, Doc," he advised, "makes for strange bedfellows. Though you know that already as well, don't you? Sure you do. What with the two of you being such good friends and all, because there is nothing stranger than the two of you being friends—damn. You and Justin? Lord." Pete sat down to lie down on his blanket and close his eyes.

"Does this mean I don't get ride home?" Michael confirmed.

"It means you get to live, Doc," Pete assured, "to where an hour ago Peter was going to kill you but settled for his rum instead so he'd be sure not to care if you lived or died. No, you don't get your goddamn airplane ride. Stupider than I think you are to believe that bullshit. But thanks for the information, and thanks for reminding me. Hank," he said, "Doc here's apparently a pilot. Thinks he can fly one of those airplanes out of here himself. How long it take you to put the distributor caps back on, should you have to take them off?"

"Twenty minutes?" Hank shrugged. "Give or take."

"That's too long," Pete said. "It doesn't take but a second or two to unlock a pair of cuffs, so be a good fellow, won't you, and chain the Doc up to his favorite tree over there for Peter so the rest of us can get some sleep—that all right with you, Doc?" he asked. "Wouldn't want to upset that killer Italian temper of yours while I lie here unsuspecting with my eyes closed only to have my head bashed in by some rock you got sitting close enough to you to grab—go ahead and try it, Doc. Do it. And then take off in one of those airplanes. Shit. You really are an arsehole, aren't you? Stupid, and a loud mouth coward to boot. Shit," he said again. "Jean Paul answer that broadcast of Justin's?" he asked Hank before he fell asleep. "Is that it?"

"Before we even got into Cairo with the jeeps," Hank said. "Waiting for us when we got in."

"That's too bad," Pete said. "I kinda liked him, I did. Aye, well, we'll see what Nel turns over and take it from there. The Doc might be heading back to Cairo faster than he thinks so we can get on with things here. That he might be."

Chapter Thirty-Three

The Fezzan
March 13

"Oh, my!" Joanna gasped as she stood on the long, narrow balcony outside her room overlooking the vast marble world sprinkled with twisted trees and chips of white sand glittering like ice in the sun.

"It is pretty, isn't it?" Pierre agreed proudly.

Pretty? Joanna touched the balcony rail warm with captured heat. "Well, I don't know," she said. "I ... don't know ..."

"Miraculous, oui," Pierre nodded. "Glorious. Though the hillside is not marble, this structure is, yes."

Hillside. Joanna stared out at the jagged white mountain so close and tall she could not see the top of it as it disappeared into the sunlight.

"A composition principally of limestone," the funny little priest was busy explaining, "not uncommon in the desert—"

"What's not uncommon?" Joanna asked, absently.

"The wall, Mademoiselle," he said.

Wall? Joanna looked at him. "Wall? What wall?"

"That one," he pointed to the mountain. "Her trees are olive, some of them a thousand years old. Cyprus, naturally. Date, fig—"

"I don't understand," Joanna interrupted. "Are we in a valley, some sort of valley?"

"Valley?" Pierre smiled. "What valley is this?"

Well, Joanna hardly knew what valley. How could she? She looked around at what wasn't at all familiar, but seemed as if it should be, and in an odd way, it almost was.

"I ..." she said.

"Do you mean like Egypt, Mademoiselle?" Pierre asked. "Egypt and her Valley of Kings? Have you been to Egypt, Mademoiselle?"

Yes, Joanna had been to Egypt. She was in Egypt ... wasn't she? She frowned because where she had been in Egypt it certainly did not look anything like this.

"Perhaps you are thinking about Rome?" Pierre pursued. "Has Mademoiselle never been to Rome to see her coliseum? Or Greece, her amphitheater?"

"Rome?" Joanna stared out over the balcony, uncomfortable with the mountain so close particularly now that the priest had mentioned it was a wall, and what an unpleasant thought that was. Surely, it couldn't really be a wall, could it? Any more than she could be in Rome, could she? Surely, he wasn't trying to tell her she had been spirited away from Egypt all the way to Rome, was he? "I'm in Rome?" she gaped at him.

"No, Mademoiselle," Pierre chuckled. "A comparison only, an example. This is a valley of the gods, oui. Jupiter. Venus, Apollo, and, of course," he smiled, "Diana. Goddess of the moon, the hunt, children," he nodded. "The Egyptian artifacts are restricted to the house, and are decorations only like mon capitaine and his Germans."

That all sounded too terribly involved to Joanna. "Why are you calling it a wall?" she asked.

"The hill?" Pierre said. "Because that is what it is? That is what it is like?" he shrugged. "All around us like a wall."

"All around ..." Joanna repeated. She leaned over as far as she could to see to the side but she couldn't see much that looked any different to her.

"Oui," Pierre continued talking. "Protecting her magnificent display of Roman splendor and opulence." He laughed. "That is what this is, Mademoiselle, yes," he assured, his hand sweeping out. "A gateway, a temple, a meeting house, a city. Mon capitaine is unsure, but then he is an architect, not an archeologist. And really what does it matter anyway, eh? It does not. Come ..." he drew her away from the balcony rail back into the cooler sunshine of her room. "Come explore Pierre's castle. Come see where you are inside, and perhaps tomorrow we will look outside. The Roman and his ruins are scattered from one end of this desert to the other. But this house is still unique, and it is the house I want you to see. It was resurrected by the Moors, renovated by a man from Istanbul ..."

"What?" Joanna said.

"Istanbul," Pierre smiled. "Constantinople to the Eastern Roman Kings. A seaport in Turkey. Rome was an Empire, Mademoiselle, not merely a city. You must know this. A very famous and wealthy shipping owner restored this home for his thousand wives. I do not know his name. If I did, I have forgotten it. It was so long ago, four-hundred years at least. So many guests Pierre had before then, so many guests since. He cannot remember all of them ..."

Joanna snatched her hand away and he laughed again, teasing her with that ugly little wink of his. "Mon capitaine does the same thing. That is interesting to me, curious for a race of man who believe in God to believe also in the supernatural. Tell me, what is frightening to you? That Pierre has been here forever, since the time of the Roman Kings. That he is telling the truth? Or that he is telling a lie?"

Joanna hardly cared either way. "You said I could see the house. I want to see the house. I don't care who built it."

"The Romans, oui," Pierre nodded, "and the Moors. A Moor is of a race similar to the Arab, Mademoiselle, if you do not know this. A pagan, if he has not found God, a Muslim, if he has. An ancient people. Descendants of the Arab and mysterious Berber who populated the whole of the coast of Afrika across the Straits of Gibraltar to Spain."

"The house," Joanna said firmly. "Show me the house."

"Of course," Pierre smiled.

They went out into the library where Joanna had met the Captain the day before, and thank heavens he was not there now, as Pierre had promised her he would not be. Pierre discouraged Joanna from exploring the library however, and that was fine with her. She was not interested in exploring anything, just wanting to see where she was. The library was huge, even larger than Joanna remembered. Overwhelming and intimidating in its size it looked like a church. The only thing she could think of as she stared up at the domed ceiling high above her head. Her room a box by comparison to this one, her ceiling was rather flat except in the chamber off the loo where the priest slept. Until he told her that and showed her his sleeping room, Joanna hadn't even thought of where he lived or slept. Why would she? She should have been upset to learn he was living so close to her, just around the corner in her room, but she wasn't, and like everything else she was feeling she wasn't quite sure why.

There was another room off the library, adjacent to hers. Half the size of the library and four times the size of hers, it, too, had a high domed ceiling, and those same French windows lining two walls, not only one wall as they did in her room. It was practically empty except for a large bureau, and equally large bed, a crucifix of wood and gold lying on top of a small night table.

"Oh," Joanna stopped short at the sight of the crucifix. "Is this your room?"

"Pierre's?" Pierre smiled. "No, as I explained to Mademoiselle, I am sleeping in the small room until Mademoiselle is completely well."

Joanna meant did he sleep there otherwise. Honestly, one of these days people were going to stop speaking to her as if she was stupid. She was not stupid. "Never mind," Joanna said. She picked up the crucifix that was very pretty and quite heavy, and unfortunately, not really the sort of thing she should consider using to bash in someone's head. She sighed.

"A reasonable question though to ask," Pierre agreed. "It is very simple like one could expect for a priest."

Yes. "It's big," Joanna said aloud.

"Yes," Pierre said. "Space is deceiving when it is empty, and mon capitaine likes space. He removed most of the furnishings from this room, as he did from the library. Antiques are ghosts of the past he claims. They haunt him, he cannot think."

Joanna was not listening. Bigger and brighter than her room, it was cooler with the cross breeze. She hesitated in approaching the windows though where she could see the balcony through them, but also the mountain wall that did appear to be surrounding them, at least on two sides. "May I go outside?"

"On the balcony? Do you want to?" Pierre asked.

Joanna was considering it. "Can we change rooms?"

"Pardon?" Pierre said.

"Can we change rooms?" Joanna asked. "You can have mine, and I'll take this one—you'll still be close," she assured when he did not answer her. "For God's sake, they're not that far apart. It's just ... well, it's more respectable," she said if he wanted to know the truth. She wasn't entirely comfortable with knowing he slept around the corner in the small room he called an alcove or something like that, even if she wasn't upset about it.

"Yes," Joanna decided. "Yes, I think I would like to have this room and you can have mine. We'll exchange."

Pierre smiled. "This room? No, you cannot have this room, Mademoiselle. It is mon capitaine's room, and he not only likes his space, he likes his privacy. The crucifix, oui," he indicated the cross she clutched in her hand, "that is Pierre's. I gave it to mon capitaine for the simple reason le Christ is a ghost of the past who should haunt him."

He was an absolute beast. "Beast!" Joanna threw the crucifix on the floor.

Pierre chuckled, evil in his laugh and twinkling eyes. "You said you wanted to see the house, Mademoiselle. This room is part of it ... and, yes, it was Pierre's room," he agreed. "It is simply on loan to mon capitaine, as yours is on loan to you—"

"I don't care!" Joanna hissed. "I hardly meant ... well, I certainly hardly meant ..." she took two wild, faltering steps forward, two wilder, faltering steps backwards, as she tried to collect her bearings and simply get out of there.

"I mean, I hardly knew!" Joanna crashed into what turn out to be a wardrobe trying to get through it, fight and find her way out, a row of Captains standing at attention, meeting her, greeting her, dressed in white, beige, green, black, and blue—"Pink?!" Joanna stared at the gaudy pink strip running down the leg of the dark green trousers. "Pink?!" she clutched them.

"Oui, pink, Mademoiselle," Pierre agreed. "Is there something about the color pink you do not like?"

What is he? An organ grinder? Joanna heard Michael crack in her head. She stared at Pierre.

"Pink is for Panzer, Mademoiselle," Pierre explained. "The color of the Panzer. Mon capitaine is a Panzer Commander—or he was," he snickered. "Mon capitaine is too much like Pierre to be anything but what he is. He does not listen any better than Pierre, and neither does he care to learn."

"I want to go," Joanna whispered.

"Oui, of course," Pierre gestured, "come. Leave that. Pierre will take care of it …" he pushed the clothes back inside, straightening them neatly. "Panzer is armor, Mademoiselle, tank. This black one?" he pointed at something, Joanna had no idea what. "That is Panzer. No buttons to hinder the man or his operation. Very practical, very attractive, and very …" he winked, "a very nice target to shoot at here in the desert, and therefore very stupid like all Germans are … as they are morbid, oui. That is the word. Morbid. A man whose favorite color is black is morbid. He is not flamboyant as mon capitaine thinks he is. He is not exotic, or dramatic … he is morbid."

"I want …" Joanna closed her eyes.

"Oui, you want to go," Pierre nodded. "We are going … you see? The door is right here …"

They were out of the room and back into the library. "Where do those lead?" Joanna stopped.

"Pardon?"

"Those!" Joanna stumbled forward, stumbling down the stairs.

"Mademoiselle!" Pierre caught her. "Be careful, you must! Remember, there are steps—"

"I'm fine!" Joanna slapped his fluttering and flapping hands away. "I want to know where those doors go … where they lead …"

She reached them, grasping their twin latches in her hands, and the latches were huge. Joanna stared up at the doors that had to be exactly the same massive height of those found in a church. She turned sarcastically on Pierre. "Where do they go? To his toilet?"

"Pardon?" Pierre said. "No, Mademoiselle, mon capitaine's toilet is in his chambers, as is yours … would you like to go to the toilet, Mademoiselle?" he asked solicitously.

No. Any water Joanna might have had in her was sucked right out of her the moment she realized she was in the Captain's room barely spitting distance from hers. Just sucked right out of her, leaving her bone dry and breathing harshly. "Where do they go?" Joanna rattled the latches. "Where?"

"The hall, Mademoiselle," Pierre said. "Oui, the corridor. Would you like to go out into the corridor?"

"They're locked!" Joanna said.

"Oui, but a simple solution."

Pierre produced a key, and the mezzanine Joanna stepped out onto was so much more enormous than the rooms, looking up, around, and even more so looking down.

"I! Oh, my ..." Joanna said as she stared at the towering columns, brilliant pink and fat, trimmed in green and gold.

"Oui, pink, Mademoiselle," Pierre nodded as Joanna dared to touch the polished stone. "I hope you do not mind. The Moors, too, they like pink, what can Pierre say?"

"Oh, my ..." Joanna said, breathed, as she dared to step and look over the rail, down onto the highly polished floor of pink glass ... too far to jump. *Fifty*? she tried to calculate. *Maybe fifty*?

"Oui, many meters, Mademoiselle," Pierre read her face and took her by the arm. "As from your balcony, you could not entertain any idea of jumping, only to your death."

Joanna could entertain any idea she liked. "It's sand," she assured, absorbed in the flamboyancy of the hall.

"Pardon? Sand, Mademoiselle?" Pierre said. "No, it is marble."

"Outside," Joanna assured.

"No, it is marble, Mademoiselle," Pierre nodded. "The sand is simply a dusting, a little here, a little there. But the grounds are marble, Mademoiselle," he promised. "Crushed marble, a deep bed of marble, trees, and, yes, limestone to support the villa. A structure such as this could never be built on sand."

"Oh," Joanna said and frowned, thinking about that.

"But it is all right," Pierre patted her hand. "We will think of another way."

Quite. Joanna eyed the twin staircases around the mezzanine on the other side, trying to count the number of steps and coming up with thirty-five before they reached a large landing where they merged into one about half-way down.

"This is the Roman atrium," Pierre was saying, his arm up and sweeping around again, "the entrance way to his temple or palace. This floor is the mezzanine with mademoiselle's chambers, mon capitaine's, and his library, and oui, several smaller vaults—you see all the little windows, Mademoiselle?" he called Joanna's attention to the row of tiny keyhole shaped windows lining the walls below the ceiling directly above her. "From the time of the Moor until this last century the atrium, the vaults, this entire section of the villa was never open as the Roman intended, instead a secure, private box.

"Oui, like a box, Mademoiselle," he nodded. "A giant box protruding on the outside ... you will see. Inside, the same. Walls, not pillars, all around you. Can you imagine? Only those tiny windows for light?"

"Well, no, actually," Joanna said honestly, "I can't."

"Neither can Pierre," Pierre assured. "I would think ugly, not beautiful like this."

"Where do those steps go?" Joanna pointed ... well, really in both directions. One set on the left and another on the right curve of the mezzanine there were narrow staircases leading up somewhere.

"Those?" Pierre said. "To the towers," he shrugged. "A series of smaller rooms used for storage that is all. Similar to any other house."

"Oh," Joanna said. "Well, can we go down?"

"Down?" Pierre smiled. "To the outside? Yes, we can do this. Perhaps tomorrow. Down to the outside ... or even better," he waggled his finger in delight, "instead of the front, down through the gardens so much prettier."

"Gardens?" Joanna said.

"Oui, gardens, Mademoiselle," he assured. "Fifteen different gardens and a magnificent arboretum. Not too many interesting plants or trees, but magnificent colors of stones and interesting places to sit ... Come, I will show you ..."

He led her away from the sweeping staircases where she wanted to go, along the mezzanine, passed the flight of steps leading up, through one of the high arched doorways. Joanna found herself on another balcony facing the hillside, overlooking a series of broken low walls that went on and on in through trees, and, yes, what did appear to Joanna to be more stone than sand. It was interesting she supposed, certainly bright and sparkling as everything else in the sunlight. She thought of something, realized, actually. She looked at Pierre. "What did you mean we'll have to think of something else?"

He smiled. "I do not know, Mademoiselle, could you explain?"

"When you were telling me how I couldn't jump down."

"Oh," Pierre said. "Well, yes, Mademoiselle, we can walk—you do not have to jump."

"Oh," Joanna said. "Oh, of course ... well," she said. "Can we go down? Why can't we go downstairs now?"

"Did Mademoiselle notice the lights?" he ignored her, guiding her back through the arched doorway to where they had started so she could see the lights. They were boring. Ugly. Half expecting crystal chandeliers from the tone of his voice, the lights were simply large and metal woven with fat short unlit candles, suspended from thick ropes tied in the walls and hanging like nets over the center of the hall.

"I really want to go downstairs," Joanna repeated.

Pierre sighed. "No, Mademoiselle, I do not think this is wise, not today."

"I know the stairs are large," Joanna assured, only half blind.

"They are larger than large," Pierre agreed, as everything in the place was bigger than big except for perhaps her and him. "And you are not blind under your bandage, Mademoiselle," he promised her. "I swear to you, a cut above your eye, not through it. But, today is the first day you have walked any distance at all ... and, oui," he approved, very pleased, "you have walked very well, a very good exercise. But now I think it is perhaps time to take a rest. The steps are not only very large, they are marble, and they are slippery as if wet, as if ice, as if glass."

"Well, I'm going down," Joanna took a step to prove she did intend to do it.

"Mademoiselle!" Pierre implored, but then stopped. "Oui, Mademoiselle," he agreed, rather than attempt to wrestle her to the floor, "if you insist."

"Thank you," Joanna said, because she did insist even though the funny thing about steps is if you haven't walked them in a while, they seem to grow as you step.

"But carefully, Mademoiselle," Pierre reminded. "Walk carefully. Remember they are large, flat, oui, but marble, smooth like glass. Take two steps if you have to before you step down."

Two steps before stepping down were too many, and one step not enough. Joanna was already tired in spite of her insistence before she started down the stairs. Dizzy when she looked down to watch where she was going when she hadn't been dizzy at all when simply looking straight ahead. The palms of her hands sweating and damp as the soles of her bare feet before she took her first knee-rattling step, she was determined though. She grasped the smooth banister she dimly noticed was wooden not stone, but smooth and polished just the same. Longer than long, she managed what seemed like a hundred steps before she paused to take a breath less than halfway to the landing less than halfway down the stairs.

"Mademoiselle?" Pierre clung to her arm on her blind side, worrying and nagging every step.

"I'm fine," Joanna breathed, "quite fine." And she was. Exhausted, but quite fine, and certainly not hard of hearing. "What was that?" her head snapped up as a distinctly loud *crash!* rattled the air.

"Pardon?" Pierre said.

"That noise," Joanna insisted. "That ... well, *bang* actually." It was definitely some sort of bang, something banging into something else, and therefore definitely not something she had done unless she had quite unknowingly fallen down. "Well?" she demanded, after quickly checking to ensure she hadn't fallen but was standing quite firmly in place.

"The front door," Pierre shrugged, too old and small himself to pick her up and carry her away.

"The front door?" Joanna repeated. "You mean the wind?" she clutched him.

"No, I mean the front door," Pierre shrugged, as was the sound Joanna heard now that of a booted foot hitting the first of the stone steps.

Reineke did perhaps shut the front door loudly causing it to *bang* rather than *click* in place. He was not paying attention to the door.

He was thinking, obviously thinking of other far more important things because his hat was in his hand, not on his head, and he loved wearing his hat on his head, if only because he loved taking it off.

His attack on the stairs was not unusual. If he had been meant to walk in mincing little steps, he would never have been given legs so long, the same as if his head was meant to watch his feet, he never would have been given a neck to hold it up and erect. And hold his head erect he did, quickly, snapping to attention when he realized the stairs were covered with elves watching him.

To have moved the wet strands of hair hanging in front of his eyes would have been to admit they were there, and so instead up in the air went his head, behind his back went his hands, and he walked up two more steps, slowly, to the landing, watching the elves watching him. It was a ridiculous little climax in the navel of the stairs. A bruised woman choking the banister, the Holy Man contorted in a grin beside her, too ridiculous for words, except for perhaps one.

"Fräulein," Reineke acknowledged Joanna unpleasantly, the one word a dare, daring her to strangle the banister, release it, go back up, or continue down. It dared her to do anything, perhaps even breathe.

Joanna Lee enjoyed breathing. In remembering that, she, too, remembered how she had a neck. Perhaps one not as long as his, perhaps not quite as sturdy, but certainly capable of holding her head up, which she did, promptly. She stepped to walk, not run, down the stairs, since running would have been far too chancy. She was confident however that with his hair hanging in his eyes blinding him, he would be unable to tell if she hobbled, skipped, or strolled.

"Captain," Joanna croaked in reply, sounding more like a frog than a queen but that was all right. He was the one who had told her she had been ill and so perhaps he would think she had a cold. She paused one more time, to hug the newel post as the first staircase ended to merge with its twin at the landing in the middle of the stairs. But it was the Captain, though, not her, who stepped aside to allow her room to stretch for the rail. She reached it without tumbling over on her face, and she mastered the rest of the stairs, all the way down to the floor. Using a banister did not make her sissy.

Anyone with half a brain used a banister. If they weren't necessary, there would be no such thing.

A soldier approached her through a fog, opening a door and she and Pierre were outside.

"Indeed," Reineke's gaze followed them until the door shut behind them. Turning back, he looked up to where Thiele would have stood annoyed, but the mezzanine was empty. Thiele was en route to the Kufra. Reineke ascended the stairs, disappearing down the mezzanine and into his office.

"So, you see, Mademoiselle," Pierre announced happily as they stood outside in the hot, stifling air, "if the winds should come to annoy us, it would be but a breeze with such a mountain to protect us."

She was in a prison. Sun did not shine on the porch of the mansion. Only weak streams of light tried desperately to sneak their way between the tight columns encircling the porch and stone steps like bars. Cold and ancient, the marble was lifeless without the sun to illuminate it, scarred with embedded ugly black lines. The little man had lied. It wasn't beautiful, but frightening in its desolate silence and overwhelming size. The huge white wall and mountain loomed all around them, high in the blazing cloudless sky.

"I want to go back," Joanna said.

"Back?" Pierre smiled. "Oui, in a little while. Come and sit, rest for a moment ..." he took her hand. "This is the mezzanine above us. The vault that is the library, mon capitaine's and Mademoiselle's quarters. These columns the legs that support it ..."

"I don't care," Joanna snatched her hand away. "I want to go back. There's nothing to see."

"Oui, of course," Pierre bowed his head.

She would not remember the stairs.

"By tomorrow the woman's hair is to be washed," Reineke stalked back and forth. "By tomorrow the woman is to have shoes. She had difficulty walking. I saw her. Fix her!"

"She will not allow it," Pierre explained. "Two days I have argued to change the bandage on her head."

"Do it!" Reineke insisted.

"Oui, do it," Pierre shrugged. "As far as the shoes ... perhaps Anne can find a pair for her to wear ..."

"Indeed ... and as far as this!" Reineke snatched up the heavy crucifix he found on the floor of his chambers. A crucifix that had never been there before, that he had never seen before in his life, but did not have to look far to know how it happened to be there now.

"You said I could show her the mezzanine, mon capitaine," Pierre reminded. "This is the mezzanine, part of it."

"Not my quarters!" Reineke assured. "Are you out of your mind?"

"No, I am not out of my mind," Pierre shook his head.

No! He was playing games—some stupid, idiotic game!

"It is not a game, mon capitaine. Mademoiselle is frightened ... She is extremely frightened," Pierre assured. "I am very concerned about this. I have been trying to explain to her, but she is not listening, and I thought if I could demonstrate for her that though I am there with her, and you are here, she is safe. No one is hurting her—"

"Get out!" Reineke ordered.

"Mon capitaine, if you think, you will understand what I am saying—" Pierre insisted.

"And take le Christ with you!" Reineke fired the crucifix through the French windows of his quarters, over the balcony and out into the desert night, daring the wrath of the heavens and hells to strike him dead for the blasphemous act, which, they would not do.

"So now you have two panes to fix," Pierre clucked with a shake of his head. "I swear to le Christ, mon capitaine, between the two of you, you and Mademoiselle have inflicted more damage than four centuries has managed to destroy."

"Get out!" Reineke pointed.

"I am going," Pierre assured.

"Good!"

Chapter Thirty-Four

March 14–15

Joanna sat on one of the low stone walls in one of the villa's large courtyard of gardens. What particular type of stone the walls were Pierre apparently did not know or he would have told her. He knew about the gardens though, and he was right when he said she would not see roses or lilacs or grass. Instead, desert flowers were of their own variety. All fairly awkward and dull as they struggled to survive entwined around the roots of olive trees embedded in their beds of stone sand absent of color except for the incessant milky pink and yellowish white marble brightening with the sun and fading with the shadows. Pierre disagreed, telling her desert flowers were not only beautiful, but could fly.

"Did you know flowers fly in the desert, Mademoiselle?" he tempted her. "Spread their wings and take flight?"

No, Joanna did not know and was not interested. The murky fog of confusion returned to surround her in the hot bright sun hurting her eye. Pierre held a funny umbrella over their heads, but it did not help much. She felt awkward sitting with him as if she was doing something wrong.

"They do," Pierre assured her how desert flowers fly. Beautiful colorful petals people call butterflies migrate in the desert, thousands of them, along with birds and eagles, hawks and hens.

"Would Mademoiselle like to see some of these?" Pierre invited with his smile, not that Joanna's answer was important. Pierre decided that tomorrow she would see his funny hens.

"Oui," Pierre decided that tomorrow they could go for a short walk in the gardens farther away than the ones they were sitting in today.

"More gardens?" Joanna yawned, much too sleepy to try to escape this morning as she had promised herself she would do as soon as she was outside. Tomorrow however would be perfect.

"Oui, more gardens, Mademoiselle," he promised. "Prettier than these."

"In what way?" Joanna looked around, thinking of Grandfather's gardens where, when she was young, it would take John, Grandfather's man, and Maria, the cook, hours to find her hiding among the hedges. There weren't any hedges here only the gnarled trees that would work well as a cover if there were more of them. "Do they have trees, like the trees over there?"

"There are thousands of trees here, Mademoiselle," he assured. "Palm, olive, fig."

On the wall, yes, Joanna could plainly see. A fat forest of thick green leaves. But the wall that had seemed so close from the balcony of her room was really a mountain and rather far away. The grounds around the house were flat and open. She needed the trees to get to the mountain with its palm trees where they would never find her.

"And very beautiful," he maintained. "This is an oasis, Mademoiselle. An island of land in a sea of sand. You are in North Africa, as has been explained. There is a lot of sand in North Africa. Not too many trees except in very special places like this," he beamed. Very proud of his stone world regardless of how boring she considered it.

"An oasis," Joanne repeated, having heard of an oasis, even before she came to Egypt, and actually finding them much larger than she thought they would be for some reason. She shrugged and absently ate one of the olives Pierre brought along as a treat. It was tart with a large pit. She gnawed on the meat, working the pit into the side of her cheek and sucking on it like a lozenge. "How long have we been out?"

"Oh, twenty minutes?" Pierre guessed. "Perhaps a little less."

"I want to go in," Joanna said. "It's too hot out here." Which it was and she wanted to think. She could not think out there in the heat.

"Oui, of course," Pierre agreed without an argument. "We will come outside again later today when it is cooler, and perhaps earlier tomorrow morning when it also cooler, so you can spend more time outside in the fresh air."

Joanna made it to thirty minutes when they came out after dinner before it was dark. Almost an hour the next morning, when they came out much earlier, and it was not so baking hot, though not as cool as early evening the night before. Joanna decided early evening would be the best time to escape, under the cover of the trees while it was still light enough to see and find them, and under the cover of darkness from there when it fell. In the meantime, it was morning, and she got to see the hens, which were cute for hens, brown and fat like the priest and almost as talkative as he was, scolding, clucking, and pecking at her in their funny way.

"How big is the island?" Joanna popped another olive in her mouth as they sat on the low stone walls of the garden where the hens lived, walking in and out of their homes situated inside the little odd cut-outs lining the base of the walls. "I see trees over there, is that where the other gardens are?"

"Oasis," Pierre smiled. "Like an island, oui, yes, as I explained. But the sea surrounding us is sand, not water."

Joanna tried to imagine that, but couldn't. She did not remember Siwa, not its name or that she had been there at all. If she had, she would know the Siwa Oasis was very large, occupied by a town and an entire community. Cairo she remembered, but it was a city with city buildings, exotic and congested with traffic and people. "Well?" she said. "How big is it?"

"Oh, very big," Pierre said, "with many more gardens and trees, this is correct. If you could travel to the other side you would see how large."

"The other side?" Joanna picked up on that. "The other side of what? The wall?"

"Oasis," Pierre smiled. "The other side of the oasis where mon capitaine believes an entire city once stood."

"A city ..." That changed things. Presented possibilities Joanna had not considered—at least not here. She had certainly considered them once she got out of there to where there were people and things one would find in a city, yes, such as a telephone. "Can we go there?"

"To the gardens where there are more trees?" Pierre smiled. "Oui, yes, perhaps even tomorrow. You see how much stronger you are today? Every day much stronger than you were the day before."

"To the city," Joanna said. "To see the city?"

"Pardon?" Pierre said.

"The city," Joanna swallowed the olive pit she had in her mouth.

"Oh, Mademoiselle," Pierre protested.

"What?" Joanna said. "You said there was a city. I want to see it."

"The pit, Mademoiselle," Pierre insisted, annoyed and, of all things, helped himself. Started snatching up the fresh olives he had collected, and the ones from the house he had given her and she had piled up on her lap. "You know you are not supposed to eat the olive pit. Really, Mademoiselle," he shook his head, "I do not understand this. I do not understand you ..."

Oh, well, excuse her. The next time Joanna would be sure to spit the pit out on the ground. For that matter as of right now throw all of the olives on the ground since he was so clearly effected by them he was snatching and grabbing at her with those hands of his that he should really learn to keep to himself.

"We were talking about the city!" Joanna slapped his hands away proceeding, yes, to clear her lap of the whole lot of olives, sweeping them off and onto the ground.

"What city?" Pierre scoffed as he gathered the extent of the olive collection he had managed to save into the little cloth napkin he wore over his lap, pulling it closed and tying it up in a protective knot. "There is no city."

"Oh, really," Joanna said. "Well, you said there was. So what happened to it? Where did it go?" she insisted. "In the last five minutes, where did it go?"

"Nowhere," Pierre assured. "That is not what Pierre said—"

"Yes it is!"

"No, it is not!" Pierre snapped, slapping the little bundle of olives back down on his lap with his frustration. "That is what Mademoiselle heard, that is what she thinks. It is not what Pierre said. Pierre said there once was a city—*once*, Mademoiselle. Possibly once, yes, and possibly once, no—and Pierre does not want to talk about it either way," he assured as Joanna stared at him. "No, Pierre wants to talk about this, Mademoiselle," he waved the olives threateningly, "this!"

"Excuse me?" Joanna said.

"There is no excuse," Pierre corrected, "No there is not. What do you want to go to the city for, eh, Mademoiselle? So you can spit olives, swallow them or throw them on the ground?" he waved the little sack.

"Please stop doing that," Joanna requested.

"Is that what little girls do when they go to the city, eh?" Pierre insisted. "No, that is why little girls do not go to the city until they know how to behave!"

"I said, please stop doing that!" Joanna snatched the waving sack out of his hand and threw it on the ground, and the two of them sat there, her looking off in one direction, having no idea where he was looking or what he was looking at if anything. Tears clouded Joanna's eyes, both of them, the one under the bandage, and the one that wasn't.

"Mademoiselle ..." Pierre said gently when Joanna looked down on her lap, picking at her hands, the cuticles still very dry and split.

"I want to go back to the house," Joanna replied.

"Oui, this is fine," Pierre nodded, "but I think it is time you and Pierre had a talk."

"I said, I want to go back to the house," Joanna repeated. "If you don't take me I'll go there myself. I remember the way—it's right over there," she pointed only half blind. "I can see it."

"Oui," Pierre agreed.

"Well, then?" Joanna said.

"Of course." Pierre rose and smiled however forced the air might be between them as they walked. "We will come out again in the evening after dinner, before dark, as we did last evening."

"Perhaps," Joanna said.

"No perhaps," Pierre said. "Definitely, Mademoiselle. This is the exercise regimen, at least for the next few days. After that—"

"Or what?" Joanna stopped. "You'll start throwing olives again?"

"It is not Pierre who threw the olives," Pierre shook his head.

That was beside the point. "I think you're right," Joanna agreed. "I think it is time we had a talk."

"About the city?" Pierre smiled. "Or that there is no city? Which there is not."

"Fine," Joanna said. "So there is no city." She did not want to see his stupid city, anyway. It was just an idea, and since it was a bad one, she would think of another one, confident it would be much better.

"Of course it is not fine," Pierre understood more than she might think he did. "But we will talk about that too, when we talk."

"I think you're the one who's not listening now," Joanna said. "I'm the one who wants to talk to you."

Yes, Pierre knew that and he suspected it would be something about her right to do what she wanted to do, her right to decide what she wanted to do as she got stronger every day. Mentally and emotionally though her strength festered in stubbornness frustrated and stagnated by fear.

It did not matter. In another moment, none of that would matter, as they were not the only two people who cared about what they wanted, regardless of what others may want.

"Mon capitaine!" Pierre suddenly gasped and before Joanna could even finish turning around to see why he was gasping, she was drenched in water pouring down over her head drowning any sound she might make. Pierre jumped as she jumped, he almost as wet as she by the splashing water.

"God!" Joanna gasped, water streaming down her face, in her eyes, her nose, mouth, gagging her. She was soaked. Her shirt, pants, an entire bucket of cold water dumped over her head, saturating her, Pierre, and the ground around them.

"Fräulein." The Captain was in front of her, holding the emptied bucket. An Arab standing next to him took it away to hand him something in exchange. He took it and grasped her wrist, forcing her hand open, slapping the object down. It was a bar of soap.

"So far my men, Fräulein," he said, cold as the water, "have been fortunate to escape the plague lice. I suggest you do the same."

And he was gone.

"Bastard!" Joanna screamed after him. "You rotten bastard!"

Back in her room, Joanna would never stop crying, destroying everything in sight until she made herself sick enough to vomit, and when she finished choking with dry heaves she washed her hair, and it felt good, marvelous.

"Is there anything else Mademoiselle would like to do?" Pierre asked as Joanna sulked at the French windows, waiting for her hair to dry in the sun.

She did not answer him. He toddled around for a while longer, rearranging things before he sat back down asking again and that time, yes, she answered.

"What do I look like?" Joanna asked.

"Hm ..." Pierre surveyed her. "Pretty bad. But it will get better. Pierre is not concerned. Do you want to see?"

Hardly. What she looked like with bandages on was bad enough. Joanna wasn't ready to see what she looked like underneath them.

"Well, this is all right, too," Pierre agreed. "You do not have to see now. You can see at any time. Tomorrow, the day after. Each time, like you it will be better ... In the meantime, I have a new hat for you," he held up her new plaster bonnet since the other one had been ruined by the water.

"It looks different," Joanna said.

"It is different. Not quite so big. It is this week's fashion." Pierre smiled. "Each week a new fashion, how is that?"

Well, it wasn't funny. "That's not funny," Joanna said.

"No, it is not funny," Pierre agreed. "But it is true. I think we can even make a little less bandages around the eye and the chin. How is your sight? Can you see?"

"It hurts," Joanna assured.

"Because you are in the sun," Pierre said. "Trying to see in the sun with an eye that has not seen anything in a week. Come out of the sun so it will not hurt ... and so," he cautioned, "you do not hurt it."

"I'm drying my hair."

"It will dry over here, out of the direct light," Pierre assured. "There is sun over here as there is sun everywhere."

There was more sun at the windows. "No," Joanna said.

"Yes," Pierre said. "Come away now and sit over here and in one hour, less, your hair will be dry. When it is, we will put your new hat

on and see how many bandages we have to add to protect your eye—
and to keep your hat on," he winked. "We cannot have it falling off,
not even in the bed. You need it to protect your head."

Joanna had stopped listening at the hour it would take her hair
to dry. Her hair took four hours to dry. Sun, rain, snow, it took four
hours.

"Mademoiselle ..." Pierre said.

"Fine," Joanna got up and went over to sit in the chair by the
bed. "My hair takes four hours to dry. The only reason it will take an
hour is because you cut it off."

"Less than an hour, Mademoiselle," Pierre assured. "Nothing
takes four hours to dry in this desert, not even a lake if we had one;
which we do not," he winked. "It left with the city."

That was also not funny. "I don't care about your stupid city,"
Joanna reminded.

"No," Pierre agreed. "And Pierre did not cut off Mademoiselle's
hair, only what he needed."

Well, he needed a lot of it. Joanna could not believe how much
of her hair was missing when she washed it. Almost the entire right
side of her head was shaved bald, down to these bristly nubs like
Michael's beard in the morning.

"Is that what you wanted to talk to Pierre about?" Pierre asked.

Hardly. "Save it for Michael," Joanna assured, because believe
her, Michael was going to ask.

"Michael ..." Pierre said. "Yes ... Mademoiselle said something
about a Michael, I believe, once before."

Joanna scoffed. "Try a hundred times."

"A hundred times," Pierre said. "Really. Well, perhaps then it is
true Pierre has not been listening because I remember Mademoiselle
saying something about a Michael only once."

Joanna tossed her drying hair. "That's not the point."

Pierre smiled. "No. No, of course it is not. But it is perhaps
Michael Mademoiselle wishes to speak to Pierre about? Do I have
this right?"

And how. Joanna turned around and sat up straight in her chair
to face him squarely. "You think I want to escape. You think I want
to go to your city because I'm planning to escape."

"Oui," Pierre agreed. "We have talked about this," he chuckled. "That is something Mademoiselle has said to Pierre a hundred times even if she has not said it out loud each time. It is always on your face," he nodded, "in your eye. I can see it very clearly."

"Well, you see," Joanna said, "that's where you're wrong. I only told you that … well, to throw you off the track," she claimed.

"Really," Pierre said. "That is interesting because Mademoiselle had Pierre completely convinced. That is very true."

"Well, that's more to the point," Joanna said, "because I don't have to escape. Michael will be coming here."

"Really …" Pierre said.

"Yes," Joanna stopped short of saying to rescue her because she did not like to think she might have to be rescued, that was too frightening to think about. But for Michael to come there and take her home, yes. That was quite comforting to think. Even if he had to come and take her out of the sand when she climbed over the mountain since apparently there was no city for him to come to, it was still a very comforting thought. "So you can stop saying 'really' because it's true."

Pierre nodded, leaving it up to Joanna to speak again if she wanted to speak. She did.

"What did you want to talk to me about? The olives?" she sneered, finding it silly.

"Oui, Mademoiselle," Pierre said.

That figured. "You know the only reason I threw the olives away is because you … you were winging them around," she waved in demonstration. "I asked you to stop and you didn't and so I threw them away."

"Pierre was excited," Pierre explained.

"Well, what's that to do with me?" Joanna said.

"Everything, Mademoiselle," he assured. "Everything." He got up and waddled over to sit down on the bed. Joanna flinched when he got up and wasn't exactly comfortable when he sat down on the bed to study her. "Mademoiselle … " he said.

"I really do not think you should be sitting on the bed," Joanna interrupted. "I'm not sure it's proper. I mean, I realize you're old, and a priest, but I still do not think it's proper."

He ignored her. "Mademoiselle," he said, "I would like you to focus on something for me, if you can. I would like you to forget about me, this room, this space, everything. Clear your mind, and think about you, only you. While you are thinking, I want you to remember how you are a young woman, not a little girl, and to leave the frightened little girl behind you regardless of what has happened to her, what may have happened to her, and what she is so afraid will happen to her—it does not matter. I want you to think about you, only about you--just for today," he smiled. "This afternoon, a few hours. Would you like to try that? We can talk about it afterwards, if you like. What you did not like and what you did like about our little experiment. Does this sound interesting to you? A challenge you might like? One that you create, meet, and win? What do you think about what Pierre is asking you?"

What did she think?

"Mademoiselle?" Pierre encouraged. "It is really not difficult for you to answer that simple question, is it?"

That was her business. "Michael will be coming here," Joanna repeated. "That is true."

Pierre nodded. "And this Michael—" he said.

"He's not *this* Michael," Joanna interrupted. "He's Michael. Just Michael."

Pierre nodded again. "Is your friend Michael in the army?" he asked.

Oh, well, now, Joanna might be stupid in a lot of ways as she understood she was, but she wasn't quite as stupid as all of that. Her chin jutted forward, unintentionally, unknowingly, but it jutted forward and was noticeable to Pierre when it did. "You'd like to know that wouldn't you?" she said.

"Oui," Pierre agreed. "I would. Mademoiselle has mentioned Michael, as she said, and Pierre is curious, yes naturally if your friend Michael is in the army ..." he hesitated, but only briefly and not so Joanna noticed at all. "An American, Pierre understands—if Pierre understood Mademoiselle correctly."

"You certainly did," Joanna assured.

Pierre nodded but refrained from saying anything, wondering only if she knew her friend Michael was dead, killed in the courtyard.

If she had perhaps witnessed the brutality of his death, or if she knew nothing about it at all … other than he was with her. Pierre studied her, curious because if she did not know or remember his death, she should be asking where he was.

She would be asking where he was, but she wasn't. This Michael was not the man who died in the courtyard, his body burned and ashes scattered, that was someone else. So who was Michael? The other blood? The third person? The same rule would apply. She should be asking where he was and she wasn't. She was telling how he would be there.

"As far as in the army," Joanna tossed her drying head, "That's for me to know and for you to find out."

"A reasonable response, Mademoiselle," Pierre smiled, "though most would probably not speak it aloud. It's all right though," he assured, "it is however fair for Pierre to presume Michael will not like Pierre when he comes?"

"He will positively loathe you," Joanna promised.

"I am sorry to hear that," Pierre said. "I would have hoped that when your friend came and Pierre explained why he cut your hair, he would understand."

"I don't think so," Joanna said.

"And I would have hoped," Pierre said, "when your friend saw how you have been cared for and not hurt, he would say thank you and understand how Pierre was not your enemy."

"I do not think so," Joanna said a little stronger that time.

Pierre smiled. "No, of course not," he agreed. "Pierre is a collaborator. That is not too difficult to see … do you know what a collaborator is, Mademoiselle?" he asked when her resolve faded away to her blank uncertain expression.

"Well, yes," Joanna said, "sort of—I know it's not very nice," she assured. "It's not a good thing to be."

"And most would agree with that, Mademoiselle," Pierre agreed, "regardless of the nature of the collaboration. But, you see," he said, "Pierre disagrees with them. Pierre says the purpose of the collaboration is not irrelevant, it is everything. The reason, the goal— everything. I am a survivor, Mademoiselle. Oui," he assured, "I am a survivor exactly like you, and it is exactly what you are going to be.

"Now," he said, "you will listen to me, and you will be the young woman you are when your friend Michael comes to take you home, or if it is you who goes to him. You will be the young woman you are, not the frightened little girl who swallows olive pits and throws dishes because she is too afraid to do anything else."

"I really do not like you," Joanna said.

He smiled. "Oui, I know. But you will," he promised, and *whisk*! he was gone, just like that. Up, off the bed, and gone, leaving her there without a word.

Chapter Thirty-Five

Reineke laughed. He walked away from the woman into his villa and laughed a deep, honest laugh. The sight of her confused and outraged, soaked like some drenched cat, was sufficient to do away with all the nerves she had caused him these past days. Gone was the thorn in his side, the corn on his toe. He had no more reason to be frightened of her, than he was frightened of Diana …

And he was frightened of Diana. "Indeed." Reineke stopped laughing. The woman was death disguised as a child, hanging there, waiting for him to surrender to her Allies out there somewhere. The only way he could hope to emerge from this was to send her away, except she was not his to send, and send her where? Heeding the cry of the Holy Man for leniency would be a gamble with his life. He knew what this woman was, and she was not just some Allied prisoner brought to his complex for reasons and purpose unknown. She was someone, some plan. There would be nothing at the Kufra except sand, plenty of sand. Le capitaine Reineke's holiday was over. He had only three days.

"Indeed," Reineke picked up his Colonel's terse reply to the notice Reineke had decided to delay the scheduled shipment between camps. It asked pointedly how long Reineke planned to remain on radio silence.

It suggested Reineke rethink his decision to delay all of the shipments. It informed him there would soon be a tête-à-tête that regardless of how informal would require his attendance nevertheless. A certain SS Major was understandably ruffled over his mistreatment during his visit to Reineke's compound. Herr Oberst Alfred Schönfeld, Reineke's Commanding Officer, wasn't necessarily interested in SS Major Hanse Weiheber, his complaints or his demand for Reineke's arrest. Their tête-à-tête already concluded had left Weiheber additionally ruffled. But then Hauptmann Reineke's characteristics of a proud, independent peacock were not characteristics belonging to him alone. Oberst Schönfeld did not care about Reineke shooting out ceilings above the heads of SS officers. He did not care about the SS at all. He did care very much, however as to the reasons why Reineke, an intelligent, and talented officer, found it a continuing need to indulge himself in such antics. Oberst Schönfeld did not reprimand, this project had no such clause, and Reineke was not the proudest, most independent, or even the most original officer with orders for men to be shot who failed to live up to expectations, he was simply the most unruly.

Fortunately, however, Oberst Schönfeld liked Hauptmann Reineke, which was why he was urging Reineke they meet at the very same desert village recently visited by SS Major Weiheber, and Reineke had three days to comply with the request.

"Request!" Reineke dropped the communiqué on his desk. He had three days to think of an alibi, compose a defense. A point sure to be discussed was Reineke's intentions with the SS prisoner, though that would only be a formality. Schönfeld, familiar as he was with his handpicked squad, was capable of understanding, if not predicting Reineke's reaction to the SS bringing some Allied prisoners to his highly sensitive compound. Reineke taking the surviving prisoner away from the SS was undoubtedly in spite, a form of punishment for the SS indiscretion. Taking the knife away from the SS that they hoped to plunge into the project by appropriating his complex, and plunging it instead into them, leaving them to explain the loss of the prisoners to their superiors regardless of what Reineke might have to explain to his.

Reineke eyed the message. If Weiheber had attempted to fuel concerns over Reineke's stability, or worse, his loyalty, with stories of the Holy Man and his children, he would have come away severely disappointed. Schönfeld already knew of them. Earlier inquiries into the issue had been quelled with a stare and short, clipped, reminder it was Schönfeld's idea to avoid notoriety for as long as possible, and what better way to ensure this than to keep oneself disguised as a native watering hole?

"Indeed," Reineke might decide to employ that excuse again.

Incorporate this new situation into his already existing rationale, reminding Schönfeld it was the SS who insisted there was an Allied troop somewhere in the immediate area.

"You hang yourself, Herr Major," Reineke suggested. "Not I." Schönfeld was not about to question one of his top officer's decision to tread slowly under the circumstances Weiheber presented.

In the event Weiheber decided to retract his claim of Allied presence? "Indeed," Reineke moved around his library, pensive. Perhaps he would simply remind Schönfeld of his passion for security regardless. Schönfeld would probably not care if Reineke decided elephants would prove useful as a façade, as long as the munitions were where they were supposed to be. They would be. Any way possible Reineke would ensure the hijacking of the munitions from the Italians remained on schedule, whether or not delivery was delayed by a few days if he had to shoot them all.

And he just might shoot them all, beginning with the woman screaming on about her wet head. "Indeed!" Reineke abandoned the library, escaping to his quarters, but stretching out on his bed and massaging his temples made no difference.

Another door between them made no difference. He sat up. He should just get up, go back through the library, into the apartment, and shoot her. He could explain her death to the children that she had died of her illness. Diana would probably not care if she died since she already wanted her and anyone else dead even remotely linked to rousing the SS. Who would care was the Holy Man, and in retaliation, Pierre just might shoot him.

But not if Reineke shot Pierre first.

Yet, if he shot Pierre, Diana would shoot him.

And if Reineke shot Diana, Anne would definitely shoot him— or shoot at him, which, if she did, Thiele would shoot Anne, and then Reineke would have to shoot Thiele.

"Indeed!" Reineke jumped off his bed. It would be distinctly risky trying to get away with killing *two* First Officers so close together. He barely got away with the first.

"Indeed," Reineke smiled in the mirror. "'Watch my Hauptmann Reineke, for he is all that he appears to be and more.'" And so they did watch. Only Pierre liked what he saw.

Diana watched, only she liked what she saw.

Thiele, the same, and so Schönfeld lost whatever control he hoped to gain by assigning his personal aide Heinrich Thiele as Reineke's new First Officer because even if Thiele knew it all, which he did not, he would not believe it.

"Indeed," Reineke smiled in the mirror. "You cannot trust your Hauptmann Reineke, you should not. He can change, if he has to."

He could change into whatever he had to, if he had to.

"Indeed," Reineke stared through the walls of his chambers out to the message lying on his desk. Odd thing was Schönfeld knew Reineke shot and killed his First Officer and why. Odd thing was Reineke knew Schönfeld knew.

Odder yet, Reineke knew when he met them, Schönfeld, Thiele, Pierre, Diana, or Anne, like each other or not, one or the other, would someday have to shoot the other. Odd thing was Reineke knew which of them it would be who shot first.

"*Return the woman!*" Diana bore down on him from her Temple, harsh and uncompassionate as her cold, marble stone. "*Return the woman, Dieter, to the SS and let it go, do not be a fool. I will take care of the SS, not you. The Holy Man will find you dead at the foot of my statue if you defy me, a bullet through your skull. The children are dying by the thousands. You cannot exchange one life for the seventy-five under your care. Return the SS prisoner, or I will kill you. Your complex, little more than a memory buried in the sand.*"

"Indeed," Reineke picked up the message from his desk. He had only three days and not an idea in his head, or so he thought.

No, Joanna wasn't angry with the little priest for leaving her without a word to go off like that and then as suddenly show back up. She was frightened. What did he mean by a ride? A ride where? Joanna did not want to take a ride. Could see no good reason why she should agree to take a ride anywhere, especially when it was a soldier playing driver and the car was a wagen.

But Pierre was emphatic, the young soldier nodding, "*Ja! Ja!*" to Pierre carrying on in some queer, foreign speech.

"Get in, Mademoiselle," Pierre instructed her, the soldier nodding, "*Ja! Ja!*" as Joanna obeyed.

Reineke left his quarters paying no particular attention where his walk brought him. He was back again in his chambers around three o'clock, still thinking. What else was there for him to do? His most recent thoughts suggested he should interrogate the woman more fully. Demand to know everything there was to know about her so he could orchestrate an appropriate response instead of attempting to guess what significance she was to the SS who involved and endangered him with their invasion of his compound. The Holy Man would be upset, but the Holy Man was a fool if he thought le capitaine did not want to know everything, because he did.

"Indeed," Reineke rapped swiftly on the apartment door.

No one answered, so he knocked again, and no one answered.

Catch them outside? With luck in the gardens? Far away from the ears and eyes of his staff? It was better still. He could put the woman up against the wall, his hand fastened around her throat, demanding to know why he had been chosen for sacrifice.

No one moved in the gardens nearest the mansion. Reineke walked quickly to cover another garden, but it was taking too long and thoughts were beginning to grow ...

"Where is the Holy Man?" he demanded, the soldier he attacked getting as far as, "The children!" and Reineke started to run.

"Dieter!" Anne was sitting in her favorite spot on the edge of one of the wells.

"Dieter!" she jumped up, dashing to meet him as she usually did, her long black hair flying behind her.

"Where is he?" Reineke insisted, Anne's flushed face paling to confusion, her arm he twisted, hurting her.

"Dieter!" she said. "Dieter, you're hurting me!"

"Where is he?" Reineke hissed. "Where are the Holy Man and the woman?"

"At the house!" Anne's snapped, meaning the Holy Man's hut, her black eyes narrowed and voice angry and emphatic. "Dieter, let go of my arm or it's not that woman Thiele will find dead!"

"Go and get him," Reineke released her. "Do it! Go and get him—MOVE!" he barked when she stood there. "Idiot!" Was Anne turning idiot on him, also?

Apparently, for she was taking far too long, and Reineke was running again, chubby legs, all different sizes, and ages believing it a game, following along, imitating the wild stride of his boots.

He was almost to the Holy Man's house, near another well. The trees parted, he could see more children gathered in a group outside—

The sun's reflection caught the armor of the idle wagen and the soldier playing with Aliza, the two year old, seated on the ground, helmet on her head.

"Hauptmann!" the soldier jumped to attention, failing in his attempt to snatch his helmet from the child before he could be found out.

"Indeed. Where is the woman?" Reineke replied.

Not more than twenty meters away. Reineke took the helmet from Aliza for protection, but the woman was too busy braiding the hair of one of the girls to notice him. A select army of the Holy Man's elves crowding around her, listening to her highly animated and inaccurate recital of some fairy tale.

A very select army of elves. The Holy Man was not a fool. Not one child spoke, or understood the prisoner's English.

"Mon capitaine!" Pierre greeted him happily, poised to present some elaborate lie, but it was unnecessary. Somewhere in the twisted story the woman was telling, Reineke stopped thinking of interrogation and returned to not caring why the SS had brought her there. She was hardly death, hardly dangerous, to him, or anyone else. She was simply a very small, very young woman, with a big, bright white bandage wrapped tightly around her damaged head.

"Mon capitaine?" Pierre frowned.

"Diana," was all Reineke said, and walked away.

One hundred times of reassuring Joanna of her safety and his as he rushed her back to the wagen, was not enough, but Pierre gave up, abandoning Joanna to her fear.

One hundred times of reassuring himself all would be well as he hiked to meet Reineke was also possibly not enough.

Reineke confessed to Diana in her Temple how he had lost his mind.

He avoided Pierre until long past dark, hoping the little man would give up and go away. But if the Holy Man had nothing he had patience, and a temper.

Chapter Thirty-Six

"So!" Pierre exploded. "It is a trick! I should have known mon capitaine keeps Pierre waiting for such a long time for no reason except to punish him for taking Mademoiselle to the children. You think Pierre is stupid? He is not! It is mon capitaine who is stupid."

"I do not think you are stupid," Reineke dodged the rock Pierre threw. "Put those down!"

Pierre would not put anything down. "You say, Diana. Oui, come to Diana, and so Pierre comes, and where is mon capitaine, eh? Nowhere. And you say it is not a trick? Ha! It is."

"I have not had the chance to say anything," Reineke managed to get ahold of Pierre's wrist. "If you stop fighting perhaps I will have a chance. Put those down!"

"So," Pierre raised a poisoned brow at the fingers clamped around his withered bones, "Mon capitaine has changed his ways. He beats now on children and old men. Anne will have a mark by morning."

He had not meant to hurt Anne. "For which, she can blame you," Reineke gave Pierre back his arm with a huff. "I did not mean to hurt Anne." He lit a cigarette, turning the collar of his jacket up against the cool air that felt good, but cold. He should have worn his greatcoat. "What?" he said to Pierre. "I did not mean to hurt Anne!"

"No excuse," Pierre waggled his finger. "It matters not what mon capitaine meant to do, it matters what he did."

"Indeed. I have not *done* anything," Reineke assured. "I have been thinking that is all, thinking. Yes."

And he was still thinking, everything from the smallest detail to the grand plan rattling around in his head, all of it needing the Holy Man.

"Ach, thinking," Pierre was already bored. "Mon capitaine is always thinking. So much so one of these days his head is going to explode."

"Indeed," Reineke said. "A week ago you told me I never think at all."

"Oui," Pierre agreed, "and you have not stopped thinking since then."

True. A week. One week. Perhaps he was thinking too much. He never took a week to decide anything. "I am here to talk now."

The Holy Man was never satisfied, complaining regardless. "Ach, talk. What do you want to talk about, eh?" Pierre sneered. "What is it the detective who does not want to know anything, want to know now? I took Mademoiselle to the children, you know this, you caught me."

"Oui, you caught Pierre," Pierre agreed. "And big deal for you. I am taking her again. You know this now because I am telling you this now and there is nothing you can do about it."

There was, of course, something Reineke could do about it, but that was not what he was there to talk about. "Your friends," Reineke nodded. "I want to talk to you about your friends."

Pierre frowned. "Pardon? My friends? What friends? I have no friends. What are you talking about?"

"Your friends," Reineke insisted. "I am talking about your friends in the west. You have friends in the west who come this way."

"I have no such friends," Pierre waved such nonsense away. "Mon capitaine is crazy, intoxicated or something. Deranged. I do not know what he is talking about."

"I am talking about the west!" Reineke barked.

"What west?" Pierre barked back.

"Algeria!" Reineke threw his hands in the air begging Diana for her assistance but she could do nothing. She was, after all, only stone, silent on her pedestal, guardian over the rubble and ruin of her temple around them. He stared up at her.

"So now mon capitaine is a maniac, screaming in the wind," Pierre shrugged in agreement. "It will do him as much good as the punishment he hoped to inflict by keeping an old man waiting out in the cold."

The man was impossible. "Holy Man," Reineke warned, "I am not a man of your patience, or convictions."

"So now it is Holy Man," Pierre nodded to Diana. "Always when mon capitaine wants something he invokes 'Holy Man'."

"And always," Reineke countered, "when the Holy Man is interested, he pretends he is not."

"What interested?" Pierre scoffed. "Interested in what? What is there for Pierre to be interested in? Some friends he does not have? In some country to the west?"

"Algeria," Reineke assured. "Algeria. Algeria. *AL-GER-I-A!*" he screamed, and Pierre winced.

"Oui, thank you, mon capitaine," he nodded, "but the ears, please. Pierre is old, he is forgetful, but he is not deaf. Talk. Do not scream." He sat down, perched on the base of the pedestal's steps, inviting Reineke to join him.

"Thank you," Reineke said.

"But!" Pierre reminded, that deadly finger extended with its claw, "I tell you this, I tell you now, if it is a trick, I will shoot you dead."

"Indeed," Reineke blinked. "Earlier today I thought of shooting you."

"Oh, please," Pierre had no patience for this nonsense of his. "Mon capitaine will never shoot Pierre, he likes Pierre. Two months ago I tell you myself to shoot Pierre. It is better if you shoot Pierre. But you say 'no. I cannot do this. Pierre is good. A man of God ... '"

He was the witch Merlin simply French and brown. "Algeria," Reineke said, a far safer subject.

"Algeria," Pierre surveyed him. "What about it? I know nothing about Algeria, and why should I, eh? What is Algeria to me? A country, that is all."

"It is your country," Reineke nodded.

"My country?" Pierre said. "No, Algeria is not my country. Here is my country. Only here."

"And in Algeria," Reineke nodded, "are friends of yours."

"These friends again," Pierre's eyes rolled "What is it to Pierre if mon capitaine thinks I have friends? It is nothing. One friend, two friends, probably no friends," he assured, "since you are here, and so what? Pierre has too few friends living in Algeria to matter to anyone, least of all you."

"And when is the last time," Reineke suggested cleverly, "you saw them, eh, Holy Man? Your too few friends living in Algeria?"

"The last time?" Pierre considered. "A long time, oui. This morning, at least."

What? Reineke stared at him.

"That is a long time, mon capitaine. Oui, many hours ago already."

"Hours?" Reineke repeated wearily.

"Oui," Pierre assured. "So close your mouth, all right? You look too stupid with the mouth hanging open like that. What is that, eh? What kind of soldier is that? Not a very good one."

That was Pierre's opinion. "This morning," Reineke said. "You saw your friends this morning."

"I said I did, yes," Pierre said. "Why? Is this some surprise to you?"

"Should it be?" Reineke closed his eyes.

"No!" Pierre laughed. "But then mon capitaine knows Pierre, he does. And Pierre has friends, he does—friends who come as friends this time, mon capitaine," he pointed out. "Concerned naturally for the safety of Pierre and his children since mon capitaine's police have been here. I tell them for now how it is nothing. How Mademoiselle is nothing, only one of mon capitaine's whores. What I tell them later we shall have to see."

"What?" Reineke felt his brain reel. "What?" he said.

"Mon capitaine doesn't have whores?" Pierre said.

Of course he had whores. "Are you insane?" Reineke sputtered. "That child one of my whores?"

Pierre shrugged. "Oh, well, what would mon capitaine have preferred for Pierre to have said to them? That the SS brought her? Beat and raped her? A young woman? A neutral? Mon capitaine would have nothing to worry about if Pierre says this to his friends because there would be no more mon capitaine."

"Neutral?" Reineke frowned. "Are they talking of the Swiss? The Red Crescent Society? Are they sure? What would she be doing here?"

"Comme ci, comme ça," Pierre waved. "They are sure enough—as is Pierre," he assured. "She is too much Mademoiselle to be anyone of any importance to anybody. You know this. You must have realized this—and, it is why!" he clouted Reineke, "Pierre takes Mademoiselle to the children in hopes they can reach her, which Pierre cannot do no matter how hard he tries. She is too frightened, trapped in her fear, like a child in a temper tantrum who does not know what to do, which she does not."

Except continue to scream days, evening, and nights rattling Reineke's teeth and his nerves. "Talk to me about Algeria," Reineke requested. "We were talking about Algeria."

"Oui, we were," Pierre agreed, "and mon capitaine is right. Algeria is a country, and it is to the west of here."

"And in it," Reineke said, "are friends of yours."

"Oui. Not as many friends as here, but yes, I have friends, this is true. I have lived in this desert all my life, sixty-seven years."

At last. "And those friends," Reineke treaded carefully, "how far to the east would they, could they go?"

"Why?" Pierre said.

"Why?" Reineke jumped up. "Because I want to send the woman away! Is that reason enough?"

"I don't know," Pierre said. "What do my friends have to do with Mademoiselle? Nothing."

"Everything," Reineke assured. "I want her gone. I want her out of here."

"So?" Pierre said. "Send her out of here. Call your trucks to come back and take her away."

"Not to the camps," Reineke waved impatiently. "Home! Except I do not even know where her home is, I need you to tell me."

"I?" Pierre said. "And I could do this how, eh? Pierre is what? A seer? A prophet? No, he is not."

"But you could find out," Reineke insisted. "Your friends could find out."

"So, if they could," Pierre agreed. "So what."

"So if they can," Reineke snapped, "they could take her there! Home. I am talking about you, your friends taking the woman home!"

"Ah, ha!" Pierre declared. "So it is a trick. A bullet through the heads of Pierre and his friends who are so stupid they will walk right into your stupid trap. I do not think so."

"It is not a trick," Reineke groaned. "Will you stop saying it is a trick? I do not care who they are, where they come from, or where they go. I simply want the woman out of here. You have to do this for me, you must!" he insisted. "I want to send the woman home!"

"Oh," Pierre said. "Well, in that case—all right," he agreed.

"What?" Reineke blinked. "All right?"

"Oui," Pierre smiled. "All right. I will do it. Yes, naturally. To defy Diana will not be easy, but it is possible. Perhaps a good friend who does not care too much about his life could find out some information for mon capitaine."

"The east!" Reineke anxiously supplied.

"East?" Pierre said. "Why not the west, eh?"

"Because it cannot be the west," Reineke sputtered. "Do not be absurd. The woman is British. They are in the east, the French are in the west—Holy Man," he warned, "this is something you already know."

"I do?" Pierre said. "I know there are many, many English in the west that is what I know. Husbands. Wives. Children. Families—"

"Not in uniform," Reineke snapped. "That woman was in uniform. Thiele is right. She is a soldier regardless of what kind. Your friends are lying—as are you. She is no neutral."

"Ha!" Pierre said. "Thiele is not right. Mademoiselle is not a soldier *AND!*" he said. "Mon capitaine is an idiot if he thinks there are no soldiers in the west other than his, because there are. British, oui. Arab, yes. And, of course, naturally, French. Because they do not wear a uniform, mon capitaine thinks they cannot? HA! Well, I tell you this, they did wear a uniform, and they will wear one again—the uniform of France!"

They could put them on tomorrow for all Reineke cared. "I want the woman returned to where she belongs," he said. "It is not here."

"That is true," Pierre agreed. "And mon capitaine is probably right. It is probably the east."

"Thank you!"

"Though it could be more north," Pierre considered. "Oui, it could be Tobruk—Your uniformed army still does not have that one," he pointed out. "Are you sure this is the same General Rommel who took France? Because he is not doing so good here. No, he is not."

"Indeed," Reineke said.

"But you are right," Pierre nodded, "it does not matter. What matters is we cannot send Mademoiselle to Tobruk. There is fighting there, and she is a woman, and so we will send her to Egypt. Oui, to Cairo. This is what we will do."

"Cairo?" Reineke weighed that. "I had not thought of Cairo."

"No?" Pierre said. "Really? There is another country to the east of here that Pierre is not aware of?"

"Do not be coy," Reineke suggested. "Of course, there is no other country. I simply had not considered Cairo." He was not sure what he had considered other than simply sending the woman away, just away.

"No," Pierre agreed. "There is only Egypt, and in Egypt there is only Cairo. So how is mon capitaine to do this once I have his information for him? Have you thought of this?"

Him? "I?" Reineke gasped. "Not I, you! You are to take the woman."

"Oh?" Pierre said. "Oh, no, no, no, mon capitaine, wait a minute. Find out for you where the Allies are so you can avoid them? Yes, Pierre can do this. If they are out there, you will know where. If they are not, you will also know that. But to take the woman for you? No. No, Pierre has no friends who have the ability to do this."

"But you have to," Reineke insisted. "I certainly cannot take the woman to Cairo. Are you mad? It has to be you!"

"Oh?" Pierre said. "How? Pierre is not only a magician, he is also invisible?"

"Far less visible than I," Reineke assured.

"Well, yes, that is true," Pierre agreed. He frowned, thinking and deciding with a clap of his hands. "All right!" he accepted, sealing the agreement. "I will do it. I will find a friend who can assist and I will take Mademoiselle to Cairo. Now all we have to do is figure out how mon capitaine is going to explain to his army what has happened to Mademoiselle. You have thought of this, right? Where has she gone?

Where has she disappeared to? She is under your authority, mon capitaine, not mine. She is a prisoner of the SS. What are you going to tell them has happened to her? I presume they will question you on this?"

Reineke hesitated.

"And?" Pierre said. "What is your plan? Claim she has died?"

And Reineke stared down at his feet.

"No ..." Pierre said softly. "No, that is not your plan. There is something else mon capitaine is not telling Pierre."

Reineke groaned again. "It is not a trick. Before you start with saying how it is a trick, it is not a trick. The woman cannot simply disappear."

"But that is what she would do with me, no, mon capitaine?" Pierre said. "No," he nodded when Reineke did not answer him. "That is not what she would do. All right, what is it actually that mon capitaine wants to do?"

"Holy Man?" Reineke said anxiously, afraid the priest had already changed his mind.

"No, it is all right, mon capitaine," Pierre nodded. "Just tell Pierre what it is you want to do."

"My supplies," Reineke explained, started to. "No, wait!" he stayed Pierre's immediate irritation. "Allow me, please? I was scheduled to transfer the supplies that arrived Thursday. I did not do this naturally."

"Naturally," Pierre agreed. "Either because Mademoiselle was not ready to leave with the trucks or because Rommel is not yet ready to receive them. Which do you think is the reason why?"

Reineke looked at him and Pierre smiled. "Continue, mon capitaine."

"But the next shipment I have to deliver," Reineke assured. "And I was thinking ..." he hesitated again. "I was thinking how the two could possibly go together?"

"Together?" Pierre frowned. "Mademoiselle and the trucks? I do not understand. This is what mon capitaine originally planned, to send Mademoiselle by his trucks to the camps."

"Not exactly," Reineke silenced him. "My superiors are asking me about my delay. I can say I was concerned about the threat of

Allies—I *am* concerned," he assured, "about the threat of Allies. But I can fault the SS for bringing the prisoners here. They insist they are Allied spies. I can say I believed the SS claim of captured spies. I have already sent Thiele to investigate the Kufra. This can only work to our advantage."

"As an example of your fear," Pierre nodded.

"Concern," Reineke corrected, "And, yes, it is. This is a prime oasis, not yet charted? Twelve hundred kilometers from the Kufra? Almost as large an area? Fear of my compound's discovery by the Allied or French would be and is natural."

"I understand that, mon capitaine. As I understand, we are now talking about things Pierre is not interested in knowing. He has nothing to do with what mon capitaine does or does not do with Thiele, or his supplies—"

"You have everything to do with it, and you know it!" Reineke jumped to his feet. "We have been in Libya for over a year and I am the first to find this paradise?"

"Oui," Pierre chuckled. "Mon capitaine is the *first* except for the Egyptian, Roman, Moor, and Turk."

"Indeed," Reineke said coldly. "The *first* except for the Arab and the French."

"And the Jew," Pierre smiled, and Reineke paused. "Yes," Pierre said. "But this is also all right, mon capitaine. As difficult as it is for you to say Jew, not Arab, it is for Pierre to say munitions, not supplies. Both are difficult as both are true, and so both tell lies."

"We are twelve hundred kilometers from the Kufra," Reineke replied, "where the French destroyed my airstrip—"

"My French, and Germany's airstrip," Pierre agreed.

"My airstrip," Reineke snapped. "Indeed, I am German. And that is neither an apology nor a lie. My point is, the French destroyed the airstrip and never bothered to look anywhere else for German installations?"

"Of course they did," Pierre shrugged. "What would it matter? Mon capitaine was not here then to be found."

"I am here now," Reineke assured. "And by some divine chance, your French continue to be content only watching the Kufra?"

Pierre laughed. "Oh, mon capitaine wishes that were only so."

"Indeed, I wish for our plan to work," Reineke said. "I wish for our lies to be believed. I do not think anyone is going to do that without some form of proof in support of our claim of danger."

"Mon capitaine's claim," Pierre corrected. "Mon capitaine's plan, mon capitaine's lies. You are the one in danger, not Pierre."

That was only too true. If it was not from the Allied or the French and now the SS, it was also from *der Jude*. Reineke lit another cigarette uncomfortably aware of the statue Diana looming above him, muscle and power etched in her stone flesh. "We are twelve hundred kilometers from the Kufra," he said again, "and the French who are everywhere leave you to be the only Frenchman to ever find and settle here."

"Pierre is so lucky," Pierre grinned.

"I wish to be lucky," Reineke assured. "Indeed, I wish to continue being *lucky*. Why else would I advocate such caution except to ensure your French continue not to look around?"

"They will never look here," Pierre promised. "Mon capitaine is safe forever from any Allied, British or French. Diana?" he considered her statue. "There, mon capitaine may have a few problems, oui. She is not as liberal as I or you, only when it suits her needs."

"And in the meantime who the SS will question is not Diana or you, but I," Reineke assured. "They will want to know why I am safe, not why you are safe twelve hundred kilometers from a French installation, in a world where the French are everywhere."

"True," Pierre said. "But it is Paris the city that fell, mon capitaine, not her spirit or her people."

"And the answer is," Reineke ignored him, "is because I have insisted upon protecting and preserving our anonymity with the utmost vigilance, which the SS, in turn, have threatened to destroy."

"This surprises you?" Pierre said, and Reineke just looked at him again with a tired expression.

"No," Reineke said controlled, "it is simply a matter of manipulating the obvious to suit our needs."

"Pierre is trying to protect his children, mon capitaine," Pierre assured. "I do not know about you."

"The same," Reineke said. "Along with my complex, and, yes, my men. The SS are a clear danger to us both."

"Oui, mon capitaine," Pierre agreed. "You are our cloak as you are for Diana."

"And you are mine," Reineke assured.

"So back to the beginning," Pierre requested. "What does any of this have to do with Mademoiselle?"

"Horses," Reineke said.

"Pardon?"

"Horses," Reineke nodded. "For a caravan of scouts, guards—listen to me!" he asked. "It will soon be summer. You have told me of the caravans that travel the roads, every year."

"Oui," Pierre said, "of course. In search of water."

"But what if they do not travel south to the Kufra or Ghat?" Reineke suggested. "But north, away from here?"

"Why would they do this?" Pierre frowned. "The Kufra or Ghat are much closer than the coast."

"Because I want them to," Reineke said simply.

"No," Pierre shook his head. "No, I am confused, mon capitaine. There are few caravans that come this way, ever, few camels, less horses. They cannot cross the sea without risk of death."

"There are hundreds," Reineke insisted. "And they can cross the sand sea the same way I can."

"Except they do not know these roads, mon capitaine," Pierre reminded. "These are your roads I have given to you, no one else. That is true, not a lie. Anyone on those roads except for you would be killed in an instant."

"Yes," Reineke said sourly, "anyone except for the SS."

"That was not Pierre's decision," Pierre waved, "clearly. I do not understand why Diana did not kill the SS any more than you understand, except to investigate their intentions and association with you. Not everyone apparently believes in mon capitaine despite what Pierre tries to do."

"And killed by whom?" Reineke interjected. "Eh? Killed by whom, Holy Man? Who would Diana use?"

"Arabs, yes, naturally," Pierre agreed, "less attention."

"On horseback," Reineke smiled. "A reasonable masquerade."

"Perhaps," Pierre shrugged. "Until mon capitaine's Germans decide to annihilate the Arab along with der Jude and the rest of the civilized world, and then, yes, mon capitaine will have to think of someone other than the Arab for his ranks to impersonate."

Reineke ignored the bait that time. "My Colonel will not order the compound dissolved because of some Arab population potentially troublesome, or not—which!" he pointed excitedly, warming to his scheme again, "he could do if he believed the danger was from your French. So disguise your friends as Arabs on horseback, traveling my roads, and there will be no difficulty."

"I already do," Pierre assured. "And you are right. It is very simple, without difficulty."

"Indeed," Reineke just sighed, exhausted. "I surrender. I am no match for you."

"And a few real Arabs, too," Pierre laughed.

"I will take either," Reineke nodded. "It does not matter. French or Arab, I will take both, whoever is willing, however you can arrange it. I will arrange a similar tactical diversion of scouts dressed as Arabs on horseback to escort my caravan, identical in the manner that they protect my complex here."

"Except a horse is not feasible," Pierre said. "He cannot cross the dunes."

"I want horses," Reineke insisted. "I do not have two months to wait for some camel to deliver the girl or my supplies."

"Well, what you want, and what you can have are two different things," Pierre said. "To begin with, I know of no such person who can provide you with so many horses—"

"Not many, a few," Reineke corrected. "I have trucks. *Trucks!*" he insisted. "The supplies will naturally be carried on the trucks. The horses are only a diversion."

"But I know of no such person," Pierre maintained.

"But you can find one," Reineke hissed. "If anyone could, you could. Who are your horse traders, then? The highest, you claim, of the desert Sheiks. You must know of such a person, you, who claim to know everyone."

"And if I did?" Pierre said. "Why should he help you? Who are you to him? Nothing!"

"You could explain it to him," Reineke said. "Tell him of my plan for the woman's return."

"Except!" Pierre pointed, "mon capitaine has yet to talk of Mademoiselle. He is ranting only about his supplies, transferring them from here to there to where, eh, mon capitaine? The front lines! This Pierre knows. Oui," he assured, "that is what is important to you. It is your plan. This has nothing to do with Mademoiselle, but everything to do with your supplies—which are munitions, mon capitaine," he assured. "Guns and bullets to kill the very children you claim to want to protect. Their mothers, their fathers, brothers—"

"A plan that includes the woman who will travel with them," Reineke grabbed the flailing hand. "To be returned to the SS. Only the caravan will be attacked, the woman kidnapped, and the SS killed, my supplies secured safely by my men."

"Pardon?" Pierre blinked.

"By your French dressed as Arabs," Reineke assured. "There is a distinct and very real potential for trouble with the scattered nomad tribes, a point my subsequent investigation into the attack will reveal. I will advise my Colonel how going forward, further precautions must be taken to ensure it does not happen again."

"Oh," Pierre said.

Yes. Reineke took a deep breath, his body hot and perspiring in the cool air. "Well?" he asked. "I presume they will take her?"

"The Arab?" Pierre said. "Yes, of course, for slavery."

"To freedom," Reineke corrected. "The Arabs are your French."

"I understand," Pierre nodded.

Did he? "I will insist the SS come—indeed, I will demand Herr Major return and collect her personally," Reineke assured. "So what is your answer, eh, Holy Man? Will I have my masquerade of horses? In exchange for granting the woman her life?"

"I do not know," Pierre shook his head.

"What?" Reineke sputtered. "What do you *not know*?"

"I do not know that is what I do not know!" Pierre insisted. "You are talking about using soldiers, and in talking of soldiers you are talking of death."

"The SS," Reineke swore. "No one will die except for the SS."

"A difficult promise to keep," Pierre said, "when you are talking about an attack upon your caravan by bandits you have employed, and who your soldiers know nothing about. And so what will your men do? Nothing? Stand there and allow the Arab attack? No, they will fight back. Kill, as will the Arab kill until how many are dead, apart from the SS? How many Germans? How many French? Possibly even Mademoiselle herself?

"No, mon capitaine," Pierre apologized. "I am sorry, but this is not a situation you can control to the extent you wish to control it. It will be a massacre, not a rescue, and I am a priest. I know you laugh and I laugh when we say I am a priest, but I am a priest, and a priest does not kill. He does not involve himself in war. You say Algeria is my country? I tell you a priest has no country. The world is his country. It was given to him by God to help, not destroy it.

"So, no, mon capitaine," he said, "I am sorry. I will try to think of a way to help you for it is good this thing you want to do to save Mademoiselle. It proves to Pierre again how you are the man I believe you are. But killing, mon capitaine? I am sorry, I cannot kill for you."

"Not even Germans?" Reineke said quietly.

"Pardon?" Pierre said.

"Not even Germans?" Reineke seized him by that sackcloth he wore covering his twisted bones. "German soldiers? Police? Not even a Major and his Leutnant and entourage of SS?"

"Mon capitaine ..." Pierre whispered.

"I am trying to save your life," Reineke pleaded. "Diana's. I am trying to save mine. I will change the plan, think of another way—indeed, return the woman myself to the SS, if I have to. Arrange for a rendezvous with them somewhere—but I want them dead! I want the SS dead. Can you do it? Will you do it? Attack and kill the SS and return the woman to where she belongs? Could you do it if only the SS were to die?   Indeed," he said, "are you so certain you cannot kill even for your children, Holy Man? Could you kill them all if it guaranteed you the lives of your children?"

"For the children, mon capitaine," Pierre replied, and Reineke held his breath, "I could kill even you."

Reineke was certain he would. "Holy Man?" he said as Pierre moved away from him beyond the towering shadow of Diana, into the ring of trees surrounding them.

"I must go, mon capitaine," Pierre nodded, "it is very late. It is tomorrow. I am sure it is tomorrow already."

"We will talk?" Reineke anxiously verified.

"We will talk," Pierre agreed. "Once more before the sun rises, now I have to think."

"I will send my car for you," Reineke offered, afraid to let him go.

"That is not necessary," Pierre declined.

"But it's twelve kilometers," Reineke stared at those crippled legs.

"It is not necessary," Pierre repeated and vanished.

It was some time later when Pierre made himself comfortable in the library. It was Monday the 16th of March, 1942. They argued for hours until Pierre left to arrange for the horses, and Reineke was in the apartment, staring down on the woman sleeping.

"Mon capitaine is a man who sits on a fence." Pierre's voice echoed in his head, but the accusation was unfair. He did the best he could. It was Pierre's misfortune to owe him, not the other way around.

"As will you," Reineke whispered at the woman. "So if I am so wrong, how can what I do be so right?"   It could not be, and yet it was. If he counted them all, it would be nearly as many lives spared as the number of his men. And while it might eventually cost him his own, it would not be today, or even the next, and certainly not for her. He had much to do after her.

"Indeed," Reineke said. "Who are you? What are you doing here? Where are you from?" Out there in the sand, long before he arrived to find her here, he knew he would find disaster when he walked in.

"Are you France?" he wondered. Was Diana right when she claimed his compassion was guilt, his rage, battle fatigue?

"No," Reineke said. "No, you are not France." The horror of France inspired him to grant life. This woman inspired him to murder with such passion and desperation he could not explain if he thought on it for a hundred years.

One hundred years and no one will ever believe in the existence of the German Captain Reineke, for in fact he was a German, and ones like him did not exist.

"I exist," he told the woman, so strange to watch her sleeping with her mouth partially open.

"I exist," he assured, and decided to order her water heated for her bath before he woke her up to show her.